Stories From Room 113

More International Adventures

CONCORDIA INTERNATIONAL SCHOOL SHANGHAI

iUniverse, Inc.
New York   Bloomington

iUniverse books may be ordered through booksellers or by contacting:

iUniverse
1663 Liberty Drive
Bloomington, IN 47403
www.iuniverse.com
1-800-Authors (1-800-288-4677)

Because of the dynamic nature of the Internet, any Web addresses or links contained in this book may have changed since publication and may no longer be valid. The views expressed in this work are solely those of the author and do not necessarily reflect the views of the publisher, and the publisher hereby disclaims any responsibility for them.

ISBN: 978-1-4502-2032-3 (sc)
ISBN: 978-1-4502-2033-0 (ebook)

Printed in the United States of America

iUniverse rev. date: 03/15/2010

Foreword

By

Terry Umphenour

Stories from Room 113: More International Adventures is a book filled with delightful tales, through which imagination takes both the reader and the writer on an adventurous tour of the writing experience. For a second year, this project exposed the minds of eighteen eighth grade student writers from Concordia International School Shanghai (CISS) to the demanding challenge of writing and refining a 5000-word story for publication. Collectively, the stories printed on the following pages take the reader on adventures—both real and imaginary—around the globe.

Brainstorming to determine the genre and story parameters started the process. Once again, students expressed excitement at the freedom to write about a topic of their choosing. Some students expressed concerns about writing such a long story and the time it would take. The second phase of the assignment found students struggling to introduce their characters, set the scene, and make their characters come alive with individual characteristics. After considerable thought, a first tentative outline, and a brief introduction, each student read and revised the plot and the storyline that provided the conflicts needed to bring the story to its climax and conclusion.

Usually the eighth grade writing process includes an outline, a rough draft, a final draft, and proofreading. *Stories from Room 113: More International Adventures* required students to write an outline, an initial introduction, a first draft, and three additional drafts. After finishing the story's first draft, each student revised the story, ensuring that the facts remained consistent, that the story used the same tense throughout the manuscript, and that correct paragraph and sentence structure kept the story moving forward. Next, each young writer edited his or her own story to make sure that the story used active voice and that correct tense was used. The final draft provided an opportunity for each writer to proofread. Proofreading such a long story, one that needed every mistake corrected, provided many opportunities to teach the conventions necessary to bring a story to publication.

Becoming insightful learners and effective communicators remains one of the expected student learning results at CISS. *Stories from Room 113: More International Adventures* tests Concordia's curriculum to see if it provides students the skills necessary to reach this expected student-learning result. As in our first book, *Stories from Room 113: International Adventures*, only you—the reader—can determine the degree of success that each of these eighteen young writers has reached toward achieving that goal. The final stories are printed exactly as the students submitted them and may include errors—or even missed comments—that should have been deleted. In order to make this work a continuing education resource, no teacher or professional editing was added to the final submitted stories.

It is with great pride that I present *Stories from Room113: More International Adventures* for your enjoyment. I hope that you enjoy reading these imaginative, adventurous stories as much the students enjoyed writing and editing them. To learn more about this writing process and its authors or to comment on this work, contact Terry Umphenour at the following email address: terry.umphenour@ciss. com.cn.

Table of Contents

The Cost of Perfection

By

Emily Amick

The city is my remedy for my dull existence. It brings me to life. Each busy street and flashing light has something new to say. Each neatly pressed person with a cell phone smashed against his face is thinking a different thought, living a different life. Even though they all may seem exactly the same, each city slicker sees his or her bustling world fly by through a different pair of eyes, with a different perspective. And each perspective has something new to bring to the table. Maybe that thirty-three-story building around the corner is going bankrupt. Maybe the law firm over on Seventh Street is closing down next week. Maybe Randy's secretary failed to invite his haven't-contacted-since-last Christmas stepmother to Thanksgiving dinner this year. Or maybe, just maybe, the city isn't where it wants to be today. Maybe it's because of things like the way those greasy puddles form on the curbs when it rains and the way everyone seems to be screaming when all you need is peace and quiet or the way all the construction makes a five-minute walk turn into a fifteen-minute one. And maybe that's what drove Seth to do it.

I don't think he saw it coming. I don't think anyone did for that matter, but living life the way Seth did—well—I do imagine that could get pretty wearisome. Waking up at the crack of dawn each morning to find yourself repeating the exact same routine you've been keeping for the past three years could drive any sane man mad. He always seemed to be happy though. He never failed to offer every employee in the office that delightful smile of his each morning. Even Linda, who had to be the ugliest middle-aged receptionist in all of New York, got one. I found that pretty sensational considering most people in the office referred to her as "the whale," on account of her beefy five-feet-five-inch body had to be nearing somewhere around two hundred fifty pounds by now. I'm sure his handsome smile was always the highlight of her day. She even smiled back from time to time, which was insane. Before Seth came to the office, that old hag smiled once every thirty-one days...when the Fed Ex man came to drop off her monthly supply of microwavable Weight Watchers meals.

I guarantee you any women in her right mind would have dated Seth in the blink of an eye. He just had that charm to him that would sweep any girl right off her feet and into his big, burly arms. Trust me, I know from experience. His laughter thrilled me. It was possibly the most contagious thing this world possessed. He gently tossed his head back just far enough so that you could see his freshly shaven neck. When he talked, I watched the way his perfectly square jaw slowly moved up and down as he rambled on about the most mind-boggling things.

I promise you, with him, there was never a dull moment. No awkward silences ever came about. He always had something to say about everything and everything to say about nothing. It amazed me how precisely he spoke, too. It seemed as if he had spent all night thinking about the perfect way to answer each question that fluttered out from the mouth of anyone. That's what confused me the most about him. His perfection was almost inhuman. Sometimes I even thought that he was just a figment of my imagination, but others saw him too, and I'm pretty sure that not every New Yorker had gone mad.

The morning it happened was unlike most wind-whipping December mornings in Times Square. I sensed something peculiar in the air as I trudged off to yet another endless day of work. I remember every last thing about that morning: the *ting* of the bell as I walked into Starbucks to purchase my daily five-thousand-calorie latte, the group of yellow hard-hat men winking at me as I jay-walked near an intersection on

West Avenue. Their whistles profoundly astounded me because I wasn't exactly the type to get hit on. At twenty-four, I barely did anything with my bodiless straight brown hair, wore make up only on occasion, and knew that I was getting pudgier by the minute, thanks to my morning consumption from stupid Starbucks. So, in my mind, that day was going to be a good one. Even though something still didn't feel right, my self-confidence was about to burst through the ceiling.

Just like that I went from trudging through the busy streets to dramatically over-swinging my hips with each step. I felt like the city was my runway. For once in my life I felt beautiful...until I saw bumblebee-colored crime scene tape wrapped around orange barrels, invading the intersection right in front of Millton's: my office. Crimes in New York City occurred frequently, but this one stood out. Something felt utterly wrong, and suddenly a wave of loneliness swept over me. It had to be the worst feeling ever. I felt so out of place, like I was alone in a crowded room, and I hated it. It was as if everyone in the entire city knew what was going on, except for me. I recall trying to shove my way through a sea of bodies but getting nowhere. The people around me shed a million tears. Then raindrops fell, and everyone looked up. Small children stuck out their tongues and caught the recycled water as parents frantically grabbed them and ran to find shelter. I remembered everyone around me fading away. I stood there alone in the pouring rain and searched for a familiar face. But my dashing eyes found no one. Officers surrounded the scene. One of them shifted over to retrieve his radio out of his back pocket, and I saw a body sprawled out across the pavement. Not just any body...the body of Seth Alexander Hastings.

I didn't really know what to do. I mean, it's not like Seth and I were best friends or anything, but we definitely had a past, a past that made me hate myself. It all started back when he was new to the office. I remember the very first day he strode in through those big, translucent sliding doors. It was like a whole new world was introduced to Millton's Paper Company. He was the type of guy that every girl adored and every guy despised, for the same reasons of course. He was perfect. The girls saw him as absolutely gorgeous, which is exactly why all the male Millton employees hated him; he was a threat, and out of all of the beautiful-could be a model for Covergirl-flawless skinned girls in the office, I was somehow his first target. Why he didn't go for one of the "Barbie-Girl," five feet eight inches tall, blonde haired, blue eyed, ten-inch-waist accountants? Well I guess I'll never know the answer to that one, but I do know why he went for me. It was because I was "different," or at least that's what they told me. The other girls I mean. But why Seth would want someone different—someone that's not your average, young, spontaneous beauty queen? Maybe it was because he knew that I would be easy to get to; I would be a good first target. Or it was because he thought that the stupid, fat, girl would be the easiest to humiliate. But for whatever reason it was, I hated that I didn't see what he was trying to do to me sooner...or before he died for that matter.

At first I thought it was a joke. "Dana, would you like to go out with me sometime?" *Yeah right.* Part of me wanted to face the truth and admit to myself that he was probably just going to use me, but for some reason I just couldn't. I hadn't been on a date in...well, ages.

"I'd love too!" I remember myself shrieking a little too loudly in my best "pretty girl" voice. I'm pretty sure *every* woman in the office heard me and I'm pretty sure that's the exact moment that all started hating me. I felt so proud to finally get something that *they* wanted.

About a week or so later Seth and I went on that date. He picked me up at the bottom of my apartment building at seven o'clock sharp, and together we walked hand in hand trying to decide which restaurant

He said his name was Gabrielle, Gabrielle Oswald DaLenport. I knew a lot about him already. He was old. I'd say early sixties. Scars coated his face the same way socks cover my feet on cold winter days, and there was something profoundly off about him. But what I didn't know about him, what I didn't know about Gabrielle, was that he would drastically change my life.

Thick, brown gloves coated his hands. Long, gray hair smothered his head. A black overcoat was draped around his shoulders and his big toe poked through the tattered leather of his worn out boat shoes. He reminded me of the man I'd seen jingling a couple of coins around in a tin mug in front of Starbucks last week. Homeless.

"Hey boy, what's your name?" he asked me in a quiet, broken voice. Startled, I just stared at him blankly and blinked about a million times.

Where was I? I looked around. Julia was nowhere to be found. The last thing I remembered was sitting in the corner of the old diner between 7th and 8th Street. Something was terribly wrong. "Seth Hasting," was all I could manage to spill out, and that's when the panic struck. Spinning, spinning...the world around me began to disappear; in an instant, black became my only companion.

The first time I ever saw her, I declared that as the best day of my life. She gave me a shy "Hello," and ever since then she's had me. I'm not really sure if she felt the same way I did at that very moment, or even if she was attracted to me at all. But if she wasn't, then why would she have wasted all that time digging through that massive red bag of hers and pulling out what looked like a *used* tissue, to help me wipe up the coffee I'd just spilled down the front of my pale purple shirt. Since then, I've been convinced that we're soul mates.

The way her soft blonde curls bounced around when she giggled and the way she daintily threw her small head back when hysterical laughter was all she could manage to say, that's what made me love her more than anything else. Her plump red lips almost never stopped babbling. Most people found it annoying, but not me. As a matter of fact, I found it amazing. I think I found it so sensational because she was so easy to talk to. You could ask her anything from, "So how's the weather today?" to "What would you do with a million dollars?" Each time I'd be astounded by her response.

On the other hand, I've always been a man of few words. Julia always said that was good though because it made those small sentences I did say seem much more important than they actually were. I believed this because I took pride in everything she said.

Opening my eyes and jerking up right I heard a voice mumble "Ya... ya...ya, finally awake, boy?"

Well duh...I thought. *How stupid was this guy?*

"Um...yeah," I answered back. We were sitting in a small, chilled room. White was everywhere: white walls, white furniture, white lamps, and white door. I was even wearing white. *How did that happen?* Gabrielle was sitting on the other side of the room in a small—you guessed it—white chair. A red scarf with little, white snowflakes stitched on it hung from his neck. This was an addition to his disgustingly ratty outfit. His left leg was crossed over his right, and his purple bottom lip was quivering rapidly. *What was going on?* I stood up and began walking toward the door. I wanted so badly to escape from this strange man and these unfamiliar surroundings. As I twisted the cool, aluminum doorknob I could feel dents from where some angry person had fiercely forced it open. The door creaked open and a hallway appeared. To my left the hallway went on as far as my perfect eyes could see. To my right it was the same. Beyond confusion, I stepped back over the threshold of the door and back into the white washed room. Gabrielle was gone. There was only one door in the room. *Where had he gone?* I walked back out into the hallway and began walking. My hands were shaking with nervousness and I could feel ice running through my veins.

No one knew about my past, except for Julia. And I had no intent on anyone else finding out about it either. The drugs took me away and helped me forget about Marcus' death. I guess in a way, they allowed me to escape for a while, to live a carefree life, and not have to worry about how long it would be until I'd break down and cry again. Marcus and I knew each other like the back of our hands.

Our parents never really got a long well. I remember one cold, autumn night back in '91 when ma and pa got in a fight. She said she "Couldn't love a man like him no more," and he said that he, "Just couldn't handle all her theatrics any longer." I guess you could say it was a sad ending to a happy story. I mean, I was only seven years old that night and Marcus was only nine, but I still remember it so clearly. Pa started striking ma and she just didn't know what to do so she stood there and took his punches. She told us kids to go hide. Since the trailer we were living in at the time only had two bedrooms and one bathroom we opted to go hide under our beds; especially since we weren't allowed in ma and pa's room *ever*. We never really knew why though.

I remember Marcus saying that we would probably be safer in ma and pa's room because pa would never think to look for us in there. I was afraid though. I knew what he would do to us if he found us...the same thing he did to ma when he found it she bought Marcus and I each a Milky Way candy bar at the grocery store last month. Beat her. You see, he got so upset because we didn't have much growing up and he the biggest drunk I'd ever seen. The way he looked at it he could have used that two bucks to buy a can of beer at the Circle K tomorrow after work instead of using it to bring "unearned joy" to his two sons.

He met our mama dry that day. She went off to stay with her sister Mary-Ann for a while. The day she left she was wearing an immensely oversized blue t-shirt with a couple of cigarette burned holes in it, ripped up, old work boots-probably both hand-me downs from pa, and tight black sweat pants. Her string hair hung over her eye in greasy clusters and her top lip was swollen purple from where pa had punched her the night before. We were all sure that she wasn't coming back. But she did.

One Friday morning around 10:00 or so, the white aluminum door to our pale blue trailer swung open. She had only been gone for a couple days, but I hardly recognized her. Her usually greasy brown hair was now bleach blonde and straight. It ended right about her jaw line and was neatly pinned up at top with a metallic silver bobby pin. She was wearing make up for the first time, too much make up that is, in...well ever, and her pointed, black stilettos made the most graceful clicking noise and she walked across our linoleum kitchen floor. Her too tight, Barbie pink dress hugged her then frame ever so tightly. I watched her cherry red lips move as she walked over to pa, who was reading the paper on the old brown Lazy-Boy in the living room and said hello. You could tell she has been crying because from her cheekbones up, make up streaked her face. She looked happier though. Any typical *Donna Marie's Trailer Park* man would have thought she was "smokin' hot," but I thought she looked like a white trash fool.

She tried to start back up again and get us back into our normal lives, but in less than a week she was exactly the same greasy haired, make up less, person she used to be. So her and pa filed for a divorce.

Neither of them wanted custody of Mark and I and joint custody would have been worse than having no parents at all, so they left and we went to live with our Aunt Brenda. She was a widow who had lost her husband to a drunk driver so she was very protective of us. She made us read the Bible all the time and enrolled us in a private catholic school called *Saint Anthony's Catholic School.* I always wondered how she afforded it, but the bigger questions was how was this kind hearted, gentle, old woman related to my crazy, free-spirited, drunken father?

Well that's when the depression really hit me hard. But the drugs were gone now and they had been for a little over a year...or at least that's what I thought.

Was that him? No...it couldn't be. "Ma-Ma-Marcus?" The tall, blonde haired, man spun around. It was him. His smooth, tanned skinned, was luminous just like it used to be.

"Seth! Seth, what are you doing here?" In utter shock, I just stood there. I still had *no* idea where I was. "You're *dead.*" I said. "What's going on? Where are we?" *Maybe I'm dreaming.*

"I know...and so are you." He reluctantly replied.

"No." I said. And I feel to the ground for the second time that day.

And that's when they started. The flashbacks I mean. I was passed out but I could hear Julia banging on my bedroom door. After I didn't answer she barged into door. I could hear her screaming and crying. I wanted so badly to get up and comfort her. But I knew I was the reason for her tears. I was just lying there lifelessly. She ran over to the phone and dialed 9-1-1. The next thing I knew sirens were blaring and blue and red lights flashed all around me. Two very deep-voiced men lifted me up onto a stretcher. This was another horrible result of the drugs; they made me crazy. They took me over and I just couldn't get away from them. I tried the anti depressants and all the other over the counter medicine the doctors prescribed, but nothing seemed to work like the drugs. I felt horrible about them though. I don't know if Julia ever found out about them, but she definitely knew something was up.

I woke up with Marcus hovering over top of me. He looked confused. *What had I done?* There was no way he could have known about anything. I mean I quit the drugs a long time ago and he had never figured out about them. I was so afraid at that very moment though. I sensed disappointment in his voice as he said, "I know what you've been hiding." Shaking, I asked him again, where we were.

"Come on Seth, You know where we are. You just don't want to accept it."

"No, Marcus, I really don't know."

"Were in Heaven." He replied back to me. It all started to make since at that very moment. I was seeing Marcus because I was heaven. We were dead. But the one question that kept running through my head was, *how did I die?*

"But how did I die?" I hesitantly asked Marcus. Something rang in my ear and told me that it was because of the...because of the drugs. Gosh, I couldn't even stand to think about it, I was so ashamed.

"You relapsed." He said bluntly. You've been on the drugs since I died. You told me you were done with them...what happened? Oh my, gosh...he was right. It all came flooding back to me at that very moment.

I was still in shock that I was seeing Marcus for the first time in over a year. I mean I had imagined the day that I'd see him again...but they was I had seen it, was nothing like this. We were supposed to run into each other's arms and exchange one of those short, awkward brotherly hugs. We were supposed to laugh about the memories we could recall about being young boys and try figure out why ma and pa didn't want anything to do with us. But instead we just sat there awkwardly. I felt like I should say something...but nothing seemed appropriate.

Seeing Marcus made me wonder if maybe I'd see ma and pa in heaven too. I hadn't spoke to either of them in years; who knew if they were dead or alive? Well not me, that's for sure. And as much as I wondered about it day after day, part of me didn't really want to know. I mean they had abandoned me and left me with absolutely nothing, so if they were dead, then they deserved every bit of it.

Ding! "Come on," said Marcus "Let's go." I stood up and chill ran down my spine. The part of the bible that says heaven is a perfect place where you never get cold or hungry or tired, well that was just a straight up lie. I was freezing and my stomach wouldn't shut up. Not to mention that it was taking every bit of strength I had left in me to keep my eyes open. As we staggered down the bustling hallway, a million thoughts crossed through my mind. *Where are we going? Am I really in heaven?* Finally the endless, white hallway ended and we turned right. I entered through a silver doorway behind Mark to find what looked like a middle school cafeteria. Everyone was wearing white though. There were people of every race. There were short people and tall people and young people and old people. It sure didn't seem like heaven. "Tonight's special is chicken wings!" blurted Marcus. "YES! My favorite!" I guess this *was* a cafeteria after all.

"Ya never answered my question, son. How'd ya get in here?" Gabrielle asked me. Back in my subzero room, GB and I sat in our living room and talked.

"I..." I began. "I...I overdosed."

"You?" the ungodly man chuckled. "Why you'd be the last person on my mind to OD."

"Well I did!" I replied back sharply. I was biting my lip to hold back the tears when it began to bleed. I used this as an excuse to get up and go to the bathroom. I slammed the door behind me and began to bawl. I missed Julia so badly. "Why me?" I wailed through my tears.

✳ ✳ ✳ ✳

Knock! Knock! I walked over to answer the door. GB was nowhere to be found. As I clicked the doorknob open, a tall, gray-haired man greeted me. "Hello," he began. "Do you want to take a walk with me?"

Normally I would have asked the man is he was crazy, but after last night's break down, a walked seemed nice. "Well, okay." I replied.

"Grrrrrreat!" he bellowed.

He stepped into my...apartment, I guess you could call it, and took a seat on a wine stained, white sofa.

"Just give me a second to get ready."

A couple of minutes later I came back out. He hadn't moved a muscle.

We walked down the interminable hallway once again, but turned left instead this time. We were greeted by the most magnificent garden I had ever laid eyes on. Gigantic flowers appeared everywhere, and the clear blue sky streamed by overhead. It smelled like cedar wood and daffodils.

"W-what's your name," I asked.

"Gabrielle," he replied.

Okay, I thought, *everyone in heaven was named Gabrielle.*

"Oh, I'm Seth."

He chuckled, "Oh yes, I know."

Now that is just scary. How does this stranger know who I am?

"How?"

"Because I'm God, boy, and God knows everything.

Should I believe him? I mean, come on, anyone could claim to be "God."

"Oh..." was all I could manage to seep out between my parsed lips. Something in his eyes made me feel like he knew me even better than I knew myself, and that's what scared me the most about him. It wasn't his scars or his long, scratchy beard. Nor was it his incredibly deep voice or spectacularly towering height. It was those eyes. Those calm blue eyes that made me want to spill out everything I'd ever done to this mysterious, possibly Godly, man. And that's exactly what I did.

After I'd practically told this man my life story, the drugs, my parents, Marcus, everything, he didn't judge me or try to make me feel any better about anything, but instead he said once again, "Seth, I am God, and God knows everything." I started believing him at that exact moment. There was something in the tone of his voice when he said it that second time that sent chills down my spine. This man had some crazy power over me, not physically, but spiritually.

"If you're God, then why did you tell me that your name was Gabrielle earlier?" I questioned him.

"Because it is," he replied back to me with a chuckle.

I turned back from the flowers I was studying to reply to his confusing remark, but he was nowhere to be found. As a matter of fact, the only person in sight was GB. *Oh God. Not him again.*

"HEY!" His heavy voice made me want to plug my ears.

"Umm...hi," I rudely mumbled back.

"I'm glad we got to have that talk."

What the heck was this stupid man talking about now?

"What talk?" I muttered back.

"Why, The talk we just had of course!"

And that's when it clicked. Gabrielle was God. I had treated him like a complete low life and he was...he was *God.*

"Are you...no. You can't be."

"I am." A missing-tooth smile came over his face as he said that.

I opened my anxious eyelids to find myself lying in a hospital bed. The heart monitor connected to my chest instantly began beeping. Was I... *back?* No. I couldn't be.

"Baby! You're alive!" Julia screeched as she burst through the white, metal door of my hospital room with tear stained cheeks. I looked around. Everything was exactly the way it had been right before I... before I *died.* I felt a piece of paper between my fingers. It was a note. I gently opened it to find the words: *Second chances don't come easy.* It was signed GOD.

A Second Chance

By

Kristina Arslain

"Ahhh!" I screeched when the freezing white snowball smacked me in the face. I combed my black side-bangs back into place with my fingers. I piled up the snow around me into a ball and threw it back at Tammy. I ran to my abandoned snow wall that was supposed to protect me from snowballs, but then the wall collapsed after ten snowballs hit it. I quickly crammed the snow together that surrounded my size six feet, and attempted to throw it at my younger sister, Sarah. The snowball didn't even get close to hitting her because when I threw the snowball, the snow just crumbled back down onto the ground.

As I attempted to throw another snowball at Sarah, a voice yelled out, "Rae! Why don't you guys come on inside and drink hot cocoa? You four have been playing outside for over an hour."

"Don't worry, Mom. We'll be fine!" I yelled back to my excessively protective mother.

"Brrr. I'm freezing!" My nine-year-old sister yelled out ten minutes after my mother intruded on our fun.

"Me too!" Millie, Tammy's younger sister, screeched, "Can we please stop the game and go inside!"

I glanced at Tammy for confirmation. "Fine, let's all go inside and warm up."

There was hot cocoa waiting for the four of us when we came in after calling a truce to our snowball fight. We stripped ourselves from our snow-covered coats, boots, hats, and gloves, making a huge pile next to the front door. All four of us sat by the fire sipping hot cocoa and making s'mores.

"Yummy!" Millie exclaimed as she licked her fingers clean. "Thanks for those s'mores," she said to my mother.

It was pitch black outside except for the moon and the stars in the sky when Tammy and Millie left. I watched them go through the front door. They waved good-bye and scurried across the street to their house. Tammy was one of my first friends that I made when I attended Jasurga High School three months ago.

"Rae!" My mother yelled out from the kitchen. "You need to clean up the mess you made and finish your schoolwork from two days ago."

"Huh? What is there to clean up?"

"The snow that you dragged in when you dumped your clothes by the door and the gram-cracker crumbs."

Rolling my eyes, I got up and lugged our heavy vacuum all the way down the stairs to clean up the crumbs that only my mother would notice. An hour later my Dad walked through the front door. He then whispered something to my mother. *Weird*, I thought. *Usually my dad says hello and starts bugging me.*

My sister's reddish-brown hair flopped through the air as she ran to my dad. "Daddy guess what!" Sarah took a deep pause before continuing. "Today, Rae and I didn't have any school because of all the snow, so Millie and Tammy came over and played with us! It was so much fun!"

"Oh, yeah!" My father picked Sarah up and swung her onto his shoulders. Then he did his embarrassing dance moves and plopped down onto the couch with Sarah on his lap. My mother joined him and called me over.

My parents looked at each other in hesitation, "We need to have another family meeting," My mother walked over from the kitchen and took a seat on the couch next to Sarah and my dad while I sat alone on the floor next to the fire place.

Huh? Family Meeting? Oh no! The only time my family has a family meeting is when something big, bad, or ugly has, or is going to happen.

"We are aware that we have just finished unpacking all of our boxes from our last move from Greensboro, but I'm afraid I must inform you that we will be moving again," my dad said trying to sound enthusiastic.

Silence filled the room until Sarah spoke, "To where?" Sarah plopped a large fluffy marshmallow into her mouth.

"We are moving back to Greensboro. You guys will be attending Mountain Peak School again. It'll be great!" Mom said.

"Will we be living in the same house?" Sarah asked vigorously.

"No, I'm afraid not. Our old house has already been sold. Sorry honey," my father said to Sarah.

"Awww man!" Sarah pouted, but then looked up with big toothy smile on her face. "Will we be going house shopping?"

"No, there is already a house waiting for us."

Sarah's eyes grew big and teary. "But..."

"Don't worry," my dad brushed Sarah's hair away from her face. "You are going to love the house."

"That's what you always say," I murmured.

"What's with the attitude Rae; I thought you loved moving?" My mother questioned me. "We've been moving around the U.S. since you were five years old, and you've been perfectly fine with it."

I couldn't tell my parents why I had been so glad to move before. Then they would be concerned and make me see a counselor. "I like living here. Sarah and I finally have separate rooms, and we live close but not too close to school." I felt my shoulders loosen as I opened up a little to my family.

"I'm so sorry Rae, but that doesn't change anything," My mother said, looking down at me from the couch. "I think we should all go to bed and let everything sink in. We've all had a long day."

I couldn't sleep all night, so I just stared at the ceiling thinking: *How can I move back to Greensboro?* A cold jolt hit me every time I thought about going to go back to my old school.

Every time my family moved to a new place, I tried to be someone I'm not when I was at school. Since I wasn't myself I didn't know my limits, allowing me to easily inherit a negative attitude. About the time people started hating me, my parents announced that we were leaving. It was my perfect escape plan.

I always thought it would be cool to be someone else because everyone else always seemed to have the perfect life.

When I first attended Mountain Peak, I pretended to be a girly-girl. I was the most popular person in school, for a short time, until I screwed everything up. I began spreading rumors around school. It was hilarious until people figured out that I was the one that made all the rumors up. Lucky for me, my family was moving to Indiana within the same week that I

When I moved to Indiana, I realized that maybe I should just be myself. This has been my family's longest stay since I started my personality experiment. So far things have been great, people like me, and I don't have to worry about showing my true personality- and now we have to move.

✷ ✷ ✷ ✷

I woke up to the luscious scent of blueberry pancakes and bacon. "Good morning darling," My mother said. "Did you sleep well?"

"Not really," I replied back, staring at my fuzzy slippers and plaid pajamas. "When are we moving?"

"At the end of the week." My dad came walking into the dining room in a black business suit, while sipping a cup of coffee.

"Huh! Say what?" I screeched in shock. It's already Thursday, and we are going to be moving in three days! "How are we going to be able to pack in time?" I demanded, trying to make my dad realize that we would have to stay in Indiana a little longer.

"Just stop it Rae; you won't be attending school today," my dad said. "I have already contacted your school and informed them about everything. Your teachers will be sending you your homework and notes so that you can keep up in school."

"Since when do you make us skip school?" I said.

"We don't have enough time to pack everything by Saturday, so you guys are going start helping your mother pack when you get done eating," my dad replied, taking another big gulp out of his favorite mug.

"Odd..." I sat down at the end of the oak table and poured syrup onto my warm pancakes.   "Why can't we just stay here until I finish eighth grade? It's only like five months away."

"Because of my job, Rae," my father glanced at his watch. "I've got to get to work; we'll finish this conversation some other time." He picked up his briefcase and hurried out the door.

By the time my dad came home, I had almost finished packing up my whole room. All of my books, clothing, shoes, and desk supplies were all packed up in cardboard boxes. I had even packed some of my clothes in a suitcase; enough clothes for a week. It was 11:00 PM, when I was lying in bed that I heard my dad's black BMW pull into the driveway in front of our brick house.

I woke up upset that today is my last day of school. I hopped on the long, yellow bus that morning with an empty bag. I kept getting this feeling in my guts that I forgot to bring something to school because of my empty bag. During classes I unpacked my locker and hung out in the school library. To my surprise, many people still didn't know I was moving. People kept asking, "Why aren't you in class?" When I told them, their mouths dropped.

My friends were upset when they found out that I was moving tomorrow. We don't even have time to hang out between now and when I leave because neither of us have any free time.

"Here we are!" My parents screeched in unison.

There was a big, fancy gate that led us into the neighborhood. People were playing golf, walking their dogs, taking a jog, and playing tennis. There it was, the two-story house with the big door and windows. The property had a long paved driveway, a huge yard, and of course, a super cool house. I was speechless. Three months ago when I left Greensboro this neighborhood was still being built.

"Well, what do you think?" My mother asked, even though she totally knew the answer.

"What do I think? I think, where are the keys to the house?"

"Whoa!" Sarah stared out her window as her voice echoed. Sarah's eyes were wide opened, mouth dropped, and she was completely frozen.

I snatched the keys from my mother's fingers and hurried to the door. "Wow!"

The house had five bedrooms, an office, a family room, living room, kitchen, dining room, and three large bathrooms. Oh yeah, there's also a sunroom with a Jacuzzi.

"Sarah, your room is on the second floor. Go down the hall and turn right to get to your room," my dad yelled. "And Rae, yours is right across from Sarah's"

Sarah and I raced up the stairs, ran down the hall, opened the doors, and gasped. "Oh, my." That's all I could say. My room was painted to my favorite color purple. I even had my own bathroom! The view from my window was the big green backyard.

You could see the golf court from our yard, which had a trampoline. There were enough trees covering the juncture of our neighbors' yards and ours so that people couldn't see through our property without getting pricked by the needle sharp needles.

Sarah walked into my room holding a teddy bear. "Where did you get that stuffed animal from?" I asked.

"It was in my room," Sarah replied. "Feel it; it's really soft." Sarah emphasized the word soft. "You can go check my room out if you want," She said in her innocent but adorable voice.

I dashed to my sister's room. My sister's light pink room was slightly smaller, but it had more space because she didn't have as much furniture as mine, and there was no bathroom. Dang man! She received a ton of stuffed animals; they were all over the room.

My sister and I walked out of each other's rooms at the same time, and we ran around house looking at all the rooms in the house. My parent's room was a ton bigger than mine, and they had their own bathroom, a walk-in closet, and a flat screen television.

"Girls, come on down and help unload the car!" My mother yelled out from the driveway! I slowly walked down the stairs, so that I wouldn't have to bring so much stuff from the car into the house.

I was lugging my overloaded suitcase up the stairs and into my new stylish room, when I noticed how much my sister was struggling to get her suitcase up the stairs. I hurried to my sister to help her get her luggage up the steps. Whoa, her suitcase is half the size as mine, and it weighs more than mine! Geez, did she pack bricks! No wonder she couldn't get her bag up the stairs!

We finished bringing everything from the car into the house. Then we all got into the car to register Sarah and I to our new school. It took about a ten-minutes ride from my new house to Mountain Peak School.

The school hadn't changed a bit! I'm glad that my parents made an appointment with the administration office to register Sarah and I on a Saturday, because then I don't have to worry about seeing any students.

My mother went with my sister to the elementary school to get registered while my father and I went to register in the middle school building.

My father and I quietly walked into the school's office. The secretary stared at her computer screen, ignoring my father and I. Her nametag read 'Ms. Jusho.' "EXCUSE ME!" My father yelped out. I felt my face turn red. Why did my dad always have to embarrass me!

My eyes widened when the secretary looked up. She was older than I remembered. Before we had a nice and young secretary; this person looked old and cranky! "What do you want?" The old woman with gray hair and yellow-fogged glasses snapped back.

"I'm Mr. Smith, and I am here to register my daughter into the middle school." My dad replied trying to ignore the woman's rudeness. "We have an appointment with the principal."

"You're late, the principal has already gone home, but he left me some papers that you need to fill out." The secretary walked to the back room and came back with the important papers in her pale, wrinkled hands. "You need to fill out these papers and turn them in tonight if you wish or your daughter to attend school on Monday."

"Thank you very much," my father replied in a sincere voice. He gently took the papers and took a seat next to me.

NOOO! My father turned the papers in on time! I was hoping that there would be some information that he didn't know so that I would have to postpone my entry into Mountain Peak's middle school.

$$\ast \quad \ast \quad \ast \quad \ast$$

"Rae! Sarah! Get up it's time to get ready for school!" My mother knocked on our doors. "It's 7:00 AM! You have thirty minutes to get ready! Chop! Chop!"

"Ugh!" I moaned and forced myself to roll out of bed. "Five more minutes. Please!" I begged.

"No!" My mother charged into my room, opened all the curtains, and turned on the lights. "You need to get ready! NOW!"

"I'm up!" I quickly stood up in surprise of how demanding my mother got.

"Good," My mother switched back to her calm voice and left my room.

I put on a pair of dark-blue skinny jeans, a printed-shirt, and a pair of flats. I then divided my bangs from the rest of my chin-length, straightened, black hair with a thin golden headband.

I had my usual breakfast containing sweat cereal and orange juice. "Are you excited?" Sarah kept on questioning me.

I shot my sister the dirty what-do-you-think look and walked away. I grabbed my school bag and slammed the door behind me as I stomped out of the house.

People stared at my sister and me when we showed up on the bus. Then they started whispering to the person next to them while still glaring at us. I felt my stomach flip.

The front of the bus was filled with younger children. I grabbed the last open seat that didn't have another person on it. On the other hand, Sarah smiled really big and skipped closer to the back of the bus. She shoved her puny butt right next to someone that I've never seen before. The girl looked like she was my age and had dirty-blonde hair.

The girl that my sister sat next to cleared her throat super loud. "Excuse me, this seat is taken," she clearly pointed out.

My sister looked at her confused, giving her a well-duh facial expression. Oh no, I quickly faced the front of the bus and slunk down in my seat. How could my sister be so blind? Doesn't she understand that she shouldn't sit there!

The bus started to move again, meaning my sister couldn't move because no one is allowed to stand up when the bus is in motion. The anonymous girl crossed her arms and made a don't-ask-me-why-she-is-sitting-next-to-me look. My sister remained clueless and still had a smile on and looked around the bus. "I'm Sarah!" my sister persisted.

The girl smashed herself as close to the window as she could; she even put her book bag between her and Sarah. I couldn't see what else she did because people's heads were in the way.

My body jerked forward and then went slamming backwards when the bus driver made a quick stop. The doors opened, and a girl with long caramel-brown hair got on the bus like she owned the place. She wore a denim miniskirt, which had to be too short for school and a tight tang-top, with flip-flops. The girl headed towards the back of the bus. She paused for a second after she passed me and squinted at me but continued walking to the back of the bus again.

The bus began moving again, and the girl went tumbling forward until she stopped herself with her hands in front of my younger sister. The girl eyed my sister and then looked back at me and back at my sister. Her mouth dropped.

"Excuse me, you're kind of in my seat," The girl said.

"We don't have assigned seats, Brittany," Mr. Kisto, the bus driver said looking at her through the mirror. "You are going to have to find another seat."

Brittany's mouth dropped, but began slowly walking to the front of the bus looking for any open seats that were as far from the front as possible. The bus was packed, and the only open seat was by me and Johnny. When I left Greensboro, Johnny was nerd who was in the chess club. He has light orange hair, wore thick glasses, had braces, and snorted whenever he laughed. Brittany chose to sit next to me.

Brittany and I didn't say a word during the whole bus ride. We kept on examining each other and gave awkward smiles towards each other. Then all of a sudden, it hit me! She was Brittany Stape! She had changed her hair color and lost weight. The one that I had been a best friend with! We practically ran the whole eighth grade society. Everything evolved around us until I messed things up. When she found out that I was the one that started all the rumors, she got furious and everything went downhill from there.

I just stared out the window to avoid eye contact with Brittany. Either Brittany didn't remember me, or she doesn't care that I exist.

"Class, I'd like you all to meet your new classmate Rae Smith," Mrs. Juabai announced to her entire homeroom class. "Most of you guys probably know who she is because she attended Mountain Peak three months ago."

I noticed how Brittany (who was unfortunately in the same homeroom class as me) froze and then started studying me.

"So tell us a little about yourself." Mrs. Juabai took her cold hands off my shoulders and sat at her desk, giving me all of her attention.

"As you already know, I'm Rae." I did my best not to stutter from the fright of being in the same class as Brittany. "I use to go to this school before I moved to Indiana, and now I'm back here." I noticed how most of the class gasped that I would ever show my face in this school again. "Yeah..." My voice slowly trailed off.

" What about your family, do you have any siblings?" The teacher pushed me to tell more.

"I come from a family of four: me, my mom, dad, and younger sister."

"Do you like playing sports?" The teacher was starting to get on my nerves with asking so many questions.

"I do enjoy playing sports." I was about to stop but I saw Mrs. Juibai raise her eyebrows and nod her head informing me to say more. "I mostly enjoy playing volleyball and basketball."

The teacher got up from her chair and clapped her hands. "Thank you very much for sharing with us. I know it can be nerve wrecking having to stand up and talk in front of twenty-two students, especially on your first day." The teacher snorted as she laughed to her own comment.

"Yeah," I whispered taking one step away from the teacher.

"Oh, don't worry; you will have friends in no time! Cheer up!" Mrs. Juibai said. "Brittany, you will be showing Rae around the school, take her to her classes, and make her feel welcome. Rae, there is an open seat next to Nick. This will be your assigned seat from now on. Are we clear?"

"Yes, ma'am," I said doing my best not to make her mad.

The tables were placed in rows with two seats per table. Nick was my table partner. Nick was my first friend when I attended Mountain Peak a couple months ago, but we quickly separated once I met Brittany and her friends. "Hey," I said nervously as I pulled the chair out and placed my bag against the leg of the table. It was awkward talking to him, considering that I was the one that ditched him for Brittany.

Nick turned his head and smiled; then he went back to reading his book. "So, what are you reading?"

"You're the girl that went around school spreading rumors, aren't you?" Nick said going off topic, as he always did when he wanted to get his point across.

I wasn't expecting for him to bring that topic up. "That's a weird book name," I faked a chuckle. "Who's it written by?"

"Is that why you left?" Nick said making it clear that he wouldn't drop the topic.

"Umm, no."

"Then why..." Nick questioned.

"Rae, I'm overjoyed to see that you are making friends," Mrs. Juibai interrupted, "but I am trying to teach a class here."

"I'm sorry; it will never happen again." I was thankful that she interrupted our conversation, although I had a feeling that the conversation about my moving wasn't over.

Before the bell rang, the teacher announced that she wanted me and Brittany to stay behind. She had asked for Brittany to show me to my locker and help me find someone that will be able to take me to my second period class. The teacher also asked Brittany to accompany me at lunch and introduce me to all of her friends. I could see the anger in Brittany's eyes when Mrs. Juibai said that Brittany was to be my buddy and that I would be eating lunch with her. The teacher also handed me a lock, school map, and my schedule. "Brittany, go help Rae get settled into her locker," the teacher said.

I got one of the newer lockers. The newer lockers looked nicer, were bigger, and were in a better location than the old lockers. The lockers were made of metal and painted over so that if you look far away you could see our giant shark painted on the lockers. The blue shark was Mountain Peek's school logo.

"Why are you here?" Brittany blurted out. "You and I bother know that no one wants you here."

"The same reason you are here," I explained, "to learn, Duh."

"Ha ha, hilarious, I've never forgotten how you always act so innocent." Brittany paused for effect. "Everyone knows what you did, and no one is ever going to forgive you!"

Before I could yell back, the principal walked by. "You guys are going to be late for class, you better hurry up."

Brittany yanked my schedule sheet from hand. "You have study hall next in room 215." She stared at the sheet a little longer, and her eyes and mouth got bigger. "With me! Ugh! You are ruining my life!"

"Why? You afraid you won't be 'queen bee' of the eighth grade anymore?" I slammed my locker door, took my schedule sheet back, and charged off to Room 215.

"You don't have any friends. You wanna know why?" Brittany yelled in my face. "You lied to people and made people look bad!"

I began walking to class again. "I know what I did was wrong, and I can't change that, but I can change who I am now."

Today had been a horrible day! People kept on asking me about why I moved, and why I'm back! Brittany and her friends were really mean to me at lunch! They kept asking how I could ever show my face at Mountain Peak, and kept talking about how mean it was for me to spread rumors. I already know what I did was wrong, do they not see that!

During lunchtime, I waited for twenty minutes by my locker to pick me up for lunch and she never came. So I went to the cafeteria to see if she was there. I saw her and her friends were packing up their lunches and getting ready to leave! I went joined them, because I thought that they would wait for me but they didn't. They left me alone with my bagged lunch, for the whole lunch time. When I went to talk to Brittany about the lunch agreement and how she didn't follow what the teacher said, she acted all innocent as if it had slipped her mind.

I made two goals before I was about to enter the deadly doors of Mountain Peak: make at least one friend today, and get Brittany to realize how sorry I am. I was really confident about today's goals until I went into the school building. Everywhere I walked, people were whispering.

I jumped when I closed my locker door and saw Nick behind it. "Goodness Nick, you scared me!" I said in a joking manner. "What is it?"

"After class I thought about how hard it must be to be the 'new kid' in school," Nick explained, "plus be on everyone's bad side."

"Are you trying to rub it in! I already know that no one wants to be my friend."

"See now that's where you are wrong." Nick said. I was completely confused because I knew that I was right. "I've decided I would put the past behind and be your friend."

I turned to Nick. "What about everything I've..."

"It's all behind me," Nick smiled. "Everyone makes mistakes. So I'll see you later?"

I laughed. "Yeah." I can't believe he is willing to be my friend! Not that I'm not thankful, but he's insane. I guess I can check one thing of my list. Now I just need to apologize to Brittany.

All of a sudden I remembered something that I had forgotten in my locker. I ran back to my locker, grabbed a cute purse filled with a photo album (with pictures of Brittany and me), friendship bracelets, some of Brittany's favorite candies, and a sorry letter.

Right before class I dragged Brittany outside to talk. "Brittany you have a good reason to be furious with me. I messed up your social life, but I also messed up mine. I am aware that I can't control the past, but I control who I am now. I realize that I was a big Jerk."

"You told me that yesterday." Brittany rolled her eyes to inform me that I was boring her.

"I dragged you out here to ask for your forgiveness," I said searching Brittany's expression for an answer. Brittany didn't seem to believe me. "Remember all the fun times we had together: being silly, going shopping together, and always being there to support each other when we were in need!" Surprisingly Brittany seemed willing to listen to what I had to say. "Brittany do you remember?"

Brittany gave me a dirty look, "No, that was a long time ago."

I thought that Brittany would be a little more open minded and forgiving towards me. "Oh." I wasn't quite sure if I should give her the present now; after all it wouldn't help me.

"Why are you carrying two purses?" Brittany asked. "Freak."

"It was supposed to be a gift for you." I glanced at the clock in the hallway. "Here," I handed Brittany the purse.

Brittany was resistant to take the purse. Maybe she thought it was a prank—or a trap, who knows?

The bell rang, notifying everyone that class is about to start. "Girls," the teacher opened the door, "class is starting."

I kept my eye on Brittany during the whole class period. She didn't even look at her gift. The purse that I gave her just lay against the table leg on the floor. It hurt even more to realize that I might not even be able to fix my problems. Why couldn't she just give me a second chance?

★ ★ ★ ★

I was dumping my books into my bag and getting ready to go home. While I was putting on my winter jacket I thought I heard my name. I looked around, but I didn't see anyone that looked like they wanted to talk to him. *Huh, Weird.* I swung my bag around my shoulder started heading towards the door. I heard someone call my name out again. It sounded like they were going "Rae! Rae! Wait up!" Maybe I was just hallucinating; the hallways do get hectic when it's time to go home.

"Rae!" Brittany laid one hand on my shoulder and the other on her knee to support her as she bent down gasping for air.

"Um, hey. Why are you so out of breath?"

"I just got out of P.E. class, and we had those dumb fitness tests." Brittany gasped for more air. "See, look what I'm wearing!" She finally caught her breath and stopped gasping for air. "Anyway, I looked through the adorable purse that you got me."

"Yeah," I didn't know what to say because I wasn't sure if she wanted to be friends with me again.

"I also read the letter that you left in there," Brittany smiled. "And I'm willing to forgive you."

"You are!" A tear rolled down my cheeks. I tried wiping it away, but more tears took its place.

Brittany searched through her bag and pulled out a small pack of tissues. She gave me a tissue and pulled another one out for herself. Brittany also had tears coming out of her eyes. "Yeah, I don't think I could hold a grudge against you forever." Both of us giggled at the same time and walked to the bus together laughing-our-heads-off with all the memories and inside-jokes.

On the bus Brittany and I sat next to each other. Brittany searched through the purse that I got her and pulled out two bracelets. "I want to give you this friendship bracelet. You know how it works! We have to make a wish, so that when the bracelet falls off our wish will come true!" Brittany and I helped each other put the bracelets on, and we made a wish at the same time.

Survivors On Shore!
By
Alex Chen

Smoke permeated the air around me. Sweat streamed down my face in this agonizing furnace. With every breath of smoky air, it felt harder to breathe. My feet gave pained cries because the burning floor had already burned through the soles of my socks. In desperation and frustration, I thought, *Why can't I even find the front door of my home?* Suddenly, I felt a flame lick my shirt, and all I could feel was heat. In my last desire to live, I suddenly remembered to stop, drop, and roll. Lying on the ground, I rolled slightly, and the world faded into blackness.

Abruptly, I awoke and found myself on the floor. "I must've rolled off my bed," I muttered to myself. Ever since a fire had devastated our house, I had been having nightmares of fires. The dreams had seemed to vanish fairly recently, but ever since I'd stepped foot on this cursed cruise ship, the dreams had been coming back. Hot sweat dripped down my forehead as I blindly groped for anything to wipe myself. I looked around and saw that all of my articles were still in their respective places. My eyes glanced around the room and stopped when I saw my clock. It was only a little after four o'clock in the morning. As I attempted to grab my clock, I clumsily knocked it over, and it made a soft metallic "clink" on the floor. Unfortunately, the quiet noise awoke my mother.

My mother came in and drowsily asked me, "What's going on?"

I told her that I had another one of my nightmares about the fire. Fearfully, I pleaded, "Mom, make the smoke smell disappear; I can still smell smoke. This ship can't be on fire...can it?"

My mother gave a gentle rebuke, "Remember, today is only the third day on the cruise. You can't really go on like this for the whole ten days can you?"

The dream and my mother's rebuke annoyed me, so I decided to head out at that very moment.

My mother advised a stroll on the cool, windy decks on the top floor. I graciously accepted her offer, but I coolly assured her I would be safe going alone. I drowsily pressed the button to deck eight and leaned back to enjoy the ride. I plodded onto the open deck, only to be blasted by a bone chilling wind. The wind pushed against my thirteen-year-old body, blowing my normally neat, black hair in all directions. My whole body shivered with cold. I headed back to my room and decided that I might as well get some rest at this crazy late time of night.

"Hi, sleepyhead. Rise and shine time," my brother, Ryan, said cheerfully. I felt the sun's rays beam down onto my bed through the cracks in the curtains. I took a quick glance at the clock; it was already half past eleven!

My brother noticed my disbelief and quickly added, "By the way, Mom also said you weren't feeling well. Are you okay?"

I replied, "I feel perfectly fine now, but I didn't feel that way seven hours ago." Sometimes little brothers could be a headache, but when you're in situations like this, they could act just like your best friend.

My mother interrupted our conversation and suggested that I take my brother to eat lunch at the restaurant on the deck seven. I thought I wasn't famished, but in the end, I agreed to go and take a break in the food area. As I entered, I immediately noticed that my worst enemy, Daniel, stood there shovelling gooey mashed potatoes onto his plate. I attempted to walk past him, but he caught my eye and slowly lumbered toward me.

Visibly frightened, I tensed up when he stopped right in front of me. Formerly, this fourteen-year-old bully had thrown punches and chased me around the ship. This time, I stood vigilantly prepared to grab Ryan and run off before he could catch me. Today, instead of his customary bluster and strutting, Daniel lumbered up asking, "James, do you want to go swimming this afternoon?"

Immediately, I wanted to say no, but against my better judgement, I reluctantly said, "Umm, sure, I'll meet you at the top of the water-slide this afternoon." Before I left, I turned around and saw that he had a malicious grin on his face and a twinkle of mischief in his eyes. I was almost ready to decline his offer.

Later that afternoon, I started the long twenty-five foot climb to the top of a water slide. I was dumbfounded that Daniel wasn't coming up to meet me. I thought he sounded pretty sincere in his invitation earlier at lunch. Unexpectedly, strong arms grabbed me from behind and pushed me not onto the slide, but the other way and off the platform. Turning my head, I saw my assaulter, Daniel, laughing at my demise.

At the last second, I flailed my arms, desperately looking for a handhold anywhere although I knew I wasn't going to find one. Even though I tried, my effort was futile as I kept on falling closer to the edge. I heard Daniel laughing at me as I fell headfirst toward the crystal-clear water, twenty-five feet below. I could see the world passing in a blur, and I thought, *is this really how it ends?*

The water felt like concrete even from a mere twenty-five foot drop. I tried to push myself towards the surface, but my limbs weren't listening to me. Everything faded into darkness

Moving my eyelids, I could only see a very dull and plain room. As I struggled to pull off my blanket, a man who I assumed to be a doctor

walked in and informed me of the extent of my injuries. "You're actually responding fine to the treatment we just gave you."

I let out a sigh of relief, but my heart nearly skipped a beat when I turned my head around from my lying position and I saw my mom. She bent over and started hugging me. Naturally, I felt embarrassed and said, "Mom, come on!"

She said, "James, I just about worried to death when we heard you had an accident. I've been sitting at your bedside the whole time. Briefly glancing at her watch, she added, "It's been almost five hours since you fell, which is a pretty light word to describe your accident."

I felt all hot and embarrassed after her emotional statements, but, fortunately, my dad and brother came in, saving me from the moment.

My dad commented, "James, are you fine? If you are, let's go and have some fun!" I personally thought his statements sounded a bit too happy, but I could tell by his exasperated expression that he just wanted to get me out of here.

The doctor, whose name I never bothered asking, interjected, "Well, you look like you're doing fine, so as long as your parents can pay for the medical fees and sign you out, then you're fine to go!"

As we walked out in the corridor, I admired the sickbay and recognized that it was a state of the art facility. Everything looked sparkling clean, and the doctor's spotless white garment even stood out against the bleach white walls. To me though, it all felt just bland, all white, but very professional.

As my dad pulled out his wallet, a couple of business and credit cards fell out, just another symbol of my unorganized father.

Meanwhile, my dad bent over and picked up his paper business cards, since they had plastered themselves to the floor. After a quick chat at the cashier counter, our whole family walked out towards the elevator.

Back, in my room, I enjoyed the comforts of our fiery hot shower as I bathed and got ready to dinner. Earlier, my mom had promised me a dinner at the best restaurant aboard the ship, which also happened to have six-star American cuisine. In my head, I wondered, *What did I do to deserve this reward...falling twenty-five feet and causing my dad a lot of hospital bills?* This whole idea sounded quite absurd to me.

I took my sweet time as my brother begged me to go play a game of chess with him. I couldn't have cared less because I knew I would lose.

After losing yet another game of chess to my brother, I took the elevator to deck eight. My parents said they would be lingering around the bar and out-door pool area. I felt utterly bored, and I resisted the temptation to eat a hot dog because I knew I had a nice dinner coming up. At that very moment, I still wished I were in the comfortable covers of my nice twin-sized bed.

Alarm bells went off all over the ship. I grumbled, "Something probably exploded in the stinking kitchen." I looked around and saw smoke rising rapidly from the aft part of the vessel.

The loud speakers announced, "All passengers move immediately toward your assigned lifeboat stations, which were given to you during the lifeboat drill. I repeat; this is not a drill. This is an order. Abandon ship!"

I moved quickly, but many others had already dropped their plates screaming and running toward the nearest lifeboat they could find. *So much for not panicking,* I felt miserable after already being cursed so much on this blasted chunk of metal that happened to have the capability to float. I would definitely regret this later, but forgetting all of my previous training in fire drills, I ran toward the stairs to get all of my worldly possessions.

A crew member yelled, "Hey you! Where are you going?"

I briefly blew him off. "I'm going to my life boat station on the other side."

Immediately, he responded and grabbed my arm. "No, you're coming with me right now young man. I can't afford to endanger your life. I think that you're going to do a bit more than go to the other side."

Frustrated as I was, I spoke calmly. "Would you please let go of my arm? I will sue you for physical assault. Just lead the way and I'll follow."

He smirked at me and said, "Sue me when you're dead. Believe me, young man; you are making some very regrettable decisions. I will respect your privacy though."

Right after he let go of me and his back was turned, I made a break for it and ran down the stairs through a crowd of people. As soon as a darted into my hallway, I promptly regretted my decision. Smoke had already started to ooze into this hallway, but the flames had not yet spread. I decided to try my luck and find a lifeboat that hadn't left yet. After crawling out to the exit, I saw that smoke had already enveloped most of the cruise ship already in a relatively short period of time. Flames were already appearing on the upper decks around the kitchen where the fire had spread steady and fast.

I managed to catch up with one of the last crewmembers who was late getting out of the ship. I glanced over at the lifeboat, which looked basically empty. As I took a closer look, I saw Daniel situated snugly in it, and my muscles immediately tensed up, preparing to run off.

The crewmember yelled at me: "Get in or you're going to either burn, drown, or suffocate!" I was considering my options when a chunk of burning hot, fiery metal landed a mere few feet behind me. The lifeboat moved toward the surface of the water when I dove and landed in the safe confines of the lifeboat. I just hoped nothing worse could happen.

"What did you do this time to yourself Mr. Smarty pants?" Daniel snorted.

I couldn't really tell what he really tried to convey to me beneath that message, but I decided to keep myself alert and quiet. I was amazed and dismayed at how well we were getting along despite this disaster. It seemed so serenely peaceful, just like a boating expedition with just Daniel, me, and this sailor. Well, peaceful except for the fact that a huge multi-million dollar ship was sinking right behind us. I heard a bubbling noise come up from the motor, and it sounded like we were running out of gas. I was completely nerve-wracked. The sailor who identified himself as Mr. Johnson leaned over to take a look and mumbled, "I can't see what's wrong. I thought all the gas tanks were filled before departure from Vancouver."

All I heard was a splash and a scream as I saw Mr. Johnson slip over the railing of the lifeboat. Daniel walked over and looked cautiously, but there was nothing to be seen. A few seconds later, his baseball cap floated up, and we knew he was gone. We heard another electric noise that made us leap up from our seat, and we saw our radio and communications box emit thick, black smoke. I heard a loud noise, similar to a loud zapping noise.

I looked at Daniel with great hatred and enmity like I had done before, but I saw a slightly pleading look in his eyes. I wouldn't really blame him. After all, we were stuck on a lifeboat somewhere along the west coast of Canada or Alaska with the depressing view of a few other lifeboats driving towards land. Sometimes, it might just help to join up with the crowd.

By some miracle, our rudder was still intact so I decided to quickly confer with Daniel about our options. For once, he acted rationally. "I think we should attempt to steer the boat, and let the waves and current do the work. Hopefully, we can meet up with the other lifeboats. I couldn't stand trying to survive out there in the Canadian wilderness." Only around a mile or so to our east, in our view, was the coast of Canada.

I had nothing better to say, so I reluctantly replied, "Sure, I just hope all of us can get of this alive and together." The enmity and tension between us began to fade because we both knew, for the sole purpose of survival that we had to work together cooperatively.

Daniel steered the boat, and I looked around for anything that might impair our lifeboat. Suddenly, we ran into a well-hidden underwater shoal that protected the inlet of the bay. Daniel let out a stream of very inappropriate words at me. Well, it was partially my fault for not seeing that.

I visualized myself drowning, and the small boat picked up pace significantly. I heard a giant thud, and I could've sworn the lifeboat fell apart. Fortunately, our small boat slammed into a mound of sound. Even though I was showered with sand, I felt suddenly reborn at having another chance to live. I'd always believed that I would be rewarded for being such a good boy one day. We had survived the first uncalled test that had been thrown at us by nature.

I said, "I think we should try to pull the boat on shore so it won't drift away."

He nodded in quick response, but my main goal was to try to obtain some basic survival supplies if we were really going to be stuck in these woods. I felt too tired to do anything, but I knew we had to secure the boat.

We secured the boat tightly to a rock using strips of my undershirt tied together. I felt completely wiped out because we had both been awake for extremely long periods of time. As I lay on the ground, it felt just like a soothing mattress.

In the morning, I felt hungry, and Daniel complained, "Come on, let's find some food." Yawning, I replied drowsily, "Oh, just wait a while. Try to find something in the lifeboat."

I dozed off yet again, but a cool gust of air blew around me. Causing me to shiver with cold. After all, I was only wearing a thin long sleeve shirt with a windbreaker. When I glanced towards the source of all the noise, I observed that Daniel had already started to take apart the lifeboat. He looked voracious searching impressed me. As cool and composed as I usually was, I jumped up and got ready to help him.

I yelled out, "Can't you check some of the waterproof compartments on the side of the boat? Don't you know that the spare life jackets are under the seats?"

Daniel looked at me with evident confusion, "What?" Gently brushing him aside, I stepped on to the boat and grabbed a small handle on the side of the boat. After tugging with all my strength, a whole section of the side panels fell off. Inside, there were food, water, and other emergency supplies all arranged neatly and categorized in this compartment.

He jumped with joy after seeing all the food housed in the compartment. I was usually quite composed, but I was excited to have a chance at survival and yelled, "Yay!"

I asked Daniel, "Where do you think our best chances of survival lay?"

He replied, "In a GPS, if you have one that is." I looked into my pocket and found that they were empty except for a few scraps of paper. Meanwhile, Daniel searched in his backpack and said ingenious when he saw the small compass hooked onto my backpack.

I was just as surprised as he was so I asked, "Where did you find that?"

Examining the compass, he responded, "On your backpack. We should start moving south. Judging by prior knowledge, we were about to reach Ketchikan before our cruise ship sunk, so we should probably be somewhere in between Ketchikan and Prince Rupert."

All I could say was, "Wow." I was tempted to say that I never knew he had that much intelligence and logical reasoning in his minuscule brain. I added, "We should start moving now. I don't want to be confined here forever."

While packing up, I took a last look at the rest of our belongings and everything that we had left behind in this uninhabited coastline. All I could see was the ocean and our wrecked lifeboat. Meanwhile, when I turned my body towards the south, I saw miles after miles of coastline with sparse brush and other plant life. Still hoping for the best, I looked out for any smoke or a sign of any other type of human being, but all I could was a deserted landscape.

Daniel must have predicted my thoughts because he slapped me on the back. "Old fool, do you think you'll see anything out there? We're nowhere close to anywhere. Honestly, we're in the middle of nowhere, otherwise known as the Canadian or Alaskan wilderness. That depends on how far north we are."

I was dazed by the next action he executed. He held out a hand and pleaded, "Do you want to forget our past incidents and work together? We're going to need every ounce of our strength to get out of this wilderness."

I immediately snapped up the opportunity to make a new friend and replied, "Sure, I just want to make one ultimatum: since we don't completely trust each other, I believe that we should both keep a distance."

He replied, "Whatever you say. I'm just trying to point out that we need to work together in order to survive this ordeal."

After much strenuous walking and hiking on this uninhabited landscape. I wiped my head, now covered with sweat and said, "Whew, that was tough; let's take a water break."

It was evident that Daniel was in a pourer physical condition than me, and he had already been panting hard for a very long time. He didn't speak but nodded in exhaustion. I pulled out a couple containers filled with water and handed one to Daniel. I said, "Please don't drink it all. We need it to last a couple of days or until it rains.

After gulping down a humongous portion of the water, he said, "You would really drink the rain? It's probably all acidic and laden down with pollution."

I argued, "We're in the wilderness. Who would build a factory here to emit greenhouse gasses and dump chemical waste into rivers?"

Seeing his argument lost, he admitted, "Okay." Then swiftly changing topic, he said, "Let's keep on moving if you feel up to it. We should cover as much ground as we can before it gets dark."

After yet another few hours of walking, it looked like we had covered quite a lot of ground, and none of the other landscapes previously seen could be sighted from our current position. I swore my lips were shrivelling up without water. I said, "I cannot take another step; I am thirsty beyond belief."

Daniel said, "Sure! I'll get you a water bottle."

I could feel his hands in my backpack, and he handed me a half-empty water bottle. I gladly took it and downed the whole bottle without a second thought.

I said, "Boy, was that good!"

Daniel mumbled, "That was our last bottle of water."

I cried out, "What? I thought we had brought seven bottles. Don't we have a water filter?"

Daniel retorted, "If you don't remember, we already drank almost all of the water. Water filters don't filter salt water. Don't even think about drinking salt water. Your cells will attempt to dilute the salt. Then your kidney's will be overwhelmed, causing you to die."

I said, "Wow. That was blunt. How about boiling some water, we can definitely drink that."

Daniel nodded his head quickly in agreement. Somehow, he found a few plastic bags, and we filled them up at the coastline. I felt very afraid that the bags might break, and there would be no water.

This time Daniel took the initiative, "Let's set up camp here. I'm too tired and hungry to move another step."

I replied, "Yes, I know. Can you get some dry twigs? We can light a fire and boil the water."

Daniel rushed off, but he returned shortly after with an armload of wood. I quickly lit a match and lit the fire. We hung the plastic bags above the fire on a branch. Another bag caught the water moisture as it vaporized. Only the salt would stay in the bag. As I lay out my sleeping bag, I thought of my parents and hoped they were all fine. I also hoped that I could meet them soon, and they were all fine. I said, "We might as well light a fire, if anyone sees the smoke, we might be saved."

Daniel agreed and gathered some tinder and looked for some matches in the survival kit that we had brought along. We lit the fire and lay in our sleeping bags. Daniel said, "Good Night."

I replied, "Good Night." I wanted to say something about the fire, but my body was too tired and I just dozed off.

* * * *

I woke up at the middle of the night hearing loud sound followed by a trail of exhaust and a scream somewhere pretty darned close to the camp. Then, as if on cue, I heard a big crash, and then all the sound disappeared. Instinctively, I looked at the sight of the fire, and the embers were still warm with billowing smoke overhead. All of the plastic bags were melted unfortunately. Probably lit by flames.

I was deeply disturbed by the fact that the people who created that noise might be murderous gangsters, so I crawled out of my sleeping bag and quietly woke up Daniel.

"Daniel, let's go take a look. Pack everything up quickly. I heard a really loud booming noise and saw a trail of exhaust."

Daniel got up and replied with a yawn, "Sure, we can go. I doubt the importance of this event. You probably thought it was some type of missile, knowing your military- like thinking."

Angered this time, I said, "Let's just go take a quick look. It won't hurt you will it?"

This time it was Daniel who had nothing to say, and he gave me a light shove. We began to gather all of our worldly possessions in case we did not return.

The whole way in that direction was silent until Daniel casually asked, "What happens if they really are terrorists or something bad? I don't want to get taken hostage and get killed."

I had already considered the worst so I said, "Well, isn't anything better than staying outside in this wilderness?"

Daniel shook his head wearily. "Fine, let's just go. I can tell you're really *excited*."

I said, "Let's just keep on moving. We're almost to the area where I saw the exhaust trail.

Without warning, a man's voice permeated the clearing. Daniel took control and pulled both of us into the cover of some bushes and other plant life. Two men walked into view, and I heard a loud crack as the man dropped a small tube when he bent down to pack his equipment.

When he was bent down, I could clearly see his features from my hiding spot. He seemed to have a pretty strong physical build and seemed surprisingly Caucasian.

My heart was throbbing out of my chest, as I could've sworn that that man had just looked me in the eye. If he really did, he didn't show any signs of it. As he bent down to go pick up his tube, I observed that it had had many small tubes next to it, each labelled FIM-92A Stinger. Simultaneously, Daniel and I looked at each other and whispered, " Missile launchers!"

This answered all of my questions about the exhaust trails and everything else I had seen previously. I could almost assume that the loud crash and scream came from a helicopter or some other vehicle sent to investigate the smoke.

The most surprising part was that these men did not look at all like what terrorists were in movies with middle-eastern looks and went around committing crimes.

As I conveyed my thoughts to Daniel, we both laughed at the semi-racial joke. Meanwhile, the man packed all of his equipment onto the back of some vehicle that I assumed to be an ATV and drove off into the pitch-black night right in the direction of our previous camp.

I said, "Wow, that answers a lot of questions."

"Yeah, let's see if we can find that big piece of wreckage that had been shot down." Daniel added.

Scouring around the clearing, I saw some smoke from an area to the right of me so I headed over to take a look. I saw the burning wreckage of an authentic Canadian Parks and Forest ministry helicopter. I called out, "Daniel! Come here and take a look at this!" Instead, when I looked around, there was no one to be found except for the sound of some wildlife.

My heart felt like it was going to pop out of my chest, but he had disappeared into thin air, just like a magic trick. I searched for a long time around this area with no avail, until I heard footsteps; causing me to immediately dive for cover.

I saw Daniel, nervous but alive, step out and look around. I felt extremely jubilant and rushed out of my hiding spot to greet him. "Where were you?" I cried out.

Daniel said, "I..." and he became suddenly speechless and stared blankly behind me until I turned around slowly and saw a blond haired, muscular, man carrying an XM8 lightweight assault rifle pointed right at my head. I mean, I've seen this scene in movies before with terrorists wielding AK's and other modern day weapons, but I never imagined someone pointing a gun at me.

He spoke calmly but briskly, "Get up and follow me now. If you don't, there will be hell to pay." As if on cue, another man carrying an M16 assault rifle walked out from behind and jabbed the muzzle of his gun into Daniel's back.

This time the other man, a brown-haired Caucasian spoke, "You, boy, if you make one wrong move, you might find a bullet or two embedded permanently in your friend's back."

For the sake of Daniel, I knew I couldn't forsake him so I turned to see what he thought. Onto Daniel's face is plastered a look of pure terror, so I know I have no other option except to follow these terrorists.

"Ouch." I winced in pain as the young blonde man leading smacked me on the side of my head with the butt of his rifle.

Despite my peril, I kept vigilant and looked for any opening where I could run out and never be found again. Anything was better than being in the captivity of a bunch of armed madmen. Then again, what would happen to Daniel if I ran away? They would probably turn him into minced meat or decapitate him. I could never accept this fate for him because I led him into this situation in the first place, and I vowed to get us both out of this alive.

I felt abused in a way because when being a spoiled rich kid, I had never felt or experienced anything like the situation I placed myself in at the moment. Every time I moved even an inch away from where I was directed and led. I was rewarded with a painful hard cuff somewhere on my already sore body.

I was already thinking about writing my epitaph and will when we got to a juncture in the path, and the sound of rushing water pervaded my mind. *This is my chance to escape.* I wondered what would Daniel do if I jumped into the rushing waters.

Although my idea may have been smart at the time being. However these "insurgents" were just as prepared, as they tied our hands together, and a motorboat loomed out of the distance and stopped to a standstill right in front of us. Daniel and I were forced onto the small motorboat, which surprisingly had the Green-peace logo messily painted on to the side.

Seriously, how can a terrorist organization try to mimic an environmental organization?

This was definitely some type of deceit to trick authorities that they were on a "Green-peace mission." I sure hoped that these guys got caught and executed by the Canadian government or something like that.

While, I was still in my state of thought, the boat slammed to a halt as we ran into a small dock head on. I immediately cleared my mind and started observing my surroundings to watch for any opportunity to escape.

I asked, "Where are we going now?"

I was rewarded with a sudden stab as the muzzle of his gun made contact with my back. I saw a flash of black and he said, "It would be best for your own health and for others if you don't make any rude comments to your superiors."

I was tempted to tell them that they weren't my superiors, but Daniel reminded me with a cold stare that they were armed and ready to kill.

I gave up after a while after attempting to memorize the landscape. Every mile that we walked looked just like a forgery of the previous landscape.

My limbs were starting to ache after such a long walk. I thought I had seen smoke rising in the distance, but it was probably a mirage produced by my tiring eyes.

Another while after, I heard the bustle of people working and talking. We must be close to a village! Unfortunately, I hoped wrong. All that was there to be seen was a small compound that had a couple of buildings and guards patrolling the whole perimeter.

Daniel and I were taken to a small concrete building where a main leader began an interrogation process with us.

He asked, "What are your names? I want straight and honest answers."

Daniel's smart mouth answered on instinct, "So what happens if we don't?"

He replied, "I'd hope you'd get there sometime," as he cracked his knuckles. "You'll wish that you had never lived and been on that cruise ship."

We both stared at each other with the same look of fear we had earlier but this time much more intense.

I answered, "I'm James, and he's Daniel."

Daniel was shocked at my honest answer and gave me a malicious stare.

The terrorist leader seemed all the more pleased and said, "Well, well, well, already fighting amongst yourselves. You young boys have no idea what is in store for you."

He leaned over and spoke into a microphone, "Raul, come in."

This guy looked like a technology nerd as he typed into a laptop and spoke quietly with the terrorist "leader."

The leader than spoke, "Based on intelligence, you have been witnessing our activities, have you?"

I hesitated slightly and he bellowed, "Answer me, now!"

I said, "No."

His face hardened as he said, "You better give me a true statement, or we'll be sending the Canadian government your ashes."

I was completely freaked out at this statement, and I cursed and swore at him with as vulgar words as my mind could create. He just laughed and the tech nerd who seemed to be called Raul chuckled softly too.

I still kept steady though, "I didn't see you guys do anything except drop a tube. What's significant about that?"

He said, "Ah, I see, the ignorance of young ones, I shall inform you of our incredible and unthinkable plot to block off American oil supplies and cause civil turmoil in that pig of a country."

I was about to retort and I could see Daniel's face tighten, but I remembered that people tend to make mistakes when they get excited or angry.

He continued, "We will fire various missiles and set off explosions all throughout the filling stations of the Alaska Oil Pipeline. That is only the beginning! Then we shall attack the oil fields, and, eventually, we will strike the oil fields off the Gulf Coast."

This sounded extremely ideological providing that the American government didn't bomb them back to the Stone Age in the process of it. I suspected he wasn't telling us anything truly meaningful.

He kept on speaking, "Now you can watch the execution of my final plan, and then our crew will quickly dispose of you."

I yelled and cursed at him again and thrashed wildly and futilely. A young man grabbed me and tugged me into a small room with a bed and a lot of security cameras.

I looked for Daniel, only to see that he was being led to somewhere else. As one of the terrorists locked the doors, he whispered, "Have fun, young one."

I screamed at him once more but kept within reason, and I decided to think and get out. I searched all over my room, but nothing could be found, I even looked at the wires behind the security cameras and found a surprisingly carelessly set up camera. They had even used some form of wireless transmitters to send the footage from this camera to their main technology warehouse. As I looked closely, I could see a tiny keypad. I reasoned, *If I can pull the cables out, and try to transmit a message to authorities, and then plug them back in, will anyone notice?* I was willing to take this risk, as I would prefer not to be decapitated. The first number I thought of was 911. I picked up the wireless transmitter, pressed a few buttons and held the phone up to my ear. Unfortunately, there was no microphone. It was only one way. I wondered, *Maybe there's some type of hidden microphone?* It was worth the risk.

The ring tone was so soft I thought there was nothing there. As I was about to give up hope, I heard a voice say, "Hello, this is the Seattle Police Department..."

I cut him off and screamed, "Help Me! I'm in British Columbia, north of Prince Rupert. Please call someone in to save me. Please!"

The operator replied, "Sir, would you mind and calm down and repeat that. The police do not handle international affairs.

I breathed a sigh of relief because I was extremely glad that he had heard me. I still screamed, "Please, call the military. Call the FBI. Just report this incident to anyone." The phone call ended abruptly as I suspected he hung up.

I pondered over the idea of trying to ram the door until it fell down. I remembered how one of my classmates had broken a collarbone when he had smashed through a door. That threw this idea out the window. I deemed this idea hopeless, and I might as well go take a nap. I had nothing left to fight with.

I woke up, hearing a steady tapping noise. Surprisingly, it wasn't coming from the door but on the other side. I was amazed as I asked, "Hello? Who's there?"

I heard the sound of a drill as part of the wall crumbled. Just as I believed nothing better could happen, a man with the words Canadian Special Forces on his uniform crawled out. He was armed with the Canadian army standard issue, a Heckler & Koch MP5.

He whispered, "Slip out through here with me, I'm here to rescue you, your 911 call has been relayed to our government."

Previously, I thought the operator thought I prank called him, but I joyously stepped outside. It looked like we were still in the compound, so I followed him for a few more meters before I saw another opening. This time, leading to the outside door.

I stepped out of the compound and saw a whole squadron of Canadian special forces, some armed with H&K MP5s and others with C7's. One man even carried a sawed off shotgun, and another carried a lightweight SAM (Surface to Air Missile).

I asked, "Why are you armed so heavily?"

The man who I assumed to be the operation leader said, "We're here to wipe these terrorists off the face of the planet."

Protesting, I cried out, "You can't do this! My friend Daniel is still stuck in there; you have to go save him."

He said, "Okay, but orders are orders. We have to accomplish our mission with minimal risk of the endangerment of human life. We have also been ordered to keep you out of any of the trouble. You are to be protected by these two men."

They looked like the same as the others but their weapons were long sinister rifles: a Barett M82A1 auto-loading sniper rifle and a C7 automatic rifle. I always had a special interest in weapons, but I had never seen them in action. I decided, I didn't want to see them being fired.

As the men carefully stepped one by one through the hole I had been rescued from, I was told, "Follow us to the escape vehicle, so we can call for support in case of the worst."

I sure hoped that I wouldn't die at this point because I had already been rescued from this deadly prison camp. The sniper set up, standing at ease while waiting for more directions. I was already nervous enough, but the worst part was when the shooting began. It sounded like God himself was pounding and destroying a metal warehouse. As quickly as it started, everything slowed down just as quickly. I breathed a sigh of relief, but Daniel appeared in the front door with two terrorist pointing pistols at his head. A few of the Canadian Special Forces walked out and saw them but they could do nothing about it. It was a classic hostage situation.

The terrorists yelled, "If anyone shoots, two shots will pierce his brain."

No one dared to move, but the sniper besides me aimed and fired quickly, putting a round through the head of each of the terrorists. One man did not die immediately as his reactions were fast enough that he had a death grip on his rifle. He started firing and did not let go.

Daniel screamed in agonizing pain as three shots pierced his arm. The rest of the shots flew over his head as the man fell. Thick red blood dripped out slowly, and this scared me tremendously. I rushed from the safety of my cover and looked at Daniel's arm to see how he was doing." The men immediately began to bandage his arm, then picked him up, and ran towards the helicopter.

One man said, "Hop on, you don't want to get stuck here for even longer do you?"

I grinned and hopped on immediately.

Roughly three weeks after I had gotten home, my mom brought up a sensitive topic in which I hadn't talked about in a while.

She asked, "Do you want to go visit Daniel? His parents have called, saying that he is staying at the military hospital of Vancouver." Because we lived in Seattle, it was only a three-hour drive there.

I cried out, "Of course! I wouldn't know where to begin about thanking him!"

After an extremely long three hours of anxiety, I ran out of the car and hopped into the elevator and went up to the fifth floor. I had already memorized his room number, so I bounced all the way down the hall to room 518.

I said hi to his parents and they said, "We can't thank you enough for helping Daniel get through this."

I snorted, "It should be me who is thanking Daniel. His ideas save both of us."

I sat down next to his beside, and we talked about trivial matters including our miraculous survival, just like old friends.

An Empty Rice Bag
By
Angeline Chen

It started with a rice bag. Maybe if it had been full...I...Chen Liang, wouldn't be here telling you this story, and your life would go on normally. But it was empty, and as much as I wish that it had been overflowing, it won't change my history or my life story.

You probably have no idea what I'm talking about, and in a way, I don't either. All I know is that one night, too many years ago, my life changed forever.

* * * *

The sounds of wooden chopsticks scraping across three glass plates echoed around the large straw hut that I called home. I wondered when I would next eat. *Tomorrow? Next week? Next month?*

"Now, don't worry. Tomorrow we're going to eat more. You two are getting a little too chubby anyway."

Mama's wavering voice jolted me out of my reverie. My brother clutched at his growling stomach. He pinched imaginary rice kernels off his plate. There was no use. There was nothing left on his plate;

he had eaten every piece two minutes ago. I stared down at my plate, down at my reflection. Long gone was the plump face from my memory. Instead, a hollow face with puffy bags under my eyes, stress wrinkles, and sunken-down eyes replaced my once prosperous features.

I knew Mama was lying. *Plump?* I thought. *More like a rake!* It was true. This was my first meal in over two days. My ribs jutted out irregularly along the sides of my body. My knobby knees stuck out farther than my rib bones did. My lucky red bracelet with my solid gold "Year of the Rooster" charm that once strained with the effort to stay on my wrist now hung off my arm; the rooster charm seemed to weight more than I did.

"But Mama, I'm *hungry!*" Ming's whining voice stung my ears and gave my already faint mind a migraine. I gave him a death stare and kicked my little brother from underneath the table.

Evidently, he was as weak and fragile as I was. He winced and bit his lip, but he knew better than to complain to Mama about it.

Mama's tense brow furrowed in confusion as she chewed her dinner...kernel by kernel. Her eyes seemed to dart all around our shack; she looked from my brother to me and from the rusted stove to a limp, empty rice bag that crumpled on the dusty floor at Mama's feet. From wall to wall her eyes flashed, and with each flash her brow creased a little more in frustration.

"Mama?" I placed one bony hand on her stubby fingers. She jumped, like I had just electrocuted her.

I paused. "Is there something you need to tell us?" I asked tentatively, afraid of what her answer might be.

She hesitated. "Well, yes I do, actually. It's about our living conditions..." Mama's voice seemed to radiate self-hate with every word that she spit bitterly from between two rows of tightly clenched teeth.

Ming's ears perked up, and his eyes were brighter than they had been in days. He smiled from ear to ear; he obviously knew what she was going to say. He turned around and faced me. His face emitted pure excitement. Mama stared curiously at Ming.

"I knew it! *See*, Ge Ge. You didn't believe me when I said that Mama had something for us. She *always* does. Remember that one time when..."

Mama quickly cut off Ming's energetic babbling.

"No, no, honey. That's not what I was going to say..." Mama wiped her sweaty palms on her cotton pants. Her mind was going through some type of torture, and Ming and I were too young to know what to do.

In one smooth, motherly motion, Mama picked Ming up from his chair and pulled him onto her lap. Ming's face was a picture of pure disgust and horror. He shoved her off quickly.

"Ma-*Ma*, all the kids at school *already* make fun of me because you're always *hugging* me. I'm *already* five years old. Why do you and Ge Ge always treat me like a *baby*?"

Mama silently let go of Ming. She set him back down on his chair. I glared at Ming. He caught my eye, and I motioned towards the front door. My expression clearly read: Outside. *Now!*

He shrugged sheepishly and slid off his chair. As soon as we were sure Mama couldn't overhear us, I pinched his ear and dragged him to the riverside. He wailed in pain and tried to push me off.

"What was *that*?" I hissed angrily.

Ming began hesitantly but gained confidence with each word. "Well, it's true. You two always talk to me like I'm three. None of the kids at school have families that do that. You guys are *so* annoying!"

I stared at him, speechless. I grabbed him by the elbow and slugged him in the stomach as hard as I could. He gagged and held his stomach, his face a picture of remorse.

"Are you so *stupid* that you can't *see* that Mama is *having trouble* telling us something?" I roared.

Ming held his stomach, all confidence lost. He pretended to be extremely interested in a hole in his sock. He wiggled his big toe out the hole. He lifted his eyes slowly to meet my penetrating stare.

"Now you are going to *go back in there* and act like a *good son*. You'd better *watch yourself*. Mama may favor you, but *I don't*." My voice was cold and hard, and I shoved him towards the house. I watched him spring towards the front door as fast as he could; he was running away from the riverside—away from me.

I causally ambled to the house. I saw Ming jumping up and down from outside the window. Then, all of a sudden, the most beautiful sound I had ever heard wafted to my ears...the sound of a chicken calling. I ran to the house, excitedly anticipating the first taste of meat

I'd had in over two weeks. I stopped short outside the house. I prayed to God that this wasn't a perverse trick—that this would be what saved my family from starvation.

I walked into the house. I couldn't contain my smile. It spilled out over the sides as I took in my surroundings. Four other people crowded inside my house. Ming raced all over the small room, running and jumping happily. My mouth watered as the chicken clucked its way around my house. Then I heard a sound, a hissing sound I will never forget. I whipped around to the source of the sound and laughed out loud when I saw a kind-looking man pouring a large portion of rice... that my family could live off for two months...into our old, weathered, and now full rice bag.

The kind-looking man looked up and smiled at me. Then he walked back to stand next to a young girl that appeared to be a little older than I was. Mama sat with her back facing all of us, folding and unfolding a brown handkerchief in her hands.

"Shen Tai Tai, is our deal still in order?" The kind looking man's smile widened as he saw Ming chasing the chicken around the house.

I was confused. *What deal?* I looked over to my mother and heard her take in a staggered breath, spin around slowly and say in a voice cracking and full of self-loathing, "Yes. You can choose. This one is five years old. His name is Shen Ming." She pointed to Ming. Then she swiveled her pointed finger in my direction, saying, "This is his older brother, Shen Liang. He is almost ten years old. Take your pick."

The man's smile fell a little, and his forehead wrinkled. "Well, Shen Tai Tai, both of your boys are very good. I guess I'll take the younger one. He'll be easier to mold into a Chen."

Ming stopped playing with the chicken. His smile wiped away in shocked disbelief. His face went through three stages: confusion, anger, and then fear. I watched his lower lip quiver as he looked from Mama to Chen Xian Sheng.

Chen Xian Sheng and the girl reached out invitingly towards Ming. Chen Xian Sheng touched him softly on the arm, trying to tug him over. Ming let out a bloodcurdling scream, as if Chen Xian Sheng had just branded him with a red-hot iron. Ming ran away from Chen Xian Sheng and into Mama's arms. Mama let out a stream of tears. Ming wrapped his arms tightly around her neck and refused to let go.

Mama's eyes drifted over to mine, and I caught her eye. Her eyes reddened from crying tears of desperation and misery. Her tortured expression pleaded with me. I knew what to do.

With a heavy heart, I cast a look of pure sorrow and despair at Mama and stepped forward. I hung my head, hating myself.

"Take me," I whispered quietly. Tears burned behind my eyes, longing to pour out.

Chen Xian Sheng smiled wide. His eyes seemed to say: *Thank you so much.* I asked for a moment with my mother and brother. He nodded curtly and nudged the girl outside.

We didn't need to say anything. Mama and Ming hugged me, and another flood of tears filled the room. Even though it hurt me more than anything in the world, I knew that I had done the right thing. I picked up a cloth bag from the ground and threw things into it. Barely even paying attention, I picked up a handful of dust. I scowled and looked at the ground.

As I walked out of the house, I stifled another fit of crying and looked back at my home for one last time. I saw Mama and Ming's faces in the window. Ming pressed his face right onto the glass. The glass flattened his nose, and his tears blurred down the window, leaving a stream of tears leaking down the glass panes. Mama peered out at me. Even from that far away, I saw tears flowing freely from her eyes. I smiled bravely and took one last glance at them before I stepped into an ornately decorated carriage.

That would be the last time I would see them for twenty years.

A person never really expects any of the things that happen in life. I mean, he doesn't just wake up one day and say, "I want to be sold by my mother for a chicken and rice." I mean, if a person ever did that, that's great for him, but I just wasn't that type of kid. I wanted a good life.

Chen Xian Sheng, who I soon started calling "Ba," was a major public figure around town. He owned many theatres and small shops. One shop was called Zhong Sheng Dian Qi, and it sold electronics. I loved going there more than anything in the world. We lived right behind Zhong Sheng Dian Qi. Every day after school I headed over there with my friends and stared at all of the tape recorders, radios, and shiny gadgets that I had never seen before. Of course, that all changed when I was about sixteen years old.

I traced the trail of the raindrops as I sat staring out the window. I had just gotten home from school; it was my sixteenth birthday today. The conversation that I had had with my principal ran in my head, making me nervous.

I had sat in front of the principal that afternoon before I had come home from school, and she had smiled at me coldly and had asked me to sit down.

"Sit down, Chen Liang," she had said.

I sat down timidly. Her eyebrows creased and she held up a manila folder containing number of papers.

"Um...What's that, Ding Xiao Zhang," I asked politely, pronouncing "principal" very loudly. She raised her eyebrows, impressed.

"Well, good thing you have such good manners, Chen Liang. That's more than I can say for your *parents*, however," she said angrily, throwing the manila folder my way.

I picked up the manila folder warily and opened it. On it was a bunch of numbers and a lot of government mumbo jumbo. I stared at it, confused. Ding Xiao Zhang looked at my confused expression and explained, "I just got this file this morning. It basically says that your father is a capitalist."

My jaw had dropped open. "He...my father...what?" I stuttered, dumbfounded.

"He's a *capitalist*, Chen Liang," she said firmly, "and I know that you really wanted to be sports representative for our school, but we really can't let you do that if your *father* is a capitalist."

I stared at her in denial. "But then what do I...what do I do?" I choked out.

Ding Xiao Zhang furrowed her eyebrows in confusion and said strongly, "Well, Chen Liang, it's pretty easy. You're either with the Communist Party and New China, or you are part of that disgraceful family. So what are you?"

"Communist...Communist Party, of course!" I sputtered, "But I have no idea what to do!"

"Well, Chen Liang, most of the students have disowned their families; they have totally separated themselves from the evilness of their families," Ding Xiao Zhang explained.

"Oh...but I...then I divorce my family, basically?" I stuttered.

"That's right, Chen Liang," she said, nodding, "but I know how much you want this, so I'll give you until tomorrow. I will have the Red Guards come by your house tomorrow, Liang."

I just stared at her blankly for a while until she had repeated in the same disgusted voice, "They are *capitalists*, Liang. *Capitalists*. They are evil."

It had suddenly seemed like something in me had snapped. She was right. Why was I spending so much time thinking about it? If it was true—if my parents *were* capitalists, they deserved every bit of torture they got from the Red Guard.

I nodded curtly and said, "That won't be a problem, miss."

She beamed at me. "The Red Guard will hurt your parents. They were trained so that they hate capitalists, Liang. The Red Guard, as I'm sure you know, are a group of high school students in red uniforms that defend Chairman Mao and that *help* Chairman Mao in his great plan for China. Oh, but I don't need to tell you," she said proudly.

A worried expression crossed my face as I thought of the way that my parents were treated. The Red Guards were known to beat their victims fiercely. I quickly erased that thought from my mind.

I nodded once again, my head bobbing up and down quickly. Then, I stood up and walked out of the door and headed home.

And now I sat at the window, watching the rain outside whip at the trees, drumming my fingers impatiently on the windowsill. A chocolate cake with white frosting sat behind me, melting as the air conditioning cooled the large house. I looked back at the cake. *Happy 16th Birthday, Liang!* was written in pink frosting on top of the white frosting. One pitiful candle sat in the centre of the cake, the candle drooping as the frosting melted.

A key turned in the lock, and, with a loud *CLUNK*, the door creaked open. I jumped up and fumbled for a match to light a candle.

The match lit with a loud popping sound as I stared up at the dark figure standing in the doorway. Oh. It was just Chen Tai, Ba's wife.

The match burned to my callused fingers. I cursed under my breath and threw the match onto the floor, stepping on it.

"Oh! Liang–happy birth..." Chen Tai started happily, coming in with grocery bags and setting them down next to my once magnificent cake.

"Where's Ba?" I interrupted, angry.

"Oh. Um. I think he's still at work," she said, confused.

"Where?" I asked.

"Zhong Sheng Dian Qi, of course. I guess this will be another birthday with just the two of us, then," Chen Tai beamed.

I cursed again and stalked out of the room, grabbing my coat and scarf and heading towards the front door that Chen Tai had just entered from.

Chen Tai looked up from the groceries, curiously, and asked, "Why, Liang, where are you going?" She plucked the drooping candle out of the cake and lit it, setting it back down in the centre of the cake carefully.

I yanked the door open forcefully. "Getting Ba!" I threw my arms up in the air.

"But why..." Chen Tai started again.

"I might as well! This is going to be my last normal birthday!" I screamed over my shoulder, slamming the door behind me.

From behind the door I could hear Chen Tai repeat to herself, confused, "Last...normal...birthday?"

I walked into Zhong Sheng Dian Qi, not stopping to check the appliances on display in the window.

I pushed open the door angrily and saw Ba sitting behind a wooden desk with a brush and ink in his hand, recording something onto a piece of paper. He looked up expectantly.

"Oh. Liang! Happy birthday, son!" Ba said heartily, and he shuffled around his desk and pattered over to my side, pushing me into the warmth of the store. I was stunned and bit back my angry retort.

"Aren't you coming home?" I asked.

"Oh yes, of course, Liang. It's your birthday!" he said warmly, slapping me on the back.   I looked around the store. I had fallen in love with the bright shiny appliances when I was just a little boy. I knew that when I went to college, I wanted to major in electrical engineering.

Zhong Sheng Dian Qi was a place where I could let myself be...me. I was at peace with electronics, and they amazed and intrigued me. I wanted to be exactly like my dad when I grew up.

The rest of the night was the happiest night of my life. Ba and Chen Tai, along with my half-sister, Chen Zhiyi, all sang "Happy Birthday" to me, and we ate my melting cake. It was the birthday that I had always wanted. I went to sleep content, trying not to think about what would happen the next day.

The next day I came home an hour late, accompanied by ten young men. No, they weren't my friends. They were dressed in red uniforms, all bearing the Communist star on their boots.

I extended a wavering hand, and I pointed at my house, my voice stronger than I actually felt.

"I think they're all in there," I said firmly, pointing.

"OK, Chen Liang," the Red Guard leader said to me and then turned to his fellow Red Guards and said, "Come on, guys! Let's go get some capitalists!"

Red uniforms swarmed around our lavish house like bees around their beehive. I backed up, standing in the shadows of a tree. The door blasted open, kicked open by a boot bearing the Communist star. I heard Chen Tai scream.

Protesting angrily, Ba was dragged out of the house and forced down onto his knees, his head bent towards the ground. Chen Tai and Chen Zhiyi were shoved out next and placed in the same position as Ba.

"Chen Fuhai," the Red Guard leader said angrily, addressing Ba by his full name.

"Yes?" Ba said, his eyes filling up with tears.

"You disgust me, you bag of scum!" the Red Guard leader screamed, kicking Ba in the side. Ba gasped and put his hand on his rib. He lifted his shirt. Sure enough, a purple-black bruise was flowering under his shirt.

I pulled a letter out of my pocket. I scanned over it, although I already knew what it said. I recited quietly:

"Communist Party:

"I would like to separate myself from Chen Fuhai and his family. They are despicable, and I despise them for being capitalists. My love and commitment to the Communist Party is forever, and my passion for the Communist Party and Chairman Mao will never ever end. I would do anything to serve the Communist Party, and it's only fair that I let go of my family in exchange for the Communist Party. I am so ashamed to bear the last name Chen, but I will continue to bear it, for I wish to change it in the future.

"I would like to dedicate myself to the Communist Party forever.

"Salute the Revolution,

Chen Liang."

I smiled at myself. I was filled with pride and disgust. I was proud of myself for finally doing this, and my adoptive parents disgusted me.

Separating myself from my family wasn't so much a physical separation; I still lived under their roof, ate their food, and wore their clothes. They even paid my college tuition. Separation was more of a mental thing. It was mentally (and formally) stating that I was in no way related to the Chens in any way.

I strode over to Ba. His eyes widened, and he choked out between gasps, "Liang! Go...away...you'll...get...caught too...Go!"

I laughed coldly, and Ba's head whipped up weakly. He stared at me.

"Don't you see, Chen Fuhai?" I addressed him, my face filled with disgust. He blinked.

"Liang, why are you calling me by my name? I'm your father!" he shouted, angry.

My anger flared up. *"Get this into your thick skull, Chen Fuhai.* You are *not* my father. I *hate* you and everything you stand for. I'm *separating* myself from you. If you don't believe me, read this letter!" I screamed, throwing my letter at him.

He skimmed it quickly, and his eyes brimmed over with tears as he handed it back to me slowly.

"What're you doing, handing it back to me? I want you to *mail it for me."* I barked. He flinched back and stuffed it into his pocket, nodding meekly.

Chen Zhiyi stared at me with mixed emotions flying in her eyes. She seemed to be in shock, and admiration shone in her face. I returned the look sarcastically, rolled my eyes, and turned to the head Red Guard.

"That'll be all, then?" he asked, straightening up.

"Yes. Thanks, guys," I said firmly, saluting him.

He saluted me back and strode off, barking commands at his fellow Red Guards.

"Liang...I...why, Liang?" Ba stuttered, his shoulders shaking with sobs.

"I don't have to explain *anything* to you, you *traitor*," I snarled and turned away, fighting the urge to hug him and apologize.

"Liang..." Ba spoke to my back, still lying on the ground writhing in pain, Chen Tai trying to help him up.

As Ba struggled to get up, memories flashed through my mind. I remembered him taking me to school for the first time, patting me on the head and giving me a big smile while gently nudging me inside the classroom. I realized that he had genuinely loved me, and this was how I was repaying him—betrayal.

"I'm so sorry," I whispered to the cool winter air, one frozen tear escaping from my eye and rolling down my cheek, leaving one splatter of liquid on the sidewalk. I smeared the wet teardrop on the ground with my shoe. I kicked dirt onto Ba, and watched as he coughed it out. I whipped back around, my back facing him once again.

I walked away.

It was 1966, the start of the Cultural Revolution, and I was thirty-three. I folded my hands and placed them on my wooden desk contemplatively. I stared into the distance. I didn't understand why the Cultural Revolution was happening. *China used to be such a great nation*, I thought to myself as I hummed a tuneless song and drummed my fingers absently on the deep brown desk, *but now since the Cultural Revolution started, suddenly so many people are traitors. All of my friends from college – they weren't considered traitors like they are now. Anti-revolution, anti-Communist, and anti-socialist – What do those things even mean?* I thought to myself desperately.

"Chen Jiao Shou?" a voice asked timidly, and I whipped my head up, surprised. *Calm it down, Liang, it's not the Red Guard. It's just a student— obviously a Red Guard wouldn't call you "professor." And anyways, it's not like anyone can read your thoughts*, I thought to myself.

"Yes?" I asked, irritated. I smoothed out the wrinkles in my face and rearranged my angry facial features into a happy smile. I smiled at Jiang Ping, hating the red uniform he was wearing so proudly.

"Oh. Well, you aren't coming in tomorrow, right? I mean, that's what I heard from Chen Faqia," Jiang Ping stuttered, his golden badges and the yellow star on his boot shining brightly in the sunlight that cascaded through my window.

My heartbeat quickened. "What do you mean, Jiang Ping?" I asked hastily, fixing my tie absentmindedly.

Jiang Ping narrowed his squinty eyes suspiciously. He shook whatever idea he had out of his head, his short hairs barely moving as he stopped moving his head. He pasted a mysterious smile on his face and looked at me again innocently. "You know, you said you were *going out of town* tomorrow? You said something about going to your hometown. What do you have to do there?"

Now it was my turn to narrow my eyes. "I'm going there to visit my sister and her husband. Her husband, as I think you may know, is the head Red Guard in Fujian?" I retorted, pasting on a sweet smile.

Jiang Ping narrowed his eyes further, but he paused to find another hole in my story. He opened his mouth triumphantly to start another sneaky question and took in a deep breath, preparing himself for his question.

"Anyways, Jiang Ping, why did you stop by?" I cut in, right as he uttered his first syllable.

He opened his eyes wider and glared at me, though the fake smile still remained on his face, as if a happy smile was pasted onto a face with nothing but angry features. "Well, *professor*, you said that there would be an essay due tomorrow," Jiang Ping paused.

"Um. Yes, that's what I said, I guess?" I replied, confused.

"Well sir, I wasn't in class today," Jiang Ping admitted, turning red.

"Oh," I said, smirking, "but there was no Red Guard meeting today. So that means that you must have..."

"Skipped," Jiang Ping finished, "Yeah. So I was wondering what the essay topic was about. I have to get started on it if it's going to be due tomorrow. Wait—but you're not *here* tomorrow, so how can you check it? I might as well turn it in when you get back, Chen Jiao Shou."

"No. The substitute will be my old professor, and she will be grading them much harder than I regularly grade them. So you'd better make yours *good*," I threatened jokingly, giving him a stern look.

"Why, of course, sir!" Jiang Ping barked obediently, "Now...the topic?"

I nodded curtly and wrote the essay topic on a slip of paper in black ink. I smiled and handed the paper to him. Then shooed him out of my office. *Gosh, he's so annoying*, I thought to myself.

I checked my watch. It was 6:00 PM, and I hadn't even *started* packing for my trip to visit my half-sister the next day. I leapt up and looked out the window. The sun was already setting, meaning that it would be pitch-dark in about thirty minutes. I shuffled out of my office quickly and strode briskly through the cold air to my apartment.

I shoved my rusty key into the lock and turned it loudly, the door creaking open. I didn't bother closing the door and instead, scrambled into the apartment, looking fiercely for my night bag. I packed my toothbrush, my books, and brushes and ink, along with a few sheaves of paper.

I walked to the kitchen and filled another bag with food, shoving both of the bags into a larger bag. I put my thick fur coat back on, and walked back outside quickly. It was going to be a long walk to Fuzhou, and I wanted to get there as fast as I could.

I don't know how long it was, but when I finally stopped walking and looked at my watch, it was 10:00 PM. I groaned at the time and looked up from my watch. A small wooden cottage sat cozily in front of me, a crackling fire blowing smoke out of the chimney from outside. I shivered inside my two layers of pants and my three-layered shirt. I walked up hastily and knocked loudly and quickly, another burst of wind blew in from my left and the cold cut through my bones, tensing my joints.

I heard someone get up and shuffle to the door, muttering, "Who would come here at this time?"

The door swung open, and a torrent of hot air came rushing at me. I smiled as it enveloped my body, loosening my joints and warming my ice-cold skin. A woman knitting a green sweater on beside the fireplace leapt to her feet and her knitting needles dropped to the floor. A man who looked exactly like the head Red Guard should look, tensed up and his hands balled into fists protectively. His large shadow loomed over me, and I looked up at him, frightened.

"No, no, it's OK. Yang Jing, this is the person I was just telling you about," my sister said hurriedly, picking her knitting needles back up off the floor. Yang Jing—who I figured was the large figure—was blocking blocked the doorway instinctively.

"*This* is your brother?" he asked, disgusted.

I furrowed my eyebrows angrily, offended. I glared at him and shot back hotly, "What is *that* supposed to mean?"

"Oh zip it, you two," my sister said impatiently, and pulled me into her cottage quickly, shutting the cold air out.

She beamed. "I told Yang Jing you were a teacher—but I guess he's so used to seeing young men that are strapping and muscled, so I guess you came as a surprise..." my sister explained quickly.

"Chen Liang," my sister said happily, pointing to me. She swung her hand around and pointed at her husband looming in the corner of the room. "This is my *husband*, Yang Jing."

Yang Jing grunted and raised his eyebrows uninterestedly in my direction. My sister made a sound in her throat, scolding Yang Jing. He shrugged lazily.

"It's very nice to meet you too, Yang Jing," I said politely, trying to sound as gruff as I could. My voice was bitter, and my sister sensed that. She made another annoyed grunt.

"Chen Liang..." she warned, calling me by my full name.

I paused. "Chen Zhiyi," I mocked in the same warning voice.

Her stern face broke into a smile, and she wrapped her arms around my chubby stomach in a large bear hug. By the time she let go, I was gasping for breath. I stared down at my potbelly.

I didn't used to be so rotund, I thought to myself, *Ba fed me everything I ever wanted...and that was how I repaid him?*

I sat there quietly, reflecting on my past. I remembered Ba taking me to the hot spring in town and ordering me every appetizer on the list because he thought I was "too skinny."

I remember Ba showing me the newest radio or tape recorder and giving me one for free "just because I was his son". I remember the day I decided that I wanted to be just like Ba when I grew up. I remembered the day that I walked away when Ba lay on the ground with two broken ribs and covered in dirt that I had kicked upon him.

Then I remembered my status going from sports representative, to class president, to school representative...eventually I became a Communist Party member.

But all those years, I had never once contacted my adoptive father. I had never once apologized to him or explained myself to him. Even though I had officially disowned my capitalist family, I was still allowed to live under their roof, eat their food, and use their money. Separating myself from them wasn't really a physical separation; it was more of a mental separation. Sure, I lived with them and used everything that they used. But in my heart I told myself that I was a Communist; my family was capitalists; and I didn't have one shred of feeling towards them.

After going to college, I broke myself off from them physically, for I was allowed to live on campus in my dorm. My emotions toward them were still as angered as before, maybe even stronger.

But as the Cultural Revolution started, I realized that Chairman Mao wasn't our savior. All he had managed to do was destroy the family it had taken me so long to start trusting. As I sat staring up at Chen Zhiyi, I knew that she felt the same way.

"I was wondering..." Chen Zhiyi and I both started at the same time. We looked at each other and laughed awkwardly.

"You first," we both said again. We laughed once more.

"Do you know where Ba is?" I blurted out.

Her smile faded. Her hands rose to her hair, tied in a neat and prim bun at the base of her neck. She patted it nervously and glanced at Yang Jing, who seemed to have awoken from his sleep.

"Oh, whoops," I said, giving myself a mental slap.

"No, no. It's OK," Chen Zhiyi interrupted, "Yang Jing won't tell anyone, will he?"

Yang Jing raised his eyebrows and nodded. I narrowed my eyes at him.

"Just ignore him," Zhiyi said, rolling her eyes, but still wringing her hands nervously, "because he's *not* going to tell anyone *anything*, right?"

Yang Jing stood up. "I already *told you* I wasn't. Just keep talking like I'm not even here," he said impatiently, taking out a brush and some ink, and starting to write on a piece of paper.

"Wh-What…what, um…what is he doing?" I whispered cautiously, pointing to Yang Jing.

Zhiyi flipped around, looking at Yang Jing with squinted eyes. Her tense posture loosened, and she turned back to me casually. "Oh, I think he's just writing in his little journal. He does them whenever he's bored," she said with a dismissive flip of her hand.

I glanced at Yang Jing who was scribbling furiously on his paper with an innocent expression on his face. I glared and turned back to Zhiyi.

"Where-is-Ba-then?" I said as quickly as I could, trying to confuse Yang Jing. I looked over at Yang Jing. A tiny smirk was settling into his broad features.

"What? Could you repeat that?" Zhiyi said, catching my attention again.

"Where…where is Ba? You looked like you knew where he was," I said quietly.

"Oh. Yes. That's why you came," she said, nodding her head.

I nodded in return.

"But why would you want to find them after all these years, after all you did…" she started, confused.

"That was the past, Zhiyi," I interrupted quickly. "I'm different now. I promise, all I want to do is see if they're doing OK."

"Well, OK, I guess," she said reluctantly, handing me a sheet of paper with an address on it and directions.

"Here's how to get to their house from here. It's not really even that far—just about fifteen to twenty minutes by foot, and you'll be there. You can go there tomorrow. I can have one of Yang Jing's soldiers come and pick you up…" Zhiyi planned, pointing to a map of Fuzhou as she spoke.

Yang Jing looked up sharply, putting down his brush with a loud *CLACK* on the table. His face turned red with anger, and Zhiyi jumped back quickly, startled. She shot him a look.

"*What?*" she asked, irritated.

"I'm *not* lending you some of my Red Guards to go do something anti-revolutionist," Yang Jing snarled. Zhiyi took a step forward threateningly.

"This isn't anti-revolutionist, Jing. He is our *father…*" she started angrily.

"He's not *anyone's* father! He's a *capitalist* and a *traitor*. Don't you see, Zhiyi?" Yang Jing interrupted, his voice scary and loud.

"I don't care *what* you say, Jing. He's visiting our father. And there's *nothing* you can do to stop him. *Right*, Liang?" Zhiyi screamed, whipping around to face me.

"Er. Yes," I said slowly.

I picked up my backpack and backed out of the house slowly. "Well, er, I'll just be *going* then," I said timidly.

"*Now?*" Yang Jing questioned fiercely.

"Er. Yes?" I answered.

"To…*there?*" he interrogated.

I paused. "Yes?" I said, unsure.

Zhiyi slapped her hand against her forehead, frustrated.

Yang Jing's voice softened. "Stay for some tea before you go, Chen Liang. I feel like I don't know the real you yet."

I stared at him curiously. "Er. OK?" I replied.

"Wait a minute, Chen Liang. I'm going to go to the kitchen to get some hot water and tea leaves. I'll be right back," Yang Jing said sweetly. I glanced at Zhiyi.

Her shoulders were shaking with sobs.

I ran to her side. "What's wrong, Zhiyi?" I asked worriedly.

"He always does this, Liang. Get out of here, quick. He's calling his Red Guard team right now. He's going to go have them *catch you*, Liang. He knows where Ba lives. Oh gosh, oh gosh. What have I done?" Zhiyi moaned, her tears seeping through her shirt.

I stood there, frozen. She pushed me.

"Go! Go, Liang! Tell Ba I said…tell him I'm sorry," she said in a wavering voice, shoving me out of the door.

I stood in the doorway. I hugged my sister quickly and ran into the black night.

I walked around in a daze. I didn't know what had just happened. Somehow I knew that I was in danger, which made me walk a little faster. I lit a cigarette. In the dim light of the match, I saw the directions and changed course, heading for Ba's house.

I reached it at about midnight, panting and dripping with cool sweat, despite the freezing cold weather. I looked up from the paper and saw a straw house, leaning pitifully, shifting in the wind. I walked up to the door and knocked on the door.

I heard slippers pattering on dirt, and the wooden door that weighed more than the house did creaked open. An old man with thick glasses peered out into the darkness, searching for the person that had knocked upon his door so late.

I shifted out of view, suddenly scared of being seen by this old man, being seen by Ba. Ba muttered to himself and started to close the door when I stepped into the light.

The lamplight shining from inside his small hut shone down on my face, accenting and shadowing my features. Ba's eyes widened as he took in the narrow chin, the flat nose, the squinty eyes, and the short haircut of the son that he had lost so many years ago.

He gasped, a wheezy cough that made my heart ache, longing to comfort him. "Liang?" he whispered, tears leaking out of his ancient eyes.

I choked, hearing his voice for the first time. "B-Ba?" I stuttered.

"Liang!" he cried, and a green sweater arm came charging my way. I flinched, thinking he was going to hit me. A moist smell took over me, and I wondered if I smelled my own blood. I took another deep breath, but ended up with a mouthful of green wool.

I flinched again. *Is he hugging me?* I thought incredulously. Ba released me from his bear hug and held me at arm's length to examine me.

He ushered me into his hut, plopping me down on a bamboo chair. I heard the bamboo creak and snap slightly as my weight sank into it. Ba sat down across from me, beaming, his eyes full of tears.

We sat in awkward silence for five whole minutes. I tried to break the uncomfortable silence.

I drew in a deep breath and said coolly, "Zhiyi says hi. She told me to tell you that she's sorry." Ba blinked slowly, and a shy smile spread across his weathered old face.

"She's a good girl," he praised. We settled back into silence again.

Finally, when I couldn't take it any longer, I took out my bag and placed the food upon the table dramatically. Ba's eyes widened as he hungrily took in the sight of the food. He clutched at his stomach, reminding me of my little brother Ming.

Hot tears rushed to my eyes. I hadn't thought about Mama and Ming for so long now. I had found that it dulled the pain if you went on with your life without thinking about the people that you were missing, even if you missed them more than anything.

"These are for you, Ba," I grumbled, embarrassed. "It's getting late now so I'd better be heading home. I'll come visit you next weekend."

I stood up and walked towards the door. I pivoted slowly on my foot and looked Ba right in the eye. My eyes were watering, and my nose was flaring, trying to keep my tears in.

"Ba. I...I...I am so...I'm...sorry...Ba, I'm sorry," I stammered.

Ba tore his gaze from the food on the table and looked at me, alarmed. He was speechless, and he sat there, stony-faced.

"And I know that that doesn't change anything. You were and still are the closest thing I have to a father, and I...I just wanted to let you know that I was sorry," I faltered.

"Why?" he said in a hoarse voice.

"Well...because, Ba," I said, tears filling my eyes and clogging my throat, "I...I...I love you, Ba."

Ba's eyes filled up with tears, and he sat there for a second, not moving a muscle. When he finally opened his mouth to speak, his voice cracked and trembled.

"Liang. After you did what you did to me, I got banished to this home. I never understood why you did that to me after I had provided you with everything in the world. I had loved you, Liang. And after you did that to me, I tried to persuade myself into hating you. I thought it would help me let go," Ba said, pausing in between words to gasp for breath between sobs. "But I never could. See, Liang. You were the closest thing I had to a son. I loved you. And Liang? I...I...well, I still do."

My heart filled up with joy, and my solemn face broke into a smile.

"But that doesn't mean what you did was right, Liang," Ba added on.

My smile faded. "I should have known I couldn't have been forgiven *this* easily. It's OK, Ba. No matter how long it takes, no matter what I have to do, I will win your trust back somehow," I said strongly.

I stood up to go, throwing my coat back on my shoulders.

Ba stood up.

"Liang..." he whispered.

"It's OK, Ba. I understand," I said, drying my tears.

"No, Liang," he started again.

"It's OK, Ba, really," I interrupted again.

"*Liang*. It's...it's OK," he started.

I whipped around to face him. He was staring into my eyes with a passion, and his hands were clasped together behind his back. Tears wet his face, leaving clean streaks of water down his face.

"Ba..." I said, patting him on the back.

"Liang. I...I forgive you," he finished.

I crouched down on the ground, falling to my knees. Tears shook my body, and my eyes leaked more than they had ever before. Tears stained the ground, leaving dark brown spots amongst the light brown dirt that littered the floor.

I stopped in front of my building, shoulders still shaking with sobs. Young men were standing outside of my apartment building, arms crossed, standing tall. I ignored them, trying to push past them to get into my apartment.

As I neared the staircase, I pushed past one of them. One man in front of me shoved me down the stairs, and I fell down the flight of stairs, landing hard on my rear. I cursed and got up, rubbing my rear angrily.

"What was *that* for?" I demanded hotly, getting up.

A strong, cold voice came from the darkness, causing shivers to go down my spine. I stared up at Yang Jing, standing boldly in front of me. He was the one who had pushed me. I scrambled backward a couple of steps.

"Yang Jing? What are you...er...what're you doing here?" I stammered nervously.

"We got an anonymous tip," Yang Jing said, and a couple Red Guards sniggered, "that you went to go see your old capitalist family tonight."

I took a step forward. "You *wouldn't have*," I threatened.

"Oh. Whoops. It seems that *I did*," Yang Jing said, smirking. "And now, if you'll *excuse me*, I have an apartment to search."

I charged up the stairs, fighting the urge to tackle Yang Jing. However, that wasn't necessary. Another Red Guard pushed me down the stairs before I could even make it halfway to Yang Jing. Yang Jing laughed.

"Take him away, boys," he said casually. One Red Guard stepped forward and led me over to the street.

"Where are you taking me? Let go of me. What are you going to do to me?" I stuttered angrily, trying to push the Red Guard off.

He smirked and kept walking. He let go of me to wipe his sweaty hands on his pants, and I saw my only chance out. I glanced at my free arm, at him, and then down the street. *If I get caught, I'll be imprisoned for a very long time*, I thought worriedly. *Oh well. I'll take that chance.*

I took a deep breath, disguising it into a yawn, and took off running as fast as I could. My cloth shoes pounded on the sidewalk, and my staggered breath seemed to awaken the Red Guardsman from his daydream.

"Wha...Oh no!" I heard him mutter, "*Hey! Come back here!*" he shouted angrily. Heavy boots pounded on the sidewalk from a distance, and I laughed into the dark night. I ran into an alleyway and jumped over a fence.

I kept running even after I couldn't hear him anymore. I burst out laughing to myself, half out of relief and out of shock.

Soon after I had run away from the Red Guard, Yang Jing filed a report saying that nothing incriminating was found inside my apartment, and since he had no solid evidence that I had visited Ba, he had to let me go.

I stayed in Hangzhou and eventually married Xu Jie. I had known her ever since I was little. She was Zhiyi's boyfriend's little sister. She eventually gave birth to two sons, whom I loved with all of my heart. I named the eldest one Chen Tong, and I named the younger one Chen Gei.

One night, Xu Jie was out getting groceries. We had just moved into another home because our old one had collapsed. A knock came at the door.

"Come on in, Jie, it's open!" I called. The knocks still wouldn't stop.

"I said the door's open!" I repeated. The knocking was really starting to get annoying.

"Ugh," I said, getting up, "I think it's about time we got you a…"

I opened the door and everything seemed to stop. "A key…" I finished.

"Shen Liang?" an old woman, aged by stress, with a tear running down her cheek, touched my face as if she was checking to see if I was real. I let a steam of tears out.

"Mama?"

Diamond: There Is More To Life Than You Know

By

Kevin Chen

The last time I came home from school, I saw my mother lying on the floor. Dead.

"Dad! Come home, quick!"

"What's wrong Jim?"

"Mom..." Jim's voice failed.

"What? What about your mom!"

"She...she's dead."

Jim heard a loud bang through the phone. His father cursed several times and continued talking in a more desperate manner. "Listen Jim. Go outside and wait for me. I'll be back as quick as I can. And DON'T touch anything. Trust me." Jim's father tried to sound calm, but Jim knew that his father was distressed at the news. His dad hung up before Jim asked further questions.

Jim paced back and forth between the front door and his mother's lifeless body. His skin crawled as if ants climbed all over him. It had been a perfectly peaceful day until he opened the door to his house. How could any twelve-year-boy bear witness to his mother's death? Jim took a look at his mother's corpse. In the middle of the living room,

Jim's mother lay in a puddle of blood with many wounds where sharp objects like knives had been used.

Jim quickly switched his gaze to the room surrounding the scene. He then realized that a window had been shattered. He looked around and saw chairs turned over and random items spread out on the floor. The room was awfully messy. Jim turned around and exited his house with dread in showing in his face.

"What did I do to deserve this? Why not me too?" Jim demanded as he left the disturbing sight and walked to his front porch. He dug his fingernails into his arm in anger. "Why would anyone want to do such a thing?"

In the distance, Jim heard his dad's car door slam shut. "Jim!" hollered his father. Jim was sitting next to the house, tears gushing from his eyes. "Jim." Jim got to his feet and opened the door. Jim saw his dad flinch in terror.

"I..." the man was speechless.

"Call the police now, Dad!" Jim screamed. "Find Mom's murderer and kill him!"

"No," said Dad. "The police will only get in the way."

"Why?" asked Jim in disbelief.

"Jim. Please."

"No Dad! Mom is dead!" Jim shouted and burst into tears.

"You should take a walk to calm down, Jim."

Jim walked down the block with his eyes glued to the ground. A few minutes later, one of Jim's friends spotted him.

Bill walked over to Jim. "Hey Jim," Bill said with a smile.

"Hi Bill," Jim replied.

Jim and Bill had known each other for years and had always gotten along well. Their mothers were college roommates. The boys knew each other for their entire lives. Jim and Bill were almost like brothers. "What's up?" Bill asked. Jim looked extremely sorrowful.

"Nothing," Jim said quickly.

"Come on. I know something is wrong."

"Not now Bill."

"You know you can trust me," Bill said, switching his expression to a more serious one.

"Well, I don't know how to say it."

"Just tell me. I'll help you."

Jim never expected to tell anyone about the tragedy this early. He simply couldn't get it out of his mouth. "Bill," Jim said. "I don't feel like talking about it now."

"What?"

"Just leave me alone for now."

"Oh come on..."

"Please, Bill."

Looking confused, Bill shrugged his shoulders. "If you say so. See you around." Then he walked off.

Jim realized, after a while, that having someone to talk to would help a bit. However, Jim couldn't get the words out of his mouth. He headed back home, anguished.

Jim walked into his father's workroom, ready to ask a burning question.

"Dad?" Jim began.

"Yes?"

"What are we going to do?" Jim asked, "We can't just let go of Mom."

"I know, Jim." His father turned and put a reassuring hand on Jim's shoulder. "You know Jim, I feel just as awful as you do. You see this?" Jim's father held out a shiny object.

"Yes."

"This diamond was your mom's," he said. "Now it's yours."

"What?"

"Keep it."

"Thanks."

"Your welcome, Jim," he paused for a moment. "Listen, I've been getting some headaches lately. I'm going to take a little nap." Jim's father got up off his chair, ready to leave the room.

"Wait Dad!" said Jim. His question was not yet answered

"Yes?"

"You still didn't say what to do!"

Jim's father took his seat again. "Well, all we can do is dig a hole and bury her."

"But Dad!"

"There is nothing else we can do."

Jim watched his father leave the workroom to go to his own bedroom.

Jim stared at the big, plain and clear diamond, sitting simply on the table. Jim looked at it while remembering his mother. "What is the point in life if you will just die?" Jim asked. "It's not fair." Angered, Jim slammed the table in the workroom with his fist. Jim felt like his world had been shattered. "I don't get it!" Jim said in anger, "And what is up with that diamond?"

Unanswered questions filled Jim's mind. After a half an hour of thinking, Jim decided that he couldn't go for another minute without having a question answered. He raced to his father's room, slammed open the door, and yelled, "Dad!" Jim's dad woke with a terrified jump. "Dad, you're keeping something from me!" Jim yelled, "I'm not an idiot!"

"What do you mean?"

"Dad!" Jim screamed and began crying, "I...I bet you're the one who killed mom!"

"No Jim. You don't understand...

"I hate you!"

"Jim."

"What's your purpose? Why would you do it!"

"Jim."

"I'm getting out of here!" Jim said. Then he sprinted out of the house in the direction of Bill's house. After a few minutes, Jim arrived at his friend's house.

Thump, thump, thump. Jim banged Bill's house door. Jim could hear the heavy footsteps of Bill hurrying to the door. "Oh, hi Jim."

"Hi."

"Come on in, my parents aren't home."

"Thanks," said Jim. "Sorry about earlier."

"It's OK."

"I feel really messed up," Jim began. "My mom...is...dead."

Bill's eyes widened, "What happened?"

"My dad killed her."

"You sure?"

"Yes!"

"How do you know he killed her?"

"My dad killed her!" Jim became impatient, "Nothing more to it!"

"Calm down..."

"No!"

"Jim, control yourself," Bill said. "And let me finish. Tell me, did you see your dad kill your mom. I don't think that your parents hate each other that much."

"I didn't see him."

Jim and Bill talked for a long time. Bill usually guided and helped Jim through rough times. At first glance, Bill looked like a mean and nasty thirteen year old, considering his height of five foot six inches. It hid his nice and caring personality well. Bill helped Jim with his situation. Jim was ready to apologize to his father when he was about to leave the house. "You're here Jim?" Bill's cheerful mother had walked to Jim.

"I was just getting ready to leave."

"It's pretty late Jim," said Bill's mother with a smile. "You should stay for dinner."

"Oh, thanks."

Jim arrived home and headed directly to his father's bedroom. When Jim saw that the room was abandoned, he quickly checked all the rooms to the house desperately. His search for his father was a failure. When he went back into his own bedroom, he found a note:

> *I've gone looking for you. I hope we can talk this through. Wait for me. I'll be back soon.*
>
> *From, Dad*

One hundred percent satisfied, Jim knew that his father was a good guy. He knew that his father loved him. However, Jim worried about his father and decided to give him a call. He headed to the phone and dialed in the numbers of his father's cell phone. Jim and his father sorted everything out in the call. Jim's father was already on the way home.

It was evening. Jim took the diamond out of his bag. "Mom." Jim had a funny feeling that his mother's spirit was in the diamond. "Nah, how silly." Jim chuckled to himself.

All of a sudden, Jim received a swift and painful punch in his stomach. "Ouch!" yelped Jim.

A dark-cloaked man quickly took Jim's diamond. The thief smashed a window and hooked a rope onto the windowsill. Then he jumped off. Everything happened so quickly. It took Jim a few seconds until he realized that he had been robbed.

"Stop, thief!" Jim struggled to get up. He clenched his stomach in pain. He had to chase the thief. "I won't lose the diamond," Jim said. Jim made a swift jump out of the window and managed to grab the rope. A second after grabbing the rope, he let go to avoid the pain of friction against his hands. The uncontrolled drop made Jim land on his rear. Two injuries and a lost keepsake summarized Jim's misfortune.

A forest covered the backyards of many houses on his street. Jim wandered hopelessly through the trees. After about five minutes of limping, Jim found the thief lying on the ground and the diamond a few feet away. Jim flinched in terror. He snatched the diamond and quickly checked for a pulse in the thief's wrist. Nothing! Jim dropped the man's hand, terrified that he had just witnessed another death. Jim didn't have the bravery to take off the dark mask that covered the thief's face. There was no blood to prove any kill. Jim ran away from the corpse immediately.

The bright, blue sky turned dark by the time Jim arrived at his house. He planned to go to Bill's house if his father hadn't returned. Jim entered the house and walked around in the darkness. "Jim." Jim turned around and saw the door slam shut. "Who? Who is there?" Jim demanded.

"It's only me," said Jim's dad while turning on the lights.

"Dad, I'm sorry for running off."

"It's OK Jim. Is the diamond safe?"

"About that..."

"Something happened?" His father said in shock.

"No, I have it right here," Jim said, pulling the diamond out of his pocket. "It's that..."

"Tell me."

"I was attacked by this black cloaked thief," Jim began. "He punched me in the stomach and stole the diamond. Then he jumped out my window."

"How did he get in?"

"I don't know," said Jim. "But when I tried to chase him in the forest, he was..."

"He was what?"

"Dead."

Jim's dad thought for a moment, "We need to get out of here."

"Why?"

"Time to tell you the truth," his father began. "There is a group of people led by someone called Dr. Zilch. This group wants a special power."

"Why us then?"

"It's the diamond Jim!"

"The diamond?"

"They originally wanted to obtain the power that your mother manipulated."

"But why the diamond?"

"They planned to kill your mom to take her power," he said. "But just before they killed her, she stored all her power in the diamond."

"It's...it's not fair. Why do I have to ruin my life because my mom was an energy source? What are they going to use the energy for anyway?"

"Their goal is to obliterate the Earth and create a new world."

"That's impossible!"

"We have to get out of here Jim!"

"But we can't just run."

"Right now we have to. They are already after us!"

"I...want to say bye to Bill."

"We don't have time."

"I'll never see him again."

"Fine."

"Thank you."

"Do it quickly. I'll meet you by the tree on the north intersection of this road."

Jim nodded his head and ran off.

Ding-dong. Jim used the doorbell instead of banging the door this time. Bill answered, "Hi Jim."

"Can we talk outside?"

"Who is it?" Asked Bill's mother.

"It's Jim," Bill replied. "Can I go for a walk?"

"With Jim?"

"Yeah."

"Sure."

"Thanks," Bill said as he closed the door.

"I don't have much time," Jim began.

"Talk."

"Please don't tell anyone, Bill."

"You have my trust."

"Thanks. I...I have to leave."

"What do you mean?"

"My mom was this power controller. That's why people wanted to kill her."

"What?"

"My mom put the power into a diamond, and now I had to run away because I had the diamond."

"Whoa. Whoa. Slow down."

"I'm sorry, Bill."

"Tell me clearly."

"Bill, they are going to kill me."

"You can't leave like this!"

"I have to Bill. I'm sorry."

"Jim..."

"I better get going."

"Bye."

"You are a great person, Bill."

"Thanks."

"I'll come back."

"Bye."

Bill stared at Jim walking down the road until he was out of sight. He sat on the front steps crying.

Jim arrived at the tree, but no one was there. Instead, he found a note.

> *I couldn't wait for you. Go back home and into my room.*
> *You will find two hundred dollars in tens under my left pillow.*
> *Take a taxi to the train station. Buy a ticket to Prit Town. A man*
> *wearing a purple coat, blue pants and a red baseball cap*
> *will greet you. Follow him into his house and wait for me.*
> *Trust him. Ask him for directions if I don't come in forty-eight*
> *hours of your arrival. Password (ask him): The mountain over*
> *the river shines with luster. Pulverize this note.*
>
> *-Dad*
> *PS. Do everything ASAP.*

Jim stood there and reread the note a couple of times. "Dad."

Jim looked out the window of the train, while eating instant noodles. He thought about his future. What it might be like to always live undercover. Jim felt like everything that existed no longer meant anything. "Hey, kid."

Jim looked up to see a chubby man. "What are you doing all alone?" The man asked.

Jim quickly thought of an excuse. "I'm visiting my grandparents."

"What about your mom and dad?"

"They..." Jim didn't know how to answer.

"They what?"

"Um..." Jim was interrupted by the man's cell phone ringing.

"Excuse me," he said as he walked off.

Jim was relieved that he didn't blow his cover. After a few minutes, the train arrived in Prit town. Jim quickly got off the train to avoid the chubby interrogator. He walked into the town's train station, searching for a man wearing a red baseball cap. Instead of actually finding the man, the man found Jim. "Jim," the man whispered. Jim turned his head to meet the man.

"How do you know my name?" Jim asked.

"Your father."

"What is...the password?"

"The mountain over the river shines with luster," he said with a smile.

"So, what do we do now?"

"Come with me." Jim and the man went together out of the train station. Jim felt unsafe in a completely new place with a person he didn't even know, but there was nothing else for him to do. However, going with this guy meant seeing his father again.

When they got in the small black car, the man introduced himself, "You can call me Jerry."

"OK."

Jerry started the car and the two were off into their one-hour trip. Jim looked out the window aimlessly. Drowsiness took over Jim, causing him to sleep.

Jim woke up when the car arrived. Jerry led him inside of the house and showed him his room. Jim then walked outside to sit outside of Jerry's house, eagerly waiting for his father's arrival.

Two boring days had passed at Jerry's house. Many cars came by, but none stopped in front of the house. Jim lost hope in seeing his father again and sadly walked back into the house. "Jerry?"

"Yes?"

"What do I do? My dad is not here."

"You have to keep going to places."

"I'm doomed."

"Or."

"Or?"

"Or you can stay with me."

"I...I want to stay," Jim looked up at Jerry hopefully

"Nice. I wanted you to stay as well."

"Thank you." Jim didn't want to be alone again.

Over the next few days, Jim and Jerry went into a forest. Jerry taught Jim fighting skills with guns and blades. "This will be useful for defending the diamond," Jerry said. Jim learned the basic movements for the sword, and killing strokes for the knife. He practiced targets for a week. When Jim returned, he put his pistol into a drawer and headed for the shower.

On one stormy night, Jerry had an unexpected visitor. Jim watched Jerry walk up to the door after the doorbell rung. When he opened the door, Jerry saw no one there. After a strike of lightning, Jerry lay on the floor, dead. "Jerry?" Jim asked quietly.

Suddenly, a spherical object sailed through the open door. Then smoke shot out of the ball. "A smoke bomb!" Jim said, surprised.

Jim took his pistol from a drawer and ran towards the back door. Jim planned to attack the invaders from behind. Jim stopped running when he saw a familiar looking silhouette walk into the house. "That guy from the train," Jim whispered to himself.

"You go up there." Jim heard the man order to his partner. When the smoke cleared, Jim prepared to aim and fire. Jerry told Jim to attack to kill, but Jim couldn't kill after he witnessed three deaths already. Jim aimed at the head, but he couldn't get the courage to pull the trigger. Jim flinched and shot the man's legs instead. The man dropped his gun and fell to the ground, yelling in pain.

"Zach?" Came a voice from upstairs. "You alright?"

"Don't talk," Jim ordered the man called Zach. "Don't move either. You may only talk when answering my questions." Jim tried to sound tough, but he felt like he was committing crime. Jim's hands shook while pointing the pistol at Zach's head. "Who sent you?" Jim interrogated.

"Why would I tell you?"

"Because I will shoot you if you don't."

"Kid," the man chuckled.

"What?"

"You don't have the guts."

"You sure you want to talk like that?" Jim yelled. "Answer me before I shoot you!"

"Yeah right, kid," said Zach.

Jim became annoyed, causing him to pull the trigger. *Bang!* Jim shot Zach in the arm. Right at that moment, Zach's companion rushed down the stairs. He ran over to his friend only to get a bullet in his head. Jim didn't expect his reaction; he started to feel remorse. "OK. OK. I'll tell you," Zach said desperately.

"Good," said Jim while trying to keep his cool.

"His name is Dr. Zilch."

The name sounded familiar to Jim. "How did you begin to work for him?"

"He said that if I was his assistant, I could rule the world with him."

"What else?"

"Well, I asked how he would get this power, but he didn't tell me."

It rang a bell. *"The diamond,"* Jim thought. "You believed him?" Jim said.

"Yes."

"I thought adults were supposed to know better."

"I..."

"Another question," Jim began, "how did Jerry die?"

"Well you see, he gathered information about how many seconds were in-between the thunder. Then we rung the doorbell early and shot when the thunder struck."

"Smart."

"Please spare me."

"No kidding?" Jim pretended to chuckle. "You wanted to kill me."

"Please," he said. "I'm begging you."

"Where's my dad?"

"I have no idea."

"You'll have to do better than that."

"Honest!"

"If all you want is your life then you'll have to do better if you want to go out alive."

"I don't know where your dad is!"

"If you're willing to die to hide the information..."

"No! Please!"

Jim was angered that he didn't get an answer. However, he couldn't kill another man. His insides felt like collapsing and Jim started crying. Zach couldn't blink. Anyone could tell from his facial expression that he seriously didn't know the answer to Jim's question. Jim thought to himself, *"If I let him go, then he might cause trouble again. I can't trust anyone after two people close to me died. I have to kill him."*

"I'm sorry," Jim shook violently and couldn't speak clearly. "I'll have to kill..."

"NO!" He yelled in fear. Zach began to get up and run.

"Jim!" A familiar voice made Jim halt. "And you stop too." He told Zach.

"D...Dad?"

"Jim. Sorry I'm late."

"Dad."

"We need to get this place cleaned up," He turned to Zach, "You're not getting away" Then he threw Zach into the basement and locked it from the outside.

"You still have the diamond Jim?"

"Yes." Jim said while pulling the diamond out of his pocket.

"Good. Now let's start cleaning."

They shoved the bodies in the cellar for the time being. Jim cleaned the blood. He was more afraid of his position even more after the action today. However, Jim felt safe and relaxed with his dad. When they finished, Jim's father said, "They know were here. We have to keep moving."

"OK."

Jim went into his father's car. The car's clock read twelve to twelve. "Take a nap Jim," His father said. "It's late." Jim easily fell asleep in the back seat of the car.

Jim awoke in a bright room. The nearest clock read nine fifty four. Jim got out of the comfort of the bed and looked around. "A hotel," Jim said. Jim saw another bed with messy sheets. He walked to the door and took a glance out in the hallway. "Definitely a hotel," Jim said. "But where is Dad?"

Jim went back into the room and washed himself, realizing that he only had one sweaty shirt to change into. He hoped that his dad would be back soon. Jim opened his backpack and looked for the diamond. To his surprise, the diamond was gone. Jim frantically searched the whole hotel room, but there was no hint of the diamond anywhere. Jim heard the door unlock.

"Dad?" Jim asked, hiding behind his bed.

"Hi Jim," said his father. "Sorry for leaving without telling you."

"Why are we here?"

"We have to go to all the places we can find."

"Um, dad."

"Yes?"

"The diamond...is gone."

"You lost it?"

"No, I woke up, checked my bag and it wasn't there."

"Let me think," the man said. "OK, we have to get in the car. I have some snacks in the car. You can eat then. Let's go"

Jim's father checked out of the hotel quickly and got the car running. Then they were off. Jim's father was impatient because he had to stay under the speed limit. "Dang traffic!" He yelled.

The car arrived in front of a gray building. Jim's father parked the car in one turn. The two raced into the building, Jim behind his father. Jim observed that his father knew this place like the back of his hand. He knew all the turns and he never looked around. Something was up.

Jim began to get exhausted. Such a long underground passage could tire anyone.

Finally, Jim and his father made it to the destination. His father kicked open the door and ran inside. A heavy steel door slammed right in front of Jim, nearly slicing his head off his shoulders. The immobile blast door separated Jim from his father. Suddenly, the floor collapsed underneath Jim and he fell into a prison cell. Everything was dark in the cell.

"Well, well, well, what do we have here?" croaked an irritating sounding voice.

"Who...who's there?" Jim demanded.

"Why, it is only me." Lights filled the room. It revealed a stranger with a pirate hat and a long cloak. His mask concealed his identiy. "My name is Dr. Zilch."

"So you're the idiotic fool called Dr. Zilch!" Jim screamed. "I hate you! You killed my mom didn't you?"

"Well it's nice to meet you too, Jim. Now . . ."

"How do you know my name?"

"I know everything, Jim."

"What the heck? How did you kill my mom?" Jim had his fists tightly clenched to the prison bars.

"Easy Jim. You don't want to threaten me. You are confined in a cell. You will only be released if I choose to free you, so don't get me angry!" Dr. Zilch yelled. "I am in complete control Jim! Don't make me mad. You could be my next kill as quickly as that." He snapped his fingers to express how quickly he meant.

That shut Jim up for good.

"But Jim," Zilch began, "I will tell you my plans. You can't do anything about it anyway."

Jim only stared at the man.

"I'm going to use this diamond I have in my hands..." said Zilch.

"How did you..."

"SHUT UP, YOU IDIOT BOY!" Jim struggled with the volume of Zilch's words. "I'll get to it. The diamond contains your mother's spirit. That is how the thief died in the forest. However, I learned how to control the power of the diamond. I'm going to destroy the earth."

"WHAT? Wouldn't that kill you too?"

"I'm going to end the life of all. It's pointless." Dr. Zilch walked out, slamming the door shut.

When Jim was in the cell, he thought about the reasons why Dr. Zilch would even attempt to destroy the earth. Jim came up with no answers. No sane man could even think about doing such a thing. Jim thought about his dad. He thought about what was happening to him, but right now, Jim could only wait. Jim felt the lock of the chamber. He remembered the pistol and pocketknife in his backpack. Jim first tried picking the lock with his pocketknife.

"No good," he said to himself. "I need a light."

Jim rummaged through his backpack, trying to feel the texture of a flashlight. Unfortunately, Jim didn't have a flashlight on him. He took his gun and located the lock on the cell door. Jim prepared to shoot the lock, hoping for the best.

Bang!

The sound of the gun rang through the cell. Jim fell back while clenching his ears. When Jim recovered, he pushed on the cell door.

"Dang it!" Jim yelled in frustration, "Didn't help at all."

"What's all that racket in there!" said a guard working for Dr. Zilch while swinging the door open.

Jim hid from the man. He put his gun behind his back and crept in the shadows. When the guard was close enough, Jim shot him in the knee. Jim reached out of the metal bars and grabbed the keys located on the guards belt loop.

"Aw, you little brat!" the guard said while clenching his knee in pain. "You shot me!"

"I sure did," Jim said as he unlocked his cell door. "Be thankful that you're not dead. I'm not afraid to kill." Jim didn't mean it though. "Now be quiet or you will be dead!"

Jim used the silence as an advantage. The blinding light was troubling for Jim after being in the pitch-black prison for such a period of time. Jim took a sneaky glance at a map of the building. After a moment of browsing, Jim found the floor where Dr. Zilch's office was on. Jim was glad that the whole area was messy with worktables, boxes, and other trash. It made it easy to move around without being seen. Jim was glad that Jerry had trained him.

Jim looked at the stairs, trying to figure out a way to hide if someone was to come down. Then Jim saw the elevator begin to open. Jim didn't have time to think. He ran to the stairs in order to avoid being seen. Jim ran up to the fourth floor: the floor that would hold the decision of the fate of the earth. Right in front of Jim was a door. "Here I come Zilch!"

Jim opened the door, ready with his handgun. "Dr. Zilch!"

There was a pirate hat, mask, and cloak on the desk; but nothing else. Jim walked up to the desk. There was a container that appeared to be absorbing energy. The energy source was the diamond. Then the door opened behind him. Jim didn't move for a second. A soothing voice broke Jim's curiosity, "Jim, I thought they killed you. It's so good to see you alive."

"Dad. Dad is that you?" Asked Jim, standing absolutely still.

"It's me, Jim. Your dad."

Jim turned around. "Dad, I'm going to kill Dr. Zilch! For Mom! I promise."

"Jim, listen." His father said weakly. "There is something that I haven't told you all along."

"What is it?"

"It's me. I've been possessed."

"What?"

"My body. You know, Jim, this plan to steal your mom's power wasn't formed recently. The whole group was organized way before you were born."

"What? What is it?"

"I married you mother because I loved her. However, I knew she had the power within her as well. A spirit wanted this power. It took over me. That day. You know we planned your mother's death. I knew it was going to happen. I tried to fight against it, but I couldn't overpower the spirit. The reason why you didn't see me sometimes was because I could have killed you when I was possessed and couldn't control myself."

"Dad."

"I loved your mother with all my heart. I lost her because of a power hungry fool inside of me." The man lowered his head in shame. "Jim! I am Dr. Zilch!"

"I don't believe it. I can't believe it."

"Kill me! Before he takes over my body again!"

"No dad! I can't believe this!"

"Do it, or you will pay the price very soon!"

"No!"

"It's your last chance! Jim, please."

"You'll die."

"That is the point! Shoot me! I can't control the spirit of Zilch!"

"You're lying!"

"I can't hold on..." Then he collapsed onto the floor.

"Dad!" Jim cried as he ran over to his father. When Jim was close enough to his father, he sprang up and grabbed Jim's neck. "I never liked your father, Jim. He was always preventing me from freeing myself. It was extremely annoying." Dr. Zilch threw Jim onto the floor. "Pretty soon the diamond will have given me enough power to overheat the earth's core."

"No." said Jim while groaning. "I won't let you." Jim took a pocketknife out of his pocket, unfolded it, and looked up angrily towards Dr. Zilch. Jim's expression died away from angry to confused. He didn't see some nasty mad man trying to wipe the Earth from existence. Jim just saw his dad grinning slightly. Jim shook his head furiously. "STUPID SPIRIT!" He yelled and ran to the evil doctor.

"If you kill me, then your dad dies with me." Zilch said slyly.

Jim immediately stopped in his tracks. *"A dad or the world?"* Jim thought. Jim loved his dad. He couldn't kill him, but Jim couldn't let Dr. Zilch destroy everything on the earth. "AAAHHHHH!" Jim yelled. "I'M JUST A KID!" Zilch smiled wickedly. Jim gave Zilch a menacing look, "You caused all this."

"The world is in your hands, Jim."

"I don't care anymore! Die!" Jim launched his arm carrying the pocketknife at Zilch. Zilch easily read the exaggerated movement and dodged it. The knife cut clean through Zilch's desk. Jim then picked up his gun and pointed it at Zilch. "Don't move!" Jim demanded. In one second, tears started gushing out of Jim's eyes. He couldn't do it.

"Can't do it eh?" Zilch chuckled. Then he took a look at the diamond's progress. "Ah. It's done. My diamond's energy has fully transferred. If I push this button, the world will explode in ten minutes." Then Zilch slammed the button down marking the final history of the planet earth. "Whatever you do, it's too late now. You fail!" Zilch laughed hysterically.

"Shut up!" Jim raised his gun in anger. Then he pulled the trigger.

However, Zilch suddenly appeared behind Jim. Jim turned around, which was a mistake. Jim had just received a hard fist to the face. Blood dripped from Jim's nose.

"I HATE YOU!"

Jim shot his pistol madly, but nothing touched Dr. Zilch. Finally, Jim smashed the case of the diamond, hoping that the whole process would cause a malfunction. "Too bad Jim!" Dr. Zilch laughed madly. "I already have all the energy I need stored into the machine! IT'S OVER!"

Jim cried and yelled as he started to take on Dr. Zilch by fist. Jim failed and kept getting thrown into a wall while Dr. Zilch continued his laughing. There was suddenly an awkward glow from the diamond. Jim took a glance at the diamond. Even the mad doctor stopped laughing to see what was going on. The diamond then shot a huge beam of light right at Zilch. Jim couldn't believe what he just saw. It was as if the beam passed right through the body, but it took out a ghost like image of Jim's father. Jim assumed that it was the spirit of Zilch. The diamond shattered, and Jim's father collapsed.

The spirit then dissolved into the air while screaming, "NOOOOO!"

Zilch was dead.

The timer showed five minutes and five seconds remaining. Jim thought furiously about what to do next. The fate of the world pushed down on one twelve-year-old boy's shoulders. Jim thought about Bill. He remembered all the good times. He then realized that life was worth living. Jim searched for something that would stop the destruction of the earth. At the corner of his eye, Jim spied a self-destruct button. Jim walked over to the button, took a glance at the timer—now showing four minutes and fifty-one seconds—and then at his father on the floor.

"Better to save the earth then than to destroy it." Jim said between tears. He hesitated before pushing the button. *Click*. Jim pushed the button and the timer restarted and read five minutes. *"Five minutes before self destructing."* said a computer voice. Jim ran over to his father.

"Get out of here Jim," his father managed to say. "Zilch is gone."

"Dad, I really love you."

He smiled weakly, "You saved the earth." Then he closed his eyes.

The world became cold to Jim. "Dad." Jim started sobbing over the death of his father. His brain ordered him to escape. Jim had only two minutes and thirty-seven seconds to get out.

Jim raced down the stairs, nearly tripping and breaking his ankle. He ran out the door and *BOOM!*

"Where am I?" Jim asked.

"You are in a hospital," replied the doctor beside Jim.

"We picked you up at the explosion site."

Jim froze, wide eyed, and started crying. "Both my parents."

"What?"

"There all dead." Then Jim turned around in his cot.

"Poor kid."

Jim was alone in the room, crying with all his might. "I can't believe this actually happened." He punched his pillow and swore. Five minutes later, an exhausted Jim lay on the hospital bed in an uneasy sleep.

✶ ✶ ✶ ✶

Bill's family came to pick up Jim. The decision was that Jim would live with Bill's family. Jim's father was an only child, and his aunt and uncle from his mother's side lived in a completely different continent. His aunt and uncle agreed to the decision. Jim looked forward to living with his best friend. "Sorry about what happened." Bill said in the car.

"It's alright."

"But I have to thank you for saving me."

"Welcome."

"Bill stop. That bothers him." said Bill's mom.

When they arrived, Jim stayed in his room thinking. He thought about it and came up with the idea that everyone has something important in life to accomplish. It had cost Jim his parents, but he had reached his life's accomplishment; Jim had saved the world.

High School Drama

By

Kirsten Duff

Watching. I sat there with a stomach full of butterflies. With a distressed look on my face, anyone could tell that I was irked. Mimi Malone was the cause of my displeasure. She stood there with her thin, perfect sixteen-year-old body, twirling her long, curly blonde hair and babbling on with her plump light pink lips. Her elegant voice sounded as if she were an angel. I was only bothered because the self-centered girl flirted with my best friend that I loved dearly.

"Sara Dulame, you're next." I suddenly heard coming from the director. My hands instantly became sweaty.

I glared at Mimi as she told me in a bratty tone, "Good Luck."

I rolled my eyes. At that moment I knew that my worst enemy and I were competing for the same exact role. Furiously I told the director I was ready to begin. I became resolute. My goal was to knock the director off of his feet and not let Mimi get the role.

My voice shook when I told the man that I was ready. I began singing my audition song: a song that I always sang immaculately. At every audition I sang, "Put on a Happy Face," from *Bye, Bye Birdie*. The musical that year was *The Wizard of Oz*. I thought I was perfect for the charming, main character role of Dorothy. I fit the role exquisitely. My soft, short, brown hair bounced as I sang my heart out. When I finished, the director asked me the usual questions. I told him that I was fifteen years old and that I was five feet four inches tall. I loathed being short, but my theater friends always told me being short is good for being a performer.

"Thanks you very much." The director told me, while writing

I rushed off the dull massive platform, trying to get home as quickly as I possibly could. I wanted to escape from the room full of anxious children. My tense body made it difficult to move my uncoordinated feet down the stairs. Suddenly, I was lying flat on my aching back. I felt like a cartoon character with stars spinning around my head and birds singing in my ears. I heard obnoxious laughter coming from the one person that I despised the most—Mimi Malone.

"Sara's so stupid!" rang over and over in my head as Mimi tried to get every student laughing at my clumsy escape. Her high-pitched voice quickly gave me a blistering headache. Before I knew it, I couldn't see or hear anything around me.

"Can you hear me? Hello?" I heard out of nowhere. I rubbed my tired eyes, hoping I would be able to see again. The distant brown ceiling above me was the only thing in view. Being hesitant to not fall flat on my face again, I got up cautiously. I spun around in a clockwise manner and slowly got familiar with my surroundings. While examining the dark red chairs and bright lights gleaming in my eyes, I was able to gather my wits. Then I saw a fellow classmate staring at me. I didn't know who it was but I thanked them for their help. While glaring at Mimi, I gave her a dark smile. I charged out of the monstrous theater.

I rushed outside into the amazing Carmel, Indiana, weather. The soft cool wind blew against my troubled face, and the green grass surrounding the school swayed like ocean waves. Spring was my favorite time of year. With a swift motion I examined the tall school building with the golden bell on top. Every new student talked about how old-fashioned or almost fairy tale like the school looked. Slowly I turned back around and headed home.

A voice behind me called my name. At first I tried to ignore the vexing voice. I didn't need anyone picking on me and making my day more unbearable than it already was. Suddenly, a large hand rested on my shoulder and spun me around toward my intruder. Avoiding eye contact I looked straight at the ground, hiding the tears of humiliation sprinting down my rosy cheeks. The Large boy's shoes told me little about who my intruder could have been.

Unexpectedly, soft fingers reach down and touched my chin. They slowly lifted my face to look at Justin Matthews's thin, pale white features. Justin Matthews, my best friend, had been on stage next to Mimi when I tumbled down the stage steps. Just thinking about Mimi irritated me. Looking deep into Justin's gorgeous big blue eyes, I knew he was baffled about my behavior. It wasn't like me to storm out of rooms after an embarrassing incident. People are used to seeing me trip because it happens so often. It was part of who I was.

"Are you okay? You look sick. Would you like me to walk you home?" he asked me.

It was obvious he cared for me. Justin was the type of guy that was willing to do anything to help a person in need. As I wiped away the salty tears from my face with the sleeve of my old scratchy jacket, I realized that I couldn't speak. I had completely humiliated myself. I tried moving my lips, but they acted as if they were Super Glued together. A dying dog sound came out of my mouth as I tried to force words out. I didn't know what to do.

"No thanks," I told him, dropping my head to look at the ground. He gave me a warm, reassuring hug. I gave Justin a fragile smile of gratitude, removed myself from his arms, and then speedily walked away. On my way home, I thought about how foolish my disgraceful exit scene must have looked. I probably wouldn't get the role now. It showed how weak I was.

When I arrived at home, I went straight upstairs to my room without greeting my parents. I needed quiet time to think about the audition, Mimi Malone, Justin Matthews, and what repercussions tomorrow might bring. I collapsed onto my bed and cried. As I closed my heavy, red eyes, I fell asleep waiting for tomorrow.

Beep, beep sounded from the corner of my bed. I slammed my small hand down on the thunderous alarm clock. Delaying getting out of bed and facing an uncertain world, I looked around my compact blue and brown room. I examined all of my favorite play billboards hanging on the wall. The billboards reminded me of past theatrical success and gave me the strength to roll out of my comfy bed and take a shower. I thought about what kind of stares I would receive from people today. Mimi had an entire evening to spread the news. Everyone in school probably thought I'm a complete loser. After the shower I placed my soft hair in a ponytail on top of my head. I put on old, torn up jeans, and a T-shirt. As I grabbed my favorite hoodie, I ran downstairs to greet my parents.

"Today, the cast list should be posted," I heard my mother singing joyfully as I joined my obnoxious family to eat breakfast. I looked towards the corner of the kitchen to see my father dancing while music blasted into his ear. Then I saw my little brother come hopping down the stairs.

"Look Mom, I'm a frog!" he screamed.

My mother rolled her eyes and shook her head. She rapidly turned back to me with a wide smile on her face.

"Aren't you excited pumpkin," my dad asked between sips of coffee.

"Yeah," I replied with a long sigh.

My parents exchanged mysterious stares that only they would understand. I placed my empty plate into the sink. I grabbed an uncooked slice of bread out of the toaster and hit my little brother on the head while I rushed out of the door.

Upon arriving at school, I took in one, big, deep breath and headed into the building. While I gathered my books from my locker, a mysterious voice coming from behind me spooked me. I jumped and turned around to face Justin.

"Hey, Kido," he said in a jovial tone.

"What's up buttercup," I replied with a timid grin on my face.

Justin and I were the closest of friends. If people heard us talking, they would probably assume that we were brother and sister.

"Are you pumped for the cast lists to be posted?" He asked.

"Not really, yesterday was a total wreck! Do you think I have anything to look forward to? Mimi will probably get the role anyway," I replied, looking down at the floor.

"Don't think like that, Sara! Be open-minded. I mean, as long as you get in the play everything is still good, right?" he asked.

"I guess, at least I still have you to have a good time with!" I said, closing my locker and heading down the hallway. We passed Mimi on our way to our first class. She gave us a wide evil smile, which we tried our hardest to ignore.

The day went by quickly, and I was so nervous about the cast list. I had no clue what role I would get, or even if I would get a role at all. I tried following Justin's advice to keep an open mind.

After school I saw a gigantic crowd around the high school bulletin board. *Oh boy, this is going to be interesting,* I thought as I came closer to the white sheet in front of me. I cut through the crowd as I confronted the square, white paper. While I scrolled down the paper with my finger, I found my name. The paper read *Sara Dulame as the part of...*I couldn't finish reading. My heart pounded inside my chest. I felt like it was going to explode. I closed and opened my eyes anxiously and read Dorothy.

"Ah!" I howled through the hallways. I wanted to find Justin as soon as possible. I turned the corner and there he was with open arms. I screamed and took one giant leap into his large, comforting arms.

"I knew you could do it," he said while twirling me around.

Both Justin and I walked home to tell my family the good news. When I entered my ugly, little, white house, I saw my mother there with cupcakes in her hands.

"So what part did you get?" she asked.

"Common what do you think?" Justin replied. My mother quickly dropped the pan full of cupcakes and ran toward me with the biggest smile on her face. While I was getting attacked with kisses and hugs I asked my animated mother what the cupcakes were for. "For you, remember I'm your biggest fan!" she said.

"Yes, Mom, how could I ever forget?" I responded.

That night I thought about what would be running through Mimi's mind. I was shocked that she hadn't said anything to me yet. I wondered what part she was playing, or even if she was playing a part at all. All I knew was that I got the part I wanted, and tomorrow would be a better day. Happy thoughts ended in peaceful slumber.

"Ah!" I yelled as I awoke from the worst nightmare in my life. I had a dream that Mimi Malone got so angry that I was Dorothy. At one of the rehearsals, she pushed me off the stage, and I broke my leg. To make sure my leg was still intact, I threw off the covers to find my leg just the same as it used to be. I got ready for school and then headed off for another adventurous day.

Today was a typical school day. Justin and I laughed and talked. I went to all of my boring, old classes and was assigned homework. All of a sudden I saw a shadow on the ground, walking towards me. When I looked up, I noticed it was Mimi. As she threw her long, blonde hair behind her, she walked to my table and bent down so that we were face to face.

"Congratulations, I heard you got the role of Dorothy!" she told me boldly.

I was shocked. *Why was Mimi being so nice to me?* I replied in a bewildered tone, "Umm thanks, I guess."

Mimi laughed and got closer to whisper in my ear. "Don't think I'm going to be nice now that you have a better role than me. Trust me; I could upstage you any day."

My eyes froze like ice. I didn't know how to reply to a statement like that. Mimi placed a hand under the end of my food tray and flipped it upward. Spaghetti and sauce landed in my lap, and chocolate pudding ran down my blouse. Furiously, I jumped to my feet. An unnatural calm settled over the cafeteria.

"Oops, sorry, you might want to wash that off. It might stain," Mimi said, turning her back and slowly walking over to her friends' table.

I turned my head to watch her and her little friends walk out of the room like nothing was wrong. I looked at Justin and said, "Let the games begin."

I said goodbye to Justin and rushed into the bathroom like a lion attacking a deer. Quickly, I whipped the nasty smelling spaghetti off my shirt. It was a bummer that I wore white that day. I swiftly went to my locker and grabbed my navy blue sweatshirt.

I charged over to the bulletin board to find out what role Mimi was playing. I scrolled down the sheet to find that Mimi was playing the role of the wicked witch. I threw my head back and snickered. It fit her personality perfectly. I don't know why she was so upset because the Wicked Witch of Oz was also a main character.

At the end of school, I got ready for the first rehearsal. I entered the theater where it all began. I took a seat in the audience excited to get the script. While we waited, I saw Mimi enter the room from behind me. She slowly walked over and sat down in the row of seats in front of me. The whole rehearsal she never took her devilish green eyes off of me. It made me very uncomfortable knowing that she watched my every move.

When rehearsal ended, I rushed out of the theater trying to escape from the stares. This experience reminded me of the auditions. This time I was being more careful not to trip.

That night I thought about ways to make Mimi mad or jealous. I wasn't sure exactly what I wanted to do yet. I finished my homework and feel asleep exhausted from the dreadful day.

I sighed a breath of relief the next morning. I was so joyful that it was finally Friday. The day went by like any other. I talked to Justin about what I could do to Mimi, but he didn't think revenge was the right thing to do. I didn't know what I should do, believe Justin and leave Mimi alone or get back at her for all the evil things she had ever done to me. I thought hard all day, but I couldn't make up my mind. As I thought, I remembered all the dishonorable things she had ever done to me.

Once when Mimi and I were in a play together, I had gotten the main role, and she ended up in the chorus. The perfect blonde teen was furious. My class went on a camping trip. I had forgotten my shampoo to wash my hair after a hike in the woods. So Mimi offered hers to me. Of course I accepted the shampoo, but what I didn't know was that she had put hair coloring in it the day before. I took my shower and went to bed. When I woke up the next morning, I looked in the mirror to find that my brown hair had turned a dark blue. I was furious. Opening night was only one week away.

Over the weekend all I could do was think of a plan to get back at Mimi. I thought of a plan that required no work. I had gotten the main role, and she was very jealous of me. All I had to do was be the best Dorothy and show her that I could be better than she would ever be.

The second rehearsal was scheduled to be on the next upcoming Sunday. I woke up that morning ready to get Mimi back. I left my house with a determined look planted in my face. I saw my little brother in his window. His blue eyes watched me as I left the house. He didn't like it when I left because he would have to play and listen to his annoying playmates, our parents.

As I stormed into the school, I saw Justin. "Justin?" I yelled, as I scurried across the wooden platform. I opened my eyes wide to give him a hug.

"What are you doing here, bud?" I asked.

"I got put into the crew, so now I can watch every rehearsal!" he told me.

I gave him one more hug and sighed; I was relieved that I could be with my greatest pal twenty-four seven.

When I was called up on stage to sing my first song, *Somewhere Over the Rainbow*, I walked passed Mimi and giggled. I could tell by the expression on her face that she was jealous. I mean, I would be to if I didn't get to sing in the entire musical. I sang boldly; I sang my best, proud that doing nothing at all made Mimi so envious.

By the end of the day, everyone was exhausted. We all wanted to go home and take a long nap. When the director gathered everyone together, we all paid close attention.

"Tomorrow is going to be a little different. We are not going to run over the scenes like we have been doing the past couple of days. Tomorrow, we are going to do many dramatic exercises to get our bodies relaxed. I have assigned an activity where you all have partners," he said while rubbing his belly.

My mind filled with joy knowing that maybe I could be with Justin.

He continued, now scratching his dark brown beard. "I have assigned your partners for you." The whole class sighed. He continued, "Here are your partners: Molly and Emily, Justin and . . ."

"Please be me, please be me," rang over in my mind.

"Jordan."

My shoulders dropped down to the floor. I looked around and noticed that Mimi and I were the only ones left.

"Mimi and Sara," he announced to the class.

My face fell. I was extraordinarily unhappy. I couldn't image working with Mimi at all.

"Justin," I sighed, "Mimi and I can't work together. We will probably end up killing each other."

"All I have to say, kid, is good luck," he replied while snickering. He wrapped his long, tan arm around me and pulled me close to him. He walked me home, trying the whole time trying to put a wide smile across my gloomy face.

Today was the day that we had to work with our partners. When rehearsal started, almost immediately we began doing our activities. The cast did things like mirror imitations and made up our own little skits. As I examined the other students participating in their groups, all of their faces were filled with glee and excitement. It was hard for me to smile and look at Mimi without making my movements look bratty. The day ended, and Justin and I walked home as usual.

A couple months past passed, and it came very close to opening night. The director got stressed out, and the cast went insane with excitement. I woke up one morning and realized that, on the list, it said that Justin and I were partners in different activity. The day that Justin and I were supposed to have a great time acting out skits, Mimi's partner got sick. She was put into mine and Justin's group. I was so frustrated. Of course when it came time for me to have fun, Mimi had to ruin it. We practiced our skit, and then it came time to perform it.

While we were performing our skit in front of the cast, Mimi had a mysterious gleam in her eye. I couldn't figure out what she was up to. As I walked past her, she flung her long hair. Every time she flipped her hair every guy stopped and stared. I was very annoyed that she thought she was the center of attention. While I was walking to say my line to Justin, she stuck out her small black shoes in front of me. Suddenly, I took a tumble to the ground. While the popular teen was twirling her hair around her small finger, she said, "Oops, sorry didn't see you."

I screamed in pain. I held my leg like a little kid would hold onto her favorite teddy bear. Tears filled in my eyes. They sprinted down my cheeks.

Justin quickly ran to my side and held me in his arms. "Sara, what hurts?" he asked me in a hurried tone.

"My leg!" I yelled. He slowly lifted my arms off my aching leg to examine it. As I looked down to see what it looked like, I saw the worst thing I have ever seen in my life. I notice a small bone sticking straight out of my leg.

"It's broken; we have to take her to the ER to get some ex rays," Justin told the chubby director.

I will always remember the look on Justin's face when he saw the small bone sticking out of my pale leg. It looked as if he was going to cry with me. I slowly became claustrophobic with everyone staring at me. The room became dark, and this incident reminded me of the fall I experience at the auditions. This tumble was the same as my dream from a couple of nights before. I slowly passed out in Justin's arms.

I woke up in an all-white room. My eyes focused and I noticed I was in the hospital. I looked around and noticed Justin holding my hand while he was asleep. I tried to remember what happened, but it was hard. All I could recall was my leg aching in pain. I looked under the cover to make sure my leg didn't have to be amputated. All of these things reminded me of my dream.

When I looked up, I saw my family in the room. They rushed over to give me a lot of hugs.

"How are you sweetie? Is your leg still in pain? What can I do to help?" my mom asked. The room was filled with questions. Justin could tell from the look on my face that I didn't feel like talking to that large of a crowd. My whole life I have had this one problem, whenever I start explaining how I got hurt, I start to cry. So what Justin did was take them out in the hall to explain everything.

When Justin came back into the room, he explained to me that Mimi had tripped me and made me fall off the stage. My face became red and inflamed with anger.

"Is she gonna be punished?" I asked him.

"Mr. David, our director, is going to think over what will happen to her. For right now you need not to worry about her," he told me. *That's Justin, always so calm* I thought.

"Am I going to have surgery? Will I have to be kicked out of the play? Who will take my part?" I asked him.

"Whoa, not to fast Kido. Everything will fall into place. I promise," he replied.

"So you're not going to tell me anything?" I asked.

"What I will tell you is that, yes, you are going to have surgery, but everything else I have to say no clue," he told me. I turned on the television, trying to get my mind off the subject.

A half hour later, the doctor walked in and told me that I was going to have surgery tomorrow. I didn't know if I could wait till tomorrow, but I was going to have to be patient.

Justin kept me company. I thought how great it was to have Justin. We would do anything for each other. When someone falls down, we pick them up. That's what friendship is.

That night my family left and I told Justin he should probably go home. He looked bored to death even though he wouldn't tell me that. He insisted on staying with me until I fell asleep. I agreed that he could stay. I wanted someone there anyway.

I asked Justin if he could go grab a wheelchair to take me on a walk around the hospital. He quickly agreed and was on his way to ask a doctor for the ugly, rolling chair. He entered the room at the speed of light and said, "Taxi has arrived." He carefully lifted me off the white bed and placed me the chair.

Justin walked and I wheeled around the hospital to get out of the gloomy room. I decided I hated hospitals. They looked like the perfect place for a scary movie. All the white walls, white floors, white desks, white shoes, and white beds were starting to give me the creeps.

As the trip came to the end, Justin took me into the room and placed me back in my new room for the night. I quickly fell asleep from the exhausting day and prayed that my surgery would go well tomorrow.

"Ka, ka doodle do," the doctor said when he entered the room to wake me up. He had brown shaggy hair, gorgeous blue eyes, and a tall skinny body. He was extremely tan. *Hello gorgeous,* I thought as I examined him.

"Are you my doctor for today?' I asked him, still staring. *I wish I had my makeup or hair done right now. He probably thinks I'm the ugliest person alive,* I thought. I decided to look down at the sheets, so he wouldn't get completely freaked out by me.

"Why yes, I am," he told me in a cheerful tone. My face lit up. He explained to me that today I was going to have surgery at ten o'clock to get my bone back where it was supposed to be.

The handsome man left my room. A couple minutes later Justin barged into the room.

"What's your mood little dude?" he asked.

Justin was the guy that came up with new rhymes that made you laugh when you heard them.

"Nothing really, I'm just sitting here watching Television. I was waiting for you to come, but here you are, so it's all good." I told him. He came over and sat down next to me.

All of a sudden, we both jumped from out seats when there was a loud banging on the door.

I yelled, "It's open!"

The door slowly creaked open. I studied the human, and it happened to be a girl wearing a mini skirt and a green and blue tank top. As my eyes adjusted to the light entering the room, I figured out who it was.

"Mimi, is that you?" I asked.

"Yeah it is. Um...Sara, can I talk to you alone for a minute?" she replied.

I looked at Justin and said, "No whatever you have to say to me, you can say to both of us." Now I was staring into the eyes of the devil. *What could she possibly say to me? She has done enough; can't she just leave me alone,* I thought.

"Okay, well um...first of all, how are you doing?" she said. Her eyes were puffy like she had been crying.

"I'm fine; what do you want?" I asked her. I felt like a brat, but she deserved it after what she had done to me.

She said, "I just wanted you to know that I am sorry. I never meant for you to get hurt. Right now you probably aren't in the best forgiving mood. I just hope that one day you can accept my apology and that everything can go back to normal."

I stared at her. "And, you're getting at?" I asked.

She continued, "Principle Davidson has suspended me for the day. Mr. Davidson said that you should be able to pick my punishment because you were the one that got hurt." I stared at her blankly. What was I supposed to say? Was I supposed to be like: yeah, no problem, don't worry about it?

I replied, "Um...right now I'm going to have to think about it, but thanks for the apology."

She said, "Thanks um...get back to me when you figure out what you want me to do." Then she left the room.

Justin asked, "What are you going to do to her?"

I replied, "I'm not sure. I'm thinking about just letting her off the hook."

"Letting her off the hook? Are you feeling okay?" Justin asked.

"Yeah, I mean like she looked really sorry, and maybe if we can work out or problems, then we can just be equal," I told him.

"Okay...Just do what you think is right." he exclaimed

About thirty minutes passed before the nurse came into the room to get me ready for surgery. As I entered the white room full of different tools, the handsome doctor was in the corner of the room. *Everything is going to be all right,* I told myself.

I finished my surgery, and when I woke, my leg was wrapped in a light pink cast. I was told I could leave the hospital that night and go home. I was very excited to get back in my regular bed.

My parents drove Justin and I home. As I entered my comfy house, I fell asleep quickly and thought about what my day was going to be at school comforting Mimi.

On Monday I stayed home and rested. I didn't feel like going to school. The whole day I was trying to figure out if I should do something to Mimi, or just let her off the hook. That night it hit me; I knew what I should do. I decided that I would make her clean all the bathrooms in the school. She would hate that because she was so perfect. Mimi would become totally disgusted.

I called Justin later that night to tell him by brilliant plan. He told me that it was lame and that I should just forgive her. I slept well that night. I woke up the next morning with this weird feeling in my gut. I just felt like my conscious didn't want Mimi to clean the bathrooms. I thought hard and long.

I finally came to a conclusion. I decided that I would talk to Mimi and make a deal with her. I would let her just go on with her regular life, but she would have to make some changes. She would have to not make me feel like I was a "nobody," and she would have to look me in the eyes and admit to me that we were equal at acting. I knew it would be hard for her to do.

The next day I went to school, and told Mimi what she had to do. The expression on her face looked very confused.

"Are you serious? What about all the mean things I have done to you before?" she asked.

"I thought about making you... Oh, never mind what I was going to do. I just think it would be best if we started over!" I told her. I could tell that she didn't know what to say. So I opened my arms to give her a friendly hug. She thanked me with a lot of hugs for not punishing her too hard. When she told me that we were equal, she started to stutter.

Mimi took in one deep breath and said, "Sara I'm so sorry for everything I have ever done to you. I hope you can accept my apology and we could be friends. Also, my whole life I have told you that you aren't very good at acting, but that was because I was jealous because I knew you were my biggest competition. So from now on, we are equally as good at acting."

I smiled and gave her one last hug. It felt weird, but good at the same time hugging my worst enemy. We walked away down the hallway talking and laughing. From that moment I clearly understood that forgiveness was the one thing that was missing in our hearts.

Although, when we hate somebody, it might be hard to forgive them. When really all we need to do is look deep down inside of their hearts and realize that they are good. God created us wanting us to love and forgive. Even the Lord said himself, "All is good!"

Million Dollar Escape

By

Alexander Huang

Sitting down on the dusty cabinet floor, I buttoned my lab coat and combed my dazzling black hair. Loud echoes drifting in the dark, damp air indicated that my target stood somewhere outside the cabinet. A feeling of satisfaction burst inside me. *You're a genius, Harold,* I told myself. Yeah, I guess you could call me arrogant. But hey, a little bit of self-confidence helps sometimes, right? A good criminal always needs that occasional morale boost to get out of sticky situations.

A sudden yelp and a loud clank awakened me up from my daydream. A series of coughing fits and footsteps followed the unpleasant noise. Leaning against the dusty wall, I slowly lifted myself to a standing position. The previous racket that this inventor made might mean that he was actually going to leave the room (about time, too). I heard more footsteps, then a creak of the lab's wooden doors. The *clicking* sound of the door closing was the jackpot.

Making sure that my target had left the room, I cautiously opened the door and peeked outside. Good, nobody home. Stepping outside and stretching my tortured muscles (sitting down in an immobile position for two hours was certainly no easy task), I scanned the area.

Dim lighting gave the room an eerie feeling. The odd smell of burnt wood glue and chlorine followed me throughout my investigation. Tools lay scattered everywhere, in twisted conditions, as if a series of unnecessary explosions had just taken place. A mountain of useless, crumpled paperwork loomed to my left. And, in the dead center of a half-decayed worktable, sat a peculiar-looking invention of some sort; a machine, I hoped. Yes, definitely a complicated, out-of-this-world machine of some sort. *Perfect.*

Because the invention was connected to a socket in the wall, I blindly grabbed several wires and attempted to yank it free. Disappointed, I located a screwdriver, stuck it into the socket, and tried scoop the wires out. Surprisingly, the maneuver was a success; the wires slipped out rather easily and fell to the floor.

"Ingenious, Harold," I said to myself. "I'm so amazing that I scare myself."

Then, suddenly, I froze. An increasingly terrifying noise sounded in my ears. *He's coming back! Quick, escape, NOW!*

Gadget in hand, I practically hurled myself into the door. Whether it was a stroke of luck or just my sixth sense, I'll never know. The door burst open and slammed into the technician, hitting him square in the forehead. Without remorse, I ran past the thunderstruck mechanic and bolted down the hallway.

"Hey!" A few seconds later, a scream echoed down the corridor. "Give that back, you thief!"

Loud footfalls transformed into deafening stomps. Obviously he was catching up. Daring not to look back, I swerved past the first corner and sprinted blindly. The exit emerged ahead. *Just a couple more seconds, then freedom...come on!*

Heavy breathing and several curses sprang out from behind, louder than expected. Immediately a siren blared, and the originally dull color of the lab became a brilliant red. Suddenly, a cold hand grabbed my lab coat and forced me to the ground. "Think again before you mess with Kevin Mecks," growled the inventor. Rising to a kneeling position, I saw his fist in the air with an intention of pulverizing me.

WHAM!

The man's blank expression instantly became a face of pain as he fell backwards and vainly gasped for breath. Luckily I had executed an uppercut into his stomach before he could smash his fist into my chest.

"Freeze! Both of you!"

I turned back, just a bit, and spotted a single security officer with a relatively fat man, who I recognized as Jerome Jaw, founder of Engineering Corps, tapping his foot impatiently next to him. The guard wielded an intimidating pistol that pointed directly at me. I heard a couple of footsteps. Then Jerome declared in a loud voice, "By the looks of your lab coat, I assume you're a sorry participant of my Inventions Contest who needs to sabotage your fellow inventors in order to win. That is just pitiful. You're a disgrace to inventors all around the world."

Trying to hide my face with my lab coat, I challenged him, "Yeah, and what are you going to do about it?"

"I'm going to disqualify you, and then I'm going to send you to prison where you dirty rascals belong. Who are you anyway? Show yourself!"

A clammy hand gripped onto my lab coat and pulled back. But, before Jerome could get a good view of my face, I kicked him in the stomach, snatched the invention, and propelled myself toward the exit. Several gunshots rang through the hall, but I felt no pain. I lunged forward, blasting the doors open. An agile hop to the left barely saved me from the handgun's approaching doom.

My legs cramped up, and my stomach felt tied into several knots, but the risk would be too great if I stopped to rest. I ducked behind several trees outside the laboratory and ran in the direction of a thick brick wall. Before I entered the lab, I had told my partner, Bill, to wait on the other side of the wall. Hoping nature would hide me from Kevin and Jerome, I ran straight to the wall and yelled to my partner. "Bill! You there?"

It didn't take long for a familiar voice to answer, "Alive and waiting, Harold. Been waiting for at least an hour already. You were crazy slow. What happened?"

"I'll explain later. Catch whatever I'm going to throw at you and stuff it in the car. After that, sit in the car and wait for me. I don't want you to be squished into orange juice if I land on you."

"Yeah, I know that you're naturally fa..."

"Cut the joke and catch!"

I hurled the machine over the wall and searched for a way to climb over the imposing obstacle. Finally finding a satisfactory crack in the brick, I began a slow but steady ascent up the ten-foot boundary that separated me from safety.

"Hey! There!" A loud scream, followed by a single gunshot, immediately triggered an adrenaline rush. I climbed at a reckless pace. Several more gunshots rang out. I knew if I couldn't get over the wall within the next few seconds, I wouldn't live to see another day. At last, with one final heave, I launched myself over the wall and landed uncomfortably on the sidewalk. I scrambled to my feet, jumped into the waiting car, and let out a huge sigh of relief as the automobile rushed down the road.

Okay, so I'm not the best burglar around. I am just your average thirty-year-old man that wants to sabotage engineers with a dream, so that I might win an inventor's competition and collect a million dollars for a loved one. It is not easy, I tell you, but it certainly isn't the first time I've casually walked into a building and successfully took something valuable. It's the one time in my life when long legs really help.

Glancing at my dirty fingernails and rubbing my hazel-colored eyes, I turned and took one last look at the laboratory. My three adversaries were not anywhere in sight—just a long, barren road. I breathed another deep sigh of relief and counted the remaining contestants. In total, around forty-eight inventors competed in the Inventions Contest. Even after sabotaging more than one-third of the participants, about thirty remained. And, now that Jerome was aware of the criminal acts going around, security would certainly tighten.

Bill, who drove the car, turned on the radio and asked me, "Harold, do you want rock or pop this time?"

I managed a small smile as the reassurance of my partner's voice temporarily drove the troubles out of my mind. "I'd like neither. Gotta recollect myself. Give me a moment to ponder, and then we'll put on some pop music, alright?"

I heard a chuckle from Bill, "After you finish your reflections, we'll probably be out of the car. Anyways, when we get back, I'll fix you up some hot cocoa, and we can rest a bit."

Although Bill had a fiery personality, he always seemed cool and collected after an act. I liked that. That's why we're partners; we both have a problem, and although we tried to avoid death, we would both kill ourselves to do it.

Only when I thought about death, did a chill come back. Reflecting upon the day's events, I realized that today could have been my death day. I recalled the sense of fear that engulfed my arrogance when the inventor Kevin Mecks tackled me. Remembering the sounds of bullets streaking through the air when I ran to the exit sent a chill up my spine. It would definitely be harder to take down the rest of the inventors.

But the worst was yet to come.

"Welcome, my friends," Jerome boomed. "Please sit down."

I gulped down a glass of an authentic Irish whiskey and looked up at Jerome, who paced back and forth by the podium. The many participants around me stopped what they were doing and gave their undivided attention to Jerome. The fat man cleared his throat before beginning his speech.

"I'm quite happy to say that the 2008 Inventors Workshop contest is half-way complete!" He waited for the audience to applause, but he received none. Jerome smiled and continued his speech as if nothing abnormal had happened. "As we all know, the annual Inventors Workshop contest was created so that young entrepreneurs could demonstrate their skills in engineering and invention. Unfortunately, there have been recent attacks on some inventions that had great potential.

"As the head of Engineering Corps and host of the 2008 Inventors Workshop contest, I apologize to those who have suffered this fate," Jerome continued. Glancing around, I noticed several groans, and a vast amount of disapproval immediately followed. With a desperate look on his face, Jerome raised his voice. "I am currently investigating this mystery, and I have discovered that one of our *fellow participants* is responsible for the entire wreckage of our contest!"

Immediately pandemonium took place. In a furious rage, the many victims of my sabotages threw glass cups (or basically anything they could find) and began to stomp angrily. Those who were bombarded by the random assortment of airborne items began to break away from the crowd. Attempting to blend into the environment without arousing too much attention, I threw my own glass of whiskey into the fray. A loud yell from Jerome punctured the chaos. Instantly, everyone hushed and silence filled the room.

"Please do not blame anyone yet. I have only small evidence as to what he or she looks like, and we are not sure if our proof is viable. We will examine and interview each and every one of you. While you are not being examined, please enjoy the banquet and *do not* start another fight with anyone. Thank you."

A long, uncomfortable silence filled the air before everyone sighed and began to interact with one another again. As the first person followed a burly guard into a small room, everyone began to feast and chatter. Assuming a relaxed and cool posture, I took off my glasses (the only part of my costume that I was not used to) and rubbed them. While I cleaned the uncomfortable eyepiece, I took the opportunity to scan the area clearly. I spied many people whose inventions I mercilessly ambushed. Those few wore somber faces, and they sat in a corner with a beer more often than they went up and conversed with other people. Putting my glasses back on, I stood up and wobbled to the buffet.

"Hey, Connor," Kevin called from the salad bar. He shuffled up to me and produced a wide grin. When I filled the application for the Inventors contest, I gave the guard my fake ID and called myself Connor, so naturally, people called me by my fake name.

I made friends with him a while ago. The cheerful guy apparently didn't recognize me when I stole his machine yesterday, so I responded in a friendly manner. "Hey Kevin, what's up?"

"The ceiling, and then the sky and God," he cackled. Kevin chuckled to himself, and then his expression hardened. "Bad news, Connor. You know that guy who sabotages our inventions to get the one million dollars the easy way?" He expected an answer, so I nodded vigorously. "Well, he's at it again. Just yesterday he took mine and left with it."

I produced a shocked expression. "What? Are you serious, Kevin?"

"Yeah. I worked on that invention for many days and nights, and now it's gone." He shook his head. "I managed to pull the guy onto the floor, but I didn't get a good view of his face."

Inside, I felt relieved. If he had found out my identity, the million dollars worth of prize money wouldn't be in my hands, and then Elaine might...*No, no, no.* I can't let that get into my mind.

"Hey Connor, you okay?" Kevin's soft voice echoed in my mind.

Immediately I noticed Kevin staring at me with a concerned expression on his face. *Drat!* I had expressed my emotions physically in front of Kevin. *Come on, Harold, think of an excuse...!*

"I, uh, had this feeling of déjà vu," I stammered. "You know, like that eerie sense of familiarity?" It dawned upon me that I had just twisted the truth.

Kevin eyed me suspiciously. "Obviously, because it's been happening to so many people in the contest lately."

"Well, yeah, but a different type of familiarity. Like it happened to *me* before."

"It didn't happen to you though, right?" Kevin checked to make sure no one paid attention to us. "By the way, what *is* your invention? I know you're not supposed to mention it to anyone, but you can tell me, right?"

A sudden pang of anxiety exploded inside me. I had never thought of a backup plan. My main intention was to sabotage the best inventor, take his invention, sabotage other inventors that showed a possibility of winning, and then "win" the Inventions Contest. The invention I took belonged to him, so no matter what, I couldn't tell him.

I desperately groped for words. "It's...it's a secret."

Kevin shrugged and took a bite of his salad. "Anyways," he said, "I didn't get a good view of his face, but I did get a tiny strip of his lab coat, and it did have a piece of hair on it. Could be anyone's hair, but I'm still going to get it through a DNA scan tomorrow. You want to come with me?"

My heart skipped a beat. Yesterday, when I took off my lab coat, I didn't check to see if the brawl had left behind any remnants. *Oh man. Now my plan is in jeopardy.*

Collecting myself, I calmly answered, "I got something planned tomorrow. I'm going to, uh, eat with my aunt and my uncle tomorrow. Then I gotta work on my invention."

Kevin smiled. "You should get something to eat before those gluttons devour the whole banquet. I'll be at that table," he pointed to an elegant table in a corner, "and we'll talk about something more pleasant, okay?" He took another bite of his salad, combed his brown hair, and smiled one more time before striding to the corner.

Taking the tall man's advice, I walked to the buffet and began to put several delicacies on my plate. Many contestants who had already been interviewed were not present; I guess they left when I was talking with Kevin. The inventor's news about the DNA scan was quite unpleasant; it forced me to believe that another action plan was necessary.

I returned to Kevin's table just as the security guard called him into the room for examination. Chewing quietly, I observed the rest of the scientists. Most of them talked to each other with glasses of wine in their hands. The remaining few huddled in a corner, eating a lot or nothing at all. I began thinking of a plan...*The only way to stop Kevin is to either steal the cloth, ambush him, or sabotage the DNA system. I only wish I knew where he was going...*

Before I could ponder more about the following day, Kevin walked up to me and said, "It's your turn, Connor. Wish you luck." He gave me a smile, put on his lab coat, and left the banquet. *Wish me luck?*

Hoping to finish the interview quickly and return to my apartment, I scrambled into the examination room.

The first thing I noticed when I entered the room was the amount of smoke lingering in the air. Three guards tapped their feet impatiently. All of them wore black caps and bored expressions; each of them produced different facial features. One of them had blonde hair; another had a scar on his nose; and the last one had small, beady eyes. The blond one had a sense of familiarity about him. And in the middle of the smoke, Jerome sat on a wooden stool with a grim expression on his face.

Before I could make another move, the scarred guard blurted, "Sit down. Don't move." Daring not to arouse suspicion, I sat down on the offered stool and waited for something to happen.

Finally, Jerome said, "I'm sorry, but we'll have to force everything out of you. I expect each answer to meet its full potential. Do you understand?"

I nodded. *So far, so good.*

Jerome locked his eyes on me, giving me an insecure feeling. Leaning forward, he tried to get a better view of me in the mist of smoke. His eyes widened, and then he cringed.

He turned his attention to the scarred guard. "Put this one on this list." *List?*

Without another word, Jerome got out of his seat, walked behind me, and put his hand on my shoulder. "His hair is black and slim, and he's around the same height. He's got the same shoulder shape, too." The security officers blew puffs of smoke from their cigarettes and nodded.

The blonde one piped in, "Yep, and he's about the same build too. Maybe we should test him to see if he runs as fast as the one we met yesterday, aye?"

The blonde was that guard I met yesterday!

Jerome shook his head. "Let's not jump to conclusions so soon. Continue the interrogation."

Inside, I breathed a huge sigh of relief.

"What is your name?" Jerome asked.

Simple enough. "My name is Connor Kingberry, sir."

"Are you sure?"

I felt appalled at the answer. *Does he know something I don't want him to know?* "How can I not know my own name?"

Jerome replied in a mocking tone, "Very well, *Kingberry*. If you would wait, I can call a colleague of mine who happens to have access to all United States citizens' statistics. We can see if your name matches . . ." He reached for the phone and stared at me, as if hoping for me to respond in a panicky manner.

"Wait." I kept my emotions concealed and continued to talk. "You must be mistaken if you thought I'm an American citizen, sir. I'm actually Canadian. This event is very important to me, you know, so I traveled from Canada to America just to participate in this contest."

Jerome did not seem surprised by my answer; in fact, he seemed amused. "Very well...we will check into that later." Jerome paused before continuing. "Please explain your day yesterday."

Jerome kept on barraging me with seemingly simple questions, and I parried them with plausible responses. Eventually, he gave up and said, "Your answers are questionable, but I cannot deny them. I'm not going to jump to conclusions, but don't expect me to be nice to you. Keep this in mind, pal. If you're really that criminal, then soon you'll feel the wrath of Jerome Jaw." He got up and left the room. His guards followed shortly afterward.

It took me a while to realize that I could leave. A sense of loneliness crawled inside of me. I remembered the days when there was nothing but sadness in my life. When I thought I could save my wife, Elaine, from the death grasp of leukemia, my life filled with an indefinite hope. The cost of the surgery—nearly a million—was what made me become the person I am now. Hoping conceit would keep the hope running, I stole and ambushed with a sense of motivation. And now... only one month remained until Elaine, who resided in a VIP hospital, was scheduled for transplant surgery, provided the money was available. *No, this can't happen. I won't let it happen.* Even if the transplant failed, I had to try.

With a new determination, I hopped off my stool and briskly paced out, and soon I was on a taxi driving back to the apartments.

"What? You crazy or something?" Bill exclaimed.

I had expected an answer like that. "Of course I'm crazy. I'm crazy and convinced. We've *got* to stick by this new plan!"

My criminal partner snorted ignorantly and shook his head. "You really gone nuts this time, Harold." He slammed his hot cocoa mug on the coffee table and cross his arms defensively.

I sighed. Whenever I argued with Bill, it always ended up like this. "Didn't you say I was nuts last week or something? It's either we're doomed, or we might be doomed."

For a moment, I thought I felt Bill's anger burning all the way from his chair, on the other side of the small room. But surprisingly, Bill answered, "All right. But if you get me killed, you got yourself a big load of trouble."

Relieved, I slumped down in my sofa chair. Engineering Corps funded the apartment building we were in, so naturally it was exquisite. The living room composed of a rug and an elegant coffee table between Bill and me, two chairs (Bill and I obviously sat on these), and three doors—one for his room, one for my room, and one leading outside.

Gazing out the window and at the starry black sky, I tried to remember the conversation with Bill. My partner and friend always talked in a spontaneous and fast-paced manner, so I couldn't memorize much of the quarrel. I remember I had told him about how Jerome would soon find out that I lied during the investigation (Bill let out a long string of inaudible curses here), how Kevin had found the strip of my lab coat (more curses from Bill), and my new plan.

Wanting to continue the conversation, I mustered up some fake conceit and smugly said, "You're not going to die when you've got me around. Engineering Corps is nothing; we've conquered stuff way above that hunk of junk."

Bill then stared at me. His blue eyes discomforted me so much that almost immediately I gave up and averted my eyes to the ground. Finally he spoke, "You got no idea how much bad Jerome's got in his sleeve, Harold. You've doomed both of us, some way or another, and you know it." He shifted his gaze and let his words sink in. "Of course, it ain't all your fault because I followed. But what a fool I was to do so."

I sat upright, shocked. His speech convinced me that my partner actually had a serious side. Usually he joked and encouraged, even in the hardest times. Now I felt that it had all changed.

Bill stood up, and walked up to me until his short bulk towered over me. "You rest," he commanded. "According to your plan, tomorrow's going to be a big day for us. And probably our last day too." Then he retired into his room and left me to float in silence.

Bill and I were originally going to split the million in half, but for Elaine he had given up his half of the deal. Before my wife was diagnosed with leukemia, she had done many favors for Bill; he clearly wanted Elaine back as much as I did. I respected him at that, and I didn't want to let him down. *Jerome's way below your league*, I assured myself. *You're not going to let anyone down.* Repeating the phrase to myself, I trudged into my bedroom, flopped onto the bed and, without changing from my lab coat, slept uneasily.

I chomped down on a huge, meaty burger and loudly slurped a Gatorade. Some of the juicy oil dripped on my lab coat, but I didn't really care. *Lovely hamburger, you'll always be by my side.*

Bill, who drove the car, yelled, "Harold! Don't eat so loud. You know, I didn't eat yet!"

Laughing, I replied, "Hey, I'm taller than you, I get more food. Simple logic."

Bill retorted, "Yeah, well it might be your last piece of food. I'll personally make sure you won't be munching on that Big Mac when we walk into Engineering Corps."

My heart of burning flame froze and dropped into my stomach like a rock. I had completely forgot about what we planned yesterday. Because of the lack of time left, I knew I had to go—by myself—into Engineering Corps, somehow elude all the guards, and find the money. Then, I had to make a great escape, get in Bill's car, and drive up into foreign territory. I told Bill that if I had to, I would sacrifice myself to the police in order for him to escape and give the money to Elaine. Now, we were heading to Engineering Corps—to make this nightmare a reality.

Bill noticed my mood swing and shook his head. "I still think you're crossing the line between *sane* and *insane*, Harold. If you don't got the guts, then you're worm food."

"And if I have the guts, I'm a criminal superhero," I replied. Even though I feared for my life, I knew I had to do it. Calming myself, I sat at an upright position and waited.

Engineering Corps—a huge, lavish building in the shape of a gear—loomed in front of us. Behind it, several animated gears emphasized the corporation's grand style. *The building's huge,* I thought. *How am I supposed to find the prize money in there?*

Apparently, I must have physically portrayed my emotions again because Bill suddenly remarked, "Are you anxious? Remember: self-confidence. Think you got every skill in the world because you'll really need them."

The car stopped in front of the Engineering Corps gate. "Good luck," Bill said. I got out of the car, and, without turning back, walked briskly up the steps and into the abyss.

Only one guard patrolled the gate, and the gate was open. I walked up to them and asked, "I am a participant in the, uh, 2008 Inventors Workshop competition, and I would like to ask Jerome, the head of Engineering Corps, several quick questions."

The guard raised an eyebrow. "I've got lots of knowledge 'bout Engineering Corps. Go ahead and ask me."

Why do I always end up in these types of situations? I asked myself bitterly. Composing myself, I answered, "Uh, it's not like that, sir. It's a very personal matter that only Jerome himself could answer."

"He ain't got nothing that we don't know about the competition."

"Competition? I'm sorry, sir, but I'm not asking him about the *competition*, I'm asking him a *personal* question. See, he told me about it a while ago."

The guard failed to keep his "train of thought" running because he pondered for a while and then casually replied, "Oh, sure. Follow me; I'll open the front door for you." He got out of his chair and walked to the front door of Engineering Corps, and I quickly tailed behind him. Once he opened the door, I said a polite "thank you" and walked grandly into the main hallway.

Think fast and don't hesitate, Harold, I told myself. *Find a security guard, beat him up, and demand the location of the prize money. It's that simple.*

Miraculously, a lone figure appeared across the hallway, whistling loudly. I walked up to him and asked him, "Can you please show me where the bathroom is? I'm kind of desperate; I've been searching everywhere, but I can't find it."

A small grin formed across the guard's face, but he replied politely. "Here, how about I show you the way? The building's kind of complicated, so it's easy to get lost. And you don't really want to get lost when you're bursting, right?"

I nodded. If the bathroom was behind him, he would turn around and walk me there. Then I could attack him, take his garb, and squeeze out the location of the cash. The bathroom could not be behind me either, because no doors or connecting hallways existed except for the main entrance. *What a lucky day! First a rather unintelligent guard positioned at the gate, and now a gullible guy is going to give me the location of the jackpot.*

As expected, the guard whirled around and began striding back from where he emerged from. Before he could walk a dozen steps, however, I slammed his shoulders with my fists and kicked the man's legs so he toppled onto the ground. I dragged him around a corner, found a closet, and booted him in it. I then entered and locked the door.

The guard coughed and moaned in pain, but I commanded him to seal his lips. "Now," I said quickly. "I want to know one thing from you: where do you guys guard that prize money?"

It took a while before he could respond, but eventually the officer sputtered, "I'm too low of a rank to be trusted with such information!" His reply filled the room with coughs and groans.

"Well then," I said, not perturbed. From my experience, it usually took a bit more torture to get something desirable out of someone. "I guess I'll get rid of you. I have no use of you anymore."

The man screamed in terror as I put my hand in my pocket. *He probably thinks I have a pistol or something,* I thought. *Good.*

Immediately, the sentry scrambled up and spilled all the information he knew. "Second floor, room 293. Go up the first flight of stairs you see, take a left, and then go into the VIP hallway. You'll find it at the end of the hall."

I produced a grim smile. "Thanks, pal. *Now* I have no use of you anymore." Without another word, I executed a punch into his stomach, and the barely conscious man collapsed senseless.

After taking his clothes off (he had a pistol on his belt, so I took that too), putting them on, and dressing him with my clothes (just in case someone reported that a strange person in a lab coat entered Engineering Corps), I unlocked the door and strode out of the closet.

Almost immediately, I saw two guards in rather splendid uniforms rush up to me. "We heard some commotion going on over here. You okay?" asked the taller one. They were obviously officers of a higher rank than the one I mugged.

I lied, "Yeah, I had a bit of trouble getting my belt buckle tight. It always loosens and I had to pull it really hard in order for it to stay put."

He emitted a harsh, spontaneous laugh before responding, "So, you're trying to sneak away without doing work? Sounds suspicious to me, Larry."

Larry, apparently the shorter of the two, answered mockingly, "Why, yes it does, George." With a sinister smile, he turned his attention to me. "You have patrolling to do outside. We'll show you to the back door."

"And," George piped in, "If we ever see the likes of you in here again today, you've got yourself a bundle of trouble."

The two officers laughed wickedly, and began to lead me across the building. Despair instantly filled my heart. At this rate, it would be impossible to locate the safe. If I snuck into the building again, the two menacing officers might catch me and...I don't even want to know. The only solution was to call it quits and return tomorrow, although I doubted that the guard I ambushed would stay unconscious for so long.

But, just as we turned the first corner, I spied a stairwell to my right. Inside, I felt like strutting my trademark victory dance at my sheer luck. Yes, definitely a stairwell of some sort that led to the second floor. According to the guard I injured, the VIP hallway should just be to my left when I walk up the stairs.

The high-ranked guards paid no attention to me. If I could make an excuse and get up to the building, the prize would be as good as mine.

"Uh, excuse me. I have to do an errand to Jerom—"

Larry and George whirled around, and said simultaneously, "No excuses, you sloth."

That's it! A voice in me yelled. *You can take these guys on. They'd be your warm-up anyways. What right do they have to call you 'sloth?'*

Satisfied with my inner drive to batter down the two guards, I reacted with a roar. Almost immediately, I thrust my elbow into George's stomach. The guard who I ambushed flopped on the floor, writhing in pain. Astonished, Larry sprang up into a ready position, yelled a curse and reached for his pistol. But before he could grip onto it, I kneed him and stole his pistol. Being the guard with the better stamina, Larry took off down the hallway and disappeared behind a corner.

Instinctively, I ignored the fleeing sentry and bounded up the stairs. I knew he would be warning Jerome and the others above, so I had to move—and leave, hopefully—quickly.

Several guards yelled simultaneously upstairs. The alarm sounded and the entire building flashed blood red. I reached the top of the stairs, and inspected the hallway. No guards yet, but definitely footsteps. To my left emerged a huge door with the golden words "VIP" plastered on it. Assuming that to be the entrance to the VIP hall, I raced down there and entered just in time to hear someone yell, "Hey, you! Get back here!"

Heart pounding, I ran across the hallway. Assuming the guard in the closet had told the truth, the cash would be at the end of the hall. Trying to imitate an infuriated officer searching for a stealthy criminal (like me), I tromped into several meeting rooms and asked the people inside if everything was alright. Consequently, when security guards entered the VIP hallway, they didn't feel intimidated or provoked in any way. Instead, they nodded at me and left the hall.

When they left, I sprinted to the end of the hallway and entered the only room there. Inside were a huge black safe and a lot of laser sensors. Not wanting to arouse any other commotion, I slipped carefully past the laser sensors and proceeded to crack the safe.

Apparently, the safe was locked with two codes: one composed of three digits and the other composed of eight. *Don't let your ingenious brain rot, Harold. You can crack that safe in a minute! Come on, focus!*

Although my artificial conceit told me I could crack the safe in a minute, a good twenty minutes passed before I managed to decode the first code. As I began the next, the doorknob began turning and the door squeaked. My racing heart sped up a couple more beats. *If I go and attempt to stop the guard, I'd have to run through the laser sensors. But, if I stay, I only have the choice of killing him. Even if I try to shoot him, there's a chance I'd die too...*

I shook my head. Dying was not an option. I decided to take the risk and charge at the opening door. Just as the door opened to a respectable size and guard popped into view, I dashed past the laser sensors, triggered another alarm, and tackled the unsuspecting man. I grabbed my pistol and aimed it at him. "What's the code of this safe?" I yelled. The guard sat, dazed. Yet, even at gunpoint, he still hesitated to answer my question. "I...I don't know!"

"Tell me, or you die!" I tightened my grip on the pistol.

"Okay, okay! The password is 8-4-7-2-5-8-3-6-8-3."

I tightened my grip harder on the pistol. I felt lines form on the top of my head. "You think I'm an idiot or something? An eight digit code doesn't have ten digits."

"All right! Fine! Just don't kill me."

"I will if you don't stop stalling!"

The man facial features hardened, and sweat began emerging from his brow. "I only know that it's the boss's birthday...but that was also a rumor! Honest to goodness, I really don't know!"

Unimpressed, I loosened my aim at the guard and used my free fist to knock the man out. I heard more footsteps, and the cocking of rifles. Slamming the door shut, I thought to myself, *This is it, Harold...*

In the midst of the deafening alarm and the ugly howls of the guards, I pounced to the safe and began cracking it. Luckily, most of the numbers were close to each other, so it took less time to decode the vault. During the opening ceremonies of the Inventions Contest, I remembered Bill hacking into Jerome's profile and salvaging his birthday. I recalled that he was born on October the 23rd, but the year did not show up on the computer screen.

More yelling. The pounding of the boots grew louder, and I heard several meeting room doors open and close quickly. It was only a matter of time before they reached me. *Guess and check, Harold!*

Desperately, I plugged in 1-0-2-3-1-9 in the first six numbers of the code, to indicate an October 23rd sometime in the 20th century. I tried countless combinations of the last two, hoping to find a satisfactory click within the metallic coffer. Finally, at 1-0-2-3-1-9-6-6, a click sounded, and the vault door swung open. Inside was a lovely black suitcase. Upon opening it, I found hundreds of neatly stacked 100-dollar bills. *Got it!*

Just as I prepared to exit the room, the door broke open, and Jerome's three bodyguards entered the room. As I presumed, they armed themselves with rifles. In the middle, Jerome held a pistol and a wicked smile on his face.

"Ha!" Jerome roared, almost in a hysterical manner, "I knew you looked suspicious one way or another. Anyhow, without pitiful scum like you, the world—and *my* contest—is purged from a criminal world. Being in control of the police station temporarily, I have all authority to kill you right now. So, what do you have to say for yourself?"

I knew he spoke the truth, yet I didn't want to believe it. "I think... that scoundrels like you should think less about your social status and more about the world yourself!"

At this, Jerome doubled in laughter. He almost dropped his pistol on the floor. I waited uncomfortably for the fat man to stop his roaring.

With tears full of laughter, Jerome said, "You? You actually ask for me to think more about the world? Why would I even make this contest if I didn't want young inventors to prosper like me?"

"So they could work for you."

"Ha! Good venture, but no. I'm too rich to even bother about my company anymore. The whole building could blow up, and I wouldn't care one bit!" The head of Engineering Corps obviously lost his sanity.

"You don't even deserve your wealth."

"And you, my friend, don't deserve that briefcase of cash." Jerome disabled the laser sensors, walked up to me and extended a grimy hand. "Hand it over."

Aside from the thunderous ringing of the security bell, silence completely filled the room. I knew that eventually too many guards would block the only exit to the room, and doom would be inevitable, so I had to act now.

Bellowing with anger, I smashed the briefcase into Jerome's head, knocking him onto the floor. Immediately a barrage of bullets filled the air, but because they hesitated to attack with their leader in firing range, the bullets failed to puncture any skin. Instead, they clattered against the wall and fell inches away from me.

I jumped quickly to the left and charged at the guard with the beady eyes, who was in the process of reloading. Without uncertainty, he dropped his rifle and retrieved a sharp knife from his belt. Swinging wildly, he advanced. *I've got no choice,* I concluded. Pulling my pistol out, I aimed and fired at the guard.

It took me a while to realize that I had missed.

To my horror, the pistol held no more bullets. I bellowed in outrage, but nothing in my possession could stop the three guards.

With two riflemen pointing their guns at me, a berserk security officer with a knife, and a recovering Jerome pulling his pistol from his belt, I had no chance but to forfeit myself to a bleak and terrible fate.

Jerome looked at the blonde and nodded. The guard prepared to fire. "You've eluded my bullets before," the guard sneered. "But now I've got you. It's just a shame I had to kill you when you were a sitting duck."

I responded, "Killing a man when he's defenseless is cruel. You're a disgrace."

Undisturbed, the blonde man gave a last, brutal smile. Then, he aimed his rifle at my head.

BANG!

I heard a thump and nothing more.

Then, I opened my eyes, and with astonishment, I noticed Bill and two downed men. Jerome cursed and shot several bullets at Bill. My partner, unfazed, ran to the right and confronted the warden with the beady eyes. While Bill distracted the guard, I flung my briefcase at the man's back and quickly followed with a painful elbow at the same spot. Bill shouted at Jerome, "Never thought there were two of us, eh?"

"Shut your mouth!" Jerome barked as he threw his pistol at the short man. The weapon pitifully landed inches away from its target.

Bill laughed and said, "Let's get out of here."

As we ran out of the room, I noticed several limp bodies scattered across the hallway. "Now, what trick did you do this time?"

"Let's just say that inhaling the wrong type of thing hurts. The rest of them guards are hiding in the meeting rooms. They probably still think that the gas is still here."

After exiting the VIP hallway, I breathlessly said, "By the way, thanks. But don't do that again. You could have killed yourself."

"And you would have. What about Elaine, eh?"

"Yeah, I guess. Thanks again."

"Stop saying thanks! Man, when do you stop with the compliments?"

I laughed at my friend's fiery nature. Having Bill around sure made things looser. "Anyways, do you know where we are going to leave?"

"Why, the exit, I assume."

Silence engulfed us until we reached the stairwell. "What if the exit's blocked?"

"The window will do."

"What if the window's blocked?"

"How would they block a window? Are they really going to tape themselves onto the glass so they could act as a shield of something?"

"Well..."

Suddenly, loud footsteps and screams sounded upstairs. More guards! "Bill! More guards are coming."

His eyes widened. "They must've gone out of the rooms now. They'll be going for us."

As we reached the bottom, he motioned for me to follow him. We ended up in a small room with a small corridor at the side. Bill locked the door and we ventured to the middle of the room. He motioned towards the corridor. "We'll go through this corridor, and it should take us to the main entrance," he explained.

The door trembled, and vulgar yells rang through the dry air. They obviously wanted to break the door down. "Quick!" hissed Bill. We both ran into the corridor. Darkness deluged my eyesight as we ran blindly for several seconds. Then, after bumping into Bill, I heard him say, "Now, we'll open the door, and if anyone's there, I'll take him and you leave."

"No, you leave and I'll take them." I motioned for him to take the black briefcase.

"There's no time to argue! Now go!"

Bill shoved the door open and found no guards in sight. The main entrance loomed ahead. "They must all be back there, breaking the door open."

I heard surprisingly close yells and the reloading of guns. The guards were in the corridor. Bill located a sofa and threw it into the darkness. Several screams echoed. The sound of footsteps diminished into nothingness. They were clearly going to use another path or corridor to find us.

"Let's go!" Bill hissed. We sprinted down the hallway, opened the glass door, and jumped out of Engineering Corps to our freedom.

To our surprise, Jerome and two more guards stood to our left, on the grass, with their guns at hand. "Hello, *Connor,*" Jerome jeered. "We were expecting you."

"How did you..." I stammered.

"I know the place better than you do," Jerome commented. "This time, I told my guards to kill you right away if you ever touch me again."

He walked up to me and slapped my face. "I'm afraid you cannot hurt me anymore, can you?"

I growled, but did not respond. Wisely, Bill remained silent.

"I don't know why you planned to sabotage such a brilliant contest," Jerome continued. "But I expect a good answer later. You'll be off to prison anyhow, both you and your partner."

With that, my anger expanded. There was no way I could accomplish my goal at this point. In fury, I shoved Jerome back. The fat man stumbled backwards couple of steps before collapsing into his two shocked guards, knocking all three of them to the ground.

Inside, I laughed at my luck. "Bill!" I yelled. "Get to the car, now!"

With quick reaction, Bill darted down the road and out the gate. Following my own instructions, I darted through the grass in the direction of the gate.

BANG!

A loud gunshot, followed by an extreme pain in my left knee, forced me to collapse onto the ground. Jerome, the one who had shot me, slowly approached. "I've had enough of you," he said. "I'll make sure you die, one way or another."

No, I thought. *Is it truly over?* My conceit succumbed to emotion as tears spilled from my eyes. *Is everything really over?* I remembered all the times, including the recent times, that I had felt a pain, emotionally or physically. It had always ended well. *No...this time isn't different. The older you are, the bigger the challenge. I can't let Elaine go just yet...if one of us has to die, it's me.*

Forcing myself to ignore my pain, I roared and jumped up into a standing position again. The sudden movement astounded Jerome, who assumed that I wouldn't even be able to move. Ignoring Jerome, I sprinted down to the gate, even though the pain was extreme. Blood spilled out, and soon I lost the ability to function my left leg. Forcing myself to now hop on my right foot, I yelled, "Bill! Take the briefcase and leave!"

"What's going on?" Bill screamed. He sounded desperate.

I didn't answer him. Giving up to the pain, I threw the black case of money as far as I could, and then crumpled down onto the floor.

"Elaine..." I whimpered to myself. "You'll be all right."

I directed my last words at Jerome. "Take me! Do whatever you want with me, but know this: I have already completed my goal." Then, everything went black.

When I returned to the conscious world, I was in a hospital.

When I saw Jerome enter the room, I yelled and attempted to run, but the extreme pain in my leg prevented me from doing so. Looking to my left, I noticed that a cast had been placed around my leg. Seeing that I could not escape, I said, "What are *you* doing here?"

Jerome put his arm on my shoulder. "I would like to speak with you for a moment."

"Go away!"

"I'm here to confirm something. The result should please you, if you cooperate."

"I don't want anything to do with you."

Jerome sighed. "If you don't want anything to do with me, then perhaps you might want to consult with your comrade." As Jerome spoke, the door squeaked open, and Bill rushed inside. The burning expression on his face indicated that something interesting had just happened.

My friend, panting, leaned against a drawer and shook his head vigorously. "You won't guess what happened, it's something to do—"

Jerome cleared his throat. As if Bill was a TV and someone had changed the channel, my partner suddenly stopped and began talking in a less energetic tone. "Ah, well, you see, Jerome wants to confirm something with you. See, I told him about your motives, and he thought that the explanation was slightly plausible. So, he sent you here, expecting that you would eventually be able to answer his questions.

"Shortly after you fainted, you see, I saw the black briefcase fall and crash somewhere on the sidewalk," Bill recalled. "So I took that, and began to start the car, but the guards in the building had already come out. So, I was forced to surrender. Except, I told Jerome to bring you to a hospital. Shortly afterward, I told him your, ah, *story*, and he was moved by it. Anyways, for now, he has a different view of you. Still thinks you've got no manners, but he's got a respect for you. Just tell the truth, Harold, and everything will turn out just right."

I sighed, but Bill's words didn't sound like a story made up on the spot. "Sounds like Jerome told you to say that. But..." I shrugged and looked at Jerome. "All right. Ask me anything you want."

"Ah, wise decision." Jerome shifted his body in my direction and smiled. "First of all, did you begin your criminal business to fund a surgery for your wife?"

"Yeah, why?"

"That's a good thing. So, tell me about the attack on Mr. Mecks and the ambush on Engineering Corps."

I recalled everything I could about that day. Every now and then Jerome would nod in approval; sometimes, he would snap his fingers or murmur something under his breath. Finally, when I was done, Jerome closed his eyes and pondered for a couple of seconds.

When he reopened his eyes, he gave Bill and I a broad smile. "You've given me the final puzzle piece; now that it's completed, everything finally makes sense."

For a while, no one spoke; not even Bill said anything. Finally, the short thief casually walked away from the drawer he leaned on and quietly exited the room, winking and smiling at me before he left.

Jerome's face softened. "I would like to say that I am impressed and even moved at your determination to save a loved one, even though the act was clearly wrong. You sabotaged numerous people's inventions, cracked a heavily guarded safe, and even took a gunshot for Elaine. I congratulate you for that.

"I also apologize for your...crippled state," Jerome said, eying the cast. "As compensation for this and your incredible feats, I have decided to *not* send you to prison, and I will give you the prize money that you have stolen from us. If you hadn't stole it, I might have donated it to you anyways."

Immediate satisfaction and admiration flushed towards the man I had always thought savage and sordid. "Thanks a bunch. You're a good guy." I remembered the jeers the master inventor had sent me during my attack on Engineering Corps. "Sometimes."

The fat man chortled before responding. "Don't mention it. Although, I do believe you owe Engineering Corps for the poison gas mishap your friend Bill plagued upon several of my employees." Jerome frowned, and his expression hardened. "I know you're situation better than anyone else, Harold. I've been in your shoes before. However, my fate was not as beautiful as yours."

Jerome prepared to exit the hospital room. "You're pretty lucky you tried to take money from a person who knows your situation, Harold. Anyways, I guess it's time for you to have a real talk with your buddy, eh?"

As Jerome began to open the wooden door, I said, "Thanks again."

The head of Engineering Corps gave me a thumbs-up and exited the hospital room.

A few minutes later, the door opened again, and Bill stumbled into the room, panting. "Dude!" he said breathlessly. "You won't guess what happened, it—"

"You've already told me this part."

"Oh, I did? But, dude! Good news. The surgery is a success. In a few weeks, Elaine will free of cancer cells, and in a few months, she'll be able to walk and do normal things again."

A flood of emotions filled me. I cried, laughed, and blushed at the same time. It took me ten minutes to stop.

Bill grinned. "Guess you're happy, aye?"

I gave a huge nod, and then a vast smile. "Aye."

"Oh yeah," Bill said before he made his second departure, "We've got one more surprise guest for you. Bear with me, OK? I'll get you, like, a burger from McDonalds when we're done, all right?"

I nodded. Bill walked to the door, opened it slightly, and motioned for someone to enter. Kevin Mecks and Jerome entered the room.

"Hey, what's up, Harold?" Kevin said.

"The ceiling, then sky and God."

"Yeah, yeah," Kevin said jokingly, smiling at the joke he played back at the Inventors Workshop banquet. "Well, when there's good news, there's also bad news. I'm here to tell you that the inventors have recently agreed that you shouldn't be given the prize money. The million will be split among the inventors; because of this, they will not sue you."

Instantly, a wave of anger slammed against me. Did Jerome simply make a false statement, just to make me feel better? How was I going to pay for the surgery now?

I was about to protest when Jerome piped in. "That is what I said to the inventors you ambushed, to keep them from individually suing you. At your stage, that would not be good. However, I have decided to give you an extra million to fund the surgery."

Again, the flood of emotions filled my heart, toppling my anger and burning it away like a withered flame within a gust of wind. I took a big breath, sighed, and grinned. I groped for words, but I simply couldn't respond.

Surrounded by my new friends, I cried.

Elaine.

Things are finally starting to get back on track.

The Mafia Teacher

By

Judy Kong

"Yuki, think about it. You have a position and a job, mafia and police officer. Why would you want to be a teacher?"

A strict-looking man tried to persuade the silvery-haired girl, but the girl was far from listening,

She retorted against him, "I need to be a teacher. I want to!"

"Father, I really want to be a teacher, and I will!"

"Think about it you already have two jobs..."

"Well a police officer is a job, but being a member of mafia, which is your job, is not considered a job in the society."

"Wh...what!" The man grabbed Yuki's arm and jerked her around.

"You can't stop me from doing what I want to do. I'm going to be a teacher," Yuki shouted stubbornly. She stared into her father's dark brown eyes. Sparks of anger flashed between Yuki and her father.

"Why are you two so stubborn?" Her mother's imploring voice inquired softly, but Yuki and her dad remained face to face, neither willing to look away first, both determined to win.

"Mom!" Yuki yelled.

"Darling!" A pretty longhaired lady came and broke the tension between Yuki and her father.

"Mom! I really need to be a teacher!" Yuki turned away from her father who still glared at her biting his lip in anger.

"OK," Yuki's mother replied with the smile that she gave her when she had something else on her mind.

"Yuki has two jobs already!" Yuki's father almost stumbled over a chair, shouting at Yuki's mother.

"I had something I wanted you to do," said Yuki's mother, ignoring her husband's angry gestures.

"What now? Not work again!" Yuki's mother was her superior on the police force as well as her mother. She was always after her to do more work; reading, writing, and studying police work. She was tired of police work; she wanted to teach children.

"If you don't accept my condition, you can't be a teacher," Yuki's mother said in a tone of voice that left no doubt that she meant what she said.

Defeated, Yuki sighed, "Fine...what is it?"

"I'm going to send you to CAI High School to teach."

"Really? You got me a job teaching! YAY!" Yuki danced around her room, but the dancing suddenly stopped when she heard her mother's next words. She barely noticed her father shaking his head.

"Your mission is to find the high school student that is drug smuggling and arrest him."

Yuki's heart sank, police work again. She didn't say anything until her mother spoke.

"Why are you so quiet?"

"Drug smuggling?" Yuki slunk down on to her sofa and looked across the room at her father. He shrugged his shoulder at her and sat down on a chair to her right.

"I was thinking of putting you in that school as a senior high school student, but if you wish, you can go in as a teacher. You look awfully young, but you should be able to rise to the challenge of teaching. After all, you are an excellent police officer."

"Does this mean that the student who is drug smuggling could be in the class that I'm going to teach?"

"Maybe"

Yuki thought about the request that her mother gave for a moment, She thought that it wouldn't be hard to accomplish this mission. At least she would have the chance to teach.

"Alright, I'll accept it."

"Yuki, don't let either the students or the teachers know you are a police officer or a member of the mafia," her father said firmly and quietly.

Her eyes got big with surprise. "Why?"

"Because when they find out that you are a cop, the school will not treat you as a teacher, and the student's will avoid you. If they find out you are a member of a mafia family, you might be in danger.

Yuki nodded her head. She realized her father's wisdom. She hated to admit it, but her father was right.

"Now, it's already all arranged. Go to the school whenever you are ready." her mother spoke in a calm but firm voice.

Yuki stood in front of CAI High School. She had been wandering around, looking to see if there was a person to open the gate for her.

" Hey! What are you doing here! This school is only for boys!" demanded a tall stern-looking man with an angry face. He seemed to be stressed and annoyed that he had to deal with Yuki.

"Are teachers not allowed to come in also? I came here to teach room 131"

"Oh...sorry."

The guy who turned out to be a guard seemed to be ashamed of his impatience and let Yuki inside the gate.

On her way to the office, Yuki thought that it was strange that the buildings were so clean compared to the other high schools she had seen.

Yuki nervously knocked on the office door and went inside." Excuse me. I am the new teacher for room 131."

"Nice to meet you. I'm Mr. Paul. Let's go. I'll show you the way to your classroom."

" Thank you, I was little bit surprised when I saw the building of this high school, it was so clean compared to the other schools I had seen before."

"Yes, students in this school are very well mannered..."

Yuki thought she heard Mr. Paul murmuring something under his breath but soon forgot about it as she left the main office with Mr. Paul. While they were walking, Yuki suddenly realized that they were going in the opposite direction of the main high school buildings. They headed for a building that looked like it had been built long ago, and this building had a totally different appearance than the clean building that Yuki had just left.

"Uh...Mr. Paul...are you sure you're going the right direction?"

"Of course, this building is another part of CAI High School."

"Sorry, but the only building I see is nothing that looks like a school."

"The building you see is part of CAI high school, and there is only one classroom in the building. It doesn't look like a school because this building is only for temporary use."

Looking at the dark building, Yuki thought her job was not going to be easy as she had first thought it would be.

"Why is this classroom separated from the other classrooms?"

"The students in that classroom are more spoiled than other students in our school. We didn't want them to ruin our school's reputation, so we teach them here."

Yuki was shocked at the revelation that the school was just hiding the bad kids, not trying to help them. She thought about her time in high school, and the thought of these kids not having a chance to learn angered her.

"The students in this classroom will want somebody's attention. They will do anything to get some ones attention. Changing these students will be hard, but I will know what to do... I've been in their situation before..." Yuki thought while she followed the principal to the classroom.

"You can go in by yourself. I don't want to see these spoilt brats."

Yuki bit her lips when she heard the principal's last words.

She thought, "You will regret what you said when they graduate next year."

Yuki opened the classroom door. The noise level grew louder when the door got opened. Yuki was frustrated but not because of the noise that they made. She was frustrated because nobody seemed to be noticing that she came in.

She stood in the front of the class. The teacher's desk looked like it had not been used for a long time. Yuki knew how to make the students pay attention to her. She calmly walked over to the blackboard, placed her nails against it, and scratched the board repeatedly. The squeaky sound did get all of the student's attention, but Yuki was shocked again when she saw the students' expressions. Every single student gave her a bored, disinterested look.

"Let's bet on how long she stays."

A student whispered to other classmates, it wasn't loud, but Yuki heard.

"Hey, I'll take that bet, and I've got another one for you. I bet I'll fix your rude behaviors in three days."

Everybody laughed, thinking that Yuki was insane.

"Hey you better do just that. If you don't, you'll be at our mercy for the rest of the year," shouted out a student who seemed to be the boss of the class.

"I will, and you guys will become good students. Choose something you're really good at, how about soccer?" Yuki challenged the class with a sly expression on her face.

"Soccer? You are crazy! We're great with anything in sports. When you lose, you leave us alone."

Yuki knew that the students thought that she was insane, but she also knew that she was going to win this bet. If she earned her students' respect, fixing their behavior would be easier. It would only take one punch to get them all listen to her, but she didn't want to use force. She knew that the students would be ashamed that a young woman beat them, so she chose soccer.

"I'll be the referee." A student who had remained silent volunteered to be the referee of the game.

"And what is your name?"

"Michael."

"Michael..? Sure, it would be better if there is a referee, but no unfair judgments."

"I was going to do it even if you didn't let me." Michael said.

Yuki wanted to argue with Michael's last comment, but she decided to let him say anything he want, she knew that it was going to be the last rude thing that he was going to say to her.

"Hey, don't you want to give up? You don't want to be our slaves, do you?" One of the students called out. Yuki looked at this students name tag, and found out that his name was Joo ho.

The students were giving Yuki another chance, still thinking that it was impossible for Yuki to win.

"Thank you for the offer but no. When I win, you will be honor bound to change your behavior. If you want to say rude things, say them right now. You won't have any chance to say them after the game." Yuki said, as they walked to the soccer field.

With a loud 'start' from Michael, the game started.

Joo ho dribbled the soccer ball towards the goal. Yuki ran and took the ball from him and said, " If I shoot from here, it is a goal,"

"That's impossible; are you an idiot?"

It was natural for Joo ho, in fact for all of the students, to think the shot was impossible because Yuki was so far from the goal. But Yuki gave a smile and kicked the ball in front of her. Everybody watched the ball sail high into the air. The ball went exactly into the goal that Yuki had aimed for.

Joo ho flopped down on the ground when he saw Yuki shooting the goal. He couldn't think of anything, and started to get nervous about winning this game.

"Stop giving me that stupid look and stand up. We didn't even actually start yet."

The game was going to be divided into two twenty minute halves, but if Yuki shoots three goals without letting Joo ho shoot any, the game ends.

"That teacher...her power is unbelievable."

One of the students who were watching mentioned it to the others. The students all agreed with him and looked and Yuki nervously.

"Here's the ball!"

The student that ran to get the soccer ball came. After the game started, Yuki shot two more goals and won the bet. Joo ho seemed to given after Yuki shot her second goal.

"I won. You guys can't say any rude things to me from now on."

Everybody was silent. It seemed like they didn't want to accept the fact that Yuki won.

"You're not going to break your promise, are you?" Yuki asked, knowing that they would.

"Now go in to your classroom."

Everybody went in except one student, Michael.

"Why aren't you going in?"

"I don't listen to teachers," Michael replied stubbornly.

"Well, that's your choice. I was just telling you to go in because there's nothing to do here. If you want to stay here, you can."

There was a moment of silence between the two of them.

"You're denying everything I tell you to do, well, not exactly me, but you just don't want to hear anything from a person called 'teacher'. I'm only here to teach you the thing that you are to do during your twelfth grade here. I'm not one of those parents who always tells you to do something until you become successful, and I don't even want to be someone like that." Yuki said, and started heading back to the classroom.

"Oh, and just so you know, I don't push away students that want my help or attention." Yuki turned around and added. Then she walked back to the classroom.

Michael stood silently. Then he called after Yuki, "Then you should find those students... students that *need* your help."

Yuki glanced over her shoulder at Michael. He stood on the middle of the soccer field until he saw Yuki disappeared into the building.

Yuki looked over the book where all of the student information for her class was stored.

"Number one, Joo ho. His father passed away. Mother works in a restaurant. Family members include two younger brothers, one younger sister. Four suspensions! Wow!"

Yuki read out information on all of the numbered students. "Number 13...Ruchi. Absent from 21 days...21 days? If he doesn't come to school next week, he'll be expelled."

Yuki shook with anger. She promised herself that she would find the missing student before the week ended.

"Number 14, Michael. Father is CEO of S group. Mother passed away."

Yuki dropped the book on the next number. It was better just saying that she had to do it.

"Number 15, Mukuro...Girlfriend died while riding with him on a motorcycle, suspended."

Yuki closed her eyes tight. After a while she picked up the book saying 'wake up' to herself.

"Number 16, Yichiru. Both parents passed away. Lives with an eleven-year-old younger sister. Currently suspended for stealing. If there were other problems with this student, he would be automatically expelled.

Everybody in Yuki's classroom had a reason to be frustrated and angry, but Yuki chose four of the students who she felt needed the most help.

"Ruchi, Yichiru, Michael, Mukuro..." Yuki quietly talked to herself. She promised to herself that she would not let these four students get expelled.

★ ★ ★ ★

The next morning, room 131 was noisy as it always was.

"Be quiet," Yuki warned. The noise level didn't go down. Yuki felt frustrated, but that feeling disappeared when she heard one of the student's talking.

"Hey, did you see Ruchi yesterday?" the student asked, with his eyes wide open.

"Yes, I thought he was at home resting, but he was actually working in a restaurant."

In the noisy classroom, Yuki heard the conversation and listened closely.

"Is he working because of Yichiru?" another student asked curiously.

"Shut up!" Michael shouted angrily.

Yuki wanted to listen more about Yichiru and Ruchi, but she couldn't because Michael ruined the opportunity.

"Michael, how about YOU shutting up?"

Everybody's' eyes got wide. They were shocked by the fact that their teacher shouted, well, they wouldn't have been shocked if a male teacher shouted, but Yuki was a woman, a young woman. If she weren't their teacher, she might be the kind of woman that the boys wanted to date.

"Why are you guys so shocked? Is 'shut up' a shocking word for you?"

"You are a teacher. Are you allowed to use those kind of words?" Michael asked Yuki.

"I was your age once, and I wasn't a really good student as well."

"You became a teacher when you were a trouble-making student during your school years? That doesn't make sense," Joo ho commented on what Yuki said.

"I wanted to 'save' you guys from all those teachers who only care for the 'good' students."

"Stop dreaming. That's impossible," Joo ho blurted out.

"I'm the one who is deciding if it's possible or not."

Everybody suddenly became silent. Yuki went to her desk, and thought about the students' conversations about Ruchi, and Yichiru.

"Then does this mean that Ruchi is not coming to school because he is working to help Yichiru? Does this mean those two are really good friends? No, Michael stopped the students from talking about Yichiru and Ruchi, so does that mean that Michael, Yichiru, and Ruchi are good friends?'

Then she noticed interesting information in the students' information book—the back four cell phone numbers of all three students were the same.

Yuki could now understand why Ruchi didn't come to school. Ruchi and Michael decided to help Yichiru because both of his parents had passed away. Ruchi was working with Yichiru to earn more money for him, and Michael was coming to school to prevent his classmates spreading rumors about his friends, Ruchi and Yichiru.

After a tiring school day, Yuki, heard her stomach growl and looked for a restaurant near school. Yuki talked to herself while she opened the restaurant door. "It will be lonely eating by myself, but I can't skip dinner because I have nobody to eat with."

When she entered to the restaurant, a loud bell greeted her. Then, an employee of the restaurant soon came to Yuki and greeted her.

"Welcome! Here is the menu. Please press the bell if you want to order."

The restaurant was clean and filled with customers. The restaurant impressed Yuki. She thought that she would come to this restaurant more often.

While Yuki looked over the menu and thought about Ruchi and Yichiru, her phone rang.

"Hello?"

"Hey Yuki, where are you?"

It was Yuki's friend Mina. Mina had been Yuki's secretary when she worked for the mafia, but she left the mafia group because Yuki thought she was too young to become an organized crime member. "I'm in a restaurant near the school where I work."

"Who are you with?" Mina asked,

"I'm here alone. I couldn't find anyone near here to eat dinner with."

"You are going to eat dinner by yourself? What restaurant are you in? I wandered by CAI high school to meet you, but you weren't there. Now I'm in a shop near your school."

"If you come out of that shop and look right, there is a narrow way. Come out that way, and you'll see a restaurant called Sumi."

"OK."

After the call, Yuki wanted to order but she decided to wait until Mina arrived. Suddenly the loud doorbell rang, Yuki looked at the door, assuming that Mina was there. It was not Mina but a familiar looking guy. Yuki knew that she had seen him somewhere but couldn't remember where she saw him.

"I'm here." The familiar boy told the guy who seemed to be the restaurant's owner.

Yuki thought, "Who is he? I saw him some where...but where?"

"Ruchi, you're here." The owner greeted him.

Yuki remembered Ruchi after she heard the owner's greeting. Was this restaurant that ruchi worked, and the restaurant where the other students saw him?

A few minutes after Ruchi came in, the door opened. This time it was Mina.

"Hey! I'm here!"

Yuki waved her hand at Mina. Mina smiled and sat right in front of her.

"What do you want to order? I'm ordering Japanese sushi. How about you?" Yuki asked. She was not even hungry any more. Thinking about talking to Ruchi had taken away her appetite, but Mina came all the way to the restaurant eat with her, so she decided to eat first and talk to him later.

"I'll order the same thing."

Yuki pressed the bell. Ruchi came and asked what she wanted to order. Yuki wanted to sit him down and persuade him to come back to school, but she decided to wait for a better time.

"Two sushi."

Ruchi took the order and went away. Yuki watched Ruchi work while she waited for their food to come.

"Why are you looking at him?" Mina asked curiously.

Yuki explained the situation to Mina. "He is my student. He's not coming to school because of good reasons, but I have to make him come to school within a week, or he will be expelled."

After they finished eating dinner, Mina had to go first to go to a meeting. Yuki, decided to tell Ruchi that she was his teacher. Even though she knew what Ruchis' reaction was going to be, she wanted to help and would do anything to get him back to the school.

Yuki walked up to ruchi and said, "Ruchi, I need to talk to you." she wanted a conversation with him.

Ruchi looked at Yuki as if she were a crazy woman. Yuki was prepared for any reaction from Ruchi because Yuki, herself, would have reacted the same way if a stranger suddenly claimed to be her teacher. Yuki decided not to think about it in Ruchis' perspective.

"Whatever it is, can you say it quickly? I have work to do."

"OK, this is going to sound crazy, but I needed to talk to you. I'm your new teacher."

"Teacher?" Ruchi interrupted, gave her a disgusted look and turned away, ignoring her.

Yuki let out a sigh and decided to persuade his friends to help her get Ruchi back to school. She was disappointed, even though she expected Ruchi would not respond positively to her proposal.

When she left the book store, Yuki saw a man much older than Ruchi hitting him. Yuki ran across the street and came up behind the man. She grabbed hold of both of the man's arms. Using a police hold designed to subdue suspects, Yuki twisted them and forced the man to the ground. The man cried out in pain and tearfully begged her to release him.

"If I ever see you hitting one of my students again, I'll break both of your arms and have you arrested for assault." Yuki angrily blurted out the words without thinking how Ruchi might react. The man struggled to his feet and ran off, protectively holding his left arm.

Yuki pulled Ruchi up and waited for him to speak. Ruchi seemed stunned that Yuki had come to his rescue.

"You are that teacher?"

Yuki nodded. "I'm also the person that saved your life," Yuki said. "Come to school tomorrow and we'll talk about this incident further."

"Hey!Hey!Hey! You guys! Ruchi is here!" Daniel ran in to the classroom and announced that Ruchi had come back to school. Yuki saw Michael running out to the field where Ruchi talked with classmates.

"Is the vice principal coming after you?" Ruchi asked mischievously.

"Ha-ha, are you stupid? I would I run if there was a vice principal coming after me?" Michael smiled, lightly punching Ruchi's arm.

Yuki was proud of herself that she had persuaded Ruchi to come to school, even though she knew that it would be difficult persuading him to remain and come every day, but she had a good feeling about her chances.

The first class with Ruchi had started, Ruchis' attitude was just the same as the other students in the class, but at least now, the students were not talking, except two students, Michael and Ruchi.

"Come in! The bell rang ten minutes ago!" Yuki opened the window, and shouted.

"Hey there! Be quite!" Yuki shouted,

"Just do what you were doing." Michael smiled and replied.

" Hey Michael, I'm going to tear your mouth apart if you don't stop being rude to me."

"Go ahead," Michael talked back.

"Really?" Yuki asked.

"Really."

Yuki was a person that if somebody wants her to do something she would really do it. She put down the chalk, and walked up in front of Michael. "You are going to regret what you said just now." Yuki placed her hands on Michael's' face, and pinched the two sides of his cheek and pulled them outward.

"Argh!" Michael's screamed was loudly.

"Should I proceed further?"

Tears filled both eyes. "Stop! Please stop!"

Yuki released her grip, and Michael rubbed his cheeks.

After class finished, Ruchi and Yuki talked. Ruchi seemed to have started to open his mind to Yuki. Ruchi and Yuki shared experiences from their high school lives.

Ruchi thought that Yuki was a lot different than the other teachers. Even if he said rude things, she didn't hop up and get mad at him. She talked back and said things that he agreed to. He also realized that Yuki had been a student that the school ignored.

"OK, this is probably the last time I talk about Yichiru, so listen carefully. Do you know that Yichiru is now suspended because he was stealing?" Ruchi told Yuki about his friend.

"Yes," Yuki answered.

"That isn't true."

"What isn't true? Why didn't you tell school officials what you know?" Yuki asked.

"I did! I told them over and over. They didn't listen to me."

"Did you know that our school has some kind of relationship with a mafia group?"

"What? A mafia group?" Ruchi's announcement startled Yuki. She never thought a school would have a relationship with a mafia group. Maybe the mafia had smuggled the drugs and tried pinning on the crime on innocent students.

Ruchi angrily continued, "As you know, Yichiru's parents passed away, and he's living with his younger eleven-year-old sister. I think one of the members of the mafia group that has a relationship to this school saw Yichiru fighting, and they wanted him to join their Mafia group. Yichiru didn't go in because of his younger sister, and the mafia group stole a school object and made the situations look as if Yichiru stoled it,"

Ruchi paused to control his anger. "You know what the funny thing is? The funny thing is that ninety percent of the school knew that Yichiru didn't steal."

Yuki was shocked. She needed time to make all these accusations clear.

"So...does this mean that the school blamed the student because they were afraid of the mafia group? Did you tell this to me because you believe I want to help? If you did, what do you want me to do? Do you want Yichiru to come back to school, or prove that Yichiru didn't steal anything? Or do you want revenge on the mafia group?"

Yuki was angry that nobody took action of this, but she controlled her emotion and asked calmly.

"Did you tell this to me because you believe me? If you did, what do you want me to do?"

"Is it that you want Yichiru to come back to school? Or knowing that Yichiru didn't steal anything? Or a revenge to the mafia group?"

"If it's all three, what are you going to do?" Ruchi carefully asked back.

"If you want me to, I could help make all of the things you want happen," Yuki firmly replied.

"That's impossible. I know you're good at fighting, but they are Mafia's! You can't take revenge on them."

"You'll know later if it's possible or not. Anyways, do you know the mafia group's name?"

"I'm not sure. It might be wrong. I think it's called 'Black," Ruchi replied.

✴ ✴ ✴ ✴

"Hello?" Yuki was called her contact in her father's Mafia group at two o' clock in the morning.

"We are going to attack them without warning tomorrow morning."

"Oh, OK...wait. WHAT?" Yuki's contact, first seemed to agree with Yuki, but paused, demanding more information.

"You don't need to know why I'm doing this. All you do is do what I say."

Yuki knew her actions were illegal and against both her country's laws and the laws of the "mafia world," but she was not fighting for her Mafia group. She was fighting as a teacher trying to save the lives of her students.

"OK, I'll call all of our group members by 5:00."

Yuki knew that her contact didn't understand what she was up to, but he believed Yuki and knew that she had a good reason to do that, so he agreed with her even if she wasn't doing the right thing. The call ended with Yuki's last words. "Thank you"

"My decision is always right," "I'm doing this for my students, not my group."

Yuki kept thinking this over and over so that she didn't feel bad about going against the "mafia rule."

✴ ✴ ✴ ✴

During the last class period in the classroom, Yuki called on Ruchi.

"Hey, Ruchi."

145

Ruchi and Michael looked at Yuki.

"Michael I didn't call you. Why are you looking?" Yuki was just joking, but Michael actually talked back to her.

"It's your fault. You're standing in front of me."

"Anyways, Ruchi, you can be excited for tomorrow,"

"For what?" Ruchi asked.

"For what you asked me yesterday."

The bell rang, Yuki told this to Ruchi and got ready to go out of the classroom, but she had to turn around when Ruchi called her again.

"Hey teacher can I really be excited?"

"Of course." Now Yuki could tell that her students were opening their minds to her, even though their scars from previous, uncaring teachers were not yet fully cured; however, at least a bit of the scar had been cured.

✶ ✶ ✶ ✶

"Is it here?" Yuki asked her contact. She stood in the building where the Black mafia group usually held its meetings.

"Yes, I've heard that black had been in that building for quite a while." Yuki's contact replied.

"Are you sure that the black doesn't know that we are fighting them today?"

"We didn't warn them, so they won't know." The other member of the Yuki's father's mafia group answered all of Yuki's questions.

After Yuki checked that everyone was ready, she led her mafia members into the Black's building. They split into groups of ten people to a floor and Yuki decided to get the eleventh floor by herself.

"When you are finished fighting on your appointed floors, come up to where I am. You must come up. I want every single one of you back. This is not an order, I'm pleading with you.

With Yuki's last order, the members went to work. Yuki entered the elevator and stopped on the eleventh floor. When she got to the top of the building she kicked opened the door of the Black boss's room.

"Y...Yuki? What is this? You're breaking the rules of the Mafias." The boss of the black shook with fear. He knew that Yuki was in the most powerful mafia group.

"Shut up. I'm not here because of our group. I'm here as a teacher, and a police officer."

The boss of the black pulled out a knife from his desk, and aimed it at Yuki. Yuki saw this and smiled.

"A knife? Don't you know that a gun is faster than a knife?" Yuki asked the Black's boss, taking her gun out of her back pocket.

"Do you want to bet what would be faster?" Yuki walked slowly up to the Black's boss.

"Now, we throw both of these on three. Three...two...one!!" Yuki shouted out. The black boss threw the knife. This was Yuki's trick to get rid of the knife from both of them.

Yuki put the gun back in her back pocket and ran to the Black's boss. She punched him continuously, until he begged her to stop.

Yuki thought of Yichiru. Then she stepped on the boss's knee with her high heels.

"Does it hurt? You deserve it. I know a kid that has been hurt by you. Tell me all of the names of innocent people that you pinned a crime on. If I don't hear what I'm expecting, you'll never walk again."

"Mark...Tim...Jack...Mike..." the Black's boss called out names.

"Yichiru...that was the name I was expecting, make a choice. Do you want to sit in wheelchair or tell the school the truth and get Yichiru in to school again? I'll give you three seconds to decide...3...2..."

"Alright, I'll tell the truth!" The black's boss shouted out quickly, with his eyes filled with fear.

"Clear Yichiru's name by tomorrow. If you don't, I'll be back." With Yuki's last warning, she walked away from the Black's boss.

The next day, everybody was excited that Yichiru had been cleared of stealing and was coming back to school. Yuki slept at school in order to make sure that she would be at school in order to make sure that she would be at school before any of her students arrived. Yuki was tired from all the energy that she used fighting yesterday.

A few minutes before the bell rang, Ruchi and Michael stood with Yichiru was standing right in front of her.

"Thank you. You are a good teacher," Ruchi thanked Yuki for bringing all of the students back and changing them. Yuki was proud, but she had one thing left after school.

Yuki drove her car to her home after school was over.

"Mom, you knew that the student drug smuggling didn't exist, right? That was an excuse for dad to agree on."

"I thought it was unfair for you not to have a chance to follow your dream. I wanted to give you chance to do what you really want to do and see if you really could handle that job. You can be a teacher for the rest of the year, and then decide whether you want to keep on teaching or not."

Yuki smiled at her mother, and her mother nodded back.

A Legend In My Heart

By

Andrew Lee

Ring. Ring.

"Ugh, can't I just sleep a little longer," mumbled Jake with his eyes closed. Then he pushed the alarm clock onto the floor, and it shattered into pieces. "This is not good."

Suddenly, the wheels of the cars screeched against the hard concrete road. The combined noise of this eerie screech and the irritating horns took over Jake's consciousness. He threw back the covers, slid out of bed, and went to the window. The air was filled with dark gray smoke outside, and smoke entered the room through the window. Jake wondered what had happened.

"Jake, you have fifteen minutes to get to school, and the school bus just left! I don't want you to get a detention for being late for your first day of school!" he heard his mother's voice.

"Sorry, I accidentally broke my alarm clock," he replied. "What was that screeching sound all about?"

"I don't know, but I do know that you're late for school," his mother said. "Come down for your breakfast."

"Not today." Jake quickly dressed in his uniform, grabbed his bag, and headed straight out the front door. As he stepped out of his house, he couldn't believe his eyes

"Fire!" Jake shouted. He ran back into the house to inform his mother. "Get out of the house, quick!"

His mother dashed out of the house. "What happened?"

"I don't know," Jake replied. "When I came out, I saw a truck tipped over, blocking the other cars from going forward."

"How did the fire start?" his mother asked.

"Well, I saw some flames right between the wheels, and they turned out to be a fire," Jake answered.

"I guess we're going to have to let the police settle this," she said.

"How about the fire?" Jake asked.

"There's nothing we can do about it, son," she replied. "Go to school now. You're late. I'll go get help."

Jake walked around the wreck to get to the main street. "Oh no, not even a single car on this street. How am I going to get to school?"

As he walked, he felt the wind blowing against his cold red cheeks. Compared to most fifteen year olds, he was taller and heavier than average.

Since he couldn't see any cars on the street, he decided to turn around and head back home. Just then, he heard a loud sound coming from behind him. He turned around and saw a small sports car. The engines roared, and the vehicle came full speed towards Jake.

There was a big bang. It startled the entire neighborhood.

When Jake arrived at school, he raced down the hallway and began searching for his classroom. Soon, he found his room and entered it.

"Are you Jake Carter?" asked a woman.

"Yes, I am," Jake replied.

"Look at the clock. It's just five minutes until English class is over!" the woman screamed.

"But a truck tipped over..." Jake tried to explain.

She cut him off. "Go sit over there, and we can talk about detention later."

The whole class giggled and whispered to each other. Jake pretended not to mind as he walked to his assigned seat. It was his first week in Shanghai after moving from America. He hated switching schools in the middle of a school year. He found it hard to settle into a new school in the middle of the year.

When the bell rang, which indicated a five-minute break, Jake walked out of the classroom quickly to avoid being late for his next class. On his way, a boy with short blond hair caught up with him. The boy didn't wear glasses but stood taller than Jake.

"What's up, Jake?" he asked, trying to start a conversation.

"Hey, what's your name?" Jake asked with a calm voice.

"I'm Edward. Welcome to Lynnwood Worldwide School. That was Mrs. Shoddy. She's always that impatient and exaggerates. She also yells often, so don't take it so seriously," Edward said, trying to cheer Jake up.

"Oh it's fine. I'm not going to blame her for that," Jake replied.

"Looks like you're having trouble settling into the school. I understand. I always have trouble joining into a new school, especially in the middle of the year," said Edward.

"It's okay, I'll get used to it one day. Well I'm going off to my next class. Don't want to be late," Jake chuckled.

"Okay, see you after math class then," Edward said, as he got the things he needed from his locker and left.

Suddenly, a voice boomed from behind. It came from a tall, thin man with dark brown hair. His dark skin camouflaged his black eyes. The man turned out to be a police officer. "May I speak to Jake Carter?" he asked.

Jake stepped up. "I'm Jake," he replied in a shocked voice.

"We need to have a serious conversation about an incident that happened this morning. Do you mind following me back to my office? I've already explained everything to your principal," said the police officer.

Jake stood speechless, trembling with fear. After an awkward moment, he followed the police officer out of the building and into the parking lot. Then they entered the car and the police officer drove off. Finally, they arrived at the police station. It was a nice police station. The reception area was at the main entrance. As Jake followed the officer through the wide, noisy hallway, they arrived in the headquarters. It was big, and police officers walked up and down through the building. The conference room was at the corner, and the bathrooms were on other corner. On the sides were a few little rooms. As they continued walking through the hallway, they came to an end. There were four rooms. They entered the first one.

"Have a seat Jake," offered the police officer. "I'm Officer Gorden. Would you tell me in detail what happened this morning?"

"Are you talking about the fire?" Jake asked.

"No, tell me about the car incident. I heard that a car crashed hard into a building, and the driver was severely injured," explained Officer Gorden. "He claims that you ran into the street suddenly and forced him to make a sharp turn and crash into the building."

"I walked down the street looking for a cab. But I heard the sounds of a car engine behind me, so I looked back and saw a car coming right at me. Before it hit me, the driver swerved and crashed into the building," Jake replied.

As Jake described the whole incident, he noticed Officer Gorden jotting down quick notes. Jake watched the pen move across the page swiftly. Officer Gorden didn't say a word but stayed focused and concentrated on writing.

"Thanks for coming, Jake. School should be over by now. I'll send you back home," Mr. Gorden said in a friendly manner. After that, they left and headed off to the parking lot.

✶ ✶ ✶ ✶

"Sit down guys. Time for class," Mrs. Shoddy announced.

Jake walked to his seat but accidentally dropped his papers on the floor. He reached down to grab them, but a foot was stepping on them. He looked up and saw a boy with gray hair, which looked a bit plump.

"Watch where you drop your stuff, you rotten brat. You know who am I? I'm David the Great," the boy said in a serious manner with a smirk on his face.

"Oh, I'm sorry. I didn't mean to drop them at your feet," Jake replied apologetically. David lifted his foot up. Then, Jake collected the papers and went to his seat.

After school, Jake walked out of the classroom with a gloomy look. David brushed himself against Jake, knocking all of his books and papers onto the ground.

"Oops, I'm sorry. You can pick that up yourself." David walked away laughing out loud. Jake quickly packed his things without saying a word and continued walking home. The first thing he saw when he opened the door was his mother sitting on the chair waiting for him. A serious look replaced his mother's normally happy smile.

"How was school today?" she asked.

"Oh, it was fine. I made new friends today," Jake answered hesitantly.

"Is there anything you want to tell me about yesterday? The police officer just called me. Why didn't you tell me about it?" His mother raised her voice.

"I'm sorry, Mom. I just went to the police station to give the police a report about what happened during the car crash incident. It was nothing much," Jake explained.

"I know, but you still should have to told me about it. Anyways, Officer Gorden wants you to meet him in his office tomorrow morning," his mother said. "Go finish your homework and come down for dinner in an hour."

A few minutes after going into his room, he heard someone at the door. He went down to see who it was. He saw a girl with short, brown hair standing inside the front door. She was a bit shorter than Jake and held onto a luggage bag.

"Sis!" Jake ran down and helped her with her bag. "How's school? I haven't seen you for months."

"I'm loving school there," she replied. "I just came back from our interim trip. So are you enjoying your new school?"

"It's fine," Jake said.

"Hi, Mom!" Jake's sister shouted excitedly. She ran to her mom and gave her a big hug.

"Welcome back, Vanessa. Dinner is ready, so please come and eat," her mom replied, filled with joy. She was happy to see her twenty-year-old daughter returning home.

"I'm hungry now, Mom," Vanessa said.

"Alright, let's eat!" her mother shouted.

★ ★ ★ ★

The next morning, Jake rode his bicycle to the police station to meet Mr. Gorden. He met Mr. Gorden outside the police station.

"Good morning," Jake greeted Mr. Gorden while locking his bicycle aside.

"Looks like it's a nice Saturday morning today," Mr. Gorden said. "Let's head into my office now."

"Sounds good to me," Jake agreed. Then, Mr. Gorden led the way into his office.

"Unfortunately, the driver has died," Mr. Gorden said with sorrow. "We found from the doctors that this driver was drunk and didn't know what he was doing. But the reason he crashed into the walls instead of you was because the car hit the curb and swerved to the right."

Jake was shocked about that fact. "Oh, this seems a bit scary."

"Yes, be careful," warned Mr. Gorden. "Okay, have a nice day."

"Thanks, you too. See you!" Jake replied.

The next day, Jake walked to class five minutes earlier, as usual. When he entered the classroom, he saw a pack of students surrounding a table. They must be looking at something interesting. He went over to see what was happening. He saw David holding lots of random pictures. He wondered how that drew everyone's attention.

"Time for class. Everyone, return to your seats please," Mrs. Shoddy announced.

"Yeah. Heard that, you rotten brat?" David teased Jake.

"Would you please stop calling me that?" Jake asked, raising his voice slowly. He started to burst with anger.

"Oh, who's talking? It's Carter the shopping cart," David said loudly. Everyone giggled, but Jake just returned to his seat.

Mrs. Shoddy lost her patience. "Enough everyone. David, if I ever hear you saying that again, you're off to the principal's office," she smiled at David.

After the whole class settled down, Mrs. Shoddy continued on with class. Jake wondered why everyone hated him so much? While he pondered and daydreamed, Mrs. Shoddy announced the scores for the recent social studies test.

"The highest score on this social studies test is a perfect paper by Jake," Mrs. Shoddy announced. As Jake came up to retrieve his test, the whole class looked away disgustedly. "Well done, Jake. You're on a hot streak."

After class, Jake decided to talk to Edward, a boy that was loyal to him. He walked towards the taller boy and started a conversation. "Hey, Edward."

"Hi, Jake," Edward said enthusiastically.

"Don't you realize that the whole class hates me?" Jake asked.

"Yeah, I think they're jealous of your grades, "Edward replied. "But don't worry. You don't have to care about what they think."

"Okay, I got to go to P.E. class. See you." Jake turned around and headed off to his locker. As he put his things in his locker, David came by and smacked everything down. "Stop it! Please!" Jake shouted.

David chuckled softly to himself. "Oh, the shopping cart is talking."

Suddenly, Jake pushed David to the ground. "Pick my papers up!" Jake demanded. "Now!"

"Alright, alright." David picked up the papers and jammed them into Jake's locker. "I'll get you another day. Hang on there," he grinned.

Everyone looked to see what had happened. But Jake simply ignored everyone and walked to P.E. class.

"Jake, you have to run laps around the field during class while all of us are going to have fun playing," the P.E. teacher said.

"But why, Mr. Bosh?" Jake asked.

"Recall yourself about what you did beside your locker just now," Mr. Bosh replied. "I do not want to see any more violence under any circumstances, ever!"

"Fine!" Jake exclaimed. He turned around and headed off to the field. Then, he picked up speed and started sprinting. "I'm going to run all day!"

"Ouch, stop. Please!" Jake cried. As he opened his eyes, he saw some weird looking equipment around him. Many people were gathered around him and bright lights flashed on him. "Where am I?"

"You are in the Shanghai World Hospital," the doctor said. "I am Dr. Doy, and you sprained your right knee. Looks like you've got too much stress, which caused you to go unconscious."

"Well it's because a teacher just made me run laps. So I'm simply following his orders," Jake stared at Mr. Bosh.

"Next time, just make a slow jog. Don't push yourself too hard" Mr. Bosh told Jake. "If there's no other problems, I'm going to go back to the school now. Take some rest."

"Okay, now if you don't mind, please leave," Jake ordered with a serious voice. After everyone left, Jake tried getting up himself to walk around. But due to his cramp, his right knee started to hurt as soon as he moved it. "Ouch! Not again, I hate Mr. Bosh. I'll get him. I'll get him."

The next morning, he heard knocking on this door. "Come in," Jake murmured.

"Good morning, son," his mother said. "How are you feeling?"

"I'm fine, but my leg hurts a lot," Jake answered. He tried to get up again but fell down to the ground due to the unbearable pain.

"Sit down." His mother helped him to the bed. "The doctor said that your leg is going to hurt for a few days. Tell me what happened?"

"Well, Mr. Bosh, told me to run laps around the field during class," Jake explained to his mother.

"Why did you have to run instead of other students?" His mother asked.

"Because I was fighting," Jake said sheepishly. "Um, there's this boy called David who knocked all my stuff down yesterday, so I pushed him to the ground and made him pick my papers up. This wasn't the first time he did that."

"How many times must I tell you not to use any violence?" his mother screamed, arousing with anger. "Please don't let me see you doing that again."

"No, I..." Jake answered, before getting cut off.

"I'm going to go back home to clean up the house first. Take some rest, and I'll visit you again soon," his mother informed Jake. Then, she opened the door and left.

Jake rested in the hospital for three days. He spent his time reading magazines and doing some homework that Mrs. Shoddy assigned to him.

"How's your leg, Jake?" Dr. Doy asked.

"It's better. When can I get out of this stupid room?" Jake asked with a frustrated tone on his voice. "Don't you even know that I have a life?"

"If your leg is okay right now, you are free to leave the hospital," Dr. Doy replied.

"Yeah, yeah, yeah. Then I'm out of this room," Jake said disrespectfully. After that, he jumped out of the bed immediately. But he fell right down onto the floor again and grabbed his right knee. "Ouch, my leg!"

"Looks like you have to stay here for a few more days. As I said, you sprained your knee badly. I suggest you stay here for another day or two." Dr. Doy helped Jake back to his feet.

Jake continued to wait impatiently in the hospital for a few more days. Soon the pain in his leg receded. "Dr. Doy, can I leave now?"

"It depends on whether your leg is okay," Dr. Doy replied.

"Well I feel so much better now, so take me out of this stupid room right now!" Jake demanded.

"As long as you can get yourself walking, then it's fine with me," Dr. Doy said.

"Well goodbye. I'm out of here." Jake stood up and started walking out of the room. Although he still felt some pain in his knee, it was endurable. He met Edward outside of the hospital. "Hey, Edward."

"Hi Jake, how's your leg?" Edward asked.

"Oh, it's fine," Jake replied. "So who are you waiting for?" "I'm just waiting for you because I heard from Dr. Doy that you were going to be discharged from the hospital today," Edward said.

"Well do you want to go to my house for a while?" Jake offered.

"Sure!" Edward shouted. "Anyway, I have nothing to do now."

"My driver is over there, come on," Jake told him.

"Alright, let's go!" Edward cried with joy.

"Jake you're late for class again," Mrs. Shoddy said.

"Yeah, you're always late," David teased Jake.

"What do you think he does everyday that makes him late?" Vincent asked David.

"Going to the shopping center with his shopping cart?" David giggled.

"Shut up you little annoying creeps!" Jake screamed.

The whole class was amazed by Jake's courage. "Jake, watch your language please," Mrs. Shoddy informed him.

"But what about them?" Jake pouted. "It's not as if they never say anything bad. So I don't care what I say to them!"

"Zip your mouth up and return to your seat," Mrs. Shoddy instructed. The whole class was quiet. They started whispering to each other and passing remarks about Jake's temper.

"Fine!" Jake yelled. Then he walked to his seat and slammed all of his stuff on the floor.

"Jake Carter, that's enough! You are going to skip lunch today and stay in the classroom with me today!" The teacher shouted. "I don't like your attitude!"

Jake mumbled, "Big whoop."

"What did you say?" The teacher asked.

"I said big whoop!" Jake screamed.

"I am going to take you to the principal's office later, and I'll leave you to him," she replied. "But don't forget that you still have to stay here at lunch."

"Whatever," Jake said.

After class, Edward walked towards Jake. "Hey, what happened to you?"

"Don't ask, I've had enough of those people already," Jake replied.

"You've seem to have change a lot since the last time I saw you," said Edward.

"If they are not going to be nice to me, then neither am I," Jake said in a serious voice. "I just don't see why I have to be nice to them anymore."

"Well you're right, but make sure you don't overdo it," Edward suggested.

"Okay, I'm going to the principal's office now," Jake mumbled.

"See you later," Edward said.

Mrs. Shoddy walked out of the room, and Jake followed her to the principal's office. "Wait here for me," she instructed. She knocked on the door gently.

"Come in," the principal said. Jake watched Mrs. Shoddy open the door and walk in. They closed the door and started talking. Jake waited impatiently for about five minutes. Just as he was about the kick the door, it opened.

Mrs. Shoddy started at him, then she said, "Go in."

Jake opened the door as instructed. "I'm Mr. James; take a seat."

"Okay, just tell me what you want to do with me. If you want to expel me, that's fine with me too," Jake rushed.

"I'm not going to expel you. But I am definitely going to be harsh on you and teach you to become a good kid," Mr. James explained.

"You know, I have a life," Jake said replied rudely. "So please hurry up."

"Watch your manners!" Mr. James shouted unexpectedly. "This is definitely not the way to talk to and elder or any of your peers. Tonight I want you to write a one thousand word essay about manners and turn it into me tomorrow."

"Sure, if there's nothing else, I'm going to get going." Jake stood up and stomped out of the room immediately.

After he finished his next class, he loitered around and put up his things in his locker reluctantly. Then, he went to the classroom for his detention with Mrs. Shoddy.

"I'm here, Mrs. Shoddy," Jake announced, standing at the front of the room. "What do you want from me?"

"You are going to stay here and skip lunch to reflect on your behavior," Mrs. Shoddy explained. "Do you think you've done the right thing?"

"Yes," Jake defended himself.

"Are you still denying?" she asked. "I don't care what you have to say, but you are very wrong, Jake."

"Tell me what I did then," Jake requested.

"Firstly, you were rude to your classmates. Then you were still talking back and arguing with me," she replied in a nice way.

"Did you even hear what David and Vincent said?" Jake shouted.

"Yes. They are wrong, and I will deal with them too." She got out a piece of paper. "You are wrong for your rude manner, and I want you to write a one thousand essay on how to be polite. It's due tomorrow"

"But I already got a..." Jake tried to say.

"You can start on it now," she said. "I want you to finish both of your essays before going home today."

Jake picked up the pencil hesitantly and started writing his essay. "Great, now I have two essays due tomorrow," he mumbled.

★ ★ ★ ★

"Very nice essay," Mr. James complimented. "Just make sure you remember what you wrote and to do it."

"Yeah, yeah, whatever," Jake mumbled.

"I hope you understand what you've done wrong, and I don't want to see this happen again," Mr. James pointed out.

"Okay, can I go now?" Jake asked.

"Watch your manners," Mr. James informed.

"Fine!" Jake shouted frustratingly. "Goodbye!"

Jake walked out of the room and started recalling about the words that Mr. James said. "Very nice essay," he repeated in his mind. "Well of course it's nice!" Jake burst out with anger. "I spent time working on it, and my hands were hurting so badly yesterday!"

Just then, Mr. James' door opened. "Well," he said, "you deserved it."

"What do you mean, I deserved it?" Jake shouted back.

"You decided to be rude, so you have to be responsible for the consequences," Mr. James explained.

"Whatever you say," Jake said annoyingly.

"Now that is already another one thousand word essay for you tonight, Jake," Mr. James replied. "When you first joined our school, you were a really caring boy. But now . . ."

"Okay, enough of your nonsense," Jake cut him off. "If you want a thousand words, I'll give you two thousand words." He turned around and walked down the hallway.

Instantaneously, Edward walked past and greeted Jake. "Hey, Jake."

"Hi," Jake replied in an angry voice.

"What happened?" Edward asked.

"Do you really have nothing else to say?" Jake asked him.

"You're just so different, Jake," Edward said.

"You too, because you just won't stop following me like a puppy stalking me," Jake replied. "So go away."

"When you first came in, you were just so nice." Edward pointed out. "But then . . ."

"When I first came in, I wanted to throw up whenever I saw you. When I first came in, I wanted to commit suicide. When I first came in, I also wanted to ram you to the ground," Jake started shouting at Edward. "Now get away!"

"Well, make sure you watch your manners while talking to a teacher," Edward replied with a smile. "See you tomorrow." Then he turned around and left.

"Some people just don't know when to stop," Jake mumbled softly to himself.

Next, Jake walked to his locker through the loud hallway and started packing his stuff. After that, he started to stroll back home. "Why is everyone against me?" he wondered. "Did I ever offend anyone?" He cleared his mind, and he continued to walk home.

When he arrived home, his mother greeted him, "hi, Jake."

Jake remained silent but raised his hand and greeted his mother. He started walking up the stairs without replying.

"How's school today?" His mother asked. "Why are you so down?"

Jake stopped and turned around. "I'm fine, okay? Give me some personal space," Jake said in a rude way. Then, he continued to walk back up.

"Jake, what is wrong with you!" His mother shouted. "I don't want to see that attitude ever again!"

But Jake ignored his mother and walked into his room. He took out a pencil and a sheet of paper and started writing his essay.

"Run!" Mr. James shouted through the hallway. "There's a fire!"

The fire alarms were on, and everyone was running out of the school. They covered their ears, crouched down, and everyone started to panic. Jake followed the crowd and ran out of the building as fast as possible. Smoke filled the air, and it was almost impossible to see.

After everyone exit the building, the teachers started counting off. "I'm missing one more," Mrs. Shoddy said in a serious voice.

"Look up there!" One of the kids pointed up at the rooftop.

"He's going to commit suicide!" Another kid shrieked. "Oh no!"

"Cool!" A small little boy said. "He's about to do the high building jump, like what I saw on the television. Awesome!"

"David!" yelled Mrs. Shoddy. "Get down now!"

"No!" David shouted. "There is fire everywhere. I'd rather die now."

"Ugh," Jake mumbled. "Let me give him a lesson." He walked into the building and started going up to the rooftop.

"Jake!" Mr. James yelled. "Where are you going? Come back!"

Jake ignored him and ran up the stairs. Finally when he reached to the top, he realized that the fire was blocking the entrance. He knew he had to do something since he's all the way up here. Without any hesitation, he opened the door.

"No! Don't, Jake!" David bellowed.

But it was too late. Jake used his arms to cover his face and jumped in, going through the huge fire. "Ah!" Jake screamed.

Jake's arm was burning and he was in real pain. But he stood upright and grabbed David towards him. Then, he brought him towards the door.

"How are we going to get through this?" David asked

"Of course we're going to jump through that door," Jake replied. "What else are we going to do? You want me to teleport you or throw you down the building?"

"Can we go down another way?" David trembled with fear.

"Hey, I'm not Superman. So don't expect me to hug you and fly down." Jake stripped a piece of his shirt and wrapped it around David's head.

"Hey what are you doing to me?" David asked while struggling. "Are you going to kill me?"

"Relax," Jake replied. "Now, I'm going to push you through the door."

"What!" David cried. "I'm not going through that fire."

Jake ignored him and pushed him through. Then, Jake covered his face with his arms and jumped right through too. "Ouch!" Jake fell to the floor.

"Are you alright?" David asked.

"Yes," Jake replied.

"How's your arm?" David picked up Jake's arm and observed it.

Jake flinched. "I'm fine, let's get out first."

David helped Jake to his feet and held him tightly. He brought Jake down the stairs, through the hallway, and out the building. When they arrived at the door, all the teachers rushed towards Jake and David to help them.

"Good job, Jake," Mr. James complimented. "That was brave of you. But don't do that again because I don't want anything to happen to you."

"Okay," Jake replied softly. "I just wanted to help."

"Be careful next time. So how's your arm?" Mr. James asked.

"I'm fine," Jake said. "Just a little scratch."

"Let me send you to the nurse," Mr. James offered.

"Oh, alright," Jake said.

Mr. James led him to the school nurse, who was checking on David's arm. The nurse observed Jake's arm, and then said, "You should be fine. Just a burned your skin a bit."

The nurse took some water and washed his wound.

"Ouch!" Jake cried out.

"Hold on there, you're fine, " the nurse reassured him. Then she applied some medicine on his Jake's arm. After that, she put on a bandage on his arm. "Alright, Jake."

"Okay, thanks," Jake said while looking at his arm.

"Great, well tell us if it gets any worse, Jake," Mr. James said. "Alright, go home and take some rest. School has been canceled for a week, so I'll see you next week."

"Wait!" Jake called out.

Mr. James turned around.

"Thanks," Jake paused, "for everything. Thanks."

"Mr. James smiled at him. Then he turned around and walked away.

After that Jake started walking home while David was still getting some treatment on his arm. Edward caught up with Jake and walked with together with him. "Yesterday, I thought that you changed to a completely mean kid. But after what you did just now, I realized that you're still the same old Jake."

"What?" Jake tried to avoid the conversation.

"I know you still care about people," Edward explained.

"What makes you think so?" interrogated Jake.

"Just look at yourself," Edward pointed out. "If you were heartless, you wouldn't have gone up there to save David."

"Well..." Jake said.

"You just turned a bit hot tempered because everyone was all mean to you," Edward said. "Jake, I know you."

"So you do have a brain," Jake teased.

Edward laughed. "Just remember, they can say whatever they want. It won't affect you."

"Okay, Mr. Know-it-all," Jake chuckled. "See you next week."

"Bye!" Edward replied.

While Jake walked home, he recalled what Edward had said. He found out that Edward was right. He decided to change into a new person.

It had been a boring week-long holiday for Jake. The purpose of the holiday was to reconstruct the school because the fire destroyed parts of it. Jake used this break to rest his arm and also spent some of his time with his family. Finally it was once again time for school.

"Good morning, Mrs. Shoddy," Jake greeted his teacher as he walked in the classroom.

"Hi Jake," Mrs. Shoddy replied. "I'm impressed in the huge change in your personality. You've finally changed."

Jake smiled, but walked to his seat and arranged his things for class. He turned around and saw David. To his surprised, David smiled at him.

"Hey," David said. "Thanks for saving me last week."

Jake slapped him on the shoulder. "No problem man."

"Looks like you've got friends now," Edward remarked.

"Yeah," Jake laughed.

"Okay, listen up guys," Mrs. Shoddy announced. "Get into groups of four, and we will work on a project."

The whole class was filled with excitement. "What are we supposed to do?" A girl shouted out anxiously.

"Although this is English class, I want you guys to have some time to relax," Mrs. Shoddy explained. "I want you guys to construct a dream house and present it to the whole class in two weeks time."

The whole class was very excited about this project and looked forward to completing it. Then, they started breaking themselves up into groups.

"Hey Jake, you and Edward can join our group," David offered, while standing alongside Vincent.

"Sure!" Jake accepted, and he pulled Edward over.

"So why don't you guys all come to my house to work on the house today," David planned. "Let's try to get this done faster. The sooner the better."

"Sure," Jake replied.

"Alright!" Edward said enthusiastically.

"I don't mind," Vincent pointed out.

"Okay then, see you after school guys," David said.

After school, Jake decided to walk home first and tell his mother what was happening. When he reached home, he explained to his mother. "Mom, today I'm going to go to my friend's house to do a project."

"That's fine," his mother replied. "But where are you going to eat dinner then?"

"Oh," Jake said, "I think I'll eat dinner with my friends."

"See you later then. Be careful." She sent him out the door.

"See you, Mom." Jake waved at her and left.

When Jake arrived, David opened the door and greeted him. "Come on in, Jake. Edward said he had something on, so he's going to come later."

"Sounds good to me," Jake said. Then, they walked in and started working on their project. First, they designed and planned what the house was going to look like. After an hour, they decided to go for dinner.

Vincent stood up to stretch. "Guys do you want to go out to that place for dinner?" He pointed outside.

"Anything is fine," David replied. "Let's go."

They left everything at home and walked to the restaurant. By then, they were all tired and really hungry. After that, they took a sluggish stroll outside.

"Wow, this alley way looks interesting." David walked towards it.

"No, David!" Jake shouted. "Don't go in there!"

"It's okay guys," David said ignorantly. "Relax."

"Oh no, what should we do?" Vincent asked.

"I guess the only thing to do is go in there and save him," Jake replied.

Suddenly, they heard a sharp shout piercing through their ears. "It's David," Vincent yelled.

"Let's get in quick!" Jake ordered. When they got in, they were shocked. They saw dogs surrounding David.

"Guys, help me!" David panicked.

Jake didn't know what to do. He knew that he couldn't just leave. He had to do something. Something quick. Without wasting any more time, he took a deep breath and jumped toward the dogs. The dogs jumped up to him too. They met in the air and fell down to the ground. Soon, all the dogs piled up over Jake and started scratching him. "Go get help guys!"

"Alright, Jake!" Vincent shouted. "Just hang on there. Come on David!"

One by one, Jake threw the dogs off. But before he could throw the last one off, it bit him hard on both of his arm. "Get off me!" Jake burst with anger. He kicked the dog away, and it ran off together with the whole pack.

After the dogs left, Jake realized that he had been bitten not only in his arm. His leg was also bitten by the dogs. He had no strength to continue walking, and he collapsed flat onto the ground.

He looked up to the sky and saw a bright full moon. It was surrounded with many stars. This was the best night he had ever seen. The sky was dark. It kept getting darker, and darker, and darker. Soon, it became so dark that his mind shut down, and his vision faded out. Perhaps, it was the last time he would see a beautiful starry night.

✷ ✷ ✷ ✷

"I'm sorry," Mr. Doy walked out of the room crying. "I tried my best. He was severely bitten by some wild dogs."

"Jake!" David cried.

"How could this happen?" Vincent asked with sorrow.

"It was my fault. I didn't come in time," Edward took the blame.

Meanwhile, Jake's mother sat on the side crying and mourning for her son. "Jake, why did you have to leave me?"

"I'm sorry Mrs. Carter," David apologized. "It was my fault for walking into the dark alley."

But she just ignored him, as she was too sad to think about anything else.

"Let me send you home first," Mr. Gorden offered.

"Okay," she replied. She sobbed on the way out of the hospital. After she arrived home, she took a hot shower, and started looking through Jake's pictures. She cried while flipping through her son's pictures.

"Why?" She fell on her knees and cried. "Why did this all have to happen?"

The fact that Jake had died was something that she couldn't accept. It was hard for her to believe that it was true.

"Jake was a really obedient boy. He cared about people and was a really nice person to know," she said to herself. "It was a pity that he had to go. I will never forget you, Jake."

The next day, the news spread around the whole school. Posters of Jake were everywhere, and people were crying throughout the day.

After school, David, Edward, and Vincent walked home together. While walking home, they passed by the dark alley, which took Jake's life.

"I really miss Jake," David cried.

"Me too," said Vincent.

"If only I didn't walk into that dark alley," David said, "then everything wouldn't have happened.

"It's no use to say that now, David. You did go and get help. But by the time we got there, he was already lying on the ground unconscious," Vincent comforted him. "As long as you don't make that same mistake again, then I'm sure that Jake will forgive you. After all, he was a really nice boy."

"Yeah, Jake was a really nice friend," Edward replied. "He was the bravest kid I've ever met in my whole life. I will never forget what he did for all of us. He is a legend that will always be in my heart."

From high above, the sun warmed the boys as much as their newfound friendship. A joyous soul looked down from the heavens and knew that he had made a difference. His unflagging care and love toward others have made him a legend that will always be remembered in everyone's heart.

Fights and Losses With Life Afterwards
By
Eric R. Lee

"Sir, we need to be moving," a soldier said to the captain. "Your brother requires aid."

The captain replied. "The garrison will fall either way. What is the use of this?"

Soldiers milled about amongst tree trunks and leaves in silence. Eyes downcast, they searched in the dying light through the prone bodies for an injured comrade to save or a wounded enemy to kill. The Orcs had underestimated the captain's force, and the ambushers were slaughtered. Still, the losses were heavy.

The captain sat on a rotting log in the middle of the small forest and undergrowth and tended to his aches and bruises as the young soldier in dirt-stained armor stood next to him and cleaned his sword in the dark emerald and brown light.

The young soldier spoke again, "Sir, this is your own brother. Would you have him suffer the same fate as your father?"

The captain scowled and decided to ignore the question. He then asked, "Private, are you fast?" The soldier seemed startled by the change of topic but nodded. "Send word to my brother that I will be arriving at dawn. Ride by horse and take two others."

The soldier saluted and went off to the horses. The captain sat for another minute before he got off the log and wrinkled his nose. The smell of Orcs was bad enough when they were alive; being dead for some hours had not improved their odor.

The captain took off his hot and dented helmet and pushed back his sweaty long hair. His halberd, a hybrid between the spear and a battle axe, in hand, he searched the shadowy figures that moved about in the dead leaves and spotted his second-in-command who took a swig from his water skin under a tree.

"Has the private gone yet?" the captain asked, meaning the young soldier earlier.

"Yes, and he has taken a spearman and an archer, Captain Listral."

"You don't call me that, Tere. You call me Keil."

"All right, Keil," the other man said, smiling in amusement. Tere wiped his mouth on his ragged leather sleeve. "But don't you think that it shows too much favoritism to me compared to the other soldiers?"

Keil beckoned, and then he called for the other men to come near instead since no one would be able to see his gestures in the bad lighting. As the weary soldiers walked toward the captain from some distance away, Keil said offhandedly before the others were within earshot. "We've known each other for fifteen years, and half of that time was on the battlefield. It isn't too much to address each other by our first names, is it?"

"No, I guess not," Tere replied shortly.

The soldiers, four hundred in arms, four hundred and fifty if the clerics were added, gathered around the captain. The original number had been five hundred including the clerics. One hundred men were lost to the ambush of the two hundred Orcs. In the dim light it was hard to see, but Keil knew that many were injured, all stunk of sweat and Orc filth, and all were tired. The captain saw these characteristics easily despite the late-afternoon sun.

I probably look the same, he thought. He wiped his brow before he put on his helmet, which was now cool.

"Men, we will rest soon. There is one...no, two more things we shall need to do. Pile the Orc bodies and set fire to their carcasses." The captain paused, mopped his face again through his helmet, and then said, "for our own men-"

Suddenly, two figures burst out from the undergrowth and sprayed twigs and leaves onto Keil. In an instant, all the soldiers were on their guard, holding their swords and spears in attack-position. In the bad lighting it took time for the soldiers to recognize the intruders as their own men before they sheathed their blades. Then, one of the figures spoke in an urgent voice.

"Captain, our scouts have spotted that four thousand Orcs are coming this way, with them travels almost eight hundred Evonlas swordsmen and mages. They are resting at the moment. Well, at least the Orcs are. They are also merging with another army mainly consisting of elite Orc clans and Evonlasi. The second force's numbers weren't counted as they had spotted our position, but there was well over six thousand. They will be here by midnight."

Keil cursed and frowned. Then he questioned the scout. The Evonlasi came from a special place in the Barren Lands from the north where no sunlight fell through the dark red clouds, which often were splashed with blue when dry thunderstorms clashed and ash fell from the sky instead of rain. "From where are they coming?" It was unusual for the Evonalasi to group with any other race or leave their dark lands so far.

The scout gestured toward the northeast. Keil said in disbelief, "But that is where our garrison was! It must have been overrun! My brother-!" He stopped, then brought his hands to his eyes and brushed away tears.

Tere told a soldier to get a horse and ride to their own kingdom of Ristam and tell them of the threat approaching. He told another to take the swiftest horse and go after the messengers and tell them to return. Then, he turned to Keil.

"Captain? What shall we do?" Tere asked through the darkness.

Keil was silent, still in shock and trying to accept that his brother was probably dead. He took his halberd and drove the butt into the dirt and threw back his head in a soundless yell. Then he bowed his head and put it against the staff part of his halberd and mourned. He felt his eyes. Tears flowed under his fingers and smudged gray dirt circles around them. He removed his hand and stared toward the ground, tears tracing paths through blood, sweat, and dirt. His brother was his only remaining family left.

His father was the paladin leading the army of Ristam to Orc territory and was shot by multiple arrows when he led a charge through the Orcs' homeland. His mother, who loved his father dearly, served as a priestess and cleric in the army, so she could do her work and be with her husband. The camp, after the attack force was crushed, was razed to the ground by the Orcs and dark figures later revealed as Evonlasi. Keil's mother dwelt in the camp during the ill-fated offensive attack. There were no survivors save one company.

"Keil?" Tere was near him now and spoke softly into his ear. "I am sorry for your brother, but we need to go. You cannot let your men be killed and taken as prisoners by the Northern Alliance."

Keil mentally shook himself, looked at Tere, before he said to the men. "We ride now." He straightened his back and viewed the outlines of his men, then spoke in a louder voice. "We ride to the second garrison along the Battle River, Battlaia."

"What of our fallen, sir?" A soldier asked.

"Take the dog tags but burn all the bodies, lest they be dishonored by our enemies." Keil walked toward the supply horses to retrieve tinderboxes. "But be quick, and take what you can from our dead."

Two hour later, as Keil's force left the forest and made their way to Battle River, Keil thought about their destination. The small tributary was named Battle River because of the many battles fought along its banks and beyond. The Ristam kingdom and the Northern Alliance, which is consisted of the army of the Necromancer and the Eastern Orcs, fought many battles. The Northern Alliance fought to destroy the Ristam Kingdom and gain territory, while the Ristam Kingdom fought to cleanse the northern lands of threats and evil beings. Before the war between Ristam and the Northern Alliance began, since the Northern Alliance wasn't even formed at that time, many a bitter clashing of armies had took place between the Eastern Orcs and the armies of Ristam. In one of the many on-and-off wars, the war's outcome began to turn dark for the Orcs. A powerful necromancer from the north soon traveled to met with the Orc leader and offered his help.

The Orc leader accepted the Necromancer's help, and soon enough was under the necromancer's control. The Necromancer, whose name had yet to be known, created a whole army of Evonlasi and a few strange creatures he created or found. He provided those and the Orcs provided their own warriors and beasts. Thus, with an army greater than any before, the Northern Alliance crushed the invaders and drove them to Battle River. However, the main force of the whole Ristam army had gathered there, to reinforce the small invasion group. With the whole army and elves that disappeared after the battle entirely, the bloodiest and longest battle in history started. Thousands men, elves, Orcs, and Evonlasi were killed. Battle River hosted the whole battle, and was also the river that Keil's father and mother crossed in the invasion force, so many years ago.

A noise in front of the battalion's position made Keil redirect his attention to the hike. He stopped, and raised a hand while he placed the other on the shaft of his halberd. Noiselessly, the rest of the company stopped as well. Another noise, around a large bush and a tree. It sounded like breathing. Heavy breathing, as though whoever it was just ran a mile. In the gathering morning mist, a glint of armor shown through the leaves of the tree and early dawn's gloom, which bore the symbols of Ristam. A half oval, with a line running through near the base. Two dots, and a long triangle, point down, in the middle of the half oval.

Keil spoke out, "Soldiers of Ristam, why do you hide from of a captain of your own lands?" In the dead silence, his voice seemed loud.

A line of men appeared from the bushes and trees, brushing off leaves from their armor. One of them replied.

"Captain Listral? Why, it is glad to see you alive. We had received word from one of your messengers that the garrison beyond Battle River was captured by the Northern Alliance and that you were going to return to the garrison behind Battle River if the Orcs and Evonlas didn't overtake you," the soldier continued, fingering his bow and shifting his weight from leg to leg. "We were sent out as scouts to see when they would be coming. How large is the enemy force? Your messenger only would say 'A great company! Send soldiers to save my captain and friends; they are being followed by the Northern Alliance!'"

"The Northern Alliance threat consists of at least five thousand Evonlasi and two thousand Orcs." Keil reported grimly. "We-"

A great cry was heard from behind Keil. Somebody yelled out "Orcs! Evonlasi!" Then "We're under attack!" Swords flashed out of scabbards and people that surrounded Keil turned around to face the oncoming attack. There were battle cries, clashing of swords, screams of pain, and the ragged yell of the Orcs and Evonlasi. Arrows and spears zipped wildly through the darkness and over the crowding soldiers' heads, but fortunately all but one missed its mark.

"Form ranks! Form ranks!" Keil shouted. "Archers and clerics get behind the swords and spear men!" He took his horse's reins, took his halberd from his gear and charged into the fray.

The Orcs piled in from the left and the Evonlasi were charging from the right. Nine Orcs lay on the ground, and a few Evonlasi, deformed with dark molted skin, howled and burned up into ash that soon was mixed into the dirt. However, their own casualties surpassed the enemies. Swords stabbed too deep into Evonlasi once they combust soon became too hot to handle. The archers were being cut down by the Evonlasi archers who were more adapted to aiming in dark environments.

Keil directed the archers to concentrate on the Orcs and went help the melee soldiers, yelling out encouragements. They were faring badly with the Evonlasi. The Evonlasi were thought at to have came from hell itself, but a better guess was that the Evonlasi were Orcs cursed and twisted with enchantments from the Necromancer. After being through the magic performed by the Necromancer, they had new abilities and would burn up when killed. They were the elites of the Northern Alliance, bearing little armor and equipped with scimitars of cold steel made in their sand dunes.

One swing, then an Evonlas screamed and fell into the dirt as ashes. A jab and another, an Orc, fell dead. This went on, and Keil's arm felt like lead. A fellow soldier was killed next to him, shot in the neck with an Evonlas arrow. An Orc crept up through the gap made. In a few seconds the captain would have been killed, but suddenly a spear flashed through the night and protruded from the possessed Orc's chest plate.

"Keil!" Tere's yell was barely heard by Keil among the noise. "We have got to go back to the garrison behind the Battle River!" He removed his spear from the body and swung it high above his head. The heavy spear landed upon an Orc's neck and a loud crack suggested that it had broken. "We cannot hold these positions for long!"

Keil turned around and hollered. "Fall a back! Fall back to the River! Go back to the base!" He turned to face the attackers in time to see an Orc dressed in dark red and black armor swing his club towards his head. Keil raised his halberd but was too slow. He saw an arrow burry itself into the side of the Orc before blinding pain blasted onto his head. His vision blurred, and he felt himself fall off his horse. The scene spun to its side, and he saw the Orc fall to the ground with him. More pain sickened him on the other side of his head and knew no more.

Darkness...My eyes are closed. The blankets on Keil were comfortable, and he did not want to move. He stirred, half way between sleep and conscience. Something was tied around his head. Feeling it, he found that it was cloth, a bandage. Now when did that get there? Why is it there? He searched his memories to find the time when he applied bandage to his head before he remembered-

The orcs! Tere! He opened his eyes and sat up. All was bright, but unclear.

"Ah, you have awakened, captain?" A young women's voice spoke to his left, sounding kind and cheerful. Keil turned his head toward the voice, wincing at the sound.

"Yes, priestess." Keil blinked and rubbed his eyes, and his settings became clear.

He was in a small cottage room, in a soft bed. There were a few shaded windows that allowed some morning light brighten the room. White linen cloth covered him, and he found that he wore a cream colored and rather stiff shirt. The priestess beside him was dressed in a white dress with a hood. "How long have I been asleep?"

"Two days." She replied, smiling at him. "Would you like some water, captain?"

"Yes, thank you. My mouth is awfully dry." The priestess walked over to a table in a corner that Keil hadn't seen just then and poured out some water, then handed it to him. He drank it and thought for a while. Two days. That's enough time for the Orcs to lay siege to the garrison. Wait, am I at the garrison? "Where am I at now, priestess? And what has happened to my company?"

The priestess drew back the shades to the windows. "Welcome to Battlaia, the garrison behind the Battle River and the Ristam Kingdom's largest garrison." Through the windows Keil could see a garden bearing flowers with bright pedals. Beyond the garden was a stone paved street filled with people and horses. There was no horizon, just many barracks and towers—all made with white stone and cleaned.

"The general of Battlaia who knows the whereabouts of you company would like to see you," the priestess informed him. "When will you go, Captain?"

"As soon as my head clears," said Keil. "Where might I find my clothes?"

The priestess went out and came back with some in five minutes. After he said his thanks and the priestess left, Keil reluctantly came out from under the warm blankets.

Ten minutes later, Keil was dressed in a fine tunic and pants, which had Ristam's coat of arms embroidered onto it. As he walked through the clean city to the tallest tower's base, Keil noticed that there were very few women and children among the populace. Men were all over the city, and almost all were in plate armor with long swords or bows at their side. This truly is a great war city, he thought as he marveled the organized way the barracks were made. There was over fifteen thousand men at arms housed in these buildings and more companies appeared to be coming every day.

With all the barracks, war towers, and supply houses, the main tower, which they call the High Tower, was relatively easy to find. Keil's first impression of the general was that he stood straight and thin like a rapier, unmoving and almost blended in with the stone walls behind him. Dressed in splendid silver armor, he stood at the doorsteps awaiting Keil.

"Greetings, Captain." The general spoke in a firm, grave tone, and his eyes reflecting all the battles he has been through. "And welcome to

Battlaia. I am Hervac, Commander of Battlaia, and fourth seating in King Vernarus's Royal Court."

General Hervac began to walk down the few steps at the doorway and talked as he went. Two guards bearing twin shields dressed in armor with ribbons of fine silk coming from their helmets followed silently behind him.

"Greetings, General Hervac. I am Captain Listral," Keil said, who bowed with his right hand faced up and in front of him, as was custom in Ristam. "Your city is filled with splendor. However, it might be destroyed by the upcoming battle."

The general had reached the bottom of the steps and now stood in front of Keil. He sighed, and then placed a hand on Keil's shoulder. "Have you eaten, Captain Listral?"

"Not yet sir." For the first time in the morning, Keil felt hunger gnaw at his insides.

"Then let us go eat; It is nearing midday," General Hervac said. He led the way to the stables and picked out four horses from many others.

He gave two of the horse to the guards, and by the way that the horses allowed the guards to mount them told Keil that the horses were the guard's personal steeds. Another he led to Keil's hand, and then mounted the last one.

They rode to the nearby mess house to eat. The horses were tethered to a rail with hay bags slung onto it next to the tower. Keil ate with gusto, as the food in Battlaia was splendid compared to the dried meats and partially rotten fruit he had eaten the past few months.

"So tell me about the Northern Alliance threat," said the general. They had finished eating and were back at the High Tower in General Hervac's office. His back was faced toward Keil and the bright light made only his was silhouette visible. Keil wanted to first know about his company, but before he could bring it up, the general, as if he had read Keil's minds, spoke again. "After that I will tell you how your company is."

Keil groped in his mind of the exact numbers, but so much time has passed. He found it, fumbled with it, and then remembered. "Ten thousand Orcs and Evonlasi." He cleared his throat and spoke again. "The North Alliance's attack force is ten thousand Orcs and Evonlasi, some mounted, and many are elite clans." He waited for the general to say something in reply but nothing came. At length, Keil was about to ask about Tere and his men before General Hervac turned around.

"Battlaia has fifteen thousand spears. We have enough men to repel them. However, seeing as they have not attacked, I believe they have set up a camp someplace in the woods, and I have sent battalions out to search for it. You company was among them." He left the windowsill and went to his wooden desk. Papers covered the desk, along with candle wax, a short dagger, and an ink bottle with its pen. General Hervac sorted through the papers and piled them up to one side of the desk. As he moved the papers, Keil took note that he had said "was" instead of "is". His pulse quickened. Finally, General Hervac extracted a wrinkled paper that had torn edges and handed it to Keil.

The note was written in a very messy handwriting that showed it was written in a hurry and some places were covered with smudged dirt. It read:

General Hervac- we have found the Northern Alliance's makeshift base. Their numbers are consisting of...is more than what our scouts reported. They are receiving reinforcements and by our luck...just as three thousand Evonlasi were outside the barricade. We have been joined by the battalion led by Captain Anvil but...circled us and we are not being able to return. We are being overwhelmed. We will not return.

Give my best regards to Captain Listral.

The "..." were the places where dirt made the writing illegible. As Keil read his hands shook, not paying attention to what General Hervac said while he read.

"This was the last communication we had with your company. The soldier that brought it was injured and his horse spent..." General Hervac noticed that Keil seemed to be reading the note a second time and was not hearing what he said. He paused and waited for Keil notice the lack of voice in the background.

Keil looked up from the note. His face was pale and haggard. He felt weak inside, as once more, within the span of less than a week, another person of great importance to him is about to die or dead. "When was this received?" he implored, speaking in a hoarse voice.

General Hervac watched Keil softly put the paper back onto his desk. Keil spoke again. "When did you know of this?"

"The note itself was received yesterday," General Hervac said. "As the soldier resided into unconscious and it took one day for him to come around and tell us about the message." Keil sank into a small chair in one corner of the room and placed his head in his hands. "I have already sent two battalions to see if they can break the encirclement and rescue your company but no word has been received since I issued the order."

Tere is likely to be dead by now. They must have been encircled since the day I was brought here. Keil sat upright as the office door suddenly slammed open and a soldier in mail armor ran in. He held a drawn sword in one hand and used the other to wipe the blood of his face, and was about to say something before an arrow flew into his back. The soldier fell on his face, and an Evonlas archer accompanied with two Orc swordsmen stood in his place.

In an instant, General Hervac grabbed the dagger resting on his desk and hurled it at the Evonlas archer. Keil jumped to his feet and threw a chair at one the Orcs and grabbed his halberd. An Orc charged toward the general as the other parried a blow from Keil. The Evonlas was reduced to ashes as Keil knocked the battle axe from the Orc's scraggy hand and removed his head with the blade side of his halberd.

"What has happened?" General Hervac said. He wiped his sword clean and stepped over his dead opponent. "How did they get here?"

Before Keil could express his own bewilderment, another Orc came in through the doorway. He threw a knife at General Hervac, who swung his sword at a tight arc and whacked the knife right back at the Orc. Keil went up and stabbed the Orc right before the knife went through its shoulder.

Keil kicked the Orc down the stairway and then turned to see General Hervac look out the window once more.

The general spoke out in amazement. "The whole Northern Alliance camp seems to be down there!" Keil came beside him and looked down. Bearing dark red and silver banners, Evonlas leaders led their own kind and companies of Orcs. Catapults built of entirely rusting metal rested outside the gates, unattended, as they have already broken in. No sounds of battle could be heard through the glass and being so high in the tower.

General Hervac charged down the stairs with Keil at his heels. Hopping over the ashes and bodies, they traveled downwards, jumping over broken sections and wall rubble. By the time when they got to the bottom, a whole company of soldiers had joined up.

The first level of the High Tower was in destruction. Bodies of soldiers littered the floor, covered by ashes from blazing fires. The roof was broken in places with burning rubble under each hole. No sunlight flowed through the dark smoke, making arrows unnoticeable until they had struck.

The High Tower was obviously a main outpost for the Northern Alliance to capture. Orcs and Evonlasi rushed through the doorway, slaying all in their way. Though more soldiers emerged from staircases and rooms, they were un-commanded, charging toward enemies recklessly, to be cut down with arrows or cold steel.

General Hervac called all soldiers to him. He rallied them with yells that echoed in the lobby of the High Tower. Keil yelled for the archers to cut down sections of the enemy ranks one by one. Slowly, as the number of archers increased, they were able to hold back the Orcs in the confined space of the doorway while the general made a charge line.

And he was finally done. The archers continued their fire until the soldiers had reached too near to the Evonlasi and Orcs. The soldiers, all bearing Ristam's coat of arms on their shields and armor, charged with battle cries, brandished swords and axes, or thrust out spears. As the fires died down, sunlight lighted the indigo patterns against silver on their helmets and their soot covered faces.

The Orcs stepped with heavy footsteps, crashing to the ground with leaden armor. Dark red and gray, like their banners, colored their armor. Wielding double-bladed axes and crude, heavy swords, they roared and ran to bash the oncoming soldiers. Archers stood behind, thinner than the warriors in front, mainly consisting of Evonlasi. The Evonlasi that did charged had thin black bands covering where their eyes were, but was unhindered by it and bore weightless mail armor. Their scimitars were already caked with dried blood, and they were wrapped in molted and ashy skin.

The two sides met, in the middle of the hall. Men that were hit in the head by axes flew onto their backs and moved no more. Orcs slashed by swords or pierced by spears let no sound out save deep throated grunting. Tiny tongues of flame licked the area where Evonlas skin was pierced, and slowly burst through the inside and exploded the whole body into ash along with their armor and weapon.

General Hervac and Keil were infront, fighting fiercely, and were rewarded when they burst out of the doorways and down the steps. But to their dismay, they were still cut off from the main army of Battlaia.

Keil lead another charge and was in the middle of fighting when the soldiers began to yell with joy.

"Captain Listral!" a voice somewhere in battle cried out. "Captain Listral, your company has returned!"

Keil jumped onto a stone ledge nearby and saw a sight that made him hopeful and joyous. It was his company, unmistakeable with a man in broken armor slashed with his spear. Behind him were soldiers of Ristam who were charging with battle cries and slew an enemy for each sword stroke. They fell on the Northern Alliance's rear, taking them by surprise. Their shields, although dented and with many arrow stubs, held enemy attacks from breaking through it. Spears bearing banners of the company and Ristam killed enemies at a distance and supported sword-wielding companions.

"Tere!" Keil called to let them know where they were. "Move toward us!"

The man dressed in dented armor looked toward Keil's direction. It was Tere. He had a bandage across an eye and had dirt mixed with blood on his face. Tere nodded, and directed the company to fight toward the High Tower's doorsteps.

Keil watched longer, but then he realized he must help fight. He leaped from the ledge and raised his halberd high above his head. The Evonlas he was aiming for did not look up until his shadow was on him. For a moment Keil seemed to be hanging in the air, before he brought the blade side down upon the head of the Evonlas and landed amid its hot ashes. He dealt wide strokes, spinning his halberd far, for he had jumped too far, and was in the middle of the sea of Orcs and Evonlas.

By the time he had killed some twenty Northern Alliance troops, his arms felt like lead, and he could barely lift his weapon, Keil finally reached back to where the company was. Someone called his name, and he saw Tere beckoning for him to draw back. Keil ran toward the middle and the company, and soldiers nearby done the same. Once they reached the middle, archers let loose a torrent of arrows toward oncoming Orcs and demons.

Keil grasped Tere's arm. "How," he asked, shouting in the background noise, "are you alive? How did you come just in time?" Tere grinned and said that he'll tell him later as he went on to lead an attack.

Tere's and General Hervac's companies had already merged together, and with a greater number, they began to fight toward the main army of Battlaia. Flames came out of almost every window frame along the streets. Bodies, ashes, glass, arrows, armor, dropped and broken weapons covered the streets. Not one ivory stone could be seen. Cries echoed through the smoke blackened air, and slowly the sun was about to disappear.

"Volley!" A cry beyond some ten lines of enemies caught Keil's ears. The archers were about to fire! Quickly, he yelled back.

"Wait!" he cried. Five arrows were let loose at once, but fortunately only the enemy was harmed. "Cease fire! You're aiming toward your own men! Cease fire, I said!" Another arrow had been fired and this time it passed a hair's width from Keil's cheek. "I am Captain Listral, and I tell you that your own general is with me here, so by what loyalty you have to your general and this city, cease fire!"

The Orcs and Evonlas in front of Keil attacked with inhumane strength and panic; they were being sandwiched between the two sides. Keil took a page from Tere's book and told all soldiers to pull back while calling for the archers to fire at the charging enemies. The enemy in between their company and the army of Battlaia was now three lines thick. Both sides charged, and they slashed through the foul beings before almost attacking their own comrades.

Now, with an army behind them, the only job now was to push the Northern Alliance out of Battlaia. Keil was with Tere when suddenly the Orcs began drawing back. Keil was about to charge forward as they seemed to have gained the upper hand, when Tere caught his arm. Keil looked toward him to see him pointing at the ranks of the enemy. Over the shoulder of the seemly retreating Orcs, Keil spied Evonlas archers taking aim at him and the soldiers next to him.

"Don't advance! Shields up!" Keil bellowed. He moved in front of Tere and raised his shield as many soldiers around him did the same. A distant whiz, then Keil felt two arrows struck his shield. Thump! Thump! Around him he heard similar sounds, though nevertheless some soldiers did not hear Keil and sprouted arrows from their chests.

As Keil lowered his shield for an instant and then snapped it back up again before three more arrows struck his shield, he felt Tere's hand slip off his arm. Keil looked from the dark gray back of his shield to the soot-covered street. Tere was kneeling down, spear by his side. But his hand was not holding his spear. An arrow had pierced through his cracked armor, zipped right past Keil's elbow.

Crimson filled the cracks in the armor, turned bright red in the afternoon sun. The dark arrow, sharp and lethal, had buried itself into Tere's stomach. All senses were numbed; the only thing Keil could see was Tere kneeling by his spear, one hand to his wound, one hand reaching, still pointing.

A soldier grabbed Tere's armor-clad shoulders and started dragging him back. Keil still watched in shock. Tere kept looking at him through hollow eyes, mouth half opened as if to say something before being dragged to the clerics. And, as fast as they left, Keil's senses returned, to the fullest at one moment. He smelled the orc filth, the smoke of demons ashes and buildings. He smelled metal and the leather of his shield. The noise was loud; Crashing of swords, yelling, and even the sound the arrows made flying through the air. Lowering his shield, Keil could see his surroundings clearer than any time before. An Evonlas archer some ten meters away loosed an arrow and reached behind for another. Adrenaline surged and time seemed to slow down. Keil felt the ground behind him and groped for Tere's spear before touching something wet. When he finally found Tere's spear and brought it to eye-level, he noticed the scarlet liquid had stained his gauntlet.

Meanwhile, the Evonlas archer reached behind him and took an arrow from a quiver on his back. As the Evonlas notched the arrow, having midnight black crow feathers tied onto its shaft and deadly stones sharpened to a point, seemed to quiver and jolt with some power though it had not been released. Keil aimed, and hurled Tere's spear with all his might toward the Evonlas archer.

The heavy spear hit its mark with a thump! The Evonlas archer loosened the bowstring instinctively and shrieked in pain before it burst forth in flames. The bow, which lied amongst its owner's ashes, ignited a moment later. The arrow still flew through the air toward Keil. Keil slumped against his shield in weariness, unable to lift it. A foot away from Keil, the arrow burst into flame in midair. Hot ashes sprayed onto Keil harmlessly.

Gathering what strength he had left, Keil stood and took up his halberd. In the last golden rays of sunlight that shot through towers and building he stood. Ash, soot and rubble; blood, bruises, and cuts all covered him. His armor did not shine through the smeared dirt, and neither did his shield, dented with arrows stuck in it. From the helmed eyes, Keil watched as an Orc grabbed a soldier by his neck and threw him against the ground. Keil closed his eyes, thought of Tere, his brother, and his parents.

His eyelids flew open in time to see the same Orc that was meters away moments ago rushing right toward his from a mere couple feet. Keil raised his heavy kite shield and knocked the Orc off its feet. It fell prostrate on the street, and Keil stabbed down at it with a snarl.

Around him, soldiers rushed forward brandishing swords and spears that glinted in the setting sun's light. Keil looked back to where Tere had been, and something burst inside.

Screaming his throat hoarse, Keil sprinted toward the Northern Alliance army as fast as his weapons and armor allowed. He crashed against Orc shields and caught Evonlas arrows on his own. Sorrow for his friend had turned into rage that fueled each sweep and stab of his halberd. He advanced still, even as soldiers drew back, oblivious to the fact that he was becoming surrounded.

Finally, his shield broke against the heavy sword of an Orc. The wood and metal exploded on his arm, some wrenched into his forearm. Keil's breath hissed in sharply, then he cringed. The Orc raised his sword against for a second blow. Keil's enemy was too close to him for a halberd to be of any use. Letting the smooth wood fall from his hand, Keil pulled out his short sword while he sidestepped the slow and heavy blow from the Orc.

He was now equipped with only a foot-and-a-half sword, wielded by an injured arm, amid hundreds of Orcs and Evonlas. As he continued to swing his sword as hard as he could, and arrow flew from enemy ranks and stuck from his thigh. Keil fell to one knee, yet still he slashed wildly. As another arrow went through his already mangled forearm completely, he dropped onto the ground. His world darkened as he felt his shoulder fall on a sword, but he was still conscience. An Evonlas swordsman came into view and raised his sword for the final blow. Keil refused to be killed, fell upon the ground, and attempted to stab the Evonlas' knee. But he had no strength left; his arm and thigh bled profusely, his shoulder was numb, and his anger was burnt out. He closed his eyes and listened to his own quick heartbeat, which had been loudened by tenfold, blocking all other sound.

He waited, yet seconds passed, and he did not feel the the sword's bite. Suddenly he felt something hot scatter upon his legs like dust. The next moment he was being dragged away from the battle. When the strength came to Keil to open his eyes, he saw he was back at the High Tower's lobby. Clerics bent over him, saying things he could not hear and began tending to his wounds.

"I'm fine" was all he could say. His jaw ached and his mind was clouded. "Where's Tere?" he asked, but no one heeded him. Keil wondered if he had simply asked in his mind.

Before long, Keil noticed the outlines of his vision blurred, spots flashed before his eyes. Then darkness closed in instantly.

When Keil came around and opened his eyes he found himself inside a familiar cottage. He moved himself to a sitting position and noticed that his left arm was heavily bandaged with wrappings stained a bit with dry blood. It also throbbed now and then, and as he put his weight on it to support himself his elbow buckled. He used his other arm to help him sit up.

It was the same cottage he woke to be in on the first day to Battlaia. There were changes though; The shaded windows glowed with light from a setting sun. Also, there was no table or the bed but mats where each laid an injured soldier. Clerics talked to one another quietly or tended to a soldier. The small room was filled with sounds of the rustle of fabric and grunts or snores among the men. There was a faint scent of blood, disinfectant, and vomit in the air.

Well, it seems that we have won after all. Keil moved aside his coverings and placed them in a crumble bunch at the edge of his mat. As he moved his legs to stand, he found that his right thigh was bandaged too. In a thought that wondered how many injuries he sustained, Keil began searching himself for more bandages. A hand closed upon his left shoulder which made it sting. Hissing in breath, Keil twisted around and shrugged of the hand of a cleric.

"Oh, I am so sorry, Captain! I...I just came to tell you that it'd be best not to move use your limbs with injuries too much." The young cleric saw Keil's discomfort and was about to fetch some painkillers before Keil stopped him.

"I'm alright," he said, his voice rusty and dry like a gust of air from the desert. "I just need some water. If you'd be as kind as to tell me where it is, I'll get it myself."

The cleric got out his own water skin and offered it to Keil. The captain looked at the water skin and struggled to say, "You keep that." The cleric put the water skin back into the folds of his robes and helped Keil up. Keil was going to say something about walking for himself before he put his weight on his right leg; a small stab of pain resulted. He staggered and the cleric caught hold of his arm. Keil slowly hobbled over to where the water was and drank down enough water to fill four water skins. As the cool water washed down his throat, he moved aside a shade to see the street.

The once gleaming white streets of Battlaia had ash piles as tall as a man's waist placed every ten yards. Each ivory stone was smudged with dirt, ashes, and, on some, dried blood. The red-orange rays of the setting sun cast long shadows wherever it seeped through buildings. In the distance, silhouettes of a couple of soldiers stood guard on top of a four-storied barrack. One of them carried a spear that held a torn banner fluttered on a breeze that nearly tore it off the spear's shaft.

Seeing the spear, Keil was reminded of Tere. He twisted around and another wave of pain stabbed at his thigh. He cursed under his breath, not about the pain but for not thinking of Tere sooner, and called for the young cleric.

"Sir?" When the cleric had arrived by Keil's side, the captain's face was disfigured with a grimace. When he turned, he had not only hurt his thigh but also hit his hip against the mouth of the water vat. "Are you alright?"

"When," gasped Keil, "did the battle end? Yesterday? And w here is my second-in-command, Lieutenant Tere?"

The cleric hesitated, then said in a low voice, "C-captain, sir, I-I..." Keil looked at him and gathered much through his face. "He...died... sir..."

Keil could not bear it. This was the second time he thought that Tere had died. He stumbled back to his mat, the cleric supporting him. He did not feel tears, but he knew that they would come later. Oh Tere, he thought, why is it that we last spoke on the battlefield in the midst of chaos and not when we could say our farewells. He turned over on the straw mat and, although he had just awoken, fell asleep.

The next day when he woke from his uneasy slumber there was a cleric that stood over him with what seemed to be a notice in hand. Keil got up and asked the cleric to see it.

"Why, o-of course, sir," said the cleric. It was the same one from yesterday, Keil noticed.

After thanking the cleric, Keil read the notice. It was for the medical staff to gather all recovered soldiers for a counter-attack on the Northern Alliance. All available personnel were to be rallied at the city gate within a day. The date also showed that he had been in a coma for three days.

Keil's initial reaction thought was to join the attack force. The second reflected that he was injured and not able to fight enemies. But the third and strongest thought that came was that he would fight, no matter what, to avenge Tere.

He sat up and tapped the nearby cleric's elbow. Once the cleric turned around, Keil asked to be enlisted into the coming counter-attack force. The cleric frowned, and politely said no and began to explain why before he was interrupted when Keil asked for some crutches. It took about ten minutes to find a pair. Keil propped himself up on them and required directions to the High Tower.

"The High Tower is quite far, sir. About two miles or so," the cleric told him. The cleric eyed Keil and could tell he planned on walking the whole way. "It'd be best to go by horseback, considering you're condition...The horses are right outside, Captain." Keil had opened his mouth to speak and the cleric had guessed his words.

"Alright. I'll ride there," Keil said as he walked outside. "And no, I will not need any help, save mounting the beast."

Keil mounted the hourse with more ease than he thought. Riding to the High Tower, however, was harder. Many buildings were damaged or destroyed; several landmarks that he had gotten used to in the short time he had stayed in Battlaia were gone. Though the High Tower ever stood against the smoky sky, tall and visible, the streets below were a mess. Twice Keil almost lost himself when he took a wrong turn. After twenty minutes, he finally arrived and, with the assistance of the crutches, went up the steps as fast as he could.

The lobby of the High Tower was still under repair. Menders were on ladders, repairing the roof, at the walls, removing arrows, and anywhere that had sustained damage. Keil looked up the staircase, sighed, and began his way up. By the time he reached General Hervac's office, his breath came in great gasps. Though Keil heard voices, he knocked anyways and opened the door when he heard the general's tired voice say "Enter".

General Hervac sat at his desk with five soldiers in front of him. The general seemed to be annoyed, his face in his palm, while the soldiers were indignant. General Hervac raised his head from his hand and, seeing that it was Keil, asked, "Have you come, too, to be assigned into the attack force?"

Keil blinked, then nodded. A soldier then said loudly, "See, general? We're not the only people who are wanting to fight again..."

"Quiet," General Hervac shot at him. The soldier opened his mouth to argue but subsided when the general glared at him. Turning his attention toward Keil, he said, "Captain, I am sorry, but you are not allowed to go to fight. At least not for now. You are an experienced captain, it'd be a waste for you to die when you could have lead many a victory..."

"I have just lost my brother and my closest friend," Keil said, trying to control himself from exploding. "If I go to my death on this attack, then I will be content, because I will have my vengeance, and if I die, it shall be on the battlefield. And after that I will be reunited with my family and dearest friend." He gritted his teeth to hold back tears.

After a moment of silence, another soldier opened up. "General, we've all lost someone one way or another." The young soldier, who Keil realized may not have even reached twenty, spoke in a voice that crackled with emotion. "Please," he said in a strangled voice. "Let us go."

The argument went back and forth for two hours. At the end, General Hervac allowed three of the five soldiers to be enlisted because their wounds were not severe, along with Keil. Keil had to debate with the general for a quarter of an hour until finally he yielded. The other two soldiers left with sour faces while General Hervac wrote a few notes to the clerics and majors to let them join.

Keil's way back down the stairs was harder, but he did not mind. He was almost glad that he had permission granted, however, recent event would not even allow him to smile. When he exited the High Tower, he thought that it was already night. Back at the cottage, however, he realized that it was just midday. The smoke blotted out the sky and made the lighting trick people to believe that it was six hours later than it really was. Nevertheless he decided to sleep. As he lowered himself onto his mat, Keil realized that despite for being awake for only a few hours that he was tired. Sleeping came rather quickly.

The next day, right after breakfast, every division was rallied at the battle-worn square right inside the battered gates of Battlaia. The Ristam Kindom managed to come up with fourteen thousand men within the short notice, ten thousand more to be sent within a few days. A strong wind blew that day, and the smoky haze that obscured the sky was blown away to reveal a cloudless forget-me-not blue expanse with a winter sun shining down on the army.

Keil was placed in his patched up company, teaching some of the new guys on some battle tatics. Keil was now able to move about without crutches; the clerics had given him a drug that numbed the senses of injury and allowed Keil to fight. Suddenly, a horn blew; the deep, rich bellow echoed across the small square and a high ranking officer called for everyone to begin moving out of the city, toward the Northern Alliance.

Marching along while shouldering his heavy pack, Keil's mind was not on the long way ahead, but at how he was on his way to avenge his family and friend. When he shifted his load, he felt two long slender weapons shove against him. One was his own trusty halberd, and one was a weapon of to remember someone. A spear, Tere's spear that he had received from his friend's will...

Twenty Years Later

A man—a veteran—limped up a hill with a had supporting his left leg. His spouse and two children followed quietly behind. The man walked past and placed a pair of flowers on a grave. The sun shone down on the carved names. Sercon F. Listral and Minsa U. Listral. Farther down the line, the man placed a flower on a small grave that read Keith N. Listral - MIA. Finally, he laid a flower on a grave, placing the flower in a niche to prevent the wind to blow it away. Tere L. Calingster. Eyes closed, the veteran recalled the battle. Minutes later, his wife pulled at his elbow.

"Keil," she said softly. "I'm sorry, Keil, but the boys are getting cold."

"Ah," Keil said. "Let us go back then, dear."

Keil stopped at the top of the hill and looked back once more; he saluted his friend. Then he turned away from the past and looked to the future.

Time Machine

By

Hagen Lee

Kyle Jackson shifted on his sofa to find a more comfortable position. He had been watching TV for the past four hours. It was well past midnight, and he was supposed to be asleep. His parents would be furious if they found out, but they're not at home. They're on a fancy cruise on the other side of the world at the moment, enjoying life, while leaving Kyle here at home, by himself, with nothing to do. So here he was, slouching like a slug without a spine on his big fluffy sofa with a bowl of popcorn in his hands. He flipped through the channels, looking for something good to watch.

BRRRIIINNNG!!! BRIIIINNNGGG!!! The phone suddenly rang. Kyle jumped, startled out of his TV stupor. He walked over to the phone, wondering who would be calling at this time of the night. A glance at his watch informed him of the time: 2:00 AM; most people would be fast asleep by now. He picked up the receiver and said in an unsteady voice, "Who's it?"

"It's me, Bruce! You have to come right now. I've got something to show you!" said a voice that Kyle recognized as Bruce Norman, his best friend.

Bruce and Kyle are best friends. But they differed completely in both appearance and interests. Kyle was a big person, thickset and almost six feet tall. He loved sports and possessed an outgoing and carefree personality. He never did his homework because he couldn't care less about academics. By contrast, Bruce's scrawny build barely reached five feet tall. His favorite subjects, science and technology, fascinated him; people at school always called him a "geek." Bruce always said that he liked sports, but he never played any. The only time he participated in any sport happened in gym class. Even then, he did his best to slack off and sit out on the side. Although Kyle and Bruce had completely different personalities and hobbies, they had struck up a fast friendship the first time they met and had remained close friends ever since.

But being Kyle's best friend didn't give Bruce the right to call him at two o'clock in the morning. Kyle groaned and made a mental note to hit Bruce when he had the chance. "It's like two... can't this wait...?"

"NO!" Bruce shouted in the receiver.

"What do you want me to come for anyway?"

"Just come, OK? I'll explain when you're here." And without another word, his friend hung up on him.

Kyle fumed. What could be so important that Bruce had to call at such a late hour to interrupt his TV time? But, knowing that his friend would never let him forget it if he didn't go, he shrugged in resignation, put on a jacket, and walked out the front door. Kyle took a bike and rode quickly to Bruce's house. Normally, he would have just cruised down the streets slowly, but he didn't want to be outside for too long. It was a cold night, and he didn't fancy a long ride down the streets in the freezing air.

Bruce was already at the front door, waiting, "What took you so long?"

"Shut up, Bruce. It's after two in the morning. Not everyone stays up all night," Kyle replied quickly, conveniently forgetting that he had been up watching TV.

"Well, anyway, you've got to see this. It's gonna blow your mind." With that he ran into his house, not bothering to see if Kyle followed him. Kyle yawned and stroll trudged after his friend. Bruce opened the door to his room and walked up to a big rectangular object with a piece of black cloth over it.

"Huh? I don't see anything…" Kyle said.

"That's because there's a cloth over it, you big oaf." With a flourish, Bruce pulled on the cloth and revealed a shiny, smooth, and silver box that stood a little over six feet in height and three feet wide. Bruce stood tall next to his newest invention, smiling in a manner that seemed like it could light up the whole room.

But Kyle seemed less impressed by his friend's newest innovation. It seemed just like a shiny fridge to him. "So that's what you called me here for? You wanted to show me this? I don't know, but for some reason, I am not impressed at all."

Bruce's smile instantly dropped a notch; he seemed to be hurt by his friend's comments. "It's not a fridge," he stated slowly, trying to contain his anger. "It's my new invention, the Chronologically Technical Transporter Time Machine X, but you can call it a time machine if you like. It is fully operational and working. But I'm still decorating the exterior, so that there won't be some idiot claiming that it's a fridge. He looked accusingly to his friend; Kyle shrugged. Once I'm finished with my design, I'm going to broadcast my invention to the world. At the age of only fifteen, I'm going to be the youngest scientist to receive a Nobel Prize. After all, it is actually quite… genius—if I say so myself. I showed it to you first because, you know, we're friends and all."

Kyle was astounded. "OK… you're telling me that that fridge is actually a time machine?" he asked.

"Stop calling it a fridge," Bruce gritted his teeth and muttered. "But yes, it is a time machine, and it's capable of taking you anywhere in the earth's timeline."

"So, you're telling me we can travel in time?" Kyle seemed shocked.

"Yes, that's exactly what I'm telling you!" Bruce exclaimed excitedly. "Think of all the good it can do. Archaeologists will be able to visit the old times and find out exactly how people lived back then. Maybe they can even bring back an artifact or two. Students will actually want to learn history because it will be so interesting! They would get to visit the actual place. And *we* could visit the future and see what happens! That would be so fun! Oh! I am so excited!" With a contented smile on his face, Bruce seemed really happy about

Kyle burst out laughing; he couldn't help it. It was all too funny.

"What are you laughing at, huh?" Bruce demanded.

"What a joke! That's the stupidest thing I've ever heard!" Kyle giggled, unable to stop his fits of laughter. "Take us back in time? Yeah right! Ha! There's something not right up there in your head."

"I take it that you don't believe me," Bruce said, indignant that his friend would think that he was delusional. He grabbed Kyle's arm and dragged him over to the time machine. Bruce was a lot smaller than Kyle, but his mixture of excitement and rage fueled his strength; he opened the door and pushed Kyle inside, following closely behind. The interior of the time machine was silver, with shining lights around the walls and knobs and buttons everywhere. In the middle of the wall was a big forty-inch plasma screen.

"Dude! What's wrong with you? I'm out o' here. This place is creepy!" Kyle recalled the time when they were seven and playing soccer with their neighbors. *It was a sunny day. The weather was amazing, and all the kids were out playing around. Kyle got all excited about soccer and decided he wanted to play. He got the ball for the first time and wanted to score. But he tripped and banged his head against the goal post. Blood spurted out like a fountain, and he ended up getting nineteen stitches on his forehead. There is still a scar there to prove his injury.* After the incident, Kyle asked Bruce if he was all right. Bruce replied that he was fine. But maybe Bruce was wrong; maybe the collision on the head did more harm than he thought; maybe Bruce got brain damage.

"Where shall we visit?" Bruce mumbled to himself, ignoring his friend's complaints. "Ah, I know, we shall go the future. "I've always wanted to see what it'd be like. This is so fun!"

"Yeah right," Kyle mumbled. The doors on the time machine had locked, and he couldn't get out. Fear and the close confines gripped him as he looked around the cramped room for a way out.

Bruce set himself to work. With his hands in a flurry, he quickly clicked different buttons and turned a few sets of knobs. After he inputted all the commands, the time machine started whirring and shaking, making a lot of noise.

"Is this supposed to happen?" Kyle asked worriedly.

"Well, since we're going to the future through time, the time machine has to take us apart atom by atom and move us through to a different dimension and rebuild us again. So this small shaking is nothing compared to the amount of work it has to do." "Oh, I see," Kyle lied. Science was not his forte.

The time machine shook more violently and bounced up and down. Bruce lost his balance and fell, hitting his head, accidentally hitting a few buttons. "Oops," Bruce mumbled and fell unconscious. The machine shook even more, and Kyle fell too and hit his head.

Kyle felt himself slowly losing consciousness. "No!" Kyle muttered, but his fall had sapped his strength, and his eyes started to dim. Everything became dark. With that, he too fainted.

Bruce opened his eyes. They were blurry and he could only make out a couple of odd shapes as he looked around. He propped himself up on his elbows and rubbed his eyes. As his vision cleared, he took a survey of his surroundings; he was in a dark room with red bricks all around him. There was a door that leads to the outside; Bruce realized the same house he resides in his own time. He wondered what it was like in the future. As he turned around, he saw a big twisted lump of metal. He walked over to study it; as he realized what it was, his disorientated expression changed to one full of alarm and distress.

"Kyle?" He demanded.

"Oh hey, Bruce. You're awake! I was just sitting there and sort of fell asleep," Kyle said sheepishly.

"You were awake? Why didn't you wake me up?" Bruce exclaimed.

"I was about to, but when I saw over to you, you were sleeping like a baby; you were drooling too! It was so sweet. That's why I didn't wake you up," Kyle laughed.

"Oh, I was drooling? Don't tell anyone, OK? No one knows about this." Bruce's face turned into a bright red hue.

"Don't worry; your secret is safe with me," Kyle promised with a snigger.

"Umm... thanks... By the way, I think this piece of metal is our time machine."

"Yeah it is," Kyle said. "When I woke up, I saw the machine burn up while it crash landed on the floor. We must have been thrown out in the process; we're lucky that we weren't in that metal piece of junk when it started melting. We'd be dead!"

"Oh no!" Bruce's face turned pale, he leaned against the wall and seemed a bit nauseous.

"Dude, it's a machine. You can build it again. We should just be glad that we didn't die."

"No! It's not that; if the time machine burned, that means we can't go back home! We're stuck here!"

"Hmm… when you put it that way, it does seem pretty bad," Kyle speculated.

"It's all your fault, Kyle! Why did you let the machine burn up, you should have–

"Done what?" Kyle exclaimed, "What am I supposed to do? I didn't have water, there was no one to help me, and I just woke up! And anyway, I'm not even shouting at you yet!"

"What do you mean? I didn't do anything wrong!" Bruce shouted.

"You didn't do anything wrong?" Kyle screamed, "Who was the one that dragged me into the time machine and then made the thing go all whirly and stuff? You think I want to be here? It's all your fault!"

"Yeah… I guess it is…" Bruce seemed close to crying. His eyes turned red, and he sat down, his hands holding his face.

Kyle looked down upon his friend with sympathy; he put a hand on his friend's shoulder and comforted him. "It's fine Bruce. I'm sorry I shouted at you; I know how you must feel about all this. But there's no point sitting around here feeling sorry for ourselves. Let's go outside and take a look. That's what we came to do, right? We might even find someone who can help us build a machine that can bring take us back; I mean, the technology now must be much better, right?"

Bruce looked up; his eyes were red, and he wiped his eyes. "Yeah, I guess so."

"Come on, let's go," Kyle said to his friend.

They opened the door walked out. What they saw took them by surprise. They had always thought that the future would be really cool, with flying cars and floating cities, and no trash lying around the streets. But what they saw was completely different. The roads weren't even paved with cement; they were just dirt lying around. There were hundreds of people walking around shops and restaurants. Merchants from their stores were shouting out about their products, trying to get people's attention. The place was filled with people and noises. It was a hectic city, and Kyle and Bruce seemed really confused.

Kyle wondered out loud, "You know, I never thought that the future looked like that. I always thought that the future would look a bit more…"

"Futuristic?" Bruce risked a guess.

"Exactly." Kyle smiled.

Their conversation was suddenly interrupted when a person on a big black horse rode along the road, plowing straight towards them, they quickly dived to the side.

"Hey! Watch it!" Kyle screamed.

"Don't say that," a person next to him whispered. "He's Sir Percy, the most powerful man in this place!"

Kyle promptly ignored him and kept on blaring out his insults, "You pig-headed fat head! What's wrong with you? You could've hurt me!"

The man on the horse suddenly stopped. He turned his horse turned around and trotted towards Kyle. "What did you say?"

"I said, you better watch it, ugly face, or I'll slap you around the head!"

"How dare you talk to me like that, you foul underling?"

The people around Kyle cringed, but Kyle simply laughed. "Underling? Who the heck says that? Anyway, who do you think you are? I can say whatever I want to you; it's called freedom of speech, you loser. Haven't you ever gone to school?"

The crowd gasped. No one ever talked to Sir Percy like that. Everyone thought that he was ugly and fat and no one likes him. But no one is brave or stupid enough to speak to him like that. Bruce slapped his forehead, feeling sorry for himself. It was not the first time that Kyle's careless mouth has gotten them into trouble.

"Freedom of speech? There is no freedom of speech, you menial worm!" The man exclaimed. He puffed out his chest and said, "I am Sir Percy, the greatest knight of this country. And I will not stand to be insulted by such low life as you!"

"Oh... you're asking for a punch, mister!" Kyle said. He lashed out with his fist and hit the knight on his stomach. Sir Percy barely even moved. He looked at Kyle with a smile.

"You want to fight?" he asked with an ominous voice. Kyle was stunned. He wasn't the toughest kid in the school, but he went to boxing lessons every week and could throw a punch. No one in his school messed with him. Kyle was ferocious in a fight. In his weekly lessons in the boxing club, they always had sparring rounds in the boxing ring. Kyle was one of the best fighters in his age. When he hits someone in the face, they stay hit. He just threw one of his hardest punches at the man, and he barely even flinched. That guy was tough, Kyle didn't fancy his chances in a fight, but his pride won't allow him to back down. So he crossed his arms and with a sneer, he said, "Yeah that's right, punk! Just don't cry to Mommy when you get beaten up."

"We'll see who will run to Mommy," Sir Percy smirked. He got off his horse and said, "I, Sir Percy, challenge thee to a duel."

"So let's go," Kyle cracked his knuckles and adopted a fighting stance. The crowd moved apart and gave the two fighters a wide berth.

With a wild battle cry, Sir Percy charged at Kyle. Kyle didn't even have a chance; the knight flipped him over with one hand and threw him at the ground. He body-slammed Kyle and knocked the breath out of him. Kyle tried to punch Sir Percy, but like lightning, the man grabbed his wrist and twisted it till his hand popped out of his joint. Kyle cried out with pain.

"Think you're so tough now, you big headed youth?" Sir Percy sneered, "You can't fight me; I've been training in the army for thirty years now. And you? You have barely even grown a beard yet. I've wasted enough time over here. I'm going back to my castle, and don't even think of following me; next time I'll break your neck." And with that, he walked towards his horse and rode away, leaving Kyle there with a broken wrist, grimacing with pain.

Bruce ran towards his friend, "Are you OK?"

"What does it look like?" Kyle groaned. "Here help me up, I need to find a doctor who can put a cast around my wrist."

Bruce offered Kyle a hand to Kyle. Kyle held on his friend's hand with his good arm and pulled himself up. He grimaced with pain as his swollen wrist brushed against his leg. "Let's ask for directions, we need to find a doctor." Kyle walked over to one of the people, "Is there doctor around?"

The person ignored Kyle; he seemed scared to talk to him after he picked a fight with Sir Percy. They walked around asking for directions, finally, one of the shop owners pointed north, "Walk for a mile or so and you will find a house, inside it is the healer. And please, don't go running around mouthing off to our knight. It's not smart."

"Thanks, I'll keep that in mind." Kyle scowled. The pair walked north towards the house. Every step was agonizing for Kyle, his wrist was in a state, with puffed up skin and a big red blotch covering his hand. His hand was twisted in an awkward angle. Kyle knew that he bit off more than he could chew. He shouldn't have challenged Sir Percy. All he got from it was a broken wrist and severely bruised ego. Strangely, Kyle thought that his dignity was hurt even more than his wrist. The agony of his broken wrist was just a physical pain, but his dignity was mental pain, which went even deeper than his broken wrist.

Finally the house came in sight; it was a strange house, unlike the other buildings. It was built with wood and bricks, this house seemed like it was made of leaves. They walked up to the house and wanted to go in. But there seemed to be no door. Bruce just knocked the wall; it was surprisingly hard for something that seemed like it was made of leaves.

A muffled voice wafted out from the house, "Kyle and Bruce, come in, I've been waiting for you."

"Umm... How?" Bruce asked.

"I tell you when you're in here. Come in, hurry, I don't have a lot of time."

"We're sort of stuck out here," Kyle said. "There doesn't seem to be a door. "Oh yeah, oops I forgot. My apologies." The wall of leaves suddenly opened up into a big hole that was wide enough for Kyle and Bruce to walk in.

Kyle and Bruce looked at each other with wonder. Then they walked in the house. The inside of the house was surprisingly bright for a place without windows; but try as they might, they couldn't fight the light source. It seemed to be everywhere, creating a weird image that doesn't have any shadows. The furniture was even stranger; everything seemed to be made of leaves. There was a leafy chair, and on it sat an old woman wearing a green gown with gold edges. She waved at the floor and the leaves on the floor rose up and formed into the shape of two chairs. Kyle and Bruce sat down; the chairs were surprisingly comfy. The leaves moved around to accommodate them no matter what position they're sitting in.

"Wow," Kyle said. "That's amazing."

"Tell me something I don't know, boy," the woman said with a smile. "I am a sorceress, this magic is easy."

"Wow..." Bruce said, "Wait a minute... when we were outside the house, you acted like you know us."

"I do know you," the sorceress said. "I could sense your presence, when you two came to this dimension, I knew that you two came from another place and you don't belong here. My magic reaches far; I like to be kept informed about this place. I also know that you picked a fight with Sir Percy, Kyle. I must say; that was courageous of you, but very foolish."

Kyle blushed, "My anger took over me. Anyway, can you heal my wrist, it hurts like crazy."

"Certainly." The sorceress waved at Kyle's wrist, a flurry of leaves flew towards his wrist. The leaves whirled around his arm and formed a cast around his wrist. Kyle's wrist was twisted back into place, it should've hurt a lot, but strangely, it didn't hurt at all, in fact, it felt really good. With a bright glow, the leaves fell off and returned to the floor. Kyle's wrist was healed, and looked as good as new. "Wow... thank you... oh yeah, I've never asked you for your name, how rude of me."

"Actually, I'd prefer it if I didn't tell you my name. From where I come form, names have powers and I wouldn't rather if you weren't tangled in this magical business. Just call me sorceress. I hope you don't take this personally."

"No harm done," Kyle said. "It's fine with me. I should be thanking you, you healed my wrist."

"Actually I have a question," Bruce interrupted.

"Ask away, dear," the sorceress said.

"Well, as you know, we aren't from around here. We were back in our time and we made a time machine."

"Quite clever, I must admit," the sorceress added.

Bruce blushed, "Thank you. Well anyway, we were planning to visit the future. But when we came here, it doesn't seem like the future."

"This is not the future. Well, it can be, but not for you. I have visited your time period before, and it is our future. I seem to recall that they call us the medieval times."

"Oh..." Bruce said. "How can that be, the calculations were completely right, nothing should have went wrong."

"Did it have anything to do with when you fell over and hit the buttons with your head?" Kyle asked.

"Ah yet...that must have been exactly what happened. The last minute changes must have reversed the generally direction of time we're traveling. The altered calculation was not exact and that must have been what caused the overload and the meltdown when we reached here."

"I see." Kyle said, another big lie. He really should start studying science.

"Um...sorceress, could we ask for a favor?" Bruce asked.

"Yes...you must want to go back to where you were from. After all, you two don't belong here." The sorceress thought for a while. "I will help you, but for a price. I want to defeat Percy and retrieve something from him.

"Defeat Percy? That's impossible!" Kyle exclaimed. "I just got beaten up by him!"

"Peace, child," the sorceress said, "Percy has a medallion that makes people around him slow and takes their strength away, but with certain wards around you, you won't be affected by his medallion. I want you to take back that medallion, that was a property of mine, but he stole it from me, and I want it back. Here is the deal, if you help me, I'll help you."

Kyle thought about it, "Fine. I'll do it."

"Are you sure?" Bruce asked, "You don't have to."

"Yes I do, that's the only way we can go back," Kyle said with a nod.

"Well, then, we'll do it tomorrow." The sorceress clapped her hands.

"Tomorrow? But...it...isn't it too early. Aren't we rushing it a bit?" Kyle stammered, he had agreed to this, but he wasn't still pretty scared.

"No. The earlier it is, the better. The medallion is mine, and I have been separated it from it for the long," the sorceress confirmed.

"Why do you want it so much anyway?" Bruce asked.

"The medallion gives the wielder incredible powers, with it, Sir Percy will do terribly bad things. It might even affect that future of yours. You wouldn't want your beautiful houses and streets to be destroyed to you?"

"Oh."

"Well anyway, that's enough talk for one day, I think you should get some rest. Tomorrow is a big day. Kyle, you have to make sure that you are ready tomorrow to fight Sir Percy," the sorceress said. "Here, sleep over there." She waved her hands once again and this time, two giant beds formed.

Kyle and Bruce lay on their beds. Like the chairs, they were incredibly comfortable.

"Good night kids," The sorceress said. She waved her hand and the lights went off. By some unknown magic, the kids were instantly asleep. The last thought in Kyle's head before he fell asleep was that he wished he could have watched TV in his own house."

"Wake up kids," the sorceress's voice sounded. "It's time."

Kyle and Bruce woke up. They felt incredibly rested. Kyle was energized and felt like he could pick up a tree and throw it across the room. The sorceress said, "Now I will put the magical wards on you for your protection."

"Sure," Kyle replied.

The sorceress started making weird hand gestures. She chanted some words of a different language. A circle of green light surrounded Kyle and disappeared. Kyle felt even better than before.

"Thanks," he said.

"Good luck," the sorceress said.

Kyle and Bruce walked out of the house. They headed south back towards the city. They asked for directions to the knight's castle. The people wondered if they were crazy. But one of the people pointed west and said, "Just walk down the road. You won't miss it."

Kyle and Bruce walked down the road; they saw the castle and gasped. The castle was magnificent. It was the biggest place they've ever seen. It had a moat, gates, walls and everything that a castle should have.

It was really cool. They walked up, and Kyle said to Bruce, "Now's the time you should stop. I have to fight the knight alone. You might get hurt. Go back to the sorceress and wait for me OK?"

"No! I can't leave you," Bruce said.

"Please, I have to do this alone," Kyle pleaded.

"Fine. I guess. But I'll kill you if you get killed in there," Bruce warned.

"Wish me good luck." Kyle grinned.

"Good luck, mate," Bruce said, "Come back in one piece eh?" And with that, he walked back to the sorceress's house.

Kyle took a deep breath and walked up to the gate of the castle. "I would like to see audience with Sir Percy."

"And who are you?" one of the guards snarled.

"I am Kyle. I come here to challenge him to a duel," Kyle announced.

"You better go before I knock you back to yesterday." The guard looked down on Kyle.

Kyle was disappointed. If he couldn't go in, the mission was ended before it even started. But just as he was about to go, Sir Percy walked to gate and said, "Let him in, he's an old… acquaintance of mine."

The gates opened and Kyle walked through. The doors closed behind him with an ominous thud. Kyle shivered and then followed the knight into the castle.

"So, even though I've told you not to come back, you want to fight me with a broken wrist?" The knight turned around and asked him.

"What broken wrist?" Kyle held up his hand for the knight to see. "See, as good as new."

The knight's eyes narrowed. "Well, I guess I'll give you another broken wrist then."

"Anyway, I challenge you to a duel...to the death."

The knight grinned, "I accept. Prepare to die!" With a wild battle cry, he charged at Kyle. Kyle jumped to the side and punched Sir Percy in the stomach. Sir Percy doubled over. "How did you...?" he sputtered.

"You're not the only one with magic." Kyle grinned.

"Foolish child, I don't need magic to beat you, I trained in the army, I can fight ten of you with ease!" He swung his arm across and whacked Kyle on the side of the head. Kyle's eyesight went blurry and he fell. The knight pushed him on the ground and viciously kicked his ribs. Percy kneeled down and reached back, preparing for the final blow. Kyle saw and mustered up all his strength to roll away. He was just in time; Percy's fist was right next to his head. If he was one second slower, he would be dead. He swept the knight's legs from under him and made him fall with a dull thud. He pushed himself right back up and punched Percy in the head. Then he swung another one onto the knight's eye.

"You think you're so tough now?" Kyle shouted.

He kicked Sir Percy in the head. He pulled the limp man up, wrapped an arm around Sir Percy, and gave him a headlock. He kept the knight incapacitated while he reached under his shirt and pulled out the medallion. He slowly put it in his pocket with one hand and he punched Sir Percy in the head repeatedly until his face was a mass of black and blue. He pushed Sir Percy down on the floor. Sir Percy closed his eyes and got ready for Kyle's final blow. It never came.

"You know, even though you're such a bad person, I just can't bring myself to kill you. I'm not cold-blooded. Now that I have your medallion, you can't do any more harm to the society. I've decided to let you go, as long as you submit," Kyle said.

The knight was really relieved that his life wasn't going to be ended, "Thank you, dear sir. What can I do to repay you?"

"Just let me go. And don't terrorize the city of London anymore. Be a good ruler, make the people happy, share some of that immense wealth of yours," Kyle replied.

"Yes, I will do that," the knight promised. "Do you have to go now?"

"Yes, I do. I don't belong here. I want to be back in my home. I'm going back today. I hope you become a good person. I really do," Kyle said.

"Good bye Kyle." Percy waved at him.

Kyle walked back to the sorceress's house. He told her everything that happened. The sorceress was delighted at Kyle's success.

"I have to say, nice job Kyle."

"Thank you, will you send us back now?" Kyle asked.

"Yes. I will do as I promised. Come here," the sorcerer said.

Bruce and Kyle walked over as they were told. The sorcerer started chanting in a magical language and make hand gestures. The leaves in her house were swirling everywhere. Surrounding them and swirling around. There was a big flash and a loud bang; everything became black. Kyle and Bruce were once again knocked out.

* * * *

They woke up back at Bruce's house. Bruce said to Kyle, "Nice job. I thought you were a goner. Percy was such a big man."

"He's too slow for me," Kyle bragged.

"Whatever, I'm just glad to be back," Bruce sighed.

"Yeah, no kidding. From now on, I'm staying at home," Kyle agreed.

Kyle put on his jacket and went home, to his relief, he found out that no time has passed since he went to the medieval times. It was still two o'clock in the morning, and everything was the way he left it. He climbed up on his bed and thought about all the things that happened. It was good to be back.

The Lost Book

By

Casey Rieschel

Fourteen-year-old Ken meandered down the brick cobbled road winding erratically among the brick, stone, and mud buildings of his hometown, Alimo. He reached the library at the western end of the town on the top of a small grassy hill. The library sat in a slight depression on the hilltop, the original site of the house of the town's first banker. Before his death, the banker had willed away the building to become a public library. Since then, once a month, a horse-drawn cart brought in new scrolls and books and took back old ones, a process set up by the deceased banker. Excitement jolted through Ken as he saw a sign advertising the arrival of a new cartload of books on the previous day.

Running up the grassy mound, heart leaping in his chest, Ken rushed through the door of the library and skidded to a halt on the worn wooden floor. He then strode past a wooden desk at which ablack-haired woman sat on a stool, looking through records of borrowed books and repairing damaged manuscripts, with nimble fingers. When Ken was younger, about nine or ten, he enjoyed spending hours watching the woman use only her hands, needles, glue, and thread to repair books harmed by careless people or animals.

Ken walked further into the dimly lit parts of the building, illuminated by evenly spaced lanterns, checking the shelves for interesting books or manuscripts and stacking them next to the moss covered stonewalls. After half an hour of searching, Ken sat down on the floor and opened his books, ready to spend hours perusing book after book, burning their contents into his ravenous mind.

His stomach finally broke his concentration with its growl for nourishment. Ken stood up, groaning with pain from his stiff muscles. After stretching his legs, Ken hurriedly returned the books to their respective shelves and prepared to exit the library. Ken gave a small smile, waved to the woman, and ran past her like the desert wind.

"Mmm," Ken murmured as the warm potato slid into his stomach, calming down the pain. Sitting down on the dirt road, he leaned against a stone house and smiled his thanks to the food seller. Ken directed his gaze to the blue sky, empty except for a few whispers of cloud floating in the breeze. The warm breeze lulled him to rest. He nodded off a few times until finally falling deeply asleep.

Ken dreamed. He was in a deserted cornfield that was covered with colorful wildflowers and resilient weeds. Detached from his body, Ken saw the lazy clouds stream endlessly above his head, at peace with the world. Suddenly, a brown cloud spread across the sky, covering the world in sepia tones. Books fell from the cloud, burning into charcoal, then charcoal into ash that blew itself across the world, covering the happy green field in a blanket of grey snow. Ken stared in horror, and a feeling of foreboding filled him as water fills a jar. A bright flash of light scattered his thoughts.

Awakened suddenly, Ken wheeled backwards as a clod of mud struck his left eye.

"What are you doing, screaming like that? Let the people sleep without your keening voice! People these days have no respect."

With that, the old woman slammed her shutter with a bang, leaving Ken groggy on the dirt road and knocking a loose chunk of mud from her wall that shattered into dust. Then Ken's surroundings and what the woman shouted out finally registered in his brain. 'Night time!'

his brain screamed as he shot down the dark road and paths between houses, racing against time to return home.

Suddenly, an old man with a wizened beard appeared like an apparition from the pitch-black night, blocking Ken's path. Ken stared at the man, surprised, and noticed he hovered very slightly above the ground. Without a word, the man, wearing a barely discernible red robe, put a blue book onto the ground. The book glowed with a soft light, though clouds coated the moon. The man disappeared into the darkness, leaving Ken alone with the book. Ken carefully took the book into his hands and admired the blue velvet cover interwoven with silver threads. Unable to resist, he opened the book, revealing completely empty pages. A ray of concentrated light burst from the open pages and blew his mind away. Darkness enveloped his world.

Ken opened his eyes to a bright day, lit by the sun already high in the sky. He sat up and fell back into a sleeping position, eyes swimming from disorientation. Ken waited several long minutes for his head to clear and then attempted to listen to his surroundings. However, other than the sound of his own breathing, he heard nothing. Everything was silent. Not even the wind blew on the...desert? Ken sat up and quickly surveyed his surroundings: enormous, endless dunes of sand, stretching endlessly across the arid land. The only patch of ground not consisting of miniscule brown or yellow particles was the dirt on which he had fallen following the opening of the book.

"Hello! Anybody here!" Ken bellowed into the distance. The towering dunes captured the sound, echoing endlessly into the distance. After spending considerable time in a vain attempt to locate a hospitable area, Ken decided to head between a pair of parallel large dunes separated by a large rift. Holding up his hand to protect from the sun's glare, Ken bent down to tie his familiar mud covered boots, only to find them replaced with a pair of strange shoes. The new shoes were made of a flexible and elastic fabric. The exotic and unknown fabric was a sandy shade and had diminutive pieces of glass that shined brightly in the sunlight. Ken removed the shoes and examined them. They seemed to be made of several layers of the strange fabric, sown together expertly at the seams. After putting the shoes back on, Ken began striding across the burning sand.

After several hours of constant walking and sweating, the sun began to set behind Ken. The fading glow illuminated the ground with a soft orange light. Ken, relieved that the sun no longer shone so harshly on his burning body, took a look at his surroundings, hoping without hope to find some water to quench his parched throat. After a few brief minutes of searching, Ken walked to a ditch next to a large dune. Ken leaned against the wall of sand, breathed in deeply, and closed his eyes. A light breeze wafted into the rift, carrying course particles of sand that brushed Ken's face. The wind grew steadily in strength, carrying more, and more sand.

Soon sand tore at his face and body, tearing small, bloodied holes on any exposed skin. Now Ken was glad for the long sleeves and pants that protected his limbs from the wind. Protectively holding his arms in front of his face, Ken ran out of the hollow, into the sandstorm. Immediately he was blown off his feet and crashed into the dunes at his side. The impact bounced Ken upward a strong stream of air tossed him high into the sky. Being blown above the sand, Ken no longer felt it tearing at him. He lowered his arms and looked below him through squinted eyes. Ken saw a sea of brown sand illuminated by moonlight that surged endlessly to all horizons. The sight astounded him.

Ken zipped through the air, borne by the current. Occasionally the peak of an especially large sand dune would poke out of the sea of sand, but soon the peak would dissolve back into the sand ocean. Ken closed his eyes and drifted into a dreamless sleep.

Smack!

"AGGH!" Ken screamed as his body smashed into the ground, sending a plume of sand hundreds of feet into the air. Ken's vision blackened, and his body went slack. Ken faintly heard himself scream on and on as agony seared his body. The last thing Ken saw was a group of people wearing clothes the color of sand. A child who looked about his age came close and, out of a hidden pocket, withdrew a vial. Though Ken's mind was foggy from pain, he instinctively knew the vial would cause him harm.

In an attempt to escape, Ken dragged his arms above him and pulled his body across the coarse sand. Without warning, the young boy jumped upon Ken's back, knocking the breath out of Ken. The boy unscrewed the vial and dumped its liquid contents into Ken's mouth. Ken immediately felt woozy. His arms and legs felt like hunks of lead, unresponsive to any command he gave them. Ken fought for control of his mind and body, but he gave up after a brief struggle. Ken was carried to a small wooden hut not very far away before falling asleep from the affects of the drug.

Ken moaned and attempted to sit up, but agony shot through his chest, and he remained in a fetal position, panting from the pain. The noise disturbed a small boy lying on the opposite side of a bright fire. Ken looked around at his surroundings and found himself inside a dim, smoky, wooden house. A small window allowed smoke from the fire to exit. The young boy awoke and, seeing Ken awake as well, began to talk.

"Hello! What's your name?

"My name is Dae."

Surprised by Dae's openness, Ken spoke, "My name is Ken. You have an odd name Dae."

"As do you Ken. I have never heard of a name like yours before. Do you come from somewhere across the desert?"

Ken chuckled uncomfortably. "Where I live, there are no deserts. Instead there are many green hills, plains dotted with plants and animals, and gentle slopes carved by small streams. I do not know how I came here, except that a book had some part in the story, but I got caught by a sandstorm and blown into the air. I became caught up in some sort of strong wind and blown to wherever we are."

"No, no, no." Dae answered. "It has been several says since you have arrived. We are now in the town of Cill. We have provided proper shelter and decent surroundings to optimize healing for your left forearm and three broken ribs. I think your left arm has already mended itself, but your ribs were fractured in several places. It will be days before they heal."

"Several days!" Ken exclaimed in shock.

"Is that too long?" Dae asked, concerned.

"No, not too long. I was simply shocked at how fast your medication works. Where I live, it takes several weeks to heal a broken arm. I am amazed that my arm healed so quickly. Can you please show me the medicine you used?"

"Medicine? What is medicine?" Dae asked, utterly bewildered.

"You don't use medicine!" Ken exclaimed, equally bewildered.

"What is medicine?" Dae persisted.

Relenting to Dae's questions, Ken answered. "Medicine is something that helps injuries heal faster or prevents an injury from becoming infected with germs."

"What are germs?" Dae questioned.

"Germs are what cause infections in people and animals and makes them sick."

Dae was obviously a very curious child by nature and continued the onslaught of questions until the fire ran low and the room became dim. The moon illuminated the room through the window until it slowly moved out of sight. As the last sliver of light fled the room, Dae was interrupted by two people wearing the same style of clothing as Dae, but with markings sown on the hem. Talking to Dae in a quick dialect that left Ken totally confused, they pointed to a small clay bowl of soup that sat in the corner of the room under the window.

Hunger washed through Ken as he saw the ice-cold soup mixed with various foreign vegetables and a few chunks of cooked meat. The shorter adult placed the bowl into Ken's hands, and Ken ravenously slurped it up. The clay pot contained more than expected and completely filled Ken's stomach. Dae suddenly stood up and ran out of the house through a wooden door that blended in perfectly into the surrounding woodwork.

Soon afterwards, Dae reappeared carrying with him a few black round patties and wooden logs. Dae threw the patties onto the remaining embers from the fire, which promptly burst into an impossibly bright flame. Sparks flew high into the air as Dae placed the wood onto the flames. The wood caught flame immediately and crackled. The patties had been burnt to a crisp and became thin disks of black separating the burning wood and powdery ashes. The adults had already left during the span of time that Ken spent looking at the flames, leaving him and Dae alone in the dark room.

"What were they talking to you about?" Asked Ken.

"Nothing," Dae replied, resolute.

"Okay then." Ken said, and then yawned. Pain from his broken ribs caused Ken to cough. He had temporarily forgotten that his ribs were broken. "I think it is time for us to sleep." Ken wheezed.

"Yeah, you need some rest," Dae said.

Dae took two thick, linen, blankets from under the bed where Ken sat. Spreading out one of the two blankets, he draped it over Ken before covering himself. After murmuring his thanks to Dae, Ken drifted into a sound sleep.

Bright sunlight shone on Ken's face. He blinked once and raised his left arm to block out the light. Groggy from his sudden awakening, Ken rolled over and fell from the bed onto the ground about half a foot below. Ken grunted from the impact and shook his mind, getting rid of the grogginess that clouded his half-awake mind. Looking around, he noticed that Dae had left. In his stead there was a bowl of the same stew Ken had eaten the previous night. Now able to see the carvings on the bowl, Ken began to examine them.

Carved onto the lid was a palace floating on top of the ocean of sand. Ken recognized it because of the occasional sand dunes poking through the surface of the ocean. The palace had large sails connected by what seemed to be long stretches of rope. Swirls representing the wind filled the sails, pushing the palace forward, or so it seemed. The palace had incredible detail put into it. Ken could see flags and their designs even though they were not much larger than grains of wheat. Part of the engraved palace was worn away by many hands, leaving only the outlines to be seen. Ken removed the lid from the top and scarfed down the stew with the spoon lying beside the bowl. After eating his fill, Ken looked into the ashes and spent a few minutes to recall what had happened the previous night.

Ken froze as he remembered Dae telling him about his broken ribs. He quickly stopped breathing, scared out of his wits, yet no pain seared his chest. Tentatively, Ken took a deep breath. There was still no pain. Ken began to bend over and froze midway expecting the pain to course through his abdomen. Instead, there were only the pins and needles feeling of an asleep foot. Ken sat, cross-legged and scratched his head. 'What happened?' Ken asked himself. 'Did someone drug me overnight? No, otherwise my whole body would feel that pins and needles effect. Then did my bones heal? No way, Dae himself said it would take at least several days before his ribs would heal from their injuries, even with the rapid recovery speeds of this...place. Then what in the world happened?' Ken thought for a while about possible causes for his rapid recovery. Ken stood up and began to push along the walls, attempting to find the door hidden among the sanded panels of wood that made up the walls.

Halfway along the second wall, the door swung silently open, letting the sunshine into the room. Ken took a step into the sun and his feet touched a cobbled road grown over with grass and lichen. Ken walked a few steps forward and spun around to observe the house where he had been staying. The house looked identical on both the outside and inside. There were wooden panels that made up the walls of the house. The roof was almost flat, a slight incline allowing rain to drip off the house and not become trapped on the roof. Sounds behind Ken caused him the whip around. Coming up the cobbled path that led into a cluster of hazy, miniscule buildings was Dae and an old man wearing a grey cotton robe. Dae and the old man talked in the quick dialect that the adults used last night. So engrossed in their talk, they did not notice Ken until Dae almost ran into him.

"Oh, sorry Ken. What brings you out here? Anything wrong with the bed? How do your ribs feel?" Dae asked with a worried voice.

"I just wanted to see the surroundings. My chest feels just fine. No problems inside the house either," Ken replied cheerfully.

Suddenly the old man jumped forward and shoved Ken against the wooden wall of the hut. Ken gasped as the air was forced from his lungs.

"Ezlo! What are you doing?" shouted Dae, completely shocked by the old man's behavior.

"No broken bones and no signs of disease or pain relievers." The old man identified as Ezlo muttered almost inaudibly to himself. Suddenly, Ezlo removed his hand from Ken's chest and spoke to Dae. "No signs of symptoms or injuries in the chest. Where are the wounds you described in such detail, Dae?" Ezlo asked dryly.

"They were here just the other night! I swear!" cried Dae, incredulously shocked by the sudden turn of events.

"I should have cracked one of this boy's ribs just now. We will see if this boy healed by himself or a stranger came into the room during the night and assisted in the healing process."

Ken collapsed against the wall where he had been pushed and coughed up blood that dripped onto the ground. This sudden noise brought Ezlo's attention back to Ken.

"Oh, I may have overdone that a little. After surviving the fall from the sky, I would have expected his body to be a bit sturdier. We better take him inside, where we can give him proper shelter and let his body rest properly."

Ezlo effortlessly hoisted Ken over his shoulder and carried him over to the cot where Ken had rested over the past few days. Ken's vision was flickering and the world was a blur. There was excruciating pain in his chest, and a vile mixture of bile and blood formed in his mouth. Ken retched all over the floor of the hut, and blacked out.

Ken awoke and slowly became aware of his surroundings. 'What happened?' Ken wondered. 'Why am I lying back down on the bed? What time is it?' A stream of thoughts rushed through his brain and only a few questions and thoughts were coherent enough to understand. Ken turned his head towards the window at the opposite end of the room. Moonlight gleamed a thin stream of light that was filtered by a thick layer of smoke from the dead fire. Ken saw Dae sleeping soundly in his corner of the hut. When he looked around, however, there was no sign of Ezlo—the man who came to help heal the ribs he had broken during the fall from the jet stream of air but had injured him instead. Ken cautiously pressed his hand against the area where Ezlo had struck.

Ken winced from the severe bruising in the area. Ken pushed his hand harder into his chest, prepared to remove it should the need arise. However, no matter how hard Ken pushed, only pain from the bruises pierced his consciousness. Now that he thought of it, Ezlo suspected that he possessed a supernatural healing ability. Ken raised the upper part of his body off the bed with the intention of fleeing outside to escape the smoke filled confines of the room. Just before Ken began raising his feet off the cot, a hidden panel swung silently downward opposite of the main door, revealing a ladder. Dae's mud-brown hair could be seen steadily climbing the ladder.

Ken silently lowered his body down and closed his eyes to a squint. A child the same general size as Dae rose up from the cot and assisted Dae and Ezlo up the ladder and then climbed down the ladder and closed the trapdoor behind him. Ezlo left the hut and came back a few minutes later carrying an armful of twigs and wood. After lighting the fire, Ezlo leaned against the wall, standing directly above the secret trapdoor, and Dae lay down at his usual sleeping place. Only the occasional hooting of owls and the crackling of the fire could be heard. These soothing sounds soon lulled Ken to sleep.

"Wake up! Wake up already!" Dae shook Ken's shoulders, causing his head to flop about like a bobble-head figure.

"What? What's so urgent?" Ken looked blearily at Dae, barely recognizing him through sleepy eyes.

"We are going to the city of Auvil! It is the greatest center for trade and knowledge for *miles*! We'll get there the same way you flew over that sea of sand. Won't it be awesome! I am so excited!"

Dae danced all over the hut and burst outside, leaving a stunned Ken lying on the bed. Ken groaned with the effort of standing up and then walked outside. Dae was running around the hut, securing the windows, covering the woodpile with a waterproof skin, and gathering blankets, dried food, water, and other necessities. Dae pointed at Ken and pointed to the supplies he had collected and three backpacks that he had procured from an unknown place. As fast as lightning Dae was running down the grass and lichen covered cobbled path. In seconds he was beyond the hill that hid part of the path from Ken's sight.

Ken sighed and trudged over to the packs that had left for him to fill. Ken split the supplies evenly across the three packs. Within an hour, there were three packs filled to the brim with travelling supplies. Ken flopped onto his stomach, His arms and back tired from the constant bending over and packing. Ken rolled over and observed the sky, slightly overcast but still a bright blue. The occasional bird flew overhead, and the rustle of the grass filled Ken's ears. Bored, Ken yawned and sprang to his feet, and then entered the house.

Wondering if Dae would mind, Ken pushed aside the wooden hut door and headed straight towards the trapdoor where Dae and Ezlo had appeared last night. Ken scrabbled at the trapdoor yet could not find a way to open it. Furious, Ken kicked the trapdoor. There was a slight click and the door swung downward. Ken's eyes widened with shock. A metal ladder ended with a tunnel dug in the same general direction as the cobbled path above. Ken took a deep breath, gripped the metal bars, and then lowered himself into the underground.

Ken's feet hit the pebbled floor of the tunnel. Placing his hands onto the wall, Ken began to walk forward unsteadily. A few minutes later, the tunnel ended with a stone wall. Ken grunted and shoved against the wall with all his might, expecting that it would take large amounts of force to push open the door. The stonewall door inched very slowly at first, but swung open very easily afterwards. Ken sprawled onto the pebbled floor. The pebbles dug into his cheeks and arms, causing them to burn. Scrambling back onto his feet, Ken saw a faint, flickering light far down the tunnel. Ken began running to the light as fast as he could. The tunnel wound and wound, turning left and right and rising and falling; it seemed that no matter how fast Ken ran, the tunnel wouldn't end. At last, Ken saw broken moss covered steps leading upward. Ken was panting and soaked with sweat from head to toe. Ken climbed to the top of the stairs, looked around, and gasped.

"Wow! This is incredible!" Ken gasped

He was standing in the middle of a grove of maple trees. There was grass underfoot that was darker than any other kind of grass he had seen. The maple trees were extremely lush and not a single leaf lay on the ground. The whole scene looked like a perfectly manicured garden. Ken cautiously began walking among the trees. As he walked, he noticed that there were small piles of leaves neatly piled up in the shadows of the trees. Then he saw Ezlo working among the trees with a rake in one hand. Ken approached Ezlo.

"Hello Ezlo."

"Boy? What are you doing here! How did you find your way to this spot?" Ezlo exclaimed.

"I saw you guys last night ascending a trapdoor in Dae's hut. I was wondering what was there, so I decided to climb down the ladder and see for myself." said Ken, calm and serene.

"So, you decided to walk down there and hope to find something?" Ezlo inquired.

"That just about sums it up," remarked Ken with a cheerful smile.

"You do understand that you must never tell anybody about this place or that passageway, you understand?" Ezlo said very firmly and with much seriousness.

"I got it. There is no need to worry so much. Anyway, why must this place be such a secret?"

"Considering you will never stop pestering me with questions, I will tell you." Enzlo chuckled and cleared his throat. "I came from a different place than this world, like you. I lived in something called a forest. It is...."

"I know what a forest is, I'm not stupid. Wait, are you telling me that I am in a completely different world? How is that possible?"

"You opened a blue velvet book with silver threads before you entered the desert, correct?"

"Y-Yes." Stammered Ken.

"Then you opened the Lost Book. It is constantly looking for the proper person to inherit it. It tests a person by sending him or her into a separate world. If that person can find the book within twenty days, then he or she will have been considered worthy of owning it and will be sent back to his or her home world. I was once tested by the blue book, but it took me twenty days and seven hours to find it, so I couldn't go back. I planted my hometown's tree saplings and grass that I accidentally brought here with me, the only reminder of my home. Now I help those who have been tested by the book by telling them its location. The book really has no originality. It always stays in the library at Auvil. However, other than that, I have no clue in what section of the library it is in. That always complicates the search. Dae's parents used to help me search for the book, but they fell ill to a fatal disease known to the locals as Ku-Se-No. It is extremely rare; only a few ever contract it. Dae was left in his guardians care, but they were abusive, so I took their place. They come visit every so often." Ezlo breathed out deeply, short of breath after telling the tale.

"So the two people that saw me on my first conscious day here were Dae's guardians?" asked Ken.

"Yes. It is unfortunate that you met them, because rumors are now flying everywhere about you. You have stayed here for seven days. It will take us an additional eight days to reach the city of Auvil. We have five days to search the library. I advise you use that time well." With that, Ezlo turned around and pointed Ken towards a path.

"Follow that until you meet another road. Then turn right. The road will lead directly to Dae's house. Never tell anybody about this meeting. If this place is noticed, the townspeople will destroy it." With that, Ezlo spun around and walked back into the grove.

Ken started with a slow walk down the road until he reached the gate, observing the trees until were partially hidden by a hill. Ken took one last look down the trail from the top of the hill and marched down. The path was protected by an iron gate that had in large letters on the front, "Do Not Enter". Ken pushed open the iron wrought gate and closed it behind him, and then set off to the right at a brisk trot. After a short while, he found himself looking at Dae running around frantically in circles, calling out his name. Ken crept off the side of the road and prowled down to the house. Ken sneaked his way behind Dae, who was now yelling Ken's name at the house's surroundings.

"Hello!" Ken shouted at Dae's ear as he grabbed hold of his shoulders.

"AAAAHHH!" Dae screamed and jumped into the air.

Ken laughed so hard it he fell to the floor. There he continued laughing, hands gripping his stomach.

"What was that for, huh? I was looking *all over* for you! Then you just have to scare me half to death! What is your answer?"

"Ken rolled on the floor and was barely able to spit out the lie before he burst into another round of laughter. "Sorry I got lost in the woods."

Dae just looked at Ken as he laughed and laughed. After several long, drawn out minutes, Ken began to calm down. He began to wheeze, the air gone from his lungs. Dae grabbed one of the three travelling packs and heaved it at Ken. Ken snatched the pack out of the air and his arms felt like they had snapped from the weight of the bag.

"Let's go." Without another word, Dae picked up the second traveling pack stomped onto the path. With a huff, Dae began to walk down the footpath. Ken sighed and wondered what he had done to upset Dae so much, and then began to jog to Dae and catch up. Ezlo was waiting for them at the fork between the main road and the stone track leading to his house.

"Hello Ken." Ezlo said warmly. "Dae, could you please hand me the pack, thanks." Ezlo shouldered the backpack that Dae wordlessly handed to him.

"Why so silent, Dae?" Ezlo asked with a worried face.

"Ask him." Dae jerked his head in Ken's direction.

"Well?" Ezlo nodded his head inquisitively towards Ken.

"I only scared him a little bit. What is so harmful about that?" Ken muttered almost inaudibly.

"He scared you? He scared you, and you decide to ignore him?" Ezlo began laughing an odd coughing laugh that grated at Ken's ears.

Continuing to laugh, Ezlo walked along the path. Dae and Ken followed him, giving each other the evil eye. Ezlo was still chuckling. After hours of walking, Ken was relatively tired. Ezlo seemed to feel the fatigue of travel the worst. He was sweating profusely and panting. Finally Ezlo stopped and grabbed at the water skin in his bag. He took several long gulps from it; water trickled down his chin. Ken and Dae stopped as well, and took gulps from their own water skins. Ken sat down and looked at his surroundings. They were surrounded by tall hills with rocky tops. The occasional wisp of dust blew by and swirled overhead. As they stood, they heard the growling of a wild beast. Ezlo was instantly alert.

"We better continue moving. There seems to be some beast located on our right side." Ezlo half whispered to both Ken and Dae.

The three travellers were nervous and wary, constantly looking around for signs of any wild creatures. They reached a crossroads with a broken post laying its side. Dae, with Ken's assistance, flipped over the signpost to read the words, but the etchings were eroded away. Ezlo stared at the road for several long seconds, debating which way to turn. Finally, he spun to the left.

"Ken, Dae, I think that the road to the village where we can buy supplies is to the left. After about forty-five minutes walking, we should reach the village. We will rest there for the night and then join the caravan over the desert. Now that we all know the plan, let's go."

Ezlo began to stride down the road. The trio walked for several silent hours. During that time, the sky became dark and the wind blew harder. More dust flew from the top of the hills, as well as a few grains from the distant desert. As they reached a yellow stone canyon, Ezlo stopped.

"Sorry, guys. I think we're lost."

"What! I thought you said the town was this way!" complained Dae loudly.

"Oh, be quiet Dae. Ezlo was not too sure about the town being to the left anyway," Ken grumbled irritably. Suddenly a blast of wind almost blew Ken down. Dae fell down on one knee, and Ezlo was on his behind.

"Sandstorm! We have to find shelter!" Dae shouted into the wind and spat sand at the ground.

"I think I see a cave in the canyon. There is our best bet." With that, Ken ran forward and helped Ezlo onto his feet.

"Thank you, my friend," Ezlo gasped. "I think that the cave ahead would be a great place for the night."

The trio swiftly moved toward the canyon. The wind was much stronger inside as it was forced to travel through the narrow space. They barely made it into the cave before a huge wave of sand roared past them. Ken was shocked. They had been seconds away from having the very meat stripped from their bones. Ken leaned against the cave wall and shuddered at the notion. Suddenly, a large rumble shook the floor and walls. Ken looked around, frightened and alarmed. Ezlo and Dae were on their feet, looking cautiously out of the cave entrance. Dae looked up and screamed. Ezlo whipped his head upward and yelled.

"Ken! Get back into the cave!" As he shouted, Ezlo roughly shoved Dae out of the cave as far as he could and ran outside himself. Ken ran into the opposite direction, into the cave. Ken looked back and saw a cascade of dark brown rocks falling, falling, falling.

"Ke . . ." Dae's voice was cut off by a thundering crash that made the very mountain seem to fall to it's knees. Ken was left in pitch-black darkness.

Ken coughed and coughed, attempting to clear the dust from his lungs, but only inadvertently inhaling more dust from the ground. Ken finally began to control his coughing and the dust settled down. Through squinting eyes Ken saw a thick fog of dust surrounding him illuminated by a shaft of light no larger than his pinkie. Half buried under the avalanche of rock was his pack. Ken yanked the pack free from its prison of rock and opened it, hoping to find the lantern undamaged. Alas, the glass was shattered into a thousand pieces and the iron frame was bent out of shape. Ken sighed, put down the wrecked lantern, and sat down. Ken wondered briefly where Dae and Ezlo were before collapsing into a deep sleep.

Ken awoke slowly, and upon opening his eyes, he found himself covered in a gray sheet of dust. Ken immediately began to gently brush the dust off to prevent it from blowing into the air. After Ken finished he stood up slowly and picked up his pack. He called out for Dae and Elzo, he heard nothing in return. Ken realized that an entire wall of rock now separated him from his friends. Ken knew it would be a futile to dig through the debris, thus he thought about what to do and decided to explore the cave. Maybe there was a way out the other end. This remote possibility lightened Ken's heart and put a spring into his step. The way was black and Ken began to walk unsteadily forward with his hands to the wall.

Ken took a long drought from his water skin and took a bit of hard bread. He had walked for several hours and had met a light breeze blowing from the ahead. There was no dust here because it was too distant from the site of the avalanche to have been affected. Ken wiped the sweat from his brow and took a long look behind him. There was a small light visible from behind him, and the wind was at his back. Ken stood up, rejuvenated from the short break and continued his silent walk under the mountain.

"Incredible!" Ken exclaimed with a loud voice, unable to help himself. Ken had walked into in a huge dome with a circular opening letting light and wind inside. Ken wandered along the ancient floor paved with smooth marble covered with thick dust. Ken looked at the dome wall and brushed away the dust. Incredibly detailed murals describing scenes from some past time decorated the walls. Ken let his gaze wander toward the center of the room. Steps led up to an obviously new wooden box lying crookedly on a slab of rock. Ken ambled up the steps and looked at the box. It was made of snugly fit together planks of wood. There were black hinges, making it clear that it was supposed to be opened. Ken grabbed the edge and pulled. It opened without a sound. Inside was the Lost Book.

Ken was shocked; he was frozen in place. Ken realized he was holding his breath and forcefully exhaled and inhaled. He hesitated, wondering if he should wait to open the book until he again found Dae and Elzo. However, Elzo's words of warning about how much time he had to find and open the book to return to his home were fresh in his mind. Another thought came to Ken's mind, the thought that perhaps the book was looking for him!

With trembling fingers, Ken picked up the book and opened it, holding it as far as he could in front of him. Ken's hands instinctively went up to his face to protect himself from the expected flash, but nothing came. Ken peered downward. The once empty pages of the black book were covered with flawlessly written words. Ken began to read the text. It was about his world and his life, except from a third person's perspective. As Ken read, he was oblivious to the changes around him. Ken heard a horse neigh and looked up, surprised. Ken saw that he was back at the road where he had first opened his book, his hometown Alimo. The road was now cobbled with multi-colored bricks. Ken ran to his house with the book in hand and burst through the door.

"I'm home!" Ken shouted. An odd looking lady looked at him curiously.

"Who in the world are you?" She asked, surprised and somewhat furious for the sudden intrusion.

"I am Ken. Where are my parents?"

"Ken? A boy named Ken disappeared around these parts thirty-seven years ago! Where have you been?"

'Thirty-seven years? I have been gone for *thirty-seven* years?' Ken's head spun, and he ran out the door bewildered. Suddenly, the world seemed very unfriendly and unfamiliar. Ken ran into a nearby alley, not bothering to shut the door to what had once been his home. He opened the book and read, desperate for something to send him back to his home and time. Ken looked around, and his surroundings changed, but nothing like the alleyway where he had hid or anything he had seen before.

It was an exotic world. Ken looked around in wonder but found it not to his liking. Ken read another passage and found himself somewhere else. Slowly, the thoughts of Alimo and Cill began to recede. He smiled to himself and marvelled. Thus, Ken's great adventure, his life, truly began.

Pursuing Goals
By
Garret Ruh

"Go!"

The crowd screamed as Brayden stole the ball and dribbled up field. He faked one defender out, blew past another, and deftly maneuvered himself into a shooting position right in front of the goal. He took aim and kicked. The goalie leaped up, ready to block the shot, but there was nothing to block. The ball still sat at Brayden's feet. As the goalie came down on his side, Brayden tapped the ball, and it rolled into the goal. The crowd roared as he turned around and jogged back to his starting position. He had scored three goals, and the game was only half over. So far, he'd had a really great game.

He looked over to the sidelines and saw his dad sitting in the bleachers cheering with the rest of the crowd. His dad was the one who had introduced him to soccer and coached him through his younger years. A high school soccer star himself, his dad was an excellent coach and taught Brayden many things about the game. One of those was the move he had just executed. Seeing his dad cheering him on had always helped him play better, even more so now that he played against competition that was almost as good as he was. "Not quite as good," he thought with a smile.

The rest of the game went smoothly with the Wolverines winning 4-1 against the Stallions. Afterwards, Brayden changed in the locker room and went out to his dad's car. His dad waited for him there.

"Great game. A hat trick in high school soccer is definitely something to be proud of," he said.

"Thanks," Brayden replied as they climbed into the car. His dad started the car, and they pulled out of the parking lot. As they drove home, Brayden thought about how lucky he was. An all-star soccer player and an "A" student, he was Jacobsville High School's model student. He had not, however, received an offer for a scholarship. He thought it might be because he had not yet started his senior year of high school. He played in a league outside of the school because high school soccer hadn't started yet.

That night, as he finished up his homework, he contemplated what the new coach would think of him. Coach Jenkins had retired after last year's season, saying that he was "too old for soccer." The school had to hire a new coach and had hired Brad Wiggin. He had a reputation for disliking really good players because of their tendency to be flashy and to show off. Brayden didn't think he was that flashy; at least he hoped he wasn't. "I guess I'll find out tomorrow," he said to himself. Tomorrow there were soccer tryouts for the school soccer team. *"And you need to get some rest, so you're not exhausted,"* he silently reminded himself.

✶　✶　✶　✶

"Listen up, gentleman," called Coach Wiggin. "I need every one of you to run ten laps around the field for a warm up. Go."

As everyone started jogging, Brayden was not impressed with the new coach. Ten laps were a few too many for a warm up. Running three or four, or even five was okay, but running ten laps would just get everyone out of breath. *On second thought,* Brayden realized, *maybe he wants to see how the team reacts when we're out of breath. It would be a good test of how they would react in the real game. Maybe the coach wasn't as incompetent as he had thought.*

After their laps, Coach Wiggin split the players up and had them demonstrate their shooting. Unfortunately for Brayden, his first shot sailed over the cross bar. When he came back from retrieving the ball, he glanced over and saw Coach Wiggin giving him a disapproving look. "I'm not making a very good first impression," he thought. After that, he made sure that all of his shots found the back of the net. Next up, they showed their "on the field" abilities in one-on-one mini games. They then moved on to passing.

The grueling practice continued for another two hours: two hours of passing, shooting, dribbling, and some other drills that used all of these skills. When it was all over, there wasn't a single person who wasn't exhausted. Surprisingly, the coach sweated right alongside them. He had run all the drills that they had and had proved that he was a very adept player as well as a good coach. However, he seemed to dislike Brayden, no matter what he did. "That might prove to be a problem," he thought as he left the field for the changing rooms.

"Yes!" Brayden exclaimed as he looked at the list posted on the bulletin board. The list identified people selected for the soccer team. Right there at the top was his name. Normally, he wouldn't have been surprised to find that he had made the team, but this year was different; a new coach, as well as a new level of playing, had added some uncertainty to Brayden's thoughts.

"Way to go man!" his friend Nick said to him with a smile. Nick had also made the team and would be playing beside Brayden as he had for the past eight years. They had been friends since elementary school and had always shared a love for soccer. Because they were both forwards, they made quite a formidable duo. They could predict each other's movements long before they actually made them. This was a result of playing together so often and for so long. They often joked that if they were the only two on the team, they could predict every play of a match exactly.

The first day of school had come a week before and caught Brayden by surprise. He had awakened at seven-thirty in the morning and had to run to school to make it on time. Having homework every night did not add to his enthusiasm and definitely detracted from the time he had to play soccer. It wasn't that Brayden disliked school, quite the contrary. He was an "A" student who excelled on all fronts and was Jacobsville High's model student. He was senior class president and the main representative for the Student-Teacher Council. Sometimes, however, it was just another thing buzzing around his head that he couldn't slap at.

They had their first school practice on Tuesday. Brayden had been playing in a league outside of school, but now he got to play with people he knew instead of strangers. Out of all the players who had tried out, Coach Wiggin selected only eighteen of them for the team. Brayden had played with many of the players who had made it before, but some of the players that gathered underneath the large scoreboard near the field were people he had never even met.

They started out as usual, running several laps and then stretching. After they had warmed up, Coach Wiggin told them to gather around for their "before practice talk" as he liked to call it. He got through the formalities of introducing himself and the other coaches, but then the talk got interesting.

"A lot of you have been playing soccer for quite a few years," he said. "You all have talent, or else you wouldn't be standing on this field today. There is one thing I want you to understand though. We will not be playing to win this year."

Coach Wiggin's announcement shocked Brayden. He noticed appalled looks from many of his teammates while others seemed confused. He thought to himself: *If we're not playing to win, why in the world are we playing? That's the whole point of soccer. You play to score; you score to win; and you win to get the rewards that come with winning. If you don't win, you're the loser, and nobody wants to be the loser. The loser is thought of as a second-rate team, a team who isn't that good.*

"This may be quite a change for some of you," the coach continued, "but it's a change you'll have to live with. Our playing this year will not be to win as many games as possible. It will be to hone our skills as players and improve our attitude towards the game." At this point, Coach Wiggin looked pointedly at Brayden.

What! How can he think I have a bad attitude towards soccer? Soccer is my life! Brayden furiously thought. Brayden's respect for the coach, which hadn't been that high in the first place, dropped a mile with this new development. Brayden couldn't wait for the practice to end.

Afterwards, he stormed off the field to the locker rooms. He changed and got his stuff and then started walking home. Along the way, he contemplated the way the season had started out. He had already made an enemy in the coach, and if there was a reason for it, he hadn't realized it yet. *If the coach doesn't like me, that could mean less playing time for me, therefore, fewer opportunities for college scouts to see me. That could severely hurt my chances of getting a scholarship.* Lost in thought, he almost missed his house.

He walked up the steps and retrieved the key hidden under the doormat. Letting himself in, he closed the door and then carried his bag up to his room. As usual, nobody was home. His parents worked a lot these days and always seemed to find a reason to work later and later hours.   In fact, they were rarely home at the same time. His mom left early in the morning and often didn't arrive back at the house until ten or eleven o'clock at night. She worked as a secretary to one of the executives in Bad Boyz, a local toy manufacturer that produced toy guns for kids. His dad worked for a small IT company that made specialized gaming computers. Brayden had never liked video games; he would rather be out on the field playing the real thing than sitting in the living room in front of the TV, watching a virtual person do all the playing. You got no exercise whatsoever by sitting on the couch.

After a dinner of eggs and toast, he went up to his room to work on homework. Everything he had heard about the amount of homework assigned in senior year was true. There was at least triple the amount of homework as there had been in previous years. At about nine o'clock, he heard his dad walk in the house. About half an hour later, so did his mother. Shortly thereafter, he heard shouting downstairs. This was pretty normal for the Jefferson household. His parents often got into long, drawn out arguments about trivial matters such as who should cook dinner. When this happened, Brayden would always ignore them and keep doing what he was doing. Tonight, however, he felt curious about why they were arguing. He quietly left his room and crept down the stairs. He could see both his parents standing in the living room pointing fingers at each other and arguing. Brayden cupped his hand over his ear and tried to listen in on their argument.

His mom was talking, "...and that's why we don't have the money. Your habit of buying everything that's advertised on TV is costing this family a lot of money. That money could be used to pay for Brayden's college. Instead, you go and spend it on the latest home gym or whatever else is on the shopping channel. We're off bad enough as it is and Brayden's college fund is even worse."

Brayden edged back up to his room. His mind reeled from these momentous revelations. *What if I don't get a scholarship? I won't be able to go to college! What if Mom and Dad decide not to live together because of this? This is my fault! I need play better so that they don't have to pay for college!* Brayden resolved, there and then, that he would get a scholarship at all costs. He didn't care about anything but his family staying together. *I will not let them separate. I won't let this happen!*

"Pass!" Nick called. Brayden spun and chipped it over the defenders' heads to Nick. Nick trapped it and sprinted up the field towards the goal. Brayden ran up to help Nick, but he didn't need any. He took a long shot and drove it into the top left corner of the net. The crowd screamed as Nick jogged back to Brayden and exchanged high fives.

"Way to go!" Brayden exclaimed as they headed back to their positions. Their first game of the school soccer season was starting out well. However, the other team, the Woodsville Wildcats, got a lucky goal on Sam Jacobs, the Mustang's goalie before the end of the game, so it went to a shoot out.

Each team was allowed to pick three players to shoot on goal. If, at the end of a round, one team had more points than the other, that team won. Brayden was the third shooter for his team, the closer. The first shooter for the Wildcats shot and scored, a nice shot to the left side of the goal. Then it was Nick's turn. He went for a curve, shooting the ball for the top right, but spinning it left. The goalie, however, realized this and made an easy save. The next shot for the Wildcats scored and so did the Mustang's shooter. The third shooter for the Wildcats, however, missed the goal completely and the ball flew a good four feet over the cross bar.

Next up was Brayden. It was all riding on him. If he shot and scored, another round would start, and the Mustangs would still be in it. If he missed, the Wildcats won. He lined up on the ball and looked at the goalie and then back down at the ball. He took a deep breath and let it out. Then he shot. He took three steps, planted his left foot, and brought his right swinging down. He hit the ball right in the middle, a perfect hit. It sailed towards to right side of the goal and almost went in. Almost. It hit the upright bar and bounced away. The Wildcats started cheering and mobbed their goalie. Brayden fell to his knees. *"I missed. How could I miss a shot that I can make in my sleep?"*

"Come on, Brayden," somebody said from behind him. He stood up and turned around to find Nick standing there. "It's one game, not the entire season. Losing one game isn't the end of the world."

"Maybe not to you," Brayden angrily snapped back at him. *He wasn't the one who had to get a scholarship to go to college.* Nick's parents were both in real estate, and his family was always more fortunate on the financial side of things. Nick was planning to study at the California Institute of Technology, and his parents had already promised to pay for his tuition fully.

"What is with you today?" asked Nick as they walked back to the school locker rooms. "You act as if every mistake is a huge, life changing event. Would it hurt to loosen up a little? Just relax."

"Easy for you to say. You aren't looking for a scholarship anytime soon." "Mind your own business," Brayden replied angrily, walking away from Nick.

As Brayden walked home, he became increasingly angry at his situation at home. *Why do I have to take my anger out on everybody else? It's not their fault I'm in this mess.* An ambulance flew by, its sirens screaming and lights flashing. *I really need to get my stuff together, or I won't have a chance getting a scholarship.*

"Nick was hit by car last night as he was walking home. The driver says he just walked out in front of the car without looking," said Carl, a friend of Nick's. Brayden was stunned.

We were talking not fifteen minutes before. "How bad is it?" he asked Carl.

"He has a broken leg and a fractured arm by the sound of it." responded Carl. Brayden was so upset that he didn't even bother going to practice that afternoon. That wasn't going to go over well with Coach Wiggin, but Brayden didn't care. All he could think about was Nick. Was it his fault that Nick had gotten hit? Was it because of the way Brayden had been talking to him before that caused Nick not to be paying attention? Brayden went to sleep that night with his mind in aturmoil of guilt and frustration.

The next few games did not go well for the Mustangs. They lost all three and had only a single goal in all. Brayden was at an all-time low. He felt terrible after what had happened to Nick and even worse that he couldn't find time to go visit him. The situation at home had worsened as well. One night, he had come home and heard his parents talking. He had listened in and heard them discussing a divorce. They weren't finalizing it yet, but they were discussing options for it.

Brayden realized that there was only one thing to do to save his parents' marriage and take his mind off of Nick. Soccer was the one way he could get a scholarship, and a scholarship was the one thing that would save his parents' marriage, or so Brayden thought. Brayden decided that the rest of his energy would go towards winning as many games and scoring as many goals as was humanly possible during the rest of the season. Soccer was now his priority.

He showed up at the next practice ready to play. However, he didn't even touch a ball all practice. Because of his lack of focus on soccer, Coach Wiggin had him sit on the sidelines watching the entire practice. Brayden was furious. How could the coach single him out again? Was it personal or just the way Brayden was playing? Whatever it was, Brayden wasn't taking it.

The next game came and went, with a win for the Mustangs finally in the books. It wasn't much of a win because the other team, the Northville Tigers, was a rather bad team that never even went above tenth place out of the league of twelve teams. Every waking hour of Brayden's life at this point was devoted to soccer. Even in class he would try to think up strategy and new moves for the team. It paid off. The Mustangs won their next few games by ever increasing margins.

As their record improved, however, Brayden's grades fell. His ultra intense focus on soccer was severely cutting into his time for studying and homework. Brayden didn't care. Soccer was what the college scouts would look at.

Brayden visited Nick after the Mustang's fourth win in a row. He was sitting in his room watching TV when Brayden came in.

"Hey man!" Nick exclaimed. "It feels like I haven't seen you forever."

Brayden replied, "Yeah, it feels that way to me too."

"Even getting hit by a car has its advantages. I get to sit in here all day playing video games and watching TV. There's even room-service," he said nodding towards a large tray of food perched on his bedside table. He leaned over and whispered, "I've convinced my parents that I can't make it to the kitchen without being in a lot of pain. For the last couple days they've been bringing all my food in to me."

Brayden was still sorry about having been so angry with Nick for no reason and wanted to apologize. "Listen, sorry about the other day when I was snapping at you. It didn't have anything to do with you. I was just frustrated and worried," he said.

Curiously, Nick asked, "About what?"

He and Nick had been best friends for years, so Brayden decided to tell him everything, starting with his parents' plans for a divorce. For twenty minutes, he described all that had happened since that first night that he had listened to his parents' argument.

Afterwards, it took Nick a couple minutes to process what Brayden had told him. Eventually he spoke up. "You know, my mom used to tell me that when the going gets tough, you keep your head up and keep going. You shouldn't let anyone or anything get in your way. Keep pursuing your goals. It always pays off in the end."

A few moments later, a nurse entered the room and told Brayden that visiting hours were over. He left the hospital and took a taxi back to his house. When he walked in the front door, his dad called to him into his office. Brayden went in and sat down on an extra chair. His dad was working on what looked to Brayden like a computer on steroids.

"I got a call from one of your teachers today," his dad said looking at him reproachfully. "It seems your grades aren't doing as well as usual. I was just wondering if anything is wrong."

Brayden replied angrily, "You're wondering if anything is wrong with me? Do you think that you and Mom arguing about every little issue that comes up would be a little upsetting to me? Guess what? It is."

His dad sighed and said, "Brayden, your mother and I only want what's best for you. That may sound clichéd, but it's true. We want you to have a better future than we have." With that, his dad got up and walked out of the room.

For ten minutes Brayden sat in the office, thinking about his dad's words. He then went to bed after an exhausting and complicated day.

From then on, every night after practice was devoted to studying and not to anything else. He would sit in his room for hours on end, studying and practicing for the upcoming finals. They were half of his grade, so he had to study for long hours to memorize the material. His favorite class was likely to have the hardest test. Math had been his favorite since he was young but had always been the most difficult course. He was in Advanced Placement Calculus, so it was bound to be an even harder test than usual.

Along with his studying, he gradually began winning the respect of the coach. He didn't celebrate at all now when he scored a goal. He would just jog back to his position and wait there until play started again. Coach Wiggin now treated him the same as every other player on the team, better sometimes. When the time came to choose a team captain, he chose Brayden. Whenever he needed somebody to demonstrate a move or shot, he asked Brayden.

Another good thing was that there seemed to be college scouts sitting in the stands for their games. There were often people, with clipboards on their knees, seen taking notes on the players. It had not been that way at the beginning of the season. Many of the players noticed and tried to improve their playing. This was one of the reasons that the Mustangs rose to second place in the league.

One night, as he was studying the writings of Shakespeare for Language Arts, he got a call from Coach Wiggin to meet the team in the school gym. He biked over to the school and went inside. There were several other Mustangs there, and more were arriving. The coach waited until everybody was there and then made the announcement.

"I am happy to tell you that we have made it into the championships. We will be facing the Oakdale Stingers two weeks from Saturday to decide who will be this year's champion." Everybody cheered and started talking amongst each other. Coach Wiggin held up his hand for silence. "I don't want any of you to get too confident. The Stingers have been the district champs for four years running. At the beginning of the season, I told you that we would not be playing to win. That still applies. I don't want you to run yourselves to exhaustion. I want you to enjoy it and maybe, just maybe, beat 'em." He smiled at that last sentence and then dismissed them. As they filtered out of the gym, Coach Wiggin pulled Brayden aside. "Can we talk?" he asked.

"Sure," Brayden said, hoping he wasn't in trouble. They walked over to the far corner of the gym, and then the coach turned around.

"I want you to know that at the beginning of the year, I didn't like you much. I thought that you were too ostentatious. The way you played, I thought you were the kind who would need a shoeshine after every goal. I must say, you proved me wrong. Your positive attitude has helped this team tremendously throughout this season. Thanks for what you've done. Keep it up. I'll see you at practice." With that, he turned around and walked out of the gym.

Brayden was pleasantly surprised. He knew the coach didn't dislike him as much, but he didn't think that he had done that much to help the team. *Well, obviously the coach thinks so.* He went and got his bike and then rode home. He had better get back to studying. He had a test tomorrow on Shakespeare, and it was going to be hard to do if he hadn't read a single one of Shakespeare's works.

"Come on," his dad exclaimed, "or we'll be late for the game."

"Just wait a minute," Brayden replied. "I can't play on an empty stomach." It was Saturday morning. Game-day. He had gotten up at six and run around the block to get loosened up for the game. He sure didn't plan on getting cramps and not being able to play. They jumped in the car and drove over to the field.

When they arrived, they saw that the Stingers had already arrived and were passing back and forth and shooting. Coach Wiggin and a couple of Mustangs were over by the bench, so Brayden grabbed his stuff out of the trunk and went over to where they were sitting.

After everyone had arrived, they went out on the field to warm up. They passed between each other for a couple minutes. Then Coach Wiggin called them over.

"Today's a big day. Let's go out there and give it our best. Enjoy the game." The starters jogged out to their positions, and Brayden walked to the center where the referee was waiting. After both captains shook hands, the ref asked Brayden if he wanted heads or tails. Brayden took tails, but it ended up heads. The Stingers would kick off first.

He walked to his position. He was absolutely buzzing with energy. This was the final game. What happened here would decide how people looked upon the team. They would either see a victorious, skilled team or a defeated and weak team. As the Stingers lined up, Brayden tensed, ready to spring forward. The referee checked that both goalies were ready and blew the whistle.

Brayden sprang forward after the ball. The Stinger's striker passed it backwards and then ran up the field. The defenseman who received the ball took a touch and then booted it back up field. The Stinger's striker slipped past the Mustang defenseman and trapped the ball neatly, then turned and shot. Brayden had never seen a soccer ball go so fast. It was a blur as it streaked into the upper right corner of the net. Sam never had a chance. Brayden kicked at the dirt. Less than half a minute into the game and they were already down a goal. This was not starting out too well.

At half time it wasn't any better. The Stingers had scored another two goals against the Mustang's one goal. Coach Wiggin gathered the team together and gave them a pep talk.

"Great playing. That's about all I can say. You guys are playing better than you've played all season. Just keep your head up. We're still in this. Heck, if it was seven to one in their favor, I would still think you guys could win. It's just the type of team you are. Once you get in the groove, you're unbeatable. Get in the groove. Now get out there and sting those Stingers right back." Everyone cheered, and they walked back out onto the field for the second half of the game.

Because the Stingers had kicked off in the first half, the Mustangs got to kick off in the second. Brayden tapped it to the other forward and then ran diagonally ahead. The forward passed it back, and a defenseman chipped it over the heads of the Stingers to Brayden who was flying down the left side of the field. He received it beautifully and ran to the corner while looking for a man in the middle. He saw one of the midfielders and centered the ball. The midfielder turned so that his back was to the goal, and threw himself into a back flip. He timed it so that when his feet were at their highest, the ball would be there too. He kicked and drove the ball into the back of the net. It was a perfect bicycle kick. The crowd screamed as the shooter landed on his feet and started jogging back to his position.

The coach had been right. Now that they were pumped up, they played a lot better. The ball spent the majority of the second half on the Stinger's end of the field. With two minutes left, Brayden managed to head a corner kick into the corner of the net. The game was tied and stayed that way until the final whistle. "*Oh no,*" Brayden thought. "*Another shootout.*"

The referee and the two coaches discussed exactly how the shootout was going to go. Again, three players from each team would be chosen to take a shot. If you won a round, you won the game. It was as simple as that. Brayden, a midfielder, and one of their forwards were chosen by Coach Wiggin to take the shot. As luck would have it, Brayden was going to shoot last again. *Great. I have to be the closer again.*

The Stingers' first player scored and so did the Mustang's forward. However, both teams' second shooters missed. The Stinger's third and final shooter lined up. He hesitated a moment and then kicked. He never had a chance. Sam was on it like a cat on a mouse. Finally, it was Brayden's turn. He walked up to the ball and took the necessary steps backwards. He looked down at the ball. It was all riding on that ball. If it went in, the Mustangs would be the district champions. If it didn't, the Stingers would have another chance to bag the game. Brayden took a couple breaths. Then he heard Nick's voice.

"Keep your head high!" Nick shouted from the sidelines. Brayden's head snapped over to look at the sidelines. There was Nick on crutches with a cast on his arm and leg. Brayden smiled. Nick had decided to come support him. He was really grateful for that. Even broken bones couldn't stop friends from helping friends. "Keep your head high," Nick had said. He had said that in the hospital too. Then, it had been advice about life. Right now, he was playing soccer.

Maybe it'll help here too, Brayden thought with an idea sparking off. He looked up at the goal and stared fiercely at the goalkeeper. He then subtly glanced at the right side of the goal.   The goalie caught the glance. He knew where Brayden was going to shoot. Brayden took a breath and ran up to the ball. He shot. The ball flew towards the goal. The goalie dived to the right. The ball, however, sailed into the left side of the net.

Brayden's teammates mobbed him instantly. The crowd cheered like crazy. Brayden was ecstatic. *We won. We actually beat them.* After everyone had gotten off of him, Coach Wiggin walked over.

"Great shot, Brayden," he said grinning as he helped Brayden to his feet. The team started walking over to the podium to receive the trophy. And what a stunning trophy it was. Newly polished, it sat on its stand, shining so much that you could barely look at it without blinding yourself.

Brayden, however, didn't care much for the cup. All he cared about was the reactions of the college scouts who had come to watch the game. He got good results in that area. Several of them came up to him and told him that they would be interested in offering him a full scholarship to the schools they represented. Brayden was overjoyed.

After the ceremony of presenting the cup had been completed, everyone headed home. Brayden walked over to his parents and told them about his scholarship offers. They looked happy, but there was also a hint of sadness in their faces. They drove home in silence. When Brayden got back to his room, he sat down on his bed and thought about what had happened. He had thought that getting a scholarship would solve his parents' financial problems and, therefore, their marriage. But they had looked sad, like something was about to happen that would hurt him emotionally. *Well, I've done all I can do. I'll just have to wait and see what happens.*

That turned out be a good strategy. As time went on, his parents started arguing less and came home earlier from work to spend time with each other. Brayden graduated from high school and went to Colgate University in New York, which had one of the best soccer programs in the country. His parents decided that they did not need a divorce and that they could resolve the remaining issues with a therapist. Brayden would remember for a long time Nick's words: *Keep pursuing your goals. It will always pay off in the end.*

Beijing Secret

By

Hannah Searcy

"China?" Hazel searched her teacher's face for an answer. "You *are* joking, right?" She sat dumbstruck thinking about people running behind her with swords in their hands. Her heart drummed fast in her chest.

I*t is okay. It isn't real,* she thought and tried to calm herself.

Professor Brent's face showed no emotion as he assured the class, "No, we are going. I have always wanted to lead an expedition, and for our interim trip this year the school administration has approved my proposal. Five students will accompany me on the China trip. The rest of the class will go with Professor David to a Native American site around here. If anyone has more questions, see me after class." He directed his last statement to Hazel, and two seconds later the bell rang. "We are leaving next week," he added as students shuffled from the room.

Hazel and a few other students made their way over to Professor Brent. After asking several questions, she darted out of the room. It didn't take her long to find her best friend's short red hair swaying through the crowd.

"Annie, wait!" She called over the bustle of the crowd. Her friend seemed to be dreaming because she didn't turn around. *That's odd,* Hazel thought as she tried to catch up with her friend.

"Move! Move!" Hazel shouted pushing her way through. The hallway was packed with students trying to escape the bustling of the crowd. Tall lockers lined both sides of the hallway. At their dorm door Hazel caught up to Annie, who turned around and started talking nonsense.

"Calm down," Hazel tried to soothe her friend, as she handed her a bottle of water from her backpack then opened the door. It seemed to work, and in a short time Annie explained herself.

"Oh my goodness Hazel, I am so excited about this trip. It will be so much fun, two whole months in a foreign country, and...and Michael will be there," she added softly, her cheeks blushing a soft pink.

Hazel smiled despite herself but then said angrily, "Why did I come to this stupid college! I should've gone to the University of California. I hate this, two months in CHINA!" she spat, sitting down hard on her bed. Hazel's soft brown hair fell across her face. She glanced up at her friend, who spoke slowly.

"Well, you came here because it was a better school for archeologists, and you wanted to be away from Hayden. Besides, this is our last year here, and after this trip we'll almost be free," Annie said.

Hazel smiled, thinking about Hayden Parkington, the boyfriend she left behind to pursue her life's dream. "Enough of this, we're leaving next week, and we should pack." Annie moved to the small closet that lined the left side of their dorm. She grabbed her suitcase and began filling it. For the next few hours they packed and repacked suitcases. All the while Annie chattered about the adventure, and Hazel complained about the hassle.

"Flight MU873 now boarding," the public address system speaker called out to all in the building.

"Come on, guys!" Professor Brent called to the small class. Robotically, Hazel picked up her carry-on and found herself walking next to Brandy, a tall blonde girl whom she and Annie disliked.

"I'm so excited! Aren't you?" Brandy asked, smiling at Hazel, who shrugged her shoulders. Brandy continued proudly, "I'm going to find a gold ring to keep."

"But you aren't supposed to keep what you find for yourself. You give it to the museums."

"Well, they don't have to know," Brandy said annoyed. Looking down on Hazel, she added, "And you aren't going to tell, right?"

Hazel shrugged her shoulders, turned away from the taller girl, and caught up to her teacher.

"Professor..." Hazel said, matching her pace with her teacher's stride. "Where are we going to dig? Where are we going to stay?"

Her teacher chuckled, "Looks like you haven't run out of questions yet." Then he added seriously, "About sixty miles west of Beijing. Some nights we will tent, and other nights we will stay with some friends." Her teacher answered as he guided Hazel to the plane and gave the flight attendant the tickets. "Get in line, class," he added.

Hazel fell in line in front of Annie. "Where are you sitting?" she asked her friend, without turning her head around.

"Row 14 seat A." Annie held out her ticket and then added miserably, "I'm next to Brandy."

"Sorry," Hazel said and checked her own ticket.

"Row 12, lucky!" Annie said excitedly. "You get to sit next to Jordan."

"Yeah, for fourteen hours. I'd rather talk to Brandy."

"Her? She's awful! The girl is spoiled rotten; she gets everything she wants and doesn't even have to ask," Annie said, as Hazel sat down in her seat. Hazel looked at her friend and her gave a sympathetic smile as she moved to her own seat.

"Yo, scoot. I got isle," Jordan said tapping Hazel on the shoulder. She scooted over a seat and bumped into an old man with gray hair and a plaid shirt.

"Careful! Kids have no respect these days," he mumbled. *Great,* Hazel thought, *I'm between a troublemaker and an angry old man. This is going to be a long flight. At least I can catch up on my sleep.*

"Wake up sleepy head. We are about to land and the seat back has to be up," Jordan gently shook Hazel. She sat up yawned, rubbed her eyes, and put the seat back into its normal position.

"Do you have everything?" Jordan asked, as she picked up her pink carry-on bag.

"I have it all here. You?" she asked looking up at the tall black-haired boy.

"Yep," he said smiling and walked down the aisle.

"Jordan!" Professor Brent's invisible hand stopped him. "Wait for the class."

Oh great, Hazel thought looking at her teacher's broad smile. *I guess the adventure has begun.*

The next couple hours proved interesting and different. Hazel and Annie saw China in a way that pictures could never do justice. They sped along crowded streets, past the Forbidden City, and finally to their destination.

"This tent is awesome! It's so cute!" Hazel squealed when she, Annie, and Brandy finished putting up the tent.

"Well, let's get our stuff," Brandy said, her eyes on Annie as she went to the bus to grab her suitcase.

"Annie, what is wrong? Did she say something on the plane?" Hazel asked softly after Brandy had gone.

"Nothing..." Annie sniffed back sobs. "She likes him!" she wailed. Hazel took Annie in her arms. "Sweetie, she doesn't mean it," Hazel said soothingly and led her friend to the bus.

"Which is yours?" Hazel asked. Annie pointed to a large back suitcase at the end of the bus and started walking towards it.

"I got it," Hazel said picking up her suitcase and Annie's. A shadow fell over her as she stepped from the bus.

"Need a hand?" Michel asked, taking Annie's suitcase. He started walking towards the tent. Hazel and Annie followed behind trying their best to wipe off Annie's face.

"Thanks Michel," Annie said, smiling at the boy. Hazel looked at Michel and took in all his features: his bright gray eyes, his short strawberry-blonde hair, and broad smile. She could see why Annie liked him.

Hazel grabbed the suitcases, shoved them into the tent, and jumped in with it. A short time later, Annie finished unpacking her suitcase and worked her way over to Hazel, sneaking past the sleeping Brandy.

"He is amazing," Annie said. She picked up one of Hazel's shirt and folded.

"Yes, I can see that," Hazel mumbled. "Go to sleep. It is going to be a long day." The two girls stretched out in their sleeping bags as sleep took them.

✳ ✳ ✳ ✳

"Up and at 'em!" The teacher's happy voice woke Hazel from an uneasy dream. To her right Annie yawned and sat up, and to her left Brandy still slept soundly.

"Should we wake her?" Annie asked Hazel softly from across the tent where she was changing into a shirt that said: *I Love China.*

"I don't know," Hazel answered, going through her stuff and pulling out a red shirt and jeans.

"Well... I-," Annie began.

"Come on girls!" Professor Brent's voice boomed in front of the tent as he shook it.

A short time later the three girls rolled out of the tent and followed their noses to the smell of bacon frying. The students filled their plates with crispy bacon and fried eggs. Hazel munched on the bacon as she took in the mountains, trees, and her campsite.

"Here we go!" Professor Brent said a short time later as the class bumped along the road. Thirty minutes later the class was standing before a tall man in his thirties.

"Hi guys! I'm Steve, and this is where we are going to dig. I want you to think of me as a co-worker, not a teacher." His voice seamed to travel through the class and all the way back to America. "I want you to get in groups of two and grab a trowel and brush, over there," he continued, pointing into a large white tent. "Go find your labeled ground and get to work," he finished, slapping his hands together as the group broke up.

"Here, catch," Annie said, tossing her a trowel and small brush and walking to their designated working area.

Hazel followed Annie to the small plot of land that served as the dig site. After taking off her shoes so she wouldn't step on anything valuable, Hazel fell to her knees and pushed the trowel into the soft dirt.

All morning she dug out spoonful after spoonful of dirt, sifting it for any remains of past civilization. Annie worked next to her, and Hazel thought that this expedition wouldn't be so bad. However, a nagging thought kept her from completely enjoying the trip. She wiped the sweat from her brow with her sleeve and smiled as she saw Annie peer at a handful of dirt, hoping to make a find of anything. *I wonder what time it is?* Hazel thought as she looked around at her fellow classmates. *I sure am hungry.* Hazel strained her ears to hear any yell or bell to signal lunchtime.

"Dinner time," Steve called, ringing a triangle bell like the ones in old west. Exhausted, the class dragged themselves into the large mess tent looking for the food. "Here ya go," Steve said in his best western accent, handing each kid a sandwich.

"Thanks," Hazel said as she walked out. "MMM...this is awesome!" Hazel bit into the fresh lettuce, chicken, and yellow mustard.

"I know," Annie agreed with mustard dribbling down her chin.

Sitting back on her heels, Hazel surveyed the work she had done over the past couple hours. The smooth surface was now cut in layers in a shallow pit. Hazel spotted her teacher walking barefoot from site to site, giving each student some pointers and help.

"Back to work already? You are doing a great job. Good work," Professor Brent said words of encouragement. She picked up her tools again.

"OH MY GOSH! I FOUND SOMETHING!" Brandy squealed, just as Hazel pushed her trowel into the ground

"What? What is it?" Annie asked. She stood up and pushed her brown her behind her ear, leaving a trail of dirt on her cheek. She walked carefully over to where a crowd now stood and peered down where she could just barely see the top of a wooden chest, poking out. out. Its top was weather worn and mud and pebbles stuck in many cracks.

"OH MY GOSH!" Brandy said again.

"Class! Class, we are going to get it the rest of the way up and open it, okay." Professor Brent instructed the students. Carefully the students wiped away the dirt and eased the trunk out of the Earth.

"It is out," Brandy said. "Let me open it." She added as she pushed her classmates to the side.

"Careful," Annie cautioned.

Glaring, Brandy bent down in front of the chest. She pushed the lid up, and it opened...revealing its riches.

"What? What happened to the treasures?" Brandy asked walking away.

"What is it?" Hazel questioned, unwrapping a scroll from another box and then the scroll from a worn leather pouch.

"I think it is a map," Michael said, taking the paper from Hazel. The class crowded around looking at the mysterious scroll.

"Let's sell the map," Jordan offered.

"No, let's find the treasure," Annie said.

"Either way, I wonder what it could be," Hazel commented.

"Excuse me, but I have a Chinese friend. He ought to be of some help," Steve volunteered.

"We will go find this friend of Steve's," Professor Brent ordered. A little time later the class bumped along a gravel road.

"Hello, my name is Xing Ming Chen," an old Chinese man said. He had wrinkles on his darkly tanned face. The class stood in an old house that served as Mr. Chen's home. Straining their necks the students tried their best to see what was going on. "Oh...I see," Chen said looking at the map. He then handed the teacher back the papers. "I help look."

"Where did Brandy and Steve go?" Hazel whispered to Annie who shrugged her shoulders.

"Come on class. Mr. Chen will come with us because he can read ancient Chinese characters. Brandy must be with Steve at the tent. Well, off we go," the teacher said, steering the class back to the bus. "And thank you, Mr. Chen for coming," Professor Brent added to the Mr. Chen. Sometime later the bus pulled in front of the tent.

"Where is Steve's truck?" Jordan asked the teacher. "We might as well look for something Brandy or Steve left," he added as the class got off the bus. Hazel walked a little left to the mess tent and scanned the ground looking for evidence to tell her where Brandy had gone. *What is that?* she asked herself picking up a folded piece of paper.

Whoever finds this, I am telling you this,
Professor...Steve and I are going to look for the treasure.

And Hazel...I told you that I would get my gold ring.
P.S. Annie, Michael is mine.
See ya later,
Brandy

"WHAT?" Hazel asked herself shocked.

"Are you okay?" Asked Michael, coming out of the shadow of the large, white mess tent.

"Yeah, I'm fine. I just found a note from Brandy. It says she and Steve are going to find the treasure," Hazel said holding the paper out of Michael's reach as she walked back to where the group gathered.

"Professor, Hazel just learned where Brandy *and* Steve have gone," Michael told their teacher.

"Thank you Michael, Hazel. Come on class, we had better go," the teacher said. The class boarded the dusty gray bus.

"Hazel, what are we going to do?" Annie asked, worried. Looking over, she saw Hazel fingering folded piece of paper. "What is that?" Annie questioned and attempted to grab the note.

"Nothing," Hazel said jerking the paper away. *What are we going to do? She could find the treasure...* "Professor, do you think that Brandy and Steve could have a copy of the map?" Hazel asked.

"I'm not sure, but let's hope they don't," Professor Brent said, as the bus made its way back to the campsite. "We'll go look for Brandy and Steve tomorrow, but now we need sleep." Professor Brent added, as the class walked to their tents.

✷   ✷   ✷   ✷

"Come on Annie, time to get up," Hazel said gently shaking her sleeping friend. Annie sat up and sleepily changed into her clothes. "Time to go on a treasure hunt," Hazel said excitedly.

"Breakfast first," Annie said, walking to the rugged picnic table. Hazel followed her friend to the group of tables where breakfast was spread. Hazel grabbed a plate and filled it with pancakes, sausage and eggs. Hazel looked at Mr. Chen's plate and saw difference in the foods they ate.

"Mr. Chen, what is that soup called?" Hazel asked the Chinese man motioning to the white soup with little pieces of what looked like rice floating in it.

"Ah, this very good; it is called Congee-rice soup." he said offering a spoonful. "Want some?"

"No thank you," Hazel said finishing her pancake with maple syrup.

"Ready class? Let's find that treasure." Professor Brent said as the class stood up. Mr. Chen and the class boarded the bus. Mr. Chen seated himself next to the bus driver and spoke using strange words that the students had never heard.

✳ ✳ ✳ ✳

"We almost there, ten minutes more," Mr. Chen said to Professor Brent without turning around. Hazel looked out of the window in excitement and fear. *What magical and amazing creatures could be here,* she wondered. Hazel suddenly felt a jerk as the bus swerved off the road. She looked around wildly before she was thrown against the seat. In a daze she put her hand to where she had been hit. Hazel winched in pain as she felt a warm liquid seep between her fingers. She looked nervously across the bus and saw Annie lying on the floor.

"Are you okay?" Hazel asked, as she inched herself near her friend who's head was bloody from her hit against the window.

"Owww...it hurts. I think I hit my head on the window," Annie said, as she tried to pick herself up.

"Shhh...lay still," Hazel said holding her head. She looked around the bus and saw her other classmates lying in their seats, holding their heads or other parts of their body.

"Hi, again, I hope this didn't hurt to much. We had to stop you before you found the treasure. Steve's friends were so kind to set up this roadblock," Brandy said smiling. "Now give us the map!"

Brandy continued looking at her teacher.

"How did you get here?" Hazel asked.

"Ha, ha, I told you that we had set up a roadblock. We knew that you would come this way," Brandy smiled in satisfaction

"I don't have it," Professor Brent said.

Why did we have to dig in the woods, what is wrong with the city.
Hazel wondered watching Brandy from where she sat in the back of
the bus.

"Brandy, why is this so important to you?" Michael asked.

"Steve, where is Mr. Chang-Ming?" Brandy asked, turning to Steve
who motioned to a tall young Chinese man. "Chang-Ming, please get
the map," Brandy ordered with a flick of her finger.

"I need the map," Chang-Ming called to everyone on the bus.

"I don't understand you, Brandy," Michael said as he handed Mr.
Chang-Ming the map. Steve, Brandy and Mr. Chang-Ming left the bus
and disappeared into the woods.

"Come on! Let's get that map back," the teacher said with a forced
smile. Hazel looked down at Annie whose face had lost most of its color
and had a white tint.

"Sir. Annie is badly hurt. She needs help," Hazel said trying to pick
up her friend.

"Let me help," Michael said, wrapping his arms under Annie and
carrying her off the bus. "We need to get her to a hospital," Michael
continued laying her down in the grass.

"I saw a motorcycle shop back there," Jordan offered pointing in the
direction of the shop. *A shop in the woods, where did that come from? This
is China. Anything can happen.* Hazel thought to herself.

"Here is what we will do. Michael will take Annie to the hospitable,
and Mr. Chen will help. Jordan, Hazel, and I will go get that treasure.
Got it?" Professor Brent said, as they walked to the shop to rent five
motorcycles.

"Bye Michael, take care. We will catch up with you in a little while,"
Professor Brent said. "We need to stop Brandy. After all Annie will get
better, but, Brandy won't, and we need to stop her. Come on guys,"
Professor Brent added, as he turned his bike down the road.

"Wahoo," screamed Hazel, as her Hazel, as her black bike sped
down the road. The three bikes zoomed past the motorcycle shop, past
the road barrier Brandy set up, and past the bus. *Look out, Brandy. Here
we come!* Hazel thought as her front wheel touched the dirt road.

"Hey look. There are tracks. Lets follow them," Jordan said as they
road along. "Stop," Jordan ordered a short time later turning off his bike.
The two students and teacher dismounted and walked along following

the tracks. Hazel motioned for Jordan and Professor Brent to follow her, and they crept up to a clearing where Brandy and Steve stood. Hiding in the bushes, Hazel peered into the clearing where Brandy and Steve were scheming.

"Okay, so does it mean to go past the wall? Or in front of it?" Brandy asked, looking over Chang-Ming shoulder, staring at the map.

"We need to go over the wall, then take a right, and go under the wall for three hundred yards. Then you will find the cave," Chang-Ming answered, looking hard at the map his black hair glistening in the morning sun.

"Good, here take this and be off. We can do the rest by ourselves," Hazel heard Steve say as the cash jingled and switched hands. Professor Brent motioned for Hazel and Jordan to follow him though the forest.

"Well, here is the wall. It looks like this forest didn't exist a long time ago," Hazel said beginning to climb.

"Hurry Hazel! They are coming," Jordan urged as Hazel threw herself over the wall and onto a path of dense vegetation. Hazel stood up just as Professor Brent landed next to her, followed by Jordan. The rustle of leaves hurried them along as they walked to the right of the tall mossy wall.

"Here guys," The teacher suddenly said, pointing to a small opening in the wall.

"Wait, I think that they are coming," Hazel whispered. The three of them froze as Brandy and Steve walked up.

"Come on Brandy, I have waited a long time for this moment, and I won't let it pass," Steve said, as he came up behind Jordan. "Oh look, it's a statue," Steve said looking at the back of Jordan's head. *Hold still. Please don't move,* Hazel thought to herself while Jordan stood a still as a rock.

"Well, there are so many thorns. I need some help," Brandy said. Hazel, Jordan, and Professor Brent ran on as soon as Steve's back was turned. The group ran down the path, hoping to reach the cave before Steve and Brandy reached them. "Stop!" Brandy screeched running after them and Steve running after her. "I want that TREASURE!" She screamed. In shock their teacher stepped back and tripped over a root, twisted his foot, and screamed out in pain.

"My leg, it's broken," Mr. Brent said struggling to get up.

"Let's get that treasure," Brandy yelled as she and Steve ran after her.

"Professor! Hurry they're going to get us," Hazel urged pulling on her teacher's sleeve.

"Go! I'll be fine. Just make sure Brandy doesn't get that treasure," Mr. Brent said pulling himself out of the way. Jordan and Hazel took off Brandy and Steve hot on their heels.

"I can't run much farther!" Hazel yelled, struggling to stay even with Jordan.

"This way!" Jordan hollered pulling Hazel into a small cave. "This is it the treasure cave," Jordan whispered.

"Is that it?" Hazel asked, walking towards a large, pile-like structure. Hazel ran her hands over the smooth surface and found the latch. "Here it is," she said slowly opening the lid. The contents glittered as the two students gazed at the golden objects. "Come on lets fill our pockets and get out of here," Hazel continued shoving gold rings, money and ornaments in her pockets and book bag. "I am sure it is safe. I think Brandy and Steve ran past the cave they were pretty far behind us and weren't paying attention." Hazel added.

"Come on, we have what we need," Jordan said as he closed the chest lid and pulled it to the back of the cave. The two students snuck out of the cave back into the sunlight and ran back to where their teacher lay against the wall. *Whew, so they didn't hurt our teacher. I guess they were too busy following us.* Hazel thought. "We have some of the treasure. Let's go," Jordan said as he pulled the teacher to his feet. The group worked their way back to their motorcycles.

"Stop right now and empty your pockets," demanded Steve coming out of the forest.

"You again, you are worse than a fly," Jordan taunted, motioning for Hazel and the Professor Brent to move to the bikes. "Well, you are not going to get them," he shouted over the rumble of the engines.

"I'll get you! Come on Brandy!" Steve shouted stamping his feet on the ground.

"Good job guys, I knew you could do it," Professor Brent said as they zoomed down the road.

"Is your leg okay Professor?" Hazel questioned over the rumble of the engine.

"It is the ankle. I'll have the doctor fix it when we get back to the hospital," the teacher answered as they turned onto the road that led to Annie, Michael and Mr. Chen.

"Annie, how are you?" Hazel asked sitting on the edge of the white hospitable bed.

"Okay I guess," Annie said turning her head to face her friend.

"Good, I am glad you are better. I have to go now. You have other visitors," Hazel said backing out of the room.

"Excuse me, but do you know when Annie Hayes will be able to leave?" Hazel asked walking up to a nurse.

"Yes, tomorrow she can leave. From what I gathered from Mr. Chen, Annie hit her head on the window, right? She nearly went unconscious from the hit and lost a lot of blood," the nurse said bustling around behind a counter. Hazel walked back to Annie's room and was met by her teacher.

"Hazel, tonight you will be sleeping in an extra bed in Annie's room. Tomorrow we will get up early so we can go to the," the teacher dropped his voice to a whisper, "museum and drop off you know what." Hazel nodded and went to get her luggage to put in Annie's room. Hazel changed into her blue pajamas and slipped into the bed.

It has been a long day. I am tired. Hazel thought rolling on her side.

"Well, Annie see you in the morning," Hazel murmured as she turned off her bed light.

"Hazel, do you think Brandy is sorry?" Annie asked in the dark.

"I don't know, but, I sure hope so. We should go to sleep it is going to be a long day tomorrow." Hazel answered.

★ ★ ★ ★

"Get up! Get up! Get up!" Annie shouted, jumping up and down on Hazel's bed. "I'm free, and it's time to go," she added as the teacher entered their room.

"Girls, we are leaving for America in ten minutes," Professor Brent said.

"What about Brandy? What about the trip?" Hazel wondered.

"Well, because Annie was nearly knocked unconscious and my ankle is twisted badly, we need to leave earlier. If Brandy doesn't want us, then she can stay. I don't believe in making a college student do something they don't want to do. It is your last year. I am sure Brandy will come back to get her college diploma," Professor Brent answered.

"I don't really want to go," Hazel muttered.

"WHAT? But, Hazel it was you yourself who said you didn't want to come to China. Why do you want to stay?" Annie asked walking over to her friend.

"I want to stay because China is awesome; the people are amazing, and the scenery is beautiful," Hazel sniffed, covering her face with her hands.

"Hazel, this is our last year in college. When we get back to the United States, we'll get an award. Professor Brent said so. Then Hazel, you can see Hayden. Come on Hazel, let's go," Annie said cheerfully.

"Oh, I guess," Hazel mumbled. Each girl quickly packed their suitcase, had a quick breakfast, and boarded the bus. As the bus rushed down the highway to the airport, Hazel found herself looking out the window. *The last time I was on a bus, Brandy nearly killed us. Even so, I don't want to leave.* Hazel thought.

"Hazel, it's okay, we can always come back, but we need to get this," Annie looked around and lowered her voice before she continued, "treasure back home."

"What about the officials?" Hazel questioned her friend.

"Professor Brent, spoke to them, and they said that is was okay to take some of it; however, we had to leave the rest with the Chinese government." Annie answered. Hazel nodded her head and settled back in her seat looking out the window.

"Well, how was that for a school trip?" Professor Brent asked, handing the two girls their tickets.

"Awesome, I guess," Hazel said, handing the patient guard her passport. "But one thing is sure, I would go back to China in a heartbeat," Hazel added taking in one last look of China's sky and it's friendly people.

"The plane is leaving in ten minutes," Michael shouted from across the room. The class quickly walked down the hall just in time as the speaker system called for final boarding.

"Yes! I get to sit next to you," Annie whispered to Hazel.

"Look who is coming," Hazel muttered back.

"Hey, Annie, Hazel," Michael asked sitting down in his seat from across the isle. "I wanted to know if you would want to..."

"Go on," Annie said with a dazzled smile on her face.

"Do you want to get a drink on Saturday?" He hurriedly finished.

"Mm hmm," Annie sighed sinking back into her seat. *I think this plane ride is going to be better than the last.* Hazel thought.

"I would like to congratulate Miss. Hazel Cook, Miss. Annie Hayes, Mr. Michael Burns, Mr. Jordan Gray, and Professor Brent Henderson for giving this museum these fine pieces of history. For their bravery of going against all odds and showing us what different cultures have to offer, I would like to give them each a medal," a large man in a black suit said speaking into a microphone. She scanned the crowed, looking to see if she could find any one she knew. *I wonder if Hayden is here?* Hazel wondered to herself.

"Come on Hazel, time to go," Annie hissed in Hazel's ear. The class walked down the steps and into a black car.

"Where are we going?" Hazel whispered to Annie who was looking out the window.

"Back to school, Professor Brent has a gift for us," Annie said, not taking her eyes off the window.

"Can't we go to the museum? I want to see how they set the artifacts up," Hazel asked. The car pulled onto the campus road. The students stepped out of the car and were engulfed by several seniors, juniors, and freshmen who had come to congratulate them.

"Over here," Mr. Brent called over the crowd. The four students pushed their way through the mob of people and into their old classroom. "Two weeks from now you will have final exams, and two days after exams, you will truly be off on your own. However, that isn't what I am going to give you. Hazel, you really grew to love China and that surprised me. Here" Mr. Brent said, and handed Hazel a small round chest.

"It's beautiful," Hazel sighed when she opened it and saw that inside the chest there was a little red model map of China with a miniature great wall and a small red temple.

"Good, I am glad you like it. This is for you Annie," he continued holding up a shirt that said *I love China*. "You were the only student that loved China from the beginning. And I saw that your old shirt was quite worn. I hope you like it."

"I do. Thank you, sir." Annie said blushing, holding the shirt tightly in her hand.

"No problem, here Michael, this is for you and Jordan," he added giving the two boys miniature model motorcycles from the trip.

"Thank you very much, but what happened to Brandy? And where did you get this stuff?" Michael asked, sitting his motorcycle on the desk.

"Steve called me this morning and said that Brandy is going to come and finish college. She'll be here next week. And I got these gifts in China right before we left," said Professor Brent.

Looks like Brandy isn't going to get her gold ring after all, Hazel thought holding her little box of China.

Of Raining Burgers

By

Jae Stelzer

Steve blinked. Hmmm, he thought. This is...original...

A two-dimensional dog raised its leg and relieved itself on Steve's two-dimensional shoe, which did not get yellow. Stick figures were black and white.

Steve punted the dog, and it went flying in a very jerky, stop-motion animation sort of way.

What kind of cheap story is this? Stick figures AND bad animation!

About to continue with these thoughts, the narrator decided otherwise. Steve felt a slight burning on the top of his head. He looked up and found that a good portion of his skull had disappeared, along with the feather in his fedora.

"What th..." Steve's mouth disappeared as the illustrator cut short Steve's exclamation.

Steve blinked. Hmmm, he thought. This is...familiar. Didn't I just do this?

He took off his overly detailed gray fedora and scratched his head, not recalling what had just happened to him. In fact, Steve didn't know where or who he was, along with how he had gotten there. As if on cue, a wandering organ player walked past. He stopped next to him and promptly played the most epic three notes of music ever composed— dun dun dunnnn!

Looking around, Steve realized that he stood on a two-dimensional sidewalk next to a two-dimensional road in a two-dimensional city. A billboard across the road from him said,: Welcome to Stickopolis. Using the amazing powers of Common Sense and Deduction, Steve reasoned that the city was Stickopolis and that the people here more or less welcomed him.

Quickly forgetting about his forgotten memories, Steve went off in search of food. All that use of Common Sense and Deduction had left him hungry!

Wandering around aimlessly, Steve absorbed the sights, sounds, and dirt of Stickopolis.

Steve marveled at the horrible quality of the skyscrapers and gawked at the misplaced ramshackle huts. The dim-witted, lethargic, and incompetent fool of an illustrator drew huts in-between skyscrapers.

Somewhere in another dimension, the illustrator shifted uncomfortably in his seat. For some reason, he felt as though someone had just insulted him.

"Ah well," the illustrator said to himself. "It's time for a random twist of fate!"

✳ ✳ ✳ ✳

THWACK! Something soft hit Steve on the back of his head, knocking off his hat. Steve spun around, about to demand whoever had hit him to show himself.

He looked upon a completely deserted street. Tumbleweed...tumbled across the road. Dust and trash created miniature whirlwinds. All was silent except for one of those gun-dueling songs that they always played in western cowboy movies.

A dark cloud rapidly approached Steve. The background music shifted to "The Imperial March" from Star Wars. Lightning strikes burst from the cloud, vaporizing rooftops and top hats and anything else that stood on top of something.

And then it happened. Like a rain of arrows, burgers started falling from the sky. There were chicken burgers and beef burgers and veggie burgers and cheeseburgers. They had everything from ketchup to eggs on them, and they totally ruined Steve's fedora, which turned a brownish color.

Steve picked his fedora up, wiped it off, and then stuck it back on his head.

"Help!" Steve heard a voice coming from somewhere behind him. "Yeah, you! Help me!"

Steve turned around and saw a ridiculously large beef burger, medium well, with what appeared to be hot sauce leaking out of it. His mouth watered. "You talking to me?"

"Yeah, I'm talking to you. Help get this burger off of me!"

Upon closer inspection, Steve saw a stickman stuck underneath the burger, which must've had at least a five-meter diameter. He didn't even hesitate. "Okay!"

Three minutes, later Steve sat contentedly in a pile of crumbs. The stickman that Steve had just rescued stood a safe distance away and stared, dumbfounded that Steve had managed to eat the ninety-pound burger. He was even more amazed at the fact that Steve hadn't blown up or even gained any weight.

"Hey, all that hot sauce made me really thirsty. Do you think it'll be raining Coke any time soon?" Steve asked.

"Sorry, no Coke."

Steve woke up to the not-so-pleasing face of the stranger he had rescued. The stranger who had gotten sick of Steve calling him, "Hey you," told Steve that his name was Bill. Steve's sarcastic reply was, "like Bill Gates?"

Steve had developed a severe stomachache, so Bill had allowed him to rest at his house. Now Steve stared at himself in the reflection of Bill's ridiculously large glasses.

"Nerd."

"Why thank you."

Scowling, Steve pushed Bill's head out of the way and stood up. Looking around, he was, once again, amazed. Bill's house, although small, seemed like some kind of spaceship command center. Computer screens dotted the walls, and wires created a thick carpet on the floor. "You sure you're not Gates?"

Ignoring him, Bill continued, "Anyways, since you're not from here, you should go see the Council. You'll need a passport to stay in Stickopolis."

"Fine."

Minutes later, Steve and Bill walked to the Council. The Council was situated on the side of the road, on the sidewalk, with a small table and a sign that said "Council" in blue and red crayon. It looked as though a first grader wrote it. All in all, the place had a cheap lemonade-stand feel to it.

"This is the all-respected Council?"

"Yeah, what's it to you?" asked a small and, once again, hidden voice.

Steve looked left. Steve looked right. Steve looked behind him.

"Down here, idiot!"

Steve looked down. Right in front of him, at waist level, stood a small boy. Stick figures do not have facial expressions, but for some reason Steve knew this little one was more than a bit peeved. In turn, a little kid calling him an idiot peeved Steve. He was about to make a rude remark, and possibly a rude gesture, when Bill cut him off.

"Good morning, Council member Hanate Wakuso Harakuro Tokugawa Teriyaki Suzuki Honda Inabe."

A state of momentary shock overcame Steve for two reasons: the little kid in front of him was a Council member and the Council member's ridiculously long name.

"What do you want?" demanded Hanate Wakuso Harakuro Tokugawa Teriyaki Suzuki Honda Inabe. Then he made a face, "I have to do my homework."

"A passport."

Hanate Wakuso Harakuro Tokugawa Teriyaki Suzuki Honda Inabe studied Steve curiously. "A passport, eh? You're not from around here, then. I'll have to speak to the other Council members."

"Are they kids like you?"

"No," Hanate Wakuso Harakuro Tokugawa Teriyaki Suzuki Honda Inabe replied. Then he walked back behind the stand.

A few minutes later, five Council members of various sizes, ages, and genders rushed out. One of them was Hanate Wakuso Harakuro Tokugawa Teriyaki Suzuki Honda Inabe. The woman on his left appeared to be in her mid two hundreds. The next person over was an old military-looking guy, complete with a belt of twenty-millimeter bullets slung across his chest, which were fed into a minigun. A little girl, using her stuffed bear as a shield, slowly inched away from the large gun. The last Council member seemed to be a mouse. Upon closer inspection, Steve discovered the Council member to be a hamster wearing a mouse costume. They all examined Steve, and he shifted uncomfortably.

"Yep, he's the one," announced the old lady. "I remember the one from last century. This one looks the same."

"Eh?" Steve asked. "What's that supposed to mean?"

All five of them stared at Steve with dead-serious expressions. In fact, they were so serious that Steve felt like laughing. Of course, he didn't.

"Hey, can we get this thing over with please? I have an essay due tomorrow and a unit test I have to cram for," complained Hanate Wakuso Harakuro Tokugawa Teriyaki Suzuki Honda Inabe. "My mom is threatening me. If I don't get an 'A' on the test, she says that I'm dead meat."

"So be it. We'll stop making this kid squirm and just tell him outright," announced the minigun toting old man.

"Okey-dokey. Steve, you are an adventurer, a quest-taker, a messenger boy, and a troublemaker. First you have to find this." The little girl held up a small photograph.

"A parakeet?"

"No, not a parakeet! It's an oriole, you idiot. It's the Oriole."

"The Oriole...I don't get it. It looks like a parakeet . . ."

"No, it doesn't. It looks nothing like a parak . . ."

"Actually," Hanate Wakuso Harakuro Tokugawa Teriyaki Suzuki Honda Inabe interrupted. "It does look a bit like a parakeet."

"Whatever! It doesn't matter! Just ask him if...I mean...when you find him."

"What do you mean if?" Steve asked. "And what do you mean by ask him? It's a bird. Bird's don't talk."

"This one does. Come back behind the booth, and we'll give you more info to start you on your quest."

After the Council had told Steve what to do, he walked back to Bill's house. Apparently, he should find "he who lacks appendages" and befriend him. For some reason, the Council thought someone without any arms or legs could somehow help him on his quest to find the Oriole. He rubbed his temples. All of this gave him a humongous migraine.

"Hey you! You look as though you could use this titanium assault umbrella! It's only ninety bucks!"

Steve looked to his right, the origin of the voice, and saw, to his complete disbelief, a man without any limbs. What was more, the limbless man had Steve's fedora on top of his head. Steve patted his head. "That's my hat! What...How...You don't have any limbs for heaven's sake!"

Realizing what he had just said, Steve scrutinized the man again. Besides the limbless part, he looked fairly normal. "Your name doesn't happen to be Larry, does it?" Steve asked. "He who lacks appendages?"

"One of my many nicknames. Along with 'cripple' and 'freak.' Oh, and saying them comes with a charge. Pay up."

"How about this. You give me my hat, and I don't beat you up. Okay?"

Larry pretended to think about this offer for a minute or two. Then he shook his head. "Nope."

Steve swung his fist at him. Larry bounced up, landed on Steve's outstretched arm, and knocked him out with a head-butt. It ended so fast that the DJ didn't even have time to turn on some fight theme music.

Steve woke up. He looked around and saw Larry sitting on a chair adjacent to him.

I'm staying in the weirdest of places these days, aren't I? "Ugh. What happened?"

"Well, I basically beat the daylights out of you using my head," Larry explained. "Then I received a message from the Council telling me that you were coming. It also said that I had to help you on your quest to find the oriole. So I dragged you into my home."

"Oh. Great. Thanks."

Larry got up and bounced over to Steve. Steve eyed him warily, wondering if Larry was going to smash his head again. Instead, Larry swung his head around like a sling and then jerked it to a sudden stop. Steve's hat, which had still been on Larry's head, came flying at Steve like a ninja star. Steve was just quick enough to dodge the projectile. The fedora lodged itself five inches into the wall.

"It didn't do that before..."

"Right. That's because I modified it a little bit for you. If you're going on a quest to find the Oriole, you'll need some tricks up your sleeves. Of course, I don't have any sleeves, so that doesn't apply to me!" with this, Larry cackled at his own joke.

Steve sighed and dislodged his hat from the wall. He closely examined it. It now had a steel brim, sharp enough to break something but not sharp enough to cut someone. He looked inside the hat and found three buttons: green, yellow, and red.

He pressed the green button. Serrated edges popped out of the hat's brim. He heard a whirring sound, and the hat started to rotate slowly in his hand. It quickly started spinning like a buzz saw, and Steve promptly cut through the bedpost with it. He clicked the green button again, and it turned off.

He pressed the yellow button. The hat hummed for a moment and then started to...retract. The brim folded up, and the crown flattened. Then the metal brim of the hat expanded and covered up the entire hat, creating a flat, circular shield. "Nice," Steve muttered to himself.

He pressed the red button. It made a very distinct clicking sound.

Larry looked up.

"You didn't just...Did you just...You pushed the red button, didn't you?"

Before Steve could reply, he heard a low beeping sound emanating from his fedora.

"Throw it out the window! Quick!"

Steve threw it out the window. It blew up. More specifically, small mechanisms in the hat combined groups of three carbon atoms, five hydrogen atoms, three nitrogen atoms, and nine oxygen atoms. The mechanisms lit the mixture, and then it blew up. Of course, it was an extremely small mixture, so it didn't vaporize the entire city, only Larry's garden.

Once the smoke cleared, Steve saw the hat sitting in the middle of a large crater. He went over and picked it up, examining it. It was undamaged. "What was that?" Steve asked.

"Nitroglycerin."

"Oh."

"Well, needless to say, don't press the red button. Just look at what happened to my poor roses!"

There was a second of silence. Then both of them burst out laughing.

Steve, Larry, and Bill met with the Council the following day. Steve told them that they were ready to go on their quest. Larry and Bill got pretty agitated about the "they" part.

"Why do I have to go?" whined Bill. "I don't want to be separated from the Internet!"

Larry joined in, "Yeah! Why does he have to go? Wait, why do I have to go? I have better things to do. Like...um...ah...never mind."

Council member Hanate Wakuso Harakuro Tokugawa Teriyaki Suzuki Honda Inabe looked at Bill. "I heard that the Oriole has the entire Star Trek collection, complete with the limited edition Start Trek lunchbox."

"Okay, I'll go."

Steve sidled up to Hanate Wakuso Harakuro Tokugawa Teriyaki Suzuki Honda Inabe. "Really?"

"Heck no."

"Well, then," announced the old man Council member with the minigun. "Time to go!"

The little girl Council member flipped a switch on the backside of her stuffed bear. The head popped open with a hydraulic hiss.

Larry looked proudly at the bear, "I made that! Nice, isn't it?"

She hit a button in the opening revealed where the bear's head came off...a big red button. It also made a very distinct clicking noise.

Larry's eyes opened very wide. "No! Don't do that! It's not finished yet..."

The three adventurers flew off, propelled by a very large spring hidden in the floor. All five of the Council members watched them go.

Steve felt the wind rushing by him. It was a rather pleasant feeling. So this is what birds feel. I should do this more often! Then he saw the ground getting bigger and more detailed. Oh.

Bill panicked. "We're gonna die! Die! I'm too young to die! World of Peacecraft: the Happiness of the Elf Queen hasn't even come out yet! I still wanted to hack the Pentagon!"

Larry, on the other hand, was not panicking. In fact, he seemed to be enjoying himself. Laughing hysterically, Larry fell head first toward the ground like some kind of insane torpedo.

Steve was probably the sanest of all of them. He thought, reflecting on the situation. Hm. Gliding or flying is not an option. We can't change our direction in the air, and even if we do manage to land on something soft, we'll still die. If only we could slow our rate of descent right before we hit the ground.

Steve's eyes lit up. He removed his hat and looked at the buttons: green button for the saw blade, yellow button for the shield, and red button for the nitroglycerin explosion. He hit the green and yellow buttons at the same time. The crown flattened, and the brim grew saw blades. Perfect.

Steve made some calculations in his head. They fell at about one hundred thirty kilometers per hour, meaning around two kilometers a minute, and around thirty meters a second. Steve estimated that the nitroglycerin explosion's shock wave had an area of effect of about twenty meters.

One second away from becoming ground paint, Steve hit the red button and threw the hat towards the ground. Half a second later the hat exploded.

Steve felt the immense shock wave hit him like a Hulk Smash. On the up side, he also felt his rate of descent decrease dramatically. Every cloud has a silver lining. Unless it's dark out. Which it wasn't.

After Steve regained enough senses to move about, he set up camp. Larry had brought with him yet another one of his inventions, which he called anti-cheese.

"See, when I add the anti-cheese to this cottage cheese," Larry had explained. "It turns into a cottage."

The reasoning for this eluded both Steve and Bill, but it worked. There, in the twenty-meter-diameter crater that Steve had made, sat a small cottage.

While Bill and Larry cooked, Steve studied them from a distance, looking for signs of hysteria or insanity. So far, the only thing that was even close to hysteria was Bill's constant flinching at the slightest of sounds. This did not surprise Steve. He was a little twitchy himself.

There was an extremely long, drawn out, and creepy knock at the door; the kind of knock that usually means, in most stories, not to open the door. Of course, nobody ever just leaves the door as is. They just have to open the door, thinking, "Maybe it's one of my friends!" it's right after that when the chainsaw murderer or a Terminator-X assassin android popped in and proceeded onto slaughtering all the people in the vicinity. Steve opened the door.

A hunchbacked old lady holding a basket of apples stood on the doorstep. Her skin seemed to have a greenish tinge to it, and her eyes were yellow. Warts decorated her long, crooked nose, and she wore a black cloak. Vultures circled overhead.

"Would you like an apple? They're wishing apples; one bite and all of your dreams will come true."

Steve stared at the hag. Then he stared at the apple, which had a skull symbol on it. "No. Go away."

"You sure? It'll make whatever you want come true. You could wish for your prince to come and whisk you away."

Steve stared at her even harder, examining her for any signs of hysteria or insanity. He didn't find any. She was serious.

Noticing his skeptical look, the old lady smiled toothily. "Ah, so you're not that kind of guy, are you? Well fine, it'll make your princess come and whisk you away."

Steve pretended to hesitate. "Yea...NO. Leave; I've already watched Snow White."

Grumbling to herself, the old crone tottered away.

Early the next morning, the three set out towards the nearest town. While walking through the forest, a bunny jumped out of nowhere and ambushed them.

"Aw, it's so cute! Can we keep it? Please?" asked Bill.

Steve sighed in exasperation. "Fine, but you have to feed it and make sure it doesn't poop on our things."

Larry gaped at Steve, absolutely horrified. "Are you crazy? That thing will eat us in our sleep!"

"No it won't!" argued Bill. "It's a very placid creature. Right little buddy?"

Both Steve and Larry inched closer to Bill's arm, eyeing it warily.

Bill followed their gazes.

"Aw, it's hugging me! With its mouth..."

The rest of Bill's sentence became lost in an incomprehensible shout as he tried to yank the bunny's fangs off his arm. Yes—fangs.

Steve and Larry joined in the fray. Shouts and censored words filled the forest, scaring off the other man-eating bunnies.

After dealing with the bunny, the three plodded along wearily. They entered a small town through its heavily guarded gates. The town clock, which looked like a really big, fake Rolex, read midday. The people hectically went about their business. Construction workers repaired parts of the town wall. Street vendors sold everything from fruits to illegal copies of the latest popular movies, such as FratMan—the Dark Brew and Day of the Dying Alive.

Steve walked up to the nearest person. "Hey, where is this?"

"This, my friend, is the second dimension."

"Yes I know that. Where is this specifically?"

"This meaning this?" the man said, pointing at the ground.

"Yeah."

"This would be the road. It's very useful."

Steve stomped away, fuming at the unhelpful answers the person had given him. He hoped that all the people in this town wouldn't answer him the same way. They did. Frustrated, he called out to Bill and Larry. "Let's go, guys."

Silence. "Guys? You there?"

Steve turned around, scanning the crowd for his companions. He immediately spotted Bill about five meters in front of him, who's huge glasses and buck teeth stuck out like a Mac in a room of Dells.

Realizing the horrible simile that he had created, the author did something called a face-palm, which involved hitting oneself in one's face with one's palm.

Annoyed by the author's rude interruption, Steve continued on with his description. Bill stood in front of a booth, examining the technological wonders displayed there. Displayed in front of him were basically really cheap things that the dealer made look really cool. For example, Bill examined an old 1989 Canon Typestar 110 typewriter put into something that looked like a cross between the Death Star and an iPod. Despite its awesome appearance, it still had paper jam problems.

"Hey Bill, don't buy that junk! That thing has been outdated for twenty years!"

Larry approached Bill and Steve. Behind him, three disgruntled stickmen carted loads of the same kind of "junk" Bill yearned to buy. Larry had gone shopping.

Steve stormed up to them. "I take my eyes off you guys for five minutes and you've loaded up on scrap metal? And you," Steve pointed accusingly at Larry. "You don't even have any legs to walk away with!"

Instead of being offended, Larry answered cheerily, "Yep! Pretty inconvenient, isn't it?" he nodded toward the carts of odds-and-ends. "That's why I'll make some!"

Steve gaped at him, a stupid look on his face. "You'll do what?"

"I'll make myself some limbs!"

Bill, who had been listening in silence, broke in. "Oh! Like in Iron Man?"

"Um, I guess..."

"Sweet! I'm helping."

For an entire week both Bill and Larry locked themselves inside the gardener's shed outside The Armadillo's Second Cousin's Goldfish, the cheapest inn that Steve could find. So cheap that Bill's pocket money would be enough to pay for a year's stay there.

The illustrator who sat across from him threw his shoe at the author. It collided with the author's head with a solid thump.

"Couldn't you think up a better name for the inn? Do you know how long it took me to figure out how to draw that inn's sign? How am I supposed to draw an armadillo's first cousin's goldfish?" the illustrator ranted. "Heck, how am I supposed to draw an armadillo? What is an armadillo?"

While Bill and Larry worked on Larry's limbs, Steve did some exploring. Still trying to figure out the name of the town, Steve kept asking around. The only answers he received were incomprehensible and mystifying riddles on completely off-topic subjects.

After six days of fruitless interrogation, Steve finally managed to find out the town's name, Pyrite.

In order to celebrate his victory over the annoying citizens of Pyrite, Steve decided to take the rest of the day off. Thirsty, Steve headed to the closest bar.

On the outside, the cheap little bar was similar to the ramshackle huts found in the slums of Stickopolis. The wood planks rotted, windows were broken in, and the roof tiling missing in large clumps. The bar's sign that hung above the door was so faded that the only indication of the building's status as a bar was a badly drawn picture of a beer mug.

Steve walked through the door and immediately felt like he had entered an Apple commercial. The inside of the bar looked completely white. So white, in fact, that Steve couldn't even tell the size of the room.

"Too...bright...eyes...burning..." Steve moaned.

"Welcome to the Infernal Candlestick County!" proclaimed a voice behind him.

Doesn't the writer have any imagination? There have been tons of voices coming from behind me lately. Why can't they ever come from in front of me?

He sighed and turned around. "Huh? Where are you? Who said that?"

"Can't you see me? I'm right in front of you!"

Steve stretched out his hand. It hit something.

"Hey! What was that for?"

Steve quickly withdrew his hand. "I can't see you. What are you, invisible or something?"

A few minutes passed by, and Steve shifted uncomfortably. "Oh! The lights are still on! It's so bright in here, no wonder you can't see me!"

The brightness of the room suddenly dimmed. Steve blinked. Now that he could actually see, the room didn't seem much like a bar at all. The walls, floor, and ceiling were all smoked glass, allowing the lights underneath them to shine through. No furniture or decorations existed in the room.

The only things there were Steve and the extremely slow stranger. Around eighty, by the looks of him, the stranger's white hair was balding on top. His long white beard would've made him look a lot like Santa Claus, but the effect was ruined due to all of the junk in the beard. Everything from rubber bands to CDs was lodged into the old man's beard, but he didn't seem to care.

"Uh, hi? What is this place?" asked Steve.

"This is the Infernal Candlestick County, boy! I already said that, so don't forget again! My name's Ike. Don't forget that either."

"So, Ike, why is this room a county?"

"It's not a county. That's just what I wanted to name it. It's really an extremely complex three-dimensional tracker system. It allows us two-dimensional beings to travel to the third dimension. It also tracks the Oriole."

"Say what?"

"I said it tracks the Oriole."

Steve blinked. That's...Oddly convenient.

"Uh, I'm going to come back later with my friends. Bye!"

Steve rushed out the door.

He sprinted back to The Armadillo's Second Cousin's Goldfish. He tripped and fell flat on his face, along with everybody else in town. Steve looked up and saw a humongous mushroom cloud coming from The Armadillo's Second Cousin's Goldfish.

He tried to get up, but he fell again. Then he realized that the ground was shaking.

Oh no. Those two idiots made an explosion this big? How the heck are we going to pay for the repair fees? Or placate the angry citizens?

Steve looked up again. He noticed a small black dot in the sky. The black dot grew larger and larger until it became the size of a stickman. It even looked like a stickman. It also looked as if the stickman shaped dot would crash into Steve at one hundred thirty kilometers an hour.

Steve whimpered and braced himself.

No intense pain came. Puzzled, Steve opened his eyes.

Larry stood in front of him.

Yes, stood.

He also danced the Macarena. Using his arms.

Steve stared, not knowing whether he should be ticked off at Larry or happy for him.

"Like 'em? Nice, aren't they? I really scared you! You thought I would land on you! You should've seen the look on your face!"

Steve decided to be ticked.

"Larry, where'd that explosion come from?" Steve asked in the nicest tone he could manage.

"Uh, me..."

"That's what I thought."

He lunged at Larry, going straight for the neck.

Larry hopped away. "I haven't finished. That was me jumping."

"When you jump you create a nuclear explosion?"

"Duh! How do you think I got up so high?"

"I see...Wait, if you're here, where's Bill?"

No reply.

"I...I told him not to but he wouldn't listen."

"What?"

"I'm really sorry, Steve! Please don't blame me!"

"What are you talking about?"

"He's...He's dead."

"Say what?"

"He was caught in the blast. I told him to go into the bomb shelter we made, but he came out just before I jumped."

"Eh? Who's dead?" asked Bill.

"Bill is!" wailed Steve. "He died in that explosion!"

"I did?"

"Yes, you did!" Steve said. "Wait, who am I talking to?"

"Bill."

"Oh, you're not dead."

"Right."

After the little reunion and the earthquake, the people around them stood up. They had all heard Larry proudly announce that he had created the explosion and the earthquake. Looking at their ruined shops and homes, then at the mushroom cloud still in the sky, the citizens came to a unanimous and instant decision: riot.

Out of breath, Steve, Larry, and Bill stumbled into the Infernal Candlestick County. The lights once again shone brightly.

"Old man!" Steve yelled into the white room. "I'm back! Dim these lights a little!"

The room dimmed, and Ike was found sitting in the middle of the room with a complex array of computers surrounding him.

Bill started to drool. He ran up to Ike, looking over his shoulder at the computer screens. Bill started to point things out and make suggestions. Nodding in agreement, Ike sat Bill down in a chair next to him. Both of them began to work diligently.

"What are you doing?" asked Steve.

"We're tracking the Oriole and opening a rift to the third dimension," replied Ike. "I thought you would need it."

"Why do we need a third-dimensional rift?"

"The Oriole is in the third dimension."

"So, why does it look like you're playing Tetris then?"

"Am not! This is an extremely complex application used to find and tear open the dimensional fabric," Ike argued, fitting a block into place. "Yes! High score!"

Bill spun around in his chair. "The portal is opening!"

Crackling blue energy lit up the room, a pinpoint of darkness at the core of it. The darkness grew steadily until it became a jagged ellipse, sucking up all light out of the room.

Ike furiously typed in commands. Light once again filled the room, only to be sucked up. Frowning, Ike whispered something to Bill and then gave him a key. He took an identical key out of his pocket. They flipped open matching lids on opposite sides of the computer table, inserted their keys into the exposed keyhole, and simultaneously turned them.

Aaron had always wanted to be an astronaut. He had spent most of his childhood dreaming about what his planet looked like from space. He graduated from college with hard earned degrees in engineering, biological and physical science, and astronomy.

He was so close to achieving his dream.

Aaron stepped out of Seraph II, the ship that had taken him and his crew to the moon. He looked proudly upon his planet, with the many cities and towns lighting up its landscape. Then he noticed something odd. In a small bundle of lights, not far from the capital Stickopolis, a light shined much brighter than any other. Even stranger, all of the lights around it went out.

As he watched, the entire planet was engulfed in darkness, yet the single bright light remained...right in the middle of the Pyrite.

"Hurry! Go through the hole!" Ike yelled at them, not looking up from his computers. "I can't keep this thing open forever!"

"What's the portal's power level?" asked Bill.

"It's...It's over nine thousand!" shouted Ike in amazement.

"How much time do we have?" Steve yelled back.

"Half a day! You have to go in, get the Oriole, and come back through!"

"What if I stay here to help?" asked Bill.

"A day and a half, if we're lucky!"

"Okay, I'll stay!"

Steve and Larry nodded. "Be right back!"

They jumped through the rift.

Subsequent to them jumping through the rift, Steve and Larry had been ambling around the third dimension for nearly a day. The two were just getting used to it. One of the most interesting anomalies happened when Steve turned ninety degrees. Turning ninety degrees was something so new to Steve and Larry that when it happened for the first few times both of them got motion sickness. There had also been accidents in which one of them turned ninety degrees and thus became so thin that the other could not see him.

Steve cocked his head in puzzlement. "Did you hear that?"

"Hear what?" asked Larry.

"Ah, nothing. I just thought I heard people crying for help."

"Really? I heard that a few minutes ago."

They walked on, heading towards the source of the sounds. As the pair got closer, they saw a huge box structure, big enough to be a mansion, looming above them. On the sides there were painted check marks with the word "NIKE" above it. It also claimed that it was size ten and made in Korea. Wherever that was.

"Whoa!" exclaimed Larry. "If that thing is size ten, then how big are the size one-hundred boxes?"

"Hey you! Can you get us out of here?" came a voice from the box. "We'll tell you about the Oriole!"

"How do you know if we're looking for the Oriole?"

"Because that's the only reason people come here."

Larry immediately began hacking away at the box with his leg, which came with a built-in eject feature. It wasn't working too well.

"Allow me," said Steve.

Steve pushed the green button, activating the buzz saw function. It cut through the box prison like a hot knife through butter. A grungy looking stickman came out, scanning the surroundings wearily. He then ducked back inside the box and brought nine more people with him.

"Uh, nice hat."

"Thanks. Now tell us where the Oriole is."

"Well, we believe it to be in the possession of the illustrator. The illustrator is said to be a giant, twenty times taller than us stickmen; it has four eyes, and all it does is eats. When it wants to, it wields the Wand of Creation, which has the ability to bring anything in the two-dimensional world into being.

The illustrator returned from the kitchen, munching on some chips. He sat himself down at his desk, pushed up his glasses, picked up his pencil, and began to do a rough draft for his next comic strip.

"We have affirmed that the illustrator lives in the very depths of The Studio, which can only be entered through The Door of Damnation at the end of the Hallway," the grungy stickman told them. "Prowling the hallway is the illustrator's vicious pet, The Clawed Tornado, but more commonly known as the Juggernaut."

The illustrator felt a furry body rubbing up against his leg. He looked down from his work and picked up his purring cat.

"How's it going, Fluffy?"

The next day, Steve and Larry trekked across the Foyer and the Living Room all the way to the Hallway.

Knees shaking in fear, Steve peeked out from around the corner into the Hallway. At the end of the Hallway he could see his goal - The Door of Damnation. The Juggernaut sat right in front of the door, staring straight at him.

"Uh-oh."

The Juggernaut charged at Steve, its footsteps making the ground shake. Its bloodcurdling roar struck terror into the hearts of Steve and his companion.

"Meow!" the Juggernaut bellowed.

The two ran across the Hallway, straight at the Juggernaut.

With a wild cry, Steve and Larry charged at the Juggernaut and straight under its legs. Once they were clear from the Juggernaut the two broke out into an all out sprint towards The Door of Damnation. Both went ninety degrees and slipped through a crack in The Door.

The Studio was littered with huge wads of used paper, old chip bags, and various articles of clothing. On the opposite side of the room sat the illustrator, who was staring at Steve and Larry in astonishment.

"I...I know you. You...You're Steve. You're Larry," the illustrator stuttered. "What are you doing here?"

"We came to find the Oriole."

"Well, I guess I could just give you guys one."

The illustrator opened a drawer in his desk and pulled out a pair of scissors. He hastily cut a small square off of a piece of paper. Then he picked up his pencil and started to draw.

"Hey Steve," Larry whispered. "That must be the Wand of Creation!"

The illustrator held up his work and examined it proudly. After giving it a complete inspection, he ambled his way over to Steve and Bill. Kneeling down, the illustrator proffered the small square of paper to Larry.

"It looks like a penguin," Steve stated blankly.

"Sorry, I've never seen an oriole before."

"Whatever. What I'm wondering is why you are helping us. Didn't you imprison those other adventurers?"

"What other adventurers?"

"Well, a while ago we broke a bunch of stickmen out of the prison NIKE."

"You what?"

"We broke them out of prison."

The illustrator did a face-palm. "There's a reason why they're in that box! Those guys are ten of Stickworld's most dangerous criminals...so dangerous that I had to trap them in the third dimension!"

"Wow. Sounds dicey. Good luck!"

"You don't get it. They've probably already gotten into Stickworld and are now wreaking havoc amongst your people. You need to stop them."

"Oh."

The illustrator picked Steve and Larry up. "Let's go."

The illustrator looked dubiously at the dimensional rift. He wouldn't be able to fit his head through it, much less his entire body.

"Great. How am I supposed to help you guys now?"

"No need," Steve grinned. "We'll take it from here."

With that, the two adventurers leaped through the portal and back into the second dimension.

"Hey," Steve began, his voice echoing eerily in the darkness. "This isn't what happened last time!"

"Where are we?" Larry muttered.

"Steve? Larry? Is that you?" came a voice from the darkness.

"Bill? Why is it so dark in here?" Steve asked.

"Well, a while ago a bunch of thugs came through the portal. They got rowdy and broke everything. We've barely been able to keep the portal open with my laptop."

"Where'd Ike go?" queried Larry.

"Bathroom."

"Do you think you'll be able to open the portal again?"

"With the equipment ruined as it is, I'm going to guess that the portal can be opened a maximum of one more time. And that's only with a twenty percent success rate."

"Good enough. Close the portal."

With a gargantuan burping sound, the pull of the third dimension faded.

"Let's go!" Larry hollered, running straight at the wall.

"Hey Larry! That's a..."

Larry barreled right through the wall, sending concrete debris flying. Light shone in from the Larry-shaped hole in the wall.

"Well," asserted Steve, "I guess that's one way to do it."

Steve opened the door and walked outside.

An hour of intense action and level-ups later, Steve and Larry were surrounded. The remaining four fugitives had jumped them while they were resting. The fugitives had armed themselves with crude wooden clubs and steel pipes. One of them had even managed to find some nunchuks.

Larry and Steve were bone-tired. Neither had enough energy to capture even one of the fugitives, let alone four of them.

"There's a word for these kinds of situations," Larry murmured. "Doomed."

The fugitives launched themselves at the doomed adventurers. Steve shut his eyes and braced himself. Larry did likewise.

Chirp!

"Eh?"

Steve and Larry slowly opened their eyes. Perched in front of them was a penguin—a very badly drawn penguin. Steve recognized it immediately.

"Oriole?"

"Yah. Dat is me," said the Oriole in an extremely good imitation of Arnold Schwarzenegger.

"What...How...How'd you get here?"

"It was de paper. I vas just looking for a time where I could make a flashy entrance."

The fugitives, who had balked when the Oriole appeared, recovered from their stupefaction.

"Ha! It's a talking penguin! What kind of cheap trick is this?" the nunchuk wielding escapee said.

Nunchuk-man charged at the Oriole.

So fast that it left an afterimage, the Oriole sidestepped and roundhouse kicked nunchuck-man twenty meters back and through three brick walls.

"Terminated," the Oriole stated in a monotone.

The three remaining fugitives backpedaled rapidly. They were so scared of the fearsome penguin that they simply decided to turn themselves in. Anything was better than being pulverized like nunchuk-man.

"We congratulate these three adventurers for their valiant efforts in obtaining the Oriole," Hanate Wakuso Harakuro Tokugawa Teriyaki Suzuki Honda Inabe began the speech to the citizens of Stickopolis. "Which have come to a success. Not only did they find the Oriole, but they also saved Stickworld from ten of the most dangerous and most wanted criminals in history."

"I award Bill," announced the minigun toting Council member. "This medal, a lifetime supply of jellybeans, and the official title of Bill of Nerdom."

Bill tentatively stepped up to receive his awards. The old man tossed him the medal and pointed to five trucks full of jellybeans across the street.

"Larry is awarded the medal, a new shop located in the mall, and the title of Larry the Un-Crippled," said the little girl Council member, who then flung the medal at him like a baseball. It connected with Larry's forehead with a solid thump.

Larry blinked. "Ow."

"Finally," Hanate Wakuso Harakuro Tokugawa Teriyaki Suzuki Honda Inabe stated. "We award Steve with the medal, his passport and citizenship here, a house, and the title of Steve the Kitten Slayer."

"What did you just call me?" Steve asked incredulously. "I think I must've misheard."

"Kitten Slayer."

The entire population of Stickopolis snickered at the exact same time. Aaron heard it from space.

Muttering to himself, Steve marched over to Hanate Wakuso Harakuro Tokugawa Teriyaki Suzuki Honda Inabe, snatched his medal and new passport, and stomped away...right into the Oriole.

"Hey Kitten Slayer," the Oriole whispered to him. "I just received a notice that there is a horde of genetically-engineered angry shape-shifting android vampire monkeys outside of town. I need you to terminate them."

Steve looked back at his two partners. They nodded at him.

"Alright," Steve sighed. "Let's go."

Hopes For Holly

By

Emily Sun

Holly scrubbed the cold, dark floor, trying to get rid of the red stain. She sighed and stared at her hand. It was all wrinkly from cleaning the long halls of Hope Orphanage. She clasped the pole next to her and rose to her feet. Then she picked up the brown bucket containing muddy, soapy water. While walking to the cabinet, she tripped over her own foot. Water spilled out and onto the floor, making a sound that echoed through the halls.

Holly stared at the puddle of water, blushing at her mistake. *Oops, I guess the other group can clean that up later,* she thought. Holly walked to the janitor's closet and placed the bucket away, carefully making sure not to spill again. Afterwards she made her way to the dining hall to grab breakfast...at five o'clock in the morning. While in line, Mrs. Somdra—Hope Orphanage Headmistress and disciplinarian—came in holding a brown stick. She slapped the instrument of pain firmly onto her hand, making a sound that made Holly shiver. Mrs. Somdra's walked through the dining hall eying each girls suspiciously. Her blond hair was tied up into a bun, and she ground her teeth at any unlucky girl she passed.

All eyes stared as Mrs. Somdra moved behind Holly. Holly's stomach tightened when she heard the constant banging from the stick. Terror filled her mind...frightened that Mrs. Somdra might strike her.

"Holly, after your breakfast come into my office. We need to discuss some important business," said Mrs. Somdra forcing a fake smile as she spoke Holly's name. "Hurry up," Mrs. Somdra added, leaving the room and disappearing into the dark hallway outside of the dining hall.

Holly stared after her. *I wonder what she wants,* she thought. A tapping on her shoulder brought her back to the attention of breakfast and that she was still in the food line.

Holly sat next to Karli and Melissa, and slowly ate her oatmeal and apple, taking as much time as possible, hoping to delay whatever waited for her after breakfast.

Sudden blaring from the orphanage's speakers interrupted Holly's conversation with Karli and Melissa. "Holly McIntyre, come immediately to Mrs. Somdra's office. NOW!" the menacing voice screamed over the dining hall speaker.

Holly clutched her hands and hid her face from fear and embarrassment. She put her tray away, rushed over to the administration building, and knocked onto Mrs. Somdra's door.

"Who is it?" demanded an angry voice.

"It's me...Holly. You asked to see me after breakfast," answered Holly. Her stomach tightened, and her knees shook.

"Get in here!" ordered Mrs. Somdra, opening the door and pulling Holly inside.

Holly sat down in the bear fur covered hair. She had never been inside Mrs. Somdra's office before. She wished she was somewhere else now. Guns hung on the walls. Red paint was splattered over a dartboard on which hung a picture of Mrs. Somdra's archenemy, Cassie Graven. Holly stared at the picture.

"Mrs. Somdra, who is Cassie Graven?" asked Holly, with a curious face.

"Talking about her brings back old, bitter memories. I remember that she and I used to be best friends. We used to play on swings when we were young and then go over to her house to make cookies. After we graduated from college, she went into a Realty business and opened up a new orphanage. It looked like a castle from outside, and the inside was so astonishing. When I went to see my old friend and rushed to give her a hug, she shocked me by acting as though that she had completely forgotten me...she called the guards and threw me out of the place. I'll always remember what she did. I've lost contact with her now...she changed my life." answered Mrs. Somdra.

"How?" Holly asked, bewildered.

"When I was in first grade, Cassie was in my class. One month after school started...my mother died. Cassie heard and she always talked to me about it and also asked if I wanted to go to her house. I said sure, and we became close friends. Her mom felt like a mother to me. Shortly afterwards, my father signed some adoption papers. He left me under the care of the Graven family. I still can't believe she has forgotten me," sighed Mrs. Somdra.

Holly never really realized that Mrs. Somdra had the same painful, regretful life as hers. *I feel sorry for her,* she thought.

"Anyways, back to why you are here," said Mrs. Somdra.

"As you know Holly, your eighth birthday is tomorrow. I was instructed by court, to tell you some extremely urgent information on your birthday," said Mrs. Somdra, staring fiercely into Holly's eyes. With a fake smile, the headmistress picked up a steel-tipped dart from a desk drawer and threw it at the dartboard, hitting the picture of Cassie Graven in the nose. "Bullseye!" screamed Mrs. Somdra.

"What do you mean ma'am?" asked Holly softly, trying to hide the fear of threatened tears.

Mrs. Somdra stared at her for a long time. "You'll find out tomorrow," said Mrs. Somdra.

Holly didn't want to know tomorrow. She wanted to know now. Whatever Mrs. Somdra had to say must be important. Maybe somebody adopted her...maybe she'll have a family again! Thoughts rushed through her head. Holly quickly grabbed Mrs. Somdra's hand, preventing the woman from throwing another dart.

"Please tell me! Please!" begged Holly, her eyes open wide with anticipation and fear.

"Only on your eighth birthday—and not a moment before," said Mrs. Somdra, jerking her hands away from Holly's grasp.

"Why won't you tell me?" sniffed Holly.

"Because it involves your father and mother!" yelled Mrs. Somdra.

"They're still alive?" questioned Holly in an astonished voice. Thoughts raced through her mind. *Was it possible?* Her heart raced as she looked to her headmistress for answers.

"I said on your birthday!" Mrs. Somdra exclaimed. She abruptly rose from her chair and left the room.

Holly stared with a blank expression on her face. *What could it be that Mrs. Somdra won't tell me now. She wants to hurt me by not telling. I wonder what it is. What does she know about my parents that I don't?*

Holly crept over to the door and looked out the hallway to check that Mrs. Somdra was out of sight. She then walked over to her desk and started looking for anything that had her name on it—or possibly her parent's names. A folder on the desk next to the couch caught her attention and drew her close. She inched towards the paper and saw that the writing on the top of the sheet read: Holly McIntyre. Parents: Deceased. Legal Guardian: Unknown.

Oh well, maybe it's all for the best, Holly thought. Suddenly the door opened, and she jumped, startled to see Mrs. Somdra staring menacingly at her. She motioned Holly to come forward, raising the stick, with a malicious express on her face.

"You ungrateful, disobedient child!" screamed Mrs. Somdra. "You ought to be spanked!"

Holly tried to run towards the door, but the swat from Mrs. Somdra's brown stick sent burning pains up the back of her legs. She fell down onto the hard floor. She cried in pain, holding her thighs below just below her bottom. Twice more than the painful implement made traumatic contact.

"Go to your room at once!" said Mrs. Somdra in a harsh tone. "Don't come out till tomorrow morning! There will be no lunch or dinner for you, today," she added.

Sobbing and rubbing pain from her legs, Holly limped to her room and sat down on the hard bed. She examined her legs and discovered thick red stripes running across the back of both her legs just below her bottom. One stripe was turning a purple color, forming a bruise.

Holly woke up at three o'clock in the morning, stretched her arms and opened her eyes to the small dim light sitting on her desk. *Another day means more chores,* she thought, glumly. Holly winced as she edged her way off the bed. She lifted her nightgown and examined her legs. A purplish bruise had formed and explained the pain. At least the stick had missed her behind, or sitting would be an agony all by itself. Holly fought back tears when she carelessly walked into furniture on her way into the bathroom.

She padded barefoot over to the long mirror above the small sink and stared endlessly at herself. *I look like one of Cinderella's ugly stepsisters. I wish I had a mom to take me away from this horrible place and take care of me,* she thought. Holly made her way downstairs in her nightgown and apron. The atmosphere around her was quiet. She saw little girls scrubbing the floor, boys wandering the halls with buckets of trash, and older boys and girls cooking food for breakfast. Holly went over to the janitor's closet and grabbed a mop. Her morning duty was to mop the floors for however long it took. She hurried the best she could. Her stomach growled, and she had no intention of missing breakfast.

At twelve o'clock the bell rang, indicating that it was lunchtime. Holly stared at the food. *Does it always have to be corn dogs and chicken?* Holly hated eating the same food every lunch and dinner. She picked up her tray and silently sat down at the table, careful not to put pressure on the back of her legs.

Mrs. Somdra walked in, guiding a small brown-haired child that seemed to be about Holly's age. She called out to everyone to listen. Holly brushed her sandy blond hair out of her face and turned towards Mrs. Somdra.

"Good day, boys and girls," she said.

"Good afternoon, Mrs. Somdra," nearly ninety children answered in unison.

"Today, we have a new girl joining us at Hope Orphanage. Please welcome Alexis Crambry," said Mrs. Somdra, as she worked her way towards Holly. "Holly, please show Alexis around. At three this afternoon, please come to my office."

Holly nodded in agreement. She hated the thought of going back to Mrs. Somdra's office, but she was eager to learn what the woman had refused to tell her yesterday. Without thinking she slid her hand and rubbed the back of her right thigh. She hoped today would go better than yesterday. After all, today was her eighth birthday. An impatient shuffle beside her brought Holly's attention back to the new girl.

"Hi, my name is Holly." Holly extended her small hand to Alexis.

"Hello, nice to meet you," answered Alexis. "Wow, it is really nice here. Is the food any good?" asked Alexis. Holly saw that Alexis was staring into her deep sea-blue eyes.

"It's okay. I mean, the first week or two you'll enjoy it. But afterwards you get tired of eating the same thing over and over again," answered Holly.

"Oh, well I guess I should go get my food now," chuckled Alexis.

Holly listened to Alexis's laugh. The laugh reminded her so much of Ella, her mother. Suddenly, Holly remembered that fateful night. Her mom and dad had rushed out the door, leaving her alone in the house. The town was surrounded by a bright glow and hot air blew in through the open door. Holly screamed out the door. People were shouting and praying, and firefighters shot water at the deathly flames. The night turned into a bitter nightmare. People came to the house and took Holly away from the house where she had lived all her life. They dropped her off at Hope Orphanage.

Holly shuddered away the memories. Now that she was turning eight, she realized that she had never had a chance to say goodbye to her own parents. *I wish I could see them again*, she thought; but she knew that it was impossible. Glumly, she finished her meal, telling Alexis the good things and the bad things about living in Hope Orphanage

Holly walked into their room. She caught Alexis viewing the brightly painted wall that Holly, Melissa, and Karli painted to make the room more vivid. She pointed a vacant bed next to her own bed, indicating Alexis could use it. Alexis then sat down on the hard mattress and opened her suitcase, dropping all the stuff onto her bed. "Hey, is that all the stuff you brought?" asked Holly.

Alexis jumped, startled by Holly's appearance. "Uh-huh, my mother and father couldn't afford to buy anything for me anymore, so they packed some clothes for me and dropped me off here without even saying good-bye. I guess they...sorry, I don't really want to talk about this," mumbled Alexis. She pulled out a shirt that said *I Love My Mom and Dad*.

"Well, I have to go talk to Mrs. Somdra. I'll see you later?" said Holly, turning to leave. Out of the corner of her eye, she saw Alexis hugging her t-shirt and crying.

Holly went over to Mrs. Somdra's office. She heard evil laughter in the background and questioned whether to knock or to quietly walk away; she regretted her choice. Mrs. Somdra cried out in a harsh tone, making known that she didn't want to be disturbed, but Holly went in anyway.

"Oh, Holly!" explained Mrs. Somdra. She quickly put the darts in her desk drawer and faced Holly, sitting in an innocent posture.

"You wanted to see me Miss," said Holly, looking Mrs. Somdra in the eye.

"Yes, I wanted to talk about your mother and father. As you know, they were killed by a wildfire that occurred in your town two years ago. Police came by your house and dropped you here without giving you any news on what had happened that night. The Will your parents' wrote mentioned that you have to be handed over to your aunt as soon as she has a place acceptable to the court. You aunt has now satisfied the court. She will come for you next week.

"Really?" asked Holly.

"Yes," answered Mrs. Somdra.

"Awesome!" exclaimed Holly. She wondered what it would be like living with someone she had never met before.

"You may go now," Mrs. Somdra added.

Sunlight peeked in through the cracks of the curtain, and a warm glow filled the room. Still in bed, Holly saw that Alexis's face was stained from tears, and her eyes were all puffy from crying herself to sleep.

"I can't believe you're leaving today," sniffled Alexis. "In the past few days I felt like we've grown to become sisters. Now I feel like I am losing someone I love again," Alexis added.

"I know," Holly said. A knocking interrupted her. A soft voice filled the room.

"Holly?" the voice said. "It's Christa, you're your aunt," she added.

Alexis looked at the door and then at Holly. She mouthed the words "go."

Holly opened the door and saw a petite lady, in her mid-thirties, staring down at her. Next to her stood Mrs. Somdra, glaring first at Holly and then at Christa. Mrs. Somdra gripped tightly onto the handle of Holly's small suitcase.

"Are you ready?" asked Christa. "You might want to change into these clothes," she added holding out an orange shirt and a pair of blue jeans.

"Thanks," said Holly, grabbing the garments. Mrs. Somdra motioned to her to quickly change. After a while, Holly went out the door. She saw Christa and Mrs. Somdra talking. She took a small glimpse at Alexis sitting on her bed, staring at the empty bed that was next to her.

"Ms. Christa? Will I be able to have a few minutes to say good-bye to Alexis?" asked Holly.

"Sure, go ahead," answered Christa, following Holly to the side of Alexis's bed.

"I am gonna miss you," said Holly, reaching down for a hug.

"Me to, I'll write you. If I can," answered Alexis, returning the hug.

"Well, I guess this is it," cried Holly.

"Yep, well, go have fun," murmured Alexis. Holly saw Aunt Christa's facial expression. It looked like guilt for being responsible for the end of Alexis and Holly's friendship. She quickly turned her body away and headed towards Mrs. Somdra, who was busy telling kids what their morning chores were.

Without turning her head back to say one last good-bye, she walked through the doorway. Outside the orphanage's heavy wooden door, a stout man awaited them, pointing to a grey Honda near the end of the street. He quickly reached toward Mrs. Somdra to take the luggage from her hand. Mrs. Somdra held on tightly, and the man kept pulling on the handle. The scene led to kids at the orphanage—watching from upper story windows—wondering who was going to win.

"Holly, please don't go!" exclaimed Mrs. Somdra. "You're one of my favorite orphan's! If you go, I'll be lonely!" she added.

"NO! I don't want to stay. I want to go," said Holly.

"Holly, I am begging you. Don't go!" said Mrs. Somdra pushing the short man down and running to grab Holly's arm.

"It's no use, Mrs. Somdra. Holly wants to stay with me," said Auntie Christa.

Auntie Christa shielded Holly from Mrs. Somdra's grab. Mrs. Somdra's stance showed that she was full of anger and frustration. She slammed the suitcase down, squishing the stout man's toes. Auntie Christa went towards the suitcase and picked it up before Mrs. Somdra could react. Holly walked towards the grey Honda and sat inside, staring at Alexis's hand waving in her direction. As the vehicle pulled out of Hope Orphanage, Holly gazed at the view outside where scenery changed from rural landscapes to small houses set side by side. *I wonder what my life is going to be like?* She thought.

"Holly! Time for dinner!" called Christa.

"Coming!" exclaimed Holly, rushing to put her hair in a ponytail. She quickly ran down the flights of stairs and sat down at the table. Auntie Christa was setting down different plates: mashed potatoes, macaroni & cheese, and grilled chicken. *More food,* Holly thought. She looked at each dish carefully. She ate her food like a young lady. She tried each dish at a time making sure not to let Auntie Christa have a wrong impression of her manners.

Shortly afterwards, Holly sat in her room. Auntie Christa sat on Holly's bed.

"Holly, would you like to hear a story?" asked Auntie Christa, getting off the bed and searching through the cabinet.

"Sure, uh...what about *Ballet Shoes*, it's my favorite book," replied Holly.

"OK, I found it," answered Auntie Christa.

Auntie Christa put her feet on the purple shaggy rug. She began reading the *Ballet Shoes*, only to see that Holly fell asleep on the soft pillow. She reached over and pulled the cover onto Holly's chest rising up and down. She kissed her on the cheek, walked to the door, and turned off the lights.

"Goodnight," whispered Auntie Christa, walking out of the room.

The car pulled into the parking lot of Sunny Hale Mall. Auntie Christa stepped out and took Holly by the hand. Holly stared at the surroundings. She saw lots of things that pleased her eyes: food stands, shops, and expensive jewelry. Auntie Christa took Holly into a small store and made her try on different clothing for Holly's first day of school, which was tomorrow. Holly stared at the variety of colors. She wished that she could buy every outfit that she saw, but she Auntie Christ firmly limited her to four outfits.

I wonder if I can ask auntie Christa if I we could drop by Hope Orphanage, she thought. While Auntie Christa was paying for Holly's clothes, Holly went up and tugged on her Aunt's arm.

"Auntie Christa?" she asked

"Yeah, hon," answered Auntie Christa.

"May we drop by Hope Orphanage today?" asked Holly.

"Why?" asked Auntie Christa, turning her attention from the cashier to Holly.

"I just want to see Alexis," replied Holly, looking down at the marble floor.

"I'll see if we could make an appointment," answered Auntie Christa, smiling at the cashier and then getting money out of her purse.

Holly looked amazed. She walked out the door and into the crowded atmosphere that surrounded her. She stared at her sweaty hands from the anxiety of getting to see her best friend once again.

"Hello? May I please get the phone number for Hope Orphanage?" asked Auntie Christa into the phone. The voice muffled numbers into her ear, making it inaudible for Holly to hear.

"Thanks," replied Auntie Christa. She quickly dialed the number onto her phone before.

"Hello?" answered a voice on the other end of the line.

"Yes, is this Hope Orphanage?" asked Auntie Christa.

"Yes," said the voice.

"May I please speak to Mrs. Somdra?" said Christa. After a while, a loud boisterous voice filled the background.

"Hello?" answered Mrs. Somdra.

"Yes, this is Christa Malone, Holly's aunt. Holly was wondering if she can come by to see Alexis today," asked Auntie Christa. Auntie Christa closed the phone silently and turned to Holly.

"She said that you could," said Auntie Christa, with a smile on her face.

"Hurray!" screamed Holly.

"Joseph, can you please take us to Hope Orphanage?" asked Christa to her driver.

"Sure," said Joseph, as he drove off from the village of Sunny Hale into the dark mountains and the vast grassy fields.

Holly stood outside the door of her old room with Jessica, the supervisor of Alexis and the girls' rooms.

"Alexis, there is someone here to see you," said Jessica.

"Who is it?" questioned Alexis.

"Somebody by the name of Holly," answered Jessica.

"Please Jessica, send her up!" cried Alexis.

"I'm already here," answered Holly.

"HOLLY!" screamed Alexis, rushing towards Holly. Alexis hugged Holly tightly. "I've missed you so much. How has your life been these past few days?"

"Absolutely...Positively...Great!" exclaimed Holly gleefully. The two girls talked for a long time about the most miraculous adventures. *I wish Auntie Christa could adopt Alexis,* Holly thought. Thirty minutes later, Holly sat in the Honda for the hour-long ride back to Sunny Hale.

Mrs. Somdra sat in the solitude of her room, going over different documents of Holly McIntyre.

"That creep!" Mrs. Somdra said shredding two papers into tiny bits and throwing them into the wastebasket. Mrs. Somdra stared gloomily at the spray-painted door, wondering how to get Holly to come back to Hope Orphanage...how to trick Holly and Ms. Malone.

"I GOT IT!" she screamed. "I FOUND OUT HOW TO GET HOLLY BACK!"

"Mrs. Somdra, is anyone in there with you?" asked Jessica.

"Nobody is here. Go away," demanded Mrs. Somdra. She carefully took Holly's parents Will and went into a small, crammed room. She grabbed the White Out and sprayed it onto the sheet of paper. Mrs. Somdra laughed maliciously as she thought how to deceive Christa. Shortly later, Mrs. Somdra sat down staring at her masterpiece.

"There," she said. She placed the folder onto her desk and quietly walking out the room, laughing at herself and how evil her plans were.

"Morning!" cried Auntie Christa, sitting down on Holly's bed and cautiously shaking Holly's shoulders.

"Mmmm," said Holly, slowly opening her eyes into the sunlight creeping in through her shades.

"We're having pancakes and cinnamon French toast for breakfast," said Auntie Christa walking towards the door and swinging her head back to look at the young girl. "Be down in fifteen minutes."

Holly stood on the polished wood floor and rubbed her feet on the soft rug that covered the bare wood. She went into the restroom to find her bathrobe. She set the bathroom on the rack and took a nice long shower. Holly went to her room and found a new shirt that Auntie Christa bought for her the other day and a pair of shorts. After putting them on, she slowly crept down to the dining room. She sat down at the table and waited for the dishes of pancakes and cinnamon French toast.

"This is really good!" she cried, taking a bite into the soft toast.

"Thanks," replied Auntie Christa, "It won the state annual fair in 1998."

"Awesome," answered Holly.

After a while, Holly and Auntie Christa received a call from Hope Orphanage.

"Maybe it is Alexis!" screamed Holly charging towards the phone.

"Maybe," replied Auntie Christa, reaching first to grab the phone. "Hello?" she asked. A murmuring.

"Who is this?" asked Auntie Christa again. During the phone call Auntie Christa nodded her head agreeing with everything the voice on the other line said.

"Mmmm," said Auntie Christa, putting the receiver down. "It was Mrs. Somdra. She wants us to come to Hope Orphanage."

"What for?" asked Holly.

"I don't know," answered Auntie Christa, putting the dirty dishes into the sink. She quickly dried her hands on the towel, walked to the garage door. Auntie Christa walked silently into the garage to grab her shoes. Auntie Christa called Joseph but realized that he was off duties on weekends. She sat in the car and patted the seat next to her motioning for Holly to sit. *Oh dear,* Holly thought, rolling down her window and sliding into the seat next to Auntie Christa.

An hour passed and Auntie Christa drove into the gates of Hope Orphanage. Holly couldn't believe that they were here again; *why had Mrs. Somdra called us to come to Hope Orphanage?* Auntie Christa found a parking spot and parked the grey Honda. She then leisurely walked into the entrance of Hope Orphanage.

"Nice to see you again!" said Mrs. Somdra, stepping out and lending a firm hand to shake. Auntie Christa took Mrs Somdra's hand and shook it gently.

"Why did you want us to come today?" asked Auntie Christa.

"Oh yes, come with me to my office," said Mrs. Somdra. Mrs. Somdra led Auntie Christa into the tiny office. Holly waited outside, looking at paintings from a long time ago. Suddenly Alexis walked by carrying a small basket of fruits.

"Alexis!" Holly cried out. Extending her arms for a hug.

"Hi Holly!" said Alexis, returning the hug.

"My aunt is here to talk to Mrs. Somdra. What are you doing?" asked Holly.

"I just went to the supermarket downtown to buy fruits for dinner tonight," replied Alexis.

"Oh, cool!" Holly said murmuring.

"Ha, ha, not really," said Alexis. "Well I gotta go give this to the cook. Talk to you later?" Alexis answered, walking towards the mess hall.

"Sure, see you!" cried Holly down the empty hall. A faint noise drew Holly to the door to listen to the conversation. Suddenly the door burst open and Auntie Christa took Holly by the hand.

"Holly isn't going to stay here anymore!" cried Auntie Christa.

"Yes she is. Didn't you see the Will?" snapped Mrs. Somdra.

"Yes I did, but my sister told me that if anything happened to her Holly would be given to me when she is eight years old," answered Auntie Christa.

"Well, apparently what she told you was wrong, because the Will mentioned that she isn't suppose to give you Holly!" Mrs. Somdra said trying to grab Holly.

"Why do you want Holly anyways?" asked Auntie Christa putting her arm around Holly and jerking Holly back.

"Because ..." Mrs. Somdra said, but she cut herself short, she didn't really think of why she wanted Holly.

"You don't even know why you want Holly? Yet still you want her?" questioned Auntie Christa.

Auntie Christa should be a lawyer! She is good at convincing and also having good comebacks, Holly thought.

"But still the Will says that Holly has to stay in Hope Orphanage," said Mrs. Somdra, raising her eyebrows.

"Let me see that!" demanded Auntie Christa grabbing the document. Auntie Christa walked over to the couch and sat down.

"You might not want to do that," said Mrs. Somdra, hiding her hands into the pockets of her pants.

"Why not?" asked Auntie Christa. "You might think that I'll find something like THIS?" she added holding up the blurred letters and the dried White Out smeared down the paper.

"Oh, that," Mrs. Somdra said. "I was hoping that you wouldn't find that," She added. Looking disgracefully at the ground.

"Well I found it. It seems you tried to trick me," said Auntie Christa inching forwards towards Mrs. Somdra.

"I...I can explain!" stuttered Mrs. Somdra. Backing up into the corner.

"This is a crime! You're going to court Mrs. Somdra," said Auntie Christa, pulling out her phone and dialing her lawyer. Once she was done she turned to Mrs. Somdra. "Be at Sunny Hale Court, ten o'clock, Saturday." added Auntie Christa.

"Holly, let's go!" Auntie Christa said in a mean tone. Dragging Holly out the door and into the car. *Why did I even come here? Wow, the two people that cared for me in my life are now fighting over me. I don't know whether to feel cared about? But on the other hand, I hope Auntie Christa will win.*

✴ ✴ ✴ ✴

Holly woke up and crept into Auntie Christa's room. She looked around and smelled the wonderful aroma that was coming out of Auntie Christa's bathroom. Her head peeked through the wooden door and into the lavender wall bathroom. She spotted Auntie Christa in a blue suit, diamond earrings, and spraying on vanilla perfume.

"Auntie Christa?" asked Holly.

"Yeah," answered Auntie Christa turning her head towards the door, and walking to unlock it.

"What should I wear today?" replied Holly.

"Whatever you want," answered Auntie Christa grinning.

"OK, thanks," Holly said, turning back towards her room.

Ten minutes passed and Holly stared down the street at two sisters who were giggling and doing cartwheels near the bench. *Oh, how I wish Alexis was here now!* She thought. Holly daydreamed as she thought of Hope Orphanage and getting rid of Mrs. Somdra and all the little girls and boys getting home. Suddenly a voice called her and brought her back to reality.

"Holly! Time to go!" said Auntie Christa, as she locked the front door and crawling into the backseat of the grey Honda.

"Coming!" Holly shouted, darting towards the car. The car took them to Sunny Hale Court first dropping by Pizza Hut for a snack. Mrs. Somdra met them at Sunny Hale Court and walked into the room without acknowledging Holly and Auntie Christa's presence. Auntie Christa sat at the front table with Holly seated next to her.

"Order!" shouted the judge, slamming her brown hammer onto the platform. Everything became silence as the hammer made a loud "BANG" when it collided with the platform. "We are here today to bring on the case of Holly McIntyre's parents Will. Will Mrs. Malone please rise to cite your story?" added the judge.

"Yes, thank you," answered Mrs. Malone. "We are called today because an incident had occurred yesterday at Hope Orphanage. Mrs. Somdra had purposely regenerated Holly's parents Will to trick us." added Mrs. Malone.

"I hope you know what you have gotten yourself into Mrs. Somdra," replied the judge, giving her the *"I am watching you"* sign.

"Mrs. Somdra please stand up!" demanded the Judge. Immediately like a dog going to his faithful owner, Mrs. Somdra stood up.

"My story is that..." Mrs. Somdra said, but then stopped. "Well. . ." she added speechless for her behavior.

"Sit back down Mrs. Somdra," shouted the Judge.

"Oh of course ma'am," said Mrs. Somdra, shuffling her feet back to her seat.

"Mrs. Somdra, you committed a crime. The child welfare department will be contacted, and go through serious discussions if they want to lay you off or keep you as headmistress of Hope Orphanage." said the Judge.

Then all of a sudden Holly burst out speaking.

"Also as a punishment, I think that Mrs. Somdra can allow no expenses into the adoption paper of Alexis," said Holly, first directing the question to the judge, then to Auntie Christa.

"Uh..." said Auntie Christa.

"I agree with the young one, we will settle this later in the afternoon, as for now case closed," said the judge slamming her hammer down onto the platform.

Holly could tell that Auntie Christa was excited about winning the case when she grabbed Holly's hand and twirled her around.

"We'll pick Alexis up tomorrow. I am really happy that we had won the case," Auntie Christa said.

After, the car drove back to Holly's new "permanent" home. *I always wanted a sister,* Holly thought. She soon drifted off into a deep sleep with thoughts about her new sister, Alexis, and also what her new life will be like calling her Auntie Christa, "Mom."

Vroom! The car zoomed to a stop in front of Hope Orphanage. Holly saw that the atmosphere was happy and all girls wore new shirts and not their plain old raggedy shirts. Alexis waited outside the colorful painted building and she sat on the staircase. When the car drove in she smiled and wave.

"Hey HOLLY!" Smiled Alexis, coming in and sitting down on the leather chair. Holly smiled back and reached over to give her new sister a hug.

"I am so glad that I can be your new sister," Alexis said enthusiastically.

"Totally, we will have the best time!" Holly said gleefully, then turning her head to the window as Alexis was singing to the radio. Holly stared at the sky and smiled, *I knew you would be here for me mom. Sorry for being a pain, and I love you so much,* she thought.

"Girls? You want to go to Pizza Hut?" asked Auntie Christa, turning her head back at the Holly and Alexis.

"Mhm!" answered Alexis.

"Yummy, yes please," replied Holly.

"Sure," replied Auntie Christa.

The next hours felt like heaven to Holly. Alexis was laughing herself silly and Holly stared at Alexis eating almost everything. *Wow,* she thought. Alexis caught Holly staring and quickly produced a silly face and then quickly turned back to eat, like a carnivore devouring his/her prey. Afterwards, Auntie Christa paid the bill and prepared for the ride back home for Alexis's and Holly's new home. Once they reached home Alexis went scavenging around the house.

"This is like a mansion!" shrieked Alexis.

"The best part is that it is OUR mansion!" screamed Holly.

"This is one of the best moments of my life," said Alexis, lying down on the grass. Her hair was fanned in different directions, her blue dress was blown by the wind, and the eyes were the deep color blue of the sky. Holly loved the feeling, and spent the whole afternoon outside, playing on the playground, riding her bike, and looking at the fields of flowers.

That night Holly stared at the ceiling. She felt like her mother was looking down on her and giving her the time of her life. Auntie Christa caught Holly staring out the window and into the stars, twinkling in the dark sky.

"Really pretty, isn't it Holly?" said Auntie Christa.

"Yea, the best thing I love about Arizona is the infinite amount of stars," answered

"Same here. Well, I'm gonna go catch some zzz's. You get a good night's rest okay?" said Auntie Christa.

"Sure," Holly answered, reaching over to her nightstand and turning off the light. Auntie Christa walked out of the room and strolled down into her bedroom.

Holly soon finally fell asleep. Her head rested on the soft, fluffy pillow. Her last thoughts were about how her life had changed for the better before she drifted off to sleep. *I love you mom! I know that you are up there and that you'll always protect me every single step that I take. I finally got a chance to say good-bye to you and I hope you can hear me when I talk to you from my thoughts. Tell dad that I miss him too, and that Auntie Christa is really neat and taking good care of me. Oh and world, get ready. Throw me whatever you want. I'm ready.* Holly thought.

Have a good life sweetie pie, popped into Holly's sleepy mind; a voice that she had heard from the past. Holly yawned and wiggled with delight. Her mother would never be far away from her, ever again.

An Unforgettable Journey

By

Meggie Wang

Cold sweat trickled down the side of Karen's brow. She felt it roll down the side of her face and then drop onto her neck. A drum beat against her chest. With every beat it felt harder to breathe, and her already shivering body shook harder. She stared into the forlorn and threatening darkness around her, desperately searching for a way out. All she saw was black. A quiet black. A frightening black. A despairing black. Karen inched backward slowly, frantically scanning the darkness for any trace of light. Her back suddenly came in contact with something cold, slimy, and distinctly solid. Startled, she turned around and let out a sigh of relief. It was only a deteriorating wall that had been overwhelmed by the growth of moss.

Still too apprehensive to move, Karen sank down into a sitting position and brought her knees to her chest in an effort to suppress her rapid breathing. Sweat soaked her clothes and made her shirt stick to her back. Karen had no idea why she was so scared. The only thing she knew was that she had to find a way out. Then Karen froze. A sudden tremor of disturbance streaked the air. Something moved.

Karen listened attentively, holding her breath in anticipation. She identified it as the sound of footsteps. They were barely audible at first but grew steadily louder and started to echo. The footsteps then increased in intensity to a volume that forced Karen to cup her hands over her ears so that the sound wouldn't burst her eardrums. The intense sound became part of her own head. Every heavy step radiated in her ears and shook her brain. It rattled her bones. It rocked her very world.

Karen opened her eyes and jerked up into a sitting position. She looked anxiously around, still expecting to see the darkness and the moss on the wall. Her breaths came rapidly, and the dream kept flashing back into her mind. Half asleep, the sound of footsteps still echoed fervently in her head. A familiar sight greeted her eyes. She was in her bed. Karen's pajamas, bed, and pillow were sopping wet from sweat. Her long, black hair stuck to her face. To Karen's right stood her half-open closet. Around it lay a chaotic mess of Karen's clothes, stuffed toys, and other articles. Farther right were her desk and a digital clock, which read 5:58 AM. Sunday morning had arrived.

Karen rose from bed and looked out her bedroom window. The small, tranquil city of Freemont, California, awoke to another weekend morning. The rising sun streaked the sky with brilliant shades of orange and pink. She marveled at the dazzling colors, but her thoughts quickly drifted back to her nightmare. Such dreams had haunted Karen for the last fourteen years of her life, and she had no clue why. Every time the dream always depicted a dark corridor and her running for her life, and the dream increased in detail and intensity as she grew older. She got used to it eventually, but the fact that it kept coming back mystified her. Seeing no point in going back to sleep again, she headed to the bathroom to take a shower.

Karen stared into the mirror. A tall, thin girl stared back. Karen studied her reflection. She had a fair-looking, egg-shaped face consisting of big, bright brown eyes, a relatively skinny nose, and a small mouth with thick lips that ended in a flat chin. Her skin was very tanned, and her long, black hair draped down past her shoulders.

"Hey, Karen, you seem sleepy. Did you have one of those dreams again?" Megan greeted Karen. Megan was Karen's best friend. They had been next-door neighbors since they were in preschool and had always been in the same school ever since. Karen thought Megan was a very trustworthy and reliable friend, and she always visited Megan when she had something on her mind or when she had a nightmare. Karen had decided to visit Megan because of the dream.

"Yeah, stupid dream woke me up at six this morning," Karen grumbled.

"Oh really? Tell me about it." Megan reached for a pencil and her special notepad. Megan always used a notepad designed just for recording Karen's dreams.

Karen thought that, in a way, this was kind of embarrassing. But on the other hand, she was glad someone was listening to her talk about her dreams and what she thought about them. Karen described in detail what she had encountered in the dream, how she felt, and what she thought was happening. Megan listened intently and furiously and scribbled words onto her notepad. Once Karen finished, Megan set the notebook down and turned to her laptop.

"I've actually been doing some research on this in my spare time," Megan explained. "And I have come to a very bizarre but still plausible conclusion."

"Let me hear it." Karen walked away from Megan's desk and sank into a beanbag cushion next to her bed.

"This will sound weird, but I think you are a descendant of an ancient Egyptian king named Ahmose," Megan speculated. "I just read it right here."

"What? How can that be possible?" Karen rose to join Megan and read the website over her friend's shoulder. "I may be Egyptian, but how likely is it that an Egyptian king was my ancestor?"

"See?" Megan pointed a finger at the screen and started following along a passage. "I can't believe it! It was all over the news, and you didn't see it?"

"Remember Megan? Our television set broke down yesterday! I'm plan to get a new TV this week," Karen said with annoyance.

"Right," Megan said flatly. "Anyway, read this part."

Karen read the section Megan pointed out to her. "No way," she said. "This is definitely not true." Karen frowned. "How do you know if what this is saying is even right?"

"I'm sure," Megan insisted. "This research was carried out by top archaeologists from the Universities of Cambridge, Yale, and Stanford."

"Okay, but that still doesn't explain why I am a descendant of this King."

"Well it has to be someone, so why not you?" Megan disputed. "The passage indicates that a curse was sealed in Ahmose's generation but will be unleashed again every 3570 years, which means right about this time period. Besides, you *are* part Egyptian."

"Alright, just suppose I *am* the descendant of this Egyptian king. Tell me more about the curse." Karen sank back into the beanbag.

"OK, get yourself comfortable. I'm going to begin," Megan said as she sat back in her chair.

"In the year 1562 B.C., in other words about 3500 years ago, there lived a young king by the name of Ahmose. At this year he was sixteen years old, and he had just become a king in his own right.

"Ahmose was a very ambitious king. After he drove the Hyksos people out of Egypt, he spent most of his reign looking for a method to live forever. He feared death very much and strived hard to find a way to live forever before his death. Hold on, the next part is irrelevant. Let me find the part where it talks about his death..." Megan straightened up in her chair, brought her face right in front of her laptop screen, and squinted her eyes in effort to read the small text.

"Got it! Okay, listen to this," Megan said abruptly after a few moments. "We're now at the part where King Ahmose is thirty-five years old.

"That year, the Hyksos people tried to regain their control over Egypt. An epic war broke out, in which King Ahmose was fatally struck. Even though he knew he would die, he denied death. Anubis, the god of the underworld, tried to retrieve Ahmose's soul. Anubis struggled for nine days to gain Ahmose's soul without success. After that, Ahmose's soul was in such a complicated state that he was neither dead nor alive but hovered between two different worlds.

"Ahmose's soul was so unstable that Anubis was no longer able to send Ahmose back to the mortal world, nor was he able to pull Ahmose further into the world of the dead. Anubis soon came to the conclusion that he could only keep Ahmose in his current state and put a seal on him, so he won't cause trouble. He put a seal on Ahmose that will last 3500 years. Once the seal breaks, Ahmose's spirit will be set free. He will repossess his body and hunt down his youngest descendant, which is probably you, Karen. His spirit will also have formidable supernatural powers. He can manipulate all the destructive natural forces and change the weather to his liking. If he succeeds in finding you, Karen, he will switch places with you. You will be sent to the world of the dead, and he will achieve immortality. Once this happens, Ahmose will have virtually unlimited power to rule and change the world as we know it."

Megan finished and swiveled around in her chair to look at Karen. An awkward silence hung in the air as this all sank in. Karen was going to be captured and then sacrificed to let someone else bring forth doomsday? That wasn't possible.

"I don't believe it," Karen finally said.

"What?" Megan appeared a little startled when Karen suddenly challenged her theory.

"I don't believe it!"

"How come?"

"Because this can't be me. I'm not the only one that's Egyptian around here. You've probably got the wrong person."

"How do you know it's not you?"

"How do you know it *is* me?"

"You are having those weird dreams. Didn't you say you thought something was after you? Couldn't it be King Ahmose?"

"No way! Even *if* I am Egyptian and I *do* have those weird dreams, what are the odds that I am actually The One?"

"Alright, for now let's just say you aren't. The archaeologists are trying to trace down Ahmose's family line, and they have gotten pretty far according to this article. More information on that is going to be released next week. For now, let's just wait for the information to come out and, in the mean time, try to see what your dreams are trying to say."

Megan rose out of her chair and, seeing her do so, Karen pushed up from her bean bag and brought herself to a standing position.

"Hopefully it's not me," Karen whispered as her eyes met Megan's.

"Yeah, hopefully," Megan whispered back.

Sensing that their discussion had come to an end this time, Karen headed out of Megan's room, went downstairs, and left the house. The fresh morning air greeted her, along with the fragrance of blooming flowers and the melody of birds singing. She decided to start on her way home when suddenly her thoughts were interrupted by a cold, wet droplet plopping onto her neck. It rained. Karen broke into a sprint. She was lucky to have long legs that were able to carry her quickly to wherever she wanted to go. Within moments, she reached her front porch, unlocked the door to her house, and stepped over the threshold. She ascended the stairs in her house and trudged right into her bedroom. She threw herself onto her bed and pondered over what just had happened in Megan's house.

What if I was the direct descendant of King Ahmose? Karen thought. *I would have to travel to Egypt, or even around the world, hunting down a spirit that could possess anybody. I'd have to destroy the curse and save the world. But I still think this sounds too much like what would happen in a movie. I need to get real. What are the odds of that happening to me? This is fake, right? Right?*

RIGHT?

Karen ran. She didn't know what she ran from. All she knew was that she had to keep running. Her legs worked to the breaking point, but she continued to push, knowing that the farther away she got from where she was, the better. Her breaths came in rapid and short intervals. Her long black hair was already drenched with sweat as it swished back and forth in rhythm to her running.

Suddenly, Karen felt one of her feet hit something. From the total abruptness of it all, she stumbled over and fell onto her stomach. The impact knocked all the air out of her, rendering her breathless. Completely terrified, she scrambled up into a sitting position and struggled to catch her breath. She then realized that she was sitting out in the open, so she leaped upright and backed up to try and find something solid. Around her, it was pitch black. There was no sign of life; neither was there any trace of an exit. She managed to find a wall to rest against, which at least brought a little comfort, but not enough to subdue her rapid breaths and her pounding heart.

Karen heard something. Her instinct told her something was wrong. Then she heard footsteps. Someone walked down the hallway and treaded her way steadily. Karen went rigid, knowing that she could do nothing. Terror immobilized her with fearful anticipation. All she could do was stay put and wait for the inevitable to happen.

"Karen! You're already late for school! Get out of bed!" A voice rang right in her ear. Startled, Karen sat straight up and opened her eyes. Her mother stood at the side of her bed. Karen was still half asleep, and blurry visions of the dream she just had flashed back and forth into her head.

"No, he's coming for me!"

"Karen! What are you talking about? YOU ARE LATE FOR SCHOOL! Are you still oblivious to the fact that you are in ninth grade?" Her mother pulled the curtains apart.

A sheath of blinding light flooded into her whole room and pierced Karen's eyes. Karen had to hold her arm over her face to avoid getting her eyes burned right out of their sockets.

"No! Stop it! I need to run!" Karen suddenly got hit with a frantic realization that she was still supposed to run.

"Karen, what is wrong?" Her mother's tone of anger suddenly changed to worry as she saw Karen in her chaotic state.

"I need to get away!" Karen leaped up, stood on her bed, and scanned the whole room, panic-struck. Her breaths came rapidly again against her will.

"Karen, it's okay; I'm here." Her mother gently took Karen's arm, helped her down, and embraced her in a hug.

Karen felt a warmness rise up in her. Everything felt okay again, even though she was in the middle of a chaotic moment. Nerves calmed, she hugged her mother back and held on tight.

"Thanks, Mom." Karen said when she finally had enough and let go.

"Karen, what was happening?" Her mom asked. With a concerned look on her face, she brushed back hair that had fallen on Karen's face.

"I'm not sure, actually. I just knew I have to run from somebody," Karen said, confused.

"It's okay Karen, nobody is chasing you. You're safe. Now you're late for school, young lady. You'd better get going. It's already 9:00 AM." Karen's mother hurried her.

"I'm sorry, Mom. I didn't get to sleep until late last night," Karen apologized. She had to get to school quickly.

"What do you mean? You went to bed last night at 9:00 PM. Do you need an earlier bedtime?"

"No Mom, I won't do this again, promise," Karen mumbled. She grabbed her backpack, slung it over her shoulders, and headed downstairs to leave the house. After she stepped out of the house, she heard her mom trying to call her back.

"Karen, hold on a moment! You haven't even eaten yet! You know breakfast is the most important meal of the day. You . . ."

That was the last she heard from her mother as she slammed the front door shut and ran to school. It was way too late to eat breakfast. She really needed to get to school. Not being at a few classes can potentially mean a lot of instructions missed. She ran.

Blinding flashes greeted her eyes as Karen entered her school building.

"It's her! It's her! It's Karen Shamenhak! She's here!" Karen heard someone shout out loud. She heard the scattered voices of people conversing excitedly. Karen was temporarily unable to see due to the fact that she was welcomed with millions of flashes. This puzzled Karen, because she had no idea why so many people looked for her, needless to mention give her a grand salutation as she entered school. What was with this whole thing? Is it a school prank on her because she came in late?

"So Miss Shamenhak, how does it feel to be The One?" A person rushed out of the crowd and held a microphone up to her mouth.

"What? What is "The One?" I don't know what you're talking about." Karen was confused.

As her vision recovered, she realized that those flashes were camera flashes. There were reporters from all kinds of news channels she recognized, and all of them jostled to get to her and stick out their microphones to her mouth.

Okay, this definitely wasn't a school prank.

"What do you mean you don't know? It was all over the news this morning! How could you have missed it?" A reporter yelled out to her.

"I seriously have no idea what you are talking about. Why are you all crowded in front of me? What's so important about me that you want to know?" Karen was now thoroughly perplexed.

"You really don't know? Alright young lady, here's the news: you are the direct descendant of King Ahmose the First, and you are the very person that will save Earth from the end of the world," the reporter stated.

Karen's heart missed a beat. This was impossible. This was *definitely* impossible. What Megan had told her about the whole 'saving the world from doomsday' thing couldn't be true.

"What? That can't be me. You've got the wrong person," Karen said firmly. She trudged back to the entrance of the school and exited. After this had happened, the last thing she wanted to do was stay in school with all the nosy reporters.

"Wait! Miss Shamenhak, we have questions for you..." The reporters behind her all chirruped. Karen ignored them and made a hurried exit out of the school. Camera shutters clicked behind her.

Despite the fact that she had run to school and was already out of breath, Karen sprinted all the way home. She tore open the door to her house and charged upstairs into her room, where she collapsed onto her bed. Her house was empty. Her parents had already gone to work, leaving the whole house in complete silence, except for the air conditioning that hummed softly.

This is all fake, She thought. *What I just saw at school is all fake. I'm just dreaming, and I'll wake up soon. Now WAKE UP!* Karen yelled at herself in her head and tried to focus on 'waking up' without success. After a while, her head throbbed and she was very fatigued. She noticed that she was nodding off...

✶ ✶ ✶ ✶

Continuous knocking awakened Karen. She sat up abruptly and glanced at her digital clock. It read 3:48 PM. She had been sleeping for about six hours.

While she marveled at the time that she had managed to sleep, Karen realized that someone had knocked on the front door to her house. She hurriedly tried to straighten her long, black hair that was tangled in chaotic bundles. She didn't want to appear shabby in case the prying reporters have come to her house. She rushed downstairs and to her rattling front door. Karen took a deep breath and allowed herself some mental preparation to face a whole crowd of reporters—if there really was a whole bunch of them at her door. Then, she whipped open the door.

It was Megan...but not only Megan. Just as Karen had expected, there was a huge crowd of reporters right behind Megan. The moment Karen opened the door the reporters started swarming with questions. Megan squeezed through the crowd, bolted in, and shoved the door close right in their faces. The door rattled as the reporters knocked frantically at it and Karen could hear yelling that got muffled by the door.

"Oh my gosh, Karen, are you okay? You skipped school today because of those reporters." Megan was panting and her hair was slightly messy. She looked truly concerned.

"Yeah, I'm okay." Karen was still startled from the reporters that had managed to gather around her house. "I just thought it was kinda weird, because I just slept from the time I got back home until just now, when you knocked."

"Wow." Megan raised her eyebrows. "Well, did you have any, you know, dreams?"

"Amazingly, no."

"Oh, well how do you feel?"

"Megan, tell me, am I really this descendant of an Egyptian King? Do I have to save the world from destruction?"

There was a long pause of silence in which Megan seemed uneasy.

"Unfortunately, yes," She said after a silence that seemed to last a century.

"How do they know it is definitely me?" Karen remained in disbelief.

"Karen, give it up. The archaeologists have substantial evidence that you truly are The One."

"I'm not ready to do this. Why me?"

"At times things just develop they way people don't expect them to. You are The One, which means you will have to save all of us."

"I can't save the world. I'm only a teenager, and I'm not doing a good job at being one either. I really shouldn't..." the sound of the front door opening cut off Karen's words. In stormed both of her parents who struggled to close the door in effort to keep reporters out. As her father finally locked the door to ensure nobody was able to barge in, he heard him whispering under his breath.

"Boy, these reporters are like vampires."

"Karen! I hurried back as soon as I could!" Her mother shouted, imminently out of breath. She ran over to Karen and embraced her with one of her motherly hugs. "Are you feeling all right? I heard you skipped school because of all of these reporters. I know what's happening."

"I'm fine," Karen managed to say flatly.

"You sure?" Her father interjected as he put his hand on her shoulders. Karen noticed the look in his eye showed extreme concern.

"Yeah," Karen said with a shrug and a smile, in effort to calm her parents down.

"My goodness, honey, you look tired," Karen's mother said.

"Maybe you should get some rest," her father added.

"Mom, Dad, it's okay. I've been doing nothing but sleeping this afternoon." Karen tried to maintain a casual mood to soothe her parents' nerves.

"Yeah, go ahead and ignore me. I'll be fine," Megan interrupted. Everybody abruptly looked in Megan's direction. She was standing off to one side with her arms folded and displayed a disgruntled attitude. Karen laughed; she knew Megan was joking around.

"Well hello, Megan. I'm sorry. " Karen's father stepped over and finally acknowledged Megan's presence. "I'm sure we all have a lot to talk about. Why don't we all calm down for now, sit down, and discuss this properly?" He motioned for everybody to sit down on the couches in the living room. Megan, Karen, her mother, and her father all took a seat.

"So, what's happening so far for you guys?" Her mother decided to start the discussion.

"I went to school and saw a million reporters taking pictures of me and trying to interview me. It was too much for me to bear with at the time, so I ran back home and realized I was tired. Then I fell asleep until just a few moments ago when Megan rang the doorbell and woke me up. Soon after, you two came sprinting in," Karen narrated her side of the story.

"I was in school this morning when I walked in and saw a bunch of reporters clustered at the door. I asked some of my friends for what was happening, and the reporters all told me they were looking for Karen. For a moment I was dazzled. I wondered why the reporters sought Karen, but then I realized that these few days it had been all over the news that they were searching for a descendant to the Egyptian King Ahmose. It was probably determined that Karen was The One," Megan said. "I was really worrying about how Karen would be overwhelmed by the reporters, so I tried calling her on her cellphone. Unfortunately, her phone was off. I tried calling her home number, but it told me it wasn't an available number. I assumed that her family had already received numerous phone calls from presses and the news, and had unplugged the phone to prevent it from ringing constantly. The only thing I could do was stand by the door so that once she came in I can help her past all the reporters. She never came, and eventually I had to go to class. At about 9:30 AM, I heard a bubbling of voices at the entrance to the school. I darted out of my classroom and took a look. Indeed, there was Karen, being overwhelmed by the mass of reporters. I tried getting through the crowd to Karen, but she was back out of the door before I had time to reach her. Afterwards, I worried about her during the whole school day. I could barely hear anything. I was thinking of what was happening to her. Then once school ended, I rushed her as quickly as possible," Megan finished.

"Indeed, I did get a lot of phone calls from reporters this morning. I just ignored them, because from watching the news these days, I know they're up to no good. I unplugged the phone because it practically wouldn't stop ringing. I thought was really strange, but I guess I was too sleepy this morning to think much of it," her mother said with a sheepish grin.

"Seems like you two went through a lot," Karen's father said. "We both apologize for not getting home earlier and leaving you home alone, Karen."

"Oh my goodness! I almost forgot!" Megan stood up abruptly. "I have a guest at my house, and she wants to see you! Come on over, Karen. We'll make it through the reporters, somehow.

Megan walked over to the door and rested her hand on the knob, ready to fling it open.

"You ready?" Megan asked.

Karen nodded.

"OK, on the count of three, we burst through and charge." Megan tightened her grip on the doorknob.

"One, two, THREE!" The door whisked open, revealing a gigantic crowd. Karen charged through and pushed away every single microphone, camera, and reporter she saw. When she looked back, she saw Megan following right after. She pushed hard, and almost knocked over a cameraman. When she finally cleared out of the crowd, she broke into a sprint to hurry to Megan's house. She heard the voices of yelling reporters echo behind her. A second pair of running footsteps behind her told her that Megan had managed to catch on and follow her. They ran all the way to Megan's house, where Megan quickly unlocked the door. She whipped it open, shoved Karen in, followed right after, and slammed it shut.

"Hello Ms. Shamenhak, it is an honor to meet you. I'm agent Lee, but you can just call me Alicia," A tall, skinny woman greeted her, "and this is Aiden." She pointed out a man next to her, who nodded in approval. Aiden wore a suit, and he had a tall and skinny form, just like Alicia.

"We know that you are The One, and we have been sent by the National Operative Squad: Elite Subdivision, or NOSES, to assist you," Alicia continued.

"NOSES? What kind of name is that?" Karen let out a snicker.

"We have received responses like that and it is totally understandable. However Ms. Shamenhak, we are here for business, not be laughed at.

We are completely serious when we say we want to help," Alicia said irritably.

"Thanks for the help, but I'm not even sure if I can even do this. Furthermore, I don't even know what I'm supposed to do," Karen said with a frown on her face.

"That's what we're here for. We have support from the archaeologists, who are specialists on the case," Alicia said.

"So, what kind of plan do you have in mind for me?" Karen said quizzically.

"Archaeologists have confirmed a location in Egypt where the tomb of King Ahmose the first lies. We are going to fly over there and do some further investigation," Alicia declared.

"And when do you plan to do this?" Karen interrogated.

"We have a private jet scheduled to take flight tomorrow afternoon," Alicia answered.

"Huh? What about school?" Karen was puzzled.

"You're saving the world now. Why do you even worry about school?" Alicia seemed baffled at Karen's oblivion to the subject.

"Okay, but I still need time to get over this. Besides, I need to ask my parents and see if they approve." Karen didn't want to be irresponsible. After all, she still cared about her parents.

"That's no problem with us. Just get everything worked out by tomorrow morning. We're going to pay you a visit at 10:00 AM and we will be expecting answers," Alicia said firmly.

"Alright, I'll do that. See you tomorrow." Karen said goodbye to Megan and then left her house.

Karen stepped out into the night air. There crickets chirped, and it was much cooler now that the sun was down. She hurried back home.

When she went back and went in the door, she saw her parents setting the table for dinner.

"It's almost time for dinner," Her father said.

Karen decided to tell her parents about what had happened while eating dinner.

"WHAT?" Her dad's mouth fell open. The turkey that he just chewed on fell out.

"If you think this is an idea of a practical joke, it isn't," Karen said seriously, "I really have to fly to Egypt and do whatever else necessary to save the world."

"Are you sure you don't have a fever?" Her mother reached over and felt Karen's forehead. Karen brushed her mother's hand away.

"No, I'm fine," she insisted, "I just need your approval to let me go on this journey."

"How long...do you think this will take?" Her mother still had a hint of disbelief in her voice.

"Mom, I'm not sure, but I don't think it will be short." Karen tried to answer the question as accurately as possible.

"What exactly are you going to do?"

"I'm going to fly to Egypt and try to find the tomb of this King that is my ancestor. I don't know the details yet."

"Honey, you can't just leave your life here behind! You have to go to school and do your chores..." She looked to Karen's dad for help, but he was already beyond words.

"I'm afraid that will have to wait, Mom. I have to save the world from destruction." Karen cut in.

A long of pause of silence followed. No one talked. The awkwardness level rose until the air itself seemed frozen. Finally, her mother let out and nervous chuckle and broke the silence.

"Honey, I'm not going to let you do such a thing. I don't even know who these agents are. What if they are trying to kidnap you?"

"Come on Mom, they are from a special organization. They mean real business and definitely won't kidnap me."

"Karen, how would you know? You are too young to see danger in everything."

Defeated, Karen left the table. She had no intention of eating anymore. She rushed upstairs into her room. Her room was in a complete state of disorder. Her closet was mostly empty, and had doors that were wide open. Most of her clothes had been tossed around various parts of her bedroom. Her desk was even more chaotic than her room. Homework sheets from days, even weeks ago were tossed all around the surface of her desk. Karen's room seemed like a third World War had broken out in it, but she didn't care. She pushed all of the unwanted articles off her bed and fell onto it with her face in her pillow. She didn't want this to happen to her. Why her? Why not someone else? Why a teenager that has a lot of problems and is not doing a good job being a teenager? Why not a person with a perfect life? Why does it have to be Karen Elisabeth Shamenhak?

Darkness. Very silent darkness. It horrified Karen. The darkness seemed to surround her and swallow her up. She was trapped in nothingness. Karen tried to run away from it, but her efforts were futile because all she ended up with was more darkness. A sound came from all the way down the hallway. She froze, trying to catch every bit of that nearly inaudible sound into her ears.

Footsteps. They were gradually getting louder. At first it only tapped softly, but after a while it turned so loud and heavy it seemed as if the world was shaking to each step. A pain in Karen's ears forced her to immediately bring her hands up to her ears and cup them. She closed her eyes in fear that she will be frightened to death if she kept them open. A sudden howl of maniacal laughter pierced the air. Alarmed, Karen opened her eyes to see two glowing red eyes staring right back.

Karen opened her eyes. She saw the blank white of her room's ceiling. It was a dream. Sitting up, she saw her room and desk. She chose once again to ignore the messy state her room was in, she looked at her digital clock. It read 9:37 AM. That was when Karen realized that in approximately twenty minutes agents would visit her. She leaped from bed and rummaged through her disorganized closet and dresser, somehow managed to find decent clothes, and darted into the bathroom to approach her daily war with her tousled hair. Twenty minutes later she emerged wearing a pair of new jeans and her best shirt. Immediately, she threw her dirty clothes back into her closet, shut the door before everything collapsed, and zoomed downstairs. She barely managed to finish breakfast in time to answer a nerve-jarring knock on her front door.

"Hello Miss Shamenhak, I hope you had a good night's sleep," Alicia said warmly.

"Hi Alicia," Karen responded. "You can call me Karen."

"I brought someone along with me too," Alicia continued. She stepped aside to reveal someone familiar.

"Megan!" Karen's heart burst with joy as she realized that her friend had also come to visit her.

"Hi Karen!" Megan said with a grin on her face. "So, what did your parents say?"

"They said no," Karen said slowly with her head hung low.

"Oh," Megan showed very obvious disappointment.

"I really want to go, though..." Karen was cut off by Megan.

"Oh! I know! What if you sneak out?" Megan suggested. "I was planning to do so anyway. I want to go with you."

"I don't think that's a good idea. I can get into serious trouble, and what about your life? You need to go to school!" Karen disregarded the idea.

"Who cares about school? Why should I go to school while my best friend is on the other side of the world risking her life to save the earth from doomsday? It is only the right thing to do for me to come along." Megan said this as if it was plain logic. "Besides, I already spent a whole hour formulating my escape plan. You're not going to let my effort go to waste, are you? You can just use the same escape plan as mine. Also, Alicia can probably help you escape since she's going to help me. Right, Alicia?" She looked to Alicia for help.

"Yes, we were expecting such a reply from your parents and have already come up with an escape plan for you. If you truly want to go and you must do so, I will support your decision," Alicia stated simply.

"I'm still not sure. I don't like the feeling of disobeying my parents," Karen said.

"Come on Karen, I am going to do that to go with you. It's all right. Alicia and I will give you support. Besides, if you don't go, who else could save the world?" Megan tried very hard to convince Karen.

"Okay," Karen sighed. "I'll sneak out and go with you," she said hesitantly.

"Okay then, let's get down to business." Alicia put on a serious tone. "We have a lot to discuss."

"So." Karen sensed Alicia's solemn manner. "Where do we start?"

"Let's start with basics," Alicia said. "Do you know why you are called 'The One' and the story behind it?"

"Yes, I think that's already covered." Karen remembered the story Megan told her just a few days ago.

"Good." Alicia appeared slightly relieved. "Just so you know what you're here for. Next, do you know what you specifically need to do to stop your ancestor?"

"No," Karen replied.

"Okay, I shall explain then." Alicia took a seat on a nearby couch. Karen did the same.

"As far as the archaeologists have gotten, they propose you have to read a scripture in ancient Egyptian and perform a ritual at the right place and right time to reseal the curse. It is probably written in hieroglyphics, but that isn't something you have to worry about because we're going to bring along skilled translators. The archaeologists have already determined that you must do this in the Temple of Abu Simbel at 8:00 PM on this Friday. The problem is that we need you there and ready to perform the ritual."

"So this is why we're going to Egypt?" Karen said after considering what Alicia just said.

"Yes, we need you there to complete the final step," Alicia proposed. "We will tell you everything you need to do, so all you have to do is listen and follow along. We're going to sneak you out in the middle of the night, so please prepare yourself."

"Alright," Karen sighed. She bounded up the stairs to her room, pulled out her personal suitcase from on top of her closet, and began packing.

Karen was awaked to the sound of tapping on her window. She immediately sprang out of bed. Her clock read 1:00 AM. She hadn't managed to fall asleep because of her restless nerves. Strangely enough, she didn't feel tired either. She rushed over to her bedroom window and opened it.

"Hi, Karen," a familiar voice whispered.

Karen immediately recognized the person at her window to be Megan.

"Hi, Megan," Karen whispered back.

"Alright, now give me your stuff. Make sure you be quiet." Megan whispered instructions to Karen. Karen tried to hurry and get her suitcase and give it to Megan while remaining as quiet as possible. Megan passed down the suitcase to somebody below her. Apparently she wasn't alone.

"Karen, come on and climb down this ladder. Hurry!" Megan whispered frantically. Her head disappeared from the window side. Karen looked out the window and downwards. Megan was climbing down a ladder that was propped up against the side of the house. On the ground were Aiden and a couple of other men dressed in suits. Karen cautiously climbed down the ladder. The men quickly grabbed the ladder and motioned for Karen and Megan to follow them. They led her to the driveway in front of her house and retreated into a van. Everybody hopped into the van, and Aiden started the engine. Off they went. Karen successfully escaped.

The van kept driving for about an hour or so, until they finally stopped at a large building. Karen noticed a gigantic sign containing the letters *NOSES* in bold, bright right font at the entrance. Aiden led them into the building and through some elaborate hallways until they met with Alicia again.

"Hello, Karen and Megan. How are you guys feeling? Sleepy?" Alicia greeted the girls.

"A bit," Karen and Megan answered at the same time. They exchanged glances and giggled at the fact that they had managed to say the same thing, in the same tone, at the same time.

"Well, good to know you two are both happy campers." Alicia smiled for a brief moment. Her expression immediately turned serious again. "We have a small plane scheduled for you guys. It's right outside. Let's get moving. There isn't much time for us to waste."

"Okay," Karen said with a yawn. She decided that she would have to sleep on the plane.

Karen took a step out into the dry, hot world of Egypt. The heat in the air made Karen break into a sweat instantaneously. She noticed that there wasn't a bit of wind; not even a faint breeze. From her plane, she was escorted to the exit of the airport in Cairo, where she met a group of archaeologists, guides, and translators. They all greeted her warmly and maintained a friendly manner as they were talking to her. All of them spoke perfect English, and Karen found it quite a pleasure to talk to them. Karen found out that the archaeologist that was leading the group was called Seb. As she further conversed with him, she found out that he knew how to speak both English and Egyptian fluently, and he knew how to interpret hieroglyphics.

Karen and Megan were ushered into an immense jeep covered with dirt. They sat in the back row, and were shortly joined by Seb.

"Alright, Miss Shamenhak, we need to tell you our plan," he said.

"Please, call me Karen," Karen was started to get annoyed at the fact that everybody kept calling her 'Miss Shamenhak' wherever she went.

"Okay, Karen," Seb appeared delighted to be allowed to address Karen by her first name. "Right now, we're going to drive you to a hotel, where you will be spending the night. Tomorrow morning we will wake you up at 8:00 AM, let you have breakfast, and then start driving to the village of Gize, where you will have to perform your ritual tomorrow night at the temple of Abu Simbel."

Karen nodded her approval to Seb's plan. Then she turned to Megan.

"This is all happening pretty quickly, you know," she started. "Just a few days ago, I was living a normal teenage life in Freemont, California. Now I am known all across the world as The One that will save the Earth from doomsday."

"Yes, it's quite overwhelming if you just think about it," Megan agreed. "Are you nervous about this whole thing? I mean, it's kind of a hit or miss situation. If you miss, the whole world is in jeopardy."

"Duh, I'm nervous." Karen made a face. "I don't know if everything will turn out fine."

"Don't worry about it Karen, you should do okay."

"Easy for you to say. You're not the one that has to undergo all the shock of realizing you're The One, and then go forth and save the world. I don't even know if I'm ready to do all this tomorrow."

"It's okay Karen, nobody ever has to be ready." Megan said with a dreamy expression on her face. Karen was distinctly reminded of the last time Megan had said that, when they were still in America. Megan wore the exact same far-fetched expression she had before. It baffled Karen. Especially those eyes. Her eyes appeared to be staring into the distance at nothing in particular, and they seemed oblivious and forlorn, almost teary.

"We have arrived!" A piercing voice shattered Karen's thoughts. Seb opened the car door and motioned for the two girls to get out.

"We have a room for you already. Here's the key. It's not that hard to get around this hotel, once you're used to it. I'm going to leave you to Aiden and Alicia now. Well, if there are no further questions, comments, or objections, I will be seeing you tomorrow." Seb casually waved goodbye to them and stepped back onto the jeep. It drove off into the distance. Alicia and Aiden then brought Karen and Megan to their room.

"Okay girls, it's not early anymore and you should be getting some rest," Alicia said gently. "We'll see you tomorrow. Don't sleep too late."

"Alright, Alicia." Karen said as she smirked to Megan. The two of them knew very well it was impossible for them to not stay up late.

"Good morning Karen!" Seb greeted her. "Did you sleep well?"

"Yes, I slept fine," Karen exchanged glances with Megan and smiled. She had been up until 3:00 AM last night with Megan, worrying over and over again about saving the world.

"Good, we are going to drive to the village of Gize. It's going to take approximately five hours to get there, so you should prepare yourselves," Alicia mentioned.

"Oh, okay." Karen said with another grin as she realized she probably would be sleeping the whole way, since she only got six hours of sleep the previous night.

"The jeeps and local authorities will be here soon," Aiden announced after hanging up on his cellphone.

"All right! Karen and Megan, make sure you have everything, because we're not coming back to this hotel," Alicia warned. At that moment, a large, black land-rover pulled up in front of them, along with a few police cars that were flashing shades of blue and red lights. Out of the driver's door came out a burly-looking man, wearing a suit.

Everyone climbed on to the land rover, which appeared to be very spacious. Other than six seats, the car also contained a big built-in monitor that was capable of going online, playing movies, get access to local cable TV, and also playing video games. There was so much space in there that Karen thought that even if five more people had to sit in the land-rover, there would be no problem with space. The moment the land rover entered the highway Karen nodded off.

Karen heard footsteps. They were very silent at first; barely audible. After a while, the footsteps got louder and assured Karen that it hadn't just been her imagination. Then they got so loud that each step boomed into her ears. Then she saw and heard it all: the glowing, red eyes, the evil laughter . . .

"Karen! Are you OK?" Megan was shaking her violently.

"Huh? What?" Karen was still partially dazed from her dream. As her vision cleared up, she saw Megan and Alicia staring right at her.

"You were talking in your sleep. You were saying things like 'No! No! Don't come closer!' and you were breathing really uneasily. Look at how much you have sweated!" Megan pointed out everything to her.

"Are you feeling sick, Karen?" Alicia frowned as she held her hand up to Karen's forehead.

"I'm fine." Karen brushed off Alicia's hand.

"Did you have one of those dreams again?" Megan wondered.

"Yeah,"

"Oh, what was it about?"

"I heard footsteps again, except I saw glowing, red eyes and I heard evil laughter."

"Wow, I think your dreams are getting more clear now that you are even closer to judgement time and all."

"Probably."

"What dreams are you two talking about?" Alicia suddenly said.

"Oh Alicia, sorry for excluding you." Megan seemed a bit surprised. "Karen's been getting strange nightmares about a dark corridor since she could remember."

"Oh really?" Alicia seemed interested. "Have they been getting more detailed?"

"Yes, most definitely." Karen nodded.

"Well, that's probably because now it's closer to the time where you will actually face your destiny and battle for the world. Karen, do you think you're ready for the task?"

"I think so," Karen simply said.

"If you don't feel confident, just remember this is a simple process. We will all be here to help you with it too. Once you get through it, you will save the world. You can do it. I know you can," Alicia said firmly.

"Thank you, Alicia." Karen felt a bit better.

"Okay, we're there. I see the temple." Megan opened the door of the Jeep then jumped out. Karen followed her out. The dry Egyptian air made its presence known again. All Karen could feel was dry. At least this time, a breeze blew by. Karen's long, black hair flittered in her face.

"Karen, we're going to enter the temple of Abu Simbel and get you ready for your ritual. Karen, remember. Don't get nervous. You will do fine." Alicia directed the girls toward a massive structure that towered over them. The temple looked very impressive. Four sitting Egyptian gods carved into stone were at the entrance. Karen entered the temple; the sights that appeared to her were even more grand. Hieroglyphics and drawing, portraying the Egyptian gods, kings, and many other holy symbols covered the wall of the temple.

She was brought into an inner area of the temple. Plenty of archaeologists hurried around and about the area, apparently preparing something. Karen could see numerous candles that had been placed around the location. If she wasn't mistaken, this is probably the place where she is going to perform her ritual. She glanced at her clock. It read 4:57 PM. She had about three hours until her time for judgment came.

"Karen, everything is prepared. I just have to tell you what to do," Seb said importantly.

"King Ahmose the first is going to awaken at approximately 8:00 PM. At that time, he is going to hurry over here, because he will still be a mummy and he needs a mortal body, which he will receive from the Egyptian gods. What I need you two to do is wait at the entrance of the temple for his appearance, and then somehow lure him to this place. Once you've done that, we will do our best to keep the mummy busy while you perform your ritual."

Seb proceeded with explaining how the ritual was done. Karen had to slit her wrist, take some of her own blood and smear it across a symbol on the temple floor. Then she had to read an incantation from Egyptian hieroglyphics that had already been properly translated for her, and do a ritual dance. That act would activate a hidden power inside the temple and seal King Ahmose with a curse.

Karen was given time to rehearse this over five times, and it was an unnerving time for her because she realized if she failed, the world was going to be destroyed. Megan did her best to comfort Karen in the process. Once they were done, it was 6:03 PM. Karen, Megan, the agents, and all the archaeologists then had a dinner that resembled The Last Supper a lot. At the table, everyone was in a solemn emotional state, knowing that this had to be done seriously. It was as if she was Jesus, and everyone was ready to say goodbye to her when the time came.

Once dinner was done, it was exactly 7:00 PM. Everything was prepared and double-checked to make sure it would work. Then everyone assumed their positions. Karen and Megan walked out to the entrance of the temple with Aiden, Alicia, and Seb.

"Well, this is it," Alicia said.

"Yeah, this is it," Seb echoed.

"Karen, you will save the world. Trust me. You won't fail. We are all here to help you. You will seal the curse successfully." Megan threw out every word of encouragement she was able to muster at the last moment.

Karen was already beyond words. She concentrated on the task ahead of her.

"Look!" Megan yelled and pointed at a cloud of dust in the distance of the desert. The sand looked as if it was being disturbed. Everyone stared at it. Soon, it became clearer. In front of the cloud of dust was a moving figure. It appeared to have a human shape and was running, flinging it's arms behind it. It was the mummy.

Karen's hearted started thumping. The running figure moved forward with astonishing speed. Within moments, the physical features were clearly visible. The loose cloth bandages, the rotting skin, the glowing, red eyes. The cloud of dust got larger, and the mummy raced closer. Karen's heart beat faster.

Eventually, the mummy screeched to a stop before them and sent up another massive cloud of dust and sand. Karen had to cover her eyes with her arm to avoid getting sand spurted into her eyes. When she looked at the mummy again, he appeared apparently confused, maybe even a little threatened at the fact that there were five people standing at the entrance of the temple, awaiting his arrival. His eyes scanned through the whole group, and then suddenly focused on Karen.

"Karen, Venez avec moi con mim," the mummy said with a surprisingly deep and rusty voice.

Karen jumped when her name was mentioned. He knew her! Seb flinched after what the mummy had said. He apparently understood the language. Although she did not understand what Ahmose had said, she knew he didn't have good intentions. She started to back away.

"Karen, he wants to take you with him. Run before he does!" Seb exclaimed.

"Go Karen, I'm right behind you!" Megan urged.

Karen broke into a run and started into the temple.

"Go! Go! Go!" She heard Megan yell after her as she followed.

At her friend's encouragement, Karen sprinted harder. She heard a distant yell of pain that sounded like a man's voice.

"Seb!" Karen yelled back as she realized her guides hadn't followed and were probably in danger.

"Karen, don't look back! Keep running!" Megan spurred her on.

Karen didn't think twice and continued to run. Suddenly, she heard a third set of footsteps echoing behind her. She looked back. Charging behind Megan was a flurry of movement with two glaring red eyes. The mummy had caught on. She ran faster.

She heard the mummy yell behind her in the same foreign language some raspy words. The voice echoed along the whole hallway. What he said she didn't understand, but apparently it made something work. Instantly, tubes that appeared to be gun barrels sprang out of the temple walls and started firing tiny darts. A dart whizzed by and barely missed Karen's head.

"Poison darts! Karen, get down low and roll through that door there! We need to get out of this place!" Megan screamed.

Trying to avoid the poison darts that zipped around the place, Karen scrunched up into a ball and pushed onto a nearby door. The door crumbled under her own weight, revealing stairs that appeared to lead deep down to a dungeon.

"Oh no!" Karen squealed as she lost control over her body. She tumbled down the stairs. Her sight was blurred by the constant rolling motion. All she managed to see was the lights in the hallway that she was spinning away from. Other than that, she saw darkness as she kept going down into the unknown.

"Oohhh man" Karen moaned as she staggered up into a standing position. She expanded her body into a full stretch and felt searing pain go down the side of her body. She hunched over and clutched her hip. She probably hurt it on the way down. She then proceeded on to check her limbs and the rest of her body for any major injuries. She was fine, other than some bruises here and there. That was when Karen realized that just moments ago she was running away from a mummy with her friend. She searched frantically around for any trace of Megan.

"Megan? MEGAN! Where are you?" Karen continued to scan around the vicinity of where she had fell. That's when she saw two, glowing red eyes. The mummy had come after her. Without second thought, she continued to run. She dashed into a dark hallway. The light behind her faded, until she eventually ran aimlessly into tendrils of darkness. Karen didn't stop. Terror drove her on, and she told herself that the farther she was from the mummy, the better. Her legs and lungs screamed at her to stop, but she ignored her body and followed what her mind was telling her.

Karen suddenly felt something stop her. Before she had time to react, she had already stumbled and fell on her stomach. The fall knocked all the air out of her. She leaped up again as if the ground were hot, and then attempted to continue running. It was then she became aware that her legs were too tired to continue. Karen collapsed onto a wall and then looked around, searching for any hint of the mummy. That's when it hit her as hard a brick. *This was her dream.* She was reliving her dream, except now it's for real. When she remembered what had happened in her dream, fear struck her and consumed her. Karen became too apprehensive to move. She scrunched herself up, wishing with all her might this wasn't happening.

Footsteps. Another wave of terror dawned upon Karen. She heard footsteps. They came from the end of the hallway, and echoed off the walls. They got closer. Karen was already immobilized by panic. She knew that with each step, the inevitable end drew her closer to it.

There he was. The bright, red eyes of the mummy illuminated the whole hallway. Karen could see his face swell with pleasure as he came closer to her. He laughed maniacally. Once the mummy came right up to her, he stopped. Karen was ready to go. *Just let it be quick. Please let it be quick.*

With a sudden sweeping motion of his left arm, the mummy grabbed Karen up by the collar. As Karen choked, she marveled at the immense strength the mummy had. For a moment, he stared right into her eyes, and Karen stared right back into his. Other than the glowing red, Karen saw triumph and great delight in his eyes. She wondered if he could see in her eyes her submissive manner. After a long moment's silence, Ahmose started slowly bringing his right arm up to Karen's face. Karen closed her eyes and prepared herself for the end.

"No! Karen!" A voice came down from the end of the hallway. Ahmose grimaced, stopped what he was doing, and looked around at the source of the voice. It was Megan. She sprinted towards them, and before Ahmose had time to react, she crushed his face with a punch and followed that with a jab in his stomach. The force of the attack made Ahmose collapse. His fingers loosened around Karen's collar as he lay on the ground and growled, evidently paralyzed by pain. Karen fell to the ground, gasped, and let out a huge cough as the restraint on her neck released. Instantly, she felt a strong hand slip into hers and pull her up.

"Come on, Karen! We need to get to the ritual site!" Megan jerked at Karen's arm and led her back down the hallway. Karen struggled to catch her breath and keep up. They ran down the hallway and reached the stairs where Megan half-dragged Karen up them. Once they reached the top, Megan instantly broke out in a full sprint. Karen wasn't ready and staggered the whole way. As she looked back, she saw that the mummy had caught up. Together, the two girls ran until they finally reached the ritual room. Megan swiveled Karen around with her arm and threw Karen onto the spot where she was supposed to perform the ritual. The mummy ran in after them, but the archaeologists standing on the sides sprang into action and kept the mummy busy with their flamethrowers.

Karen hurriedly lit a match with her shaking fingers and lit the four candles around her. She picked up the knife lying on the ground next to her and then winced as she slit her wrist. Bright red blood flowed out, and she allowed a drop to fall onto the floor. Simultaneously, a bright purple light shone through the cracks of the tiles in the floor. Karen grabbed the piece of paper that had been laid down on the floor next to her and started to read.

"Rakka schetabera." Karen had no idea what the words meant, but apparently they worked because the purple light shone brighter. At that moment, to Karen's terror, the mummy finished his wrestle with the archaeologists. He grabbed the archaeologists by their collars—just like he did to Karen—and then flung them, one by one, to the wall. The archaeologists were all knocked out. The mummy started racing towards Karen, and held out his hand, getting ready to grab Karen once again. Karen froze. Suddenly, Megan jumped into action to save Karen again. She jumped over and grabbed the mummy by the arm in effort to wrestle him away from Karen.

"Karen! Hurry up and finish!" Megan said in a rushed manner. Despite Megan's state of danger, Karen looked back to the sheet of paper and continued reading. The sheet instructed her to do a ritual dance. Karen sprang up and started doing the pre-rehearsed dance from memory.

Karen paused as Megan landed with a thud on the floor. The mummy had managed to knock her onto the ground. The whole temple now shone with purple light.

"Don't mind me Karen. Continue!" Megan encouraged as she rolled over to dodge a punch. The mummy flinched as his fist was nailed into the ground, but recovered quickly to send another flurry of punches. Karen hurried with the swishing motions of the dance, trying to get Megan out of trouble.

Karen looked around, hoping that her friend wasn't endangered. The mummy had managed to grab hold of Megan's shoulder. He flung her into the wall. Megan's face scrunched up with pain.

"No! Megan!" Karen yelled as she tried to run over and help.

"Don't, Karen! Stay and finish dancing! The ritual will stop if you leave your spot," Megan warned as Karen tried to leave the center of the temple. The mummy then landed a punch square in Megan's stomach. Megan let out a grunt and clasped her stomach. Then, her arms and legs loosened up. She was done for.

Although her insides screamed for her to go and help Megan, Karen reluctantly continued the ritual dance, finished with a majestic leap, and pushed her hand onto the floor.

The whole temple seemed to be activated the moment Karen finished. Waves of vibration spread out from the place where she had pounded the floor. Subsequently, purple wisps of mist rose out of the place where here hand was rested, and solidified into what appeared to be ghosts. The ghosts rushed to Ahmose and started dragging him into the temple. Ahmose struggled to be released, but his efforts were futile. The ghosts sank into the wall until only their arms were visible. They pulled Ahmose in. It was such a grotesque sight that Karen closed her eyes. When the sounds were completely gone, she opened her eyes again. Everything appeared tranquil. It was as if nothing had happened at all. The fire on the candles quivered and made shadows on the temple walls dance. The walls were no longer shining with purple. Megan lay there in the corner...

"Megan, get up!" When Megan remained motionless, Karen panicked and ran over. Megan had her head turned away from Karen. Karen kneeled and gently turned Megan's face so that she could see her face. Karen was appalled to find that Megan had sustained numerous injuries. She was bruised on many parts of her body. A trickle of blood rolled down the side of her head. She still appeared to not have lost her consciousness because she constantly winced, and her face was scrunched up with pain.

"No, no, no, no, no! Megan, talk to me!" Karen yelled in astonishment.

"Hey, Karen," Megan whispered casually, as if nothing was wrong. She managed a weak smile. Megan appeared to have trouble breathing.

"Megan, are you okay?"

"I'm fine. You saved the world!" Megan managed to whisper again.

"Look at you, Megan. You are heavily injured and all you care about is the fact that I got this done. That doesn't matter anymore. Come on, get up, and we'll get you to some help."

"Karen, I'm afraid I won't be going."

"What! What do you mean?"

"I'm sorry, Karen."

"No Megan, you are going to stay alive. We're going back to America, and we're going to celebrate this properly."

"Karen, I don't think I'm going back. I'm sorry." Megan's whispering got so soft that Karen was afraid that she could falter any moment.

There was a long pause of silence where the two friends stared into each other's eyes. Although no words were exchanged, Karen knew they were both thinking about the memories they had shared. She knew that she couldn't lose Megan.

"Megan, you're the only true friend I've ever had," Karen said with a quivering voice.

"You are too," Megan whispered back with a smile.

"I can't let you go."

At this moment, Karen could see Megan's lips moving, but the words were no longer audible. She had to put her ear up right next to Megan's mouth to hear.

"...Karen, I'll be fine. I'm happy that this is the way it ends. I'm glad that I did this for you. No regrets. You won't have to live without me. Remember, I will always be with you...right here." Megan summoned the last of her strength to rest a shaking finger on the part of Karen's chest near her heart.

"Megan, I'm not ready to live without you." Karen clutched Megan's hand tightly. Tears blinded her vision.

"It's Okay Karen; nobody ever has to be ready." Megan's eyes closed. Her head collapsed over to the side, and the hand that rested on Karen's chest loosened its grip and fell to the floor.

Karen felt teardrops streaming down her face. She bent over on Megan and let the tears come out. For a moment, only Megan existed with her. They were in their own world. All she could feel was Megan and the coldness of her skin.

It's raining.

The drops pattered hard on the roof, and the wind whistled.

Karen sat on her bed, with tear-stained pictures of her and Megan since preschool. She had already looked through them over and over many times, but it still didn't seem enough. It felt like every time she finished, she needed look at them again. She knew that these pictures were ones that she would never get sick of looking at.

Megan was a loyal friend. She always managed to cheer Karen up in times of hardship. She never failed to make Karen smile. She was the silver lining that Karen had looked for in her whole life. She was Karen's courageous leader, support system, and partner in crime. More tears came to Karen's eyes as she realized what a sacrifice Megan had made for her. If she weren't there, Karen would not be here by now. One of them had to go, but Megan went for her. *Her memories will stay with me forever,* Karen thought as a tear rolled down her face. *At least, for this lifetime it will...until we're together again.*

An Unknown World

By

Junny Yang

Boom!

"Mom, why don't you trust me? I'm just trying to be creative! Isn't my imagination good?" Drake shouted, as he stomped up the steep stairs.

"Drake, imagination is good, but the teachers expect you to obey the rules and what they say," his mother replied in a guilty voice.

He sat in his room, with his face down on the table, covered with his brown hair. He was the biggest joke in his high school, mainly because of his mushroom style hair, so people called him Fungi. "Why does Mom always have to like Alex better than me? Just because he's her first-born son doesn't mean she should treat him better than me," Drake murmured. He thought that he should belong to a world of imagination and creativity.

It was eleven o'clock at night, and Drake remained awake, hugging his pillow, thinking about what to do with his life. He thought of how was he going to convince his parents to see his point of view, not always his older brother's. Alex was articulate and persuasive; his mom and dad treated Alex with greater privileges.

Drake jumped on his bouncy bed, "Ugh! When am I going to get a new bed? This one is too small for me. I'm seventeen years old, 175 centimeters tall, and weigh 80 kilograms. I'm not a Lego boy or Power Ranger anymore," Drake cried.

Drake fell asleep and dreamed about a land of dragons. In his dream world there were only Drakos and Draks. The Drakos were the good ones, and the Draks were the evil ones. Drake was on a boat searching for something he has believed in for his whole life. He wanted to prove to his parents that he was not worthless, and he was actually worthy of something. The young boy found a mysterious island, never seen before, not even located on the map. He sailed swiftly, allowing Drake to quietly arrive on the shore. He was afraid that there might be some undiscovered or dangerous creatures that might harm him.

Just then he heard a growl behind a tree, so he quickly backed away. A beautiful creature popped out, getting close enough to Drake to let him to get a good look at the creature. Bright, ruby-colored scales covered the Drako, protecting the animal from attack. Two stout horns rested on top of the Drako's head. Strong, muscular legs, a tail shaped like an arrowhead, and huge marvelous bird-like wings gave the creature a majestic appearance. What a beautiful creature Drake thought, as he reached out his hand to try and touch the Drako's sharp spiny head. The Drako stood about 180 centimeters tall and had a body that extend nearly seven feet long

"Wake up, Drake! It's morning! Come down for breakfast!" Alex Shouted.

"Great...YOU just had to interrupt my sweet dream," Drake roared back as he sadly leaned on his elbow. Reflecting on his dream, Drake decided he would set out on a journey to find those Drakos and Draks. He knew they were real. He slowly walked downstairs to his breakfast as lazy as a turtle. He finished his delicious breakfast of fried eggs, bacon with black pepper on it, and pancakes with maple syrup, his favorite. When he finished his breakfast, he rushed up to his room as fast as a tiger and packed his bags. He was ready to sail out on the one-person sailing vessel that he built with his dad when he was a kid. Drake would find the Drakos and Draks. He could still picture the mysterious island he had found in his dream.

"Drake, where are you going?" his mother barged into his room.

"To a place in my dream, no one can stop me from going. I believe in this place. It's real! That world of imagination and creativity is where I belong. I'll find it, and I will return to show you that I'm actually worthy of something and not worthless!" Drake yelled back at his mother.

"And just exactly where is this place that you dreamed of?" his mother asked as she rolled her eyes at Drake.

"It's a land of Drakos and Draks. They're dragons, and they are real. I can still remember the exact location from my dream. I'm going to that spooky island. The island is an unknown world. No one has ever seen it before," Drake said stubbornly. "I'll be back in two months. Be ready to meet a Drako," he grinned.

His mom couldn't think of a way to stop Drake from going on this adventurous journey, so she had to let him go. Drake was adamant on his decision and nothing his mom said could change his mind. That very night, Drake snuck outside of his house. His footsteps were as silent as an ant's. He ran to the dock and got on his little sailing vessel.

Now I'll begin my journey to the unknown world, discovering Drakos and Draks. I will make history and impress my whole family.

After sailing for a month and a half, he ran out of food. Drake really wanted to reach the island, get some food, find the Drakos and go home. Suddenly, a fog came which frightened Drake very much. He hugged himself tightly with his arms and put his head down. After two minutes, he lifted it up to see if the fog was still there. Then he saw something very blurry, not far from his boat. The fog disappeared, and he saw an island! He finally found the mysterious island. He quickly paddled onto the bank and tied the rope attached to the boat onto a tree bunk, making sure it would not drift away.

Drake walked silently into the forest, picking some grapes and strawberries. To determine if it was poison, his dad had taught him to smell it when he was younger. Drake gobbled down the grapes. Then a Drako popped out behind the bushes.

ROAR!

Drake yelped and jumped back, "WOAH! I didn't see that coming. Are you what I'm looking for? Are you a Drako?"

"Hi, I am a Drako, and my name is Drok, your name is?" Drok asked in the dragon language.

"What did you just say? I don't understand," Drake replied anxiously.

✳ ✳ ✳ ✳

Just then the Drako touched his horns onto Drake's lips. "You have now been possessed by my spirit. You can also speak my language; therefore, we can communicate," the Drako said. "Let me repeat myself now. My name is Drok, and yours is?"

"My name is Drake. Our names are very similar," Drake replied, amused.

"We have our own language, so complicated that no one can understand unless we touch our horns to your lips. By doing that, I sacrificed half of my life to you. Which means, when you die, I'll die along with you. When I die, you will also die along with me," Drok said.

"Oh my, that's very surprising and frightening," Drake shivered.

"It is as if we were born to have a connection or something," Drok said.

"Yes, in fact, I need your help. I need to confront my family. They think I can't do anything right, and I have to show them that I can. I believed in my imagination. That's how I found you," Drake murmured.

"Really? I think you're a gentle, kind, and cunning boy," Drok smiled.

"Wow, thanks. Can you please help me, Drok? Can you fly me back to Chicago to prove to my mom that dragons are real," Drake asked.

"Sure, but why do people think that we're not real? Of course we're real! We'll show them!" Drok exclaimed with a smirk on his face.

Drok and Drake took off immediately, flying to the Pacific Coast. Drake took a nap, lying on Drok's back, careful not to fall off. As Drake brushed his hands over the Drako's scales, he knew it was hard, maybe even harder than titanium. Flying swiftly in the air, Drake dreamed about what it would be like when he arrived back in Chicago.

"Whoa! You almost shook me off. What's happening?" Drake cried.

"We're in a strong wind current. I'm trying to fly under it, but it's not working! Wherever I fly, it seems to follow us! I think someone is purposely causing this, and maybe it isn't a wind current at all!" Drok shouted.

"Try diving down! If you go fast enough, you'll go out of its sight; so it won't know where you've gone!" Drake bellowed.

"Good idea. Hold on! One, Two, Three!" Drok screamed with excitement.

They darted downwards, faster than any bullet or rocket, trying to lose the current. Drake held onto Drok's spine as hard as he could; so hard that his hands began bleeding. "Argh! Keep going. Don't worry about me!" Drake shouted, holding on tightly. Drok and Drake sped down towards the water, and then just when they were about to hit the calm sea, Drok braked and flew upwards. *Phewph.*

"Now that we've lost the stalking current, I'll go back to my sleep. Wake me up when we get there." Drake yawned.

"Yeah, that was intense," Drok whined.

"By the way, nice flying," Drake stated.

About two hours later, a fireball came shooting right beside Drake's ear. "OW! What's so hot and noisy? Was that you Drok? You better not be messing with me!" Drake shouted.

"It wasn't me! It's that big black hairy Drak!" Drok murmured angrily.

"He's been stalking us and trying to kill us! Let's get him!" Drake commanded

"How? I can breathe ice and fireballs, but you don't even have a weapon to fight," Drok questioned. "It is unlikely we will win this fight."

"I've got a small dagger in my backpack, right here. Maybe you can throw me onto his back, and I'll stab him in his eyes. Then you can finish him off." Drake said.

"Good plan. Let's do it," Drok roared bravely, stunning the Drak. Drake turned himself around carefully and crawled to the end of Drok's tail. Drok swung him towards the Drak. Just when Drake was about to fly past the black Drak, he grabbed on to one of the spikes.

"Ouch! That spiky spine cut my finger," Drake cried. He unsheathed his dagger, and then stabbed the Drak in the eyes vigorously, carving them out. All the blood was dripping into the sea. "Yeah, Ooohooo, HaaaHaaa, Yeehaa." Suddenly, the Drak breathed fire, turning some of Drake's hair in front of his forehead into dust and ashes. "That is my precious hair; now I look like a punk! Oh, you're a dead big thing."

"You have blinded me, but I can still hear and smell as well as I could see," the evil Drak grinned, trying to shake Drake off his back. Drake held on tightly, swinging left and right, injuring his kneecaps. Some of Drake's blood flew onto the Drak's lips. "That blood tastes good. I think I might have a good lunch meal."

"No! Don't you dare hurt him! I'll make you pay if you do!" Drok exclaimed.   "Oh really! Catch me if you can!" the Drak smiled. He flew forward and rolled in the air making, Drake fall.

"Ahhhhh, HELP Drok HELP!" Drake cried, frightened. *This is going to be the end of my life; I'll never see my family again. I won't even be able to show them the dragon I found.* Right on time, before Drake hit the ocean, Drok grabbed hold of Drake with his claws, rescuing him. "Thanks a lot my friend."

"Anytime," Drok smiled. "Now back to the fight! Concentrate." Drake climbed onto Drok's back, getting his mind back on the battle. "FIRE!" Drok breathed a humongous fireball at the Drak's butt, burning him.

ROAR! The Drak breathed an even larger fireball at Drok and Drake, but they dodged it because of Drok's excellent agility.

"Stop him! He's charging at us!" Drake screamed. *WUSH!* Drok breathed a big ice ball towards the Drak freezing him at his spot. He then fell straight down into the sea. Because of the great height of the fall, the Drak died by smashing into the sea on his chest with great force, crushing the ribs.

"YEA! Victory!" Drake yelled out loudly.

"Now, let's meet your parents, shall we?" Drok asked.

"I'm not so sure about that. Wait, hold on, we're there?" Drake replied, surprisingly.

"Yes, I think so..." Drok said.

"Ha, ha, ha, I bring you the dragon of my dreams. Meet Drok!" Drake said, pretending he's talking to his mom and dad. Drok laughed loudly, almost breathing out fire.

Drok and Drake landed in Drake's huge garden, full of different types of colorful flowers. They landed softly, not making one single sound. "Wait here, Drok. I'll introduce you to my cruel parents," Drake suggested.

Drok nodded, showing that he understood. Luckily, it was at night, or else Drok would've been noticed when flying in the air.

Drake ran into the house through the backdoor. His mother, father, and Alex were all there sitting on the couch, watching TV like a family. They were all quiet, like they didn't even care if Drake was still alive or not. Drake ran in front of the TV, surprising his whole family.

"Wow, I'm surprised that you made it through your journey," Alex said, laughing with his parents.

"Thanks, you are so kind to your little brother," Drake replied sarcastically.

"So Drake, where is your awesome dragon that you saw in your dreams? Did you find it? Wait, I should say, did you even see it?" his mom questioned.

"Of course I did. It's right outside, in our garden," Drake replied proudly. Drake took them outside, standing proudly beside Drok with his chin up high. "This, Mom and Dad and Alex, is my dragon. His name is Drok. You cannot understand what he is saying because he has not touched you on the lips with his horns.

"Oh my gosh! This is a beautiful dragon! I'm sorry I did not believe you before Drake. Will you please forgive me?" Drake's mom asked feeling guilty. Drake hesitated about this question. He's not sure if his mom is tricking him or if she means it.

"Yes, I can forgive you," Drake replied.

"Oh, thank you my dear…" his mother said.

"But there is one thing, you have to be fair to Alex and me, treating us equally," Drake said angrily, cutting his mother off.

"Yes, yes of course," his mom answered. All of a sudden, Drake's mom was fascinated with the dragon. She flew on Drok lots of times and was always washing Drok and feeding him. Everyday, she spent at least half of her time talking and doing several types of activities with

Drok. It stayed inside the huge garden all day, covered by the big trees, so no one would know of him.

Now Drake knows Alex is very jealous of him because of his Drako. He wants to let Alex know how bad it feels when their mother likes Drake better than him. *I bet Alex is desperate for his mom to like him better again and hate me.*

Alex also decided to find a Drako or Drak. He had no idea what the differences between them are, and he didn't even know there were two different types of dragons. He just wanted one that looked better and was much cooler than Drok.

"Hey Mom, I'm going to stay over at my friend's house for a few days. I'm getting bored of my room. Is that OK with you?" Alex asked.

"Yes, yes, whatever, just don't stay there for too long," his mom answered in a hurry trying to get back to Drok. It seemed like she didn't even care.

✶ ✶ ✶ ✶

Alex went to a smart friend of his who was a scientist and worked in a lab. He studied about the ancient times, all the mysterious creatures, like the phoenixes, the serpents, and orcs.

"Do you know anything about the dragons, like the Drakos?" Alex asked.

"Yes I do. In fact I have great curiosity in those fantastic creatures," the scientist said.

"Can you tell me where to find them?" Alex asked excitedly.

"No, sorry. I have no idea where to find it, but I'm confident that they still exist," the scientist murmured.

"Well, do you have a map or a teleport machine?" Alex questioned disappointedly.

"I can make a portal for you to get to the place of Drakos and Draks," the scientist replied cheerfully.

"That would be wonderful. Thank you," Alex said.

The scientist opened a dusty book on the bookshelf and started reading the ancient lines. The words are for summoning the portal to the unknown world of mysterious dragons. Suddenly, a portal appeared in front of the scientist's desk, just large enough for Alex to go through.

"Thanks a lot my friend. I owe you," Alex thanked.

The scientist accidentally made Alex the wrong portal; he led him to the Draks, not the Drakos. "Where is this place? I don't see any dragons," Alex said to himself. Suddenly, he saw a tail sticking out of a large bush. The tail had two spikes on the left and right side to kill the prey.

Alex carefully crawled up, and touched the tail, making the Drak wince. The Drak growled, scaring Alex back. "Hi, my name is Alex. I am very fond of you dragons. Will you come back with me to Chicago and show my brother who is stronger?" Alex asked.

The Drak simply raised his right eyebrow, showing that he did not understand what he was saying. The Drak touched his horn onto Alex's lips, uniting with Alex. "Hi, we are now united, so you can understand my language and talk to me in this language," the Drak said.

"Cool, my name is Alex. What's yours?" Alex asked.

"Mine is Borak, and we belong to the Draks," Borak answered.

"Draks? I thought there were only Drakos!" Alex exclaimed.

"No, no, no, there are two types. We are the evil ones who will overpower them and rule the world! Will you join us?"

"Yes, of course I will. Will you help me defeat my brother in a battle and kill him?" Alex asked.

"Sure, but why kill him? What did he do?" Borak replied.

"He is united with the Drakos, does that explain your answer?" Alex said.

"Yes! We'll show him whose boss," Drok and Borak laughed evilly. Borak and Drok quickly walked back through the portal before it disappeared. Once again, they were back at the scientist's place.

"Wow, I'm surprised you came back so fast! Have you found your dragon?" the scientist asked. Borak came in behind Alex and roared. "Well, I suppose that answers my question." The scientist did not ask for permission to touch the dragon, he simply just reached out his arm and touched the dragon's back, rubbing it.

The dragon growled, swinging its spiky tail at the scientist, throwing him back. The dragon leaped over, standing right on top of the scientist, preparing to tear him apart. Borak gripped him with his sharp shiny golden claws, scratching at his chest.

"Enough!" Alex yelled, "he's my friend. Don't kill him."

Borak answered with a bow.

Quickly, they flew back to their house, finding that his mom was stroking Drok's head. Alex grinned, prepared to show Borak to his mom. "Hi Mom!" Alex said surprisingly.

"You're back so early! I thought you were going to your friend's house for a sleepover?" his mom asked.

"Yes I was, but I don't want to leave our family. After all, Drake just got a dragon," Alex stated.

"Awww, you're so kind," his mom commented.

"Here, let me show you, Borak!" Alex exclaimed as Borak flew right into the garden surprising her.

"Wow, that is also a dragon! But somehow, it looks evil to me," his mom said.

"No, no, no, Drake's dragon is evil. You've been mistaken. That's why I'm here, to kill Drake and Drok!" Alex laughed.

Drake pushed passed his mom, seeing the Drak. "No! Alex you're wrong, that's a Drak. The Draks are the evil and the Drakos are the good!" Drake said.

"Well, we can settle this in a battle. Don't the good ones usually win? Hm? I think so too, so whoever wins this battle, wins! We fight to the DEATH!" Alex yelled.

"That's insane! What are you talking about Alex; don't fight with your own brother! Especially don't kill him!" Drake's mom cried.

"No, you love him more than you love me! You're supposed to treat us equally!" Alex yelled.

"Yeah well, before I found Drok, she liked you so much better that she didn't even care about me! Now shut up! We're not going to fight!" Drake shouted back. He quickly turned his back on Alex and strode swiftly away. Alex ran up behind Drake, turned him around with force, drew his arm back and with full strength, punched Drake in the face. It left a big purplish and blackish bruise.

"You did not just punch me in the face!" Drake yelled.

"Oh, I so did! What are you going to do about it? Oooooo!" Alex laughed.

"Shut up, crybaby!" Drake insulted.

"No, you shut up! Are you scared to fight me? Boo hoo hoo, who's the crybaby now?" Alex shouted.

"Fine, let's settle this fight, Saturday, in the woods, where no one will know of this fight except for us. Be prepared what you're going to face Alex." Drake said.

Drake began to prepare his armor; he bought leather armor from a store that was selling ancient weapons and armor. The armor covered all of his body, protecting him from any cuts or slashes from weapons. His weapon was a red sword with a silver handle. One the end of the handle was shaped like a dragon's head. The sword was once carried by a great warrior named, Durn, and his dragon was also named Drok.

The war between the Draks and the Drakos began about hundreds of years ago. Durn the greatest warrior of the Drakos fought with the greatest warrior of the Draks, Kael. Durn had the chance for the last killing blow on Kael but hesitated too long, because Kael was once his friend. Kael quickly swung his mace at Durn's right thigh, making him fall down. Then Kael smashed the mace at Durn's head. Since then, no one has been that close to destroying the Draks.

Drake thought of making a deal. If he wins, then the Drakos and Draks will have peace forever, and will help each other when they're in trouble. *I think that's a great idea! Also, I'm positive I will win this battle.*

Alex was way too confident. He didn't even bother to get any gear; he just wore his normal jeans and a polo shirt. *I am so going to win this fight; my little brother has never won a fight against me. Psh!* Alex spat on the floor. Alex carried his favorite weapon, a hammer which he named Storm hammer.

"Good morning kids! Today's Friday! And guess what we always do on Friday?" his mother asked cheerfully.

"We fight!" Alex bloated.

"No we don't, you silly idiot," Drake said.

"What? What fight are you guys talking about? You will not fight in my house; I'm going to lock both of you up! Now get into your rooms and don't come out. I'll lock you in with my keys!" his mother cried.

"No, you can't make us do that! We can fight however we want!" Drake said delightfully.

"I'll have spaghetti for lunch, and an awesome cheeseburger for dinner, please," Alex ordered.

"Alex! This is not the time to choose what you want for lunch and dinner. Now get into your rooms! You are both still a minor!" his mom said.

"Fine," Drake said truthfully.

"So will I," Alex said sarcastically.

"I'm sure both of you will stay in your rooms, right? If you guys ever dare sneak out and do anything stupid, you are grounded for the rest of the year!" his mom answered.

Throughout the day, Alex and Drake never spoke a word to one another. They stayed in their rooms for almost the entire day like they were hiding a secret weapon for their battle. That night, they both slept early, waiting for tomorrow, the big day!

As the sun rose, Alex and Drake woke quickly. They both dressed up. Alex and Drake put on their chest armor, and then their roman-like helm, after that their gauntlets, at last their greaves. Drake shined in gold, Alex was dressed in black. Their dragons wore in the same colored armor as their favorite companions. Alex and Drake both pick locked their doorknobs to sneak out. They snuck out at the same time, not waking their mother. Alex and Drok both dashed into the woods.

"Prepare to die, brother!" Alex screamed as he leaped in the air while drawing his storm hammer from his back and preparing to crush Drake. Drake quickly dodged to the side, unsheathing his glowing red sword out and his golden shield, which had a dragon crest, printed on the front.

"So you want to kill me, do you?" Drake asked calmly.

"Of course I do. Now stop talking before I slash your throat!" Alex shouted as he tried another blow on Drake's legs, but Drake simply jumped, and the hammer just swung past his legs. Alex pulled back his mace to his right thigh, just about to swing it upward, breaking Drake's chin. Before he swung the hammer, Drake quickly slashed Alex's weakest point, his shins. Just then, Alex collapsed to the ground, grabbing his knees and moaning.

"Ha, ha, my throat is still whole," Drake laughed sarcastically.

"SHUT UP!" Alex screamed, using all his arm muscles and pushing himself over Alex's head and punching Drake's butt.

They both fell on the ground moaning. While Drake was rubbing his butt cheeks, Alex quickly tore off two strips of his shirt and tied it onto his shins like soccer shin guards, stopping the bleeding.

Drake and Alex ran and climbed up to their dragons' back simultaneously, preparing to fight on their mounts. Both Drok and Borak growled, releasing fire at the same time. They launched into the air, grabbing hold of each other's bodies and ripping and scratching while Drok and Borak fought with their swords. "Die!" Alex yelled as he through a nicely snake shaped dagger at Drake. Drake simply blocked it with his golden shield and smiled at Alex.

"Retreat now!" Alex said. Borak struggled free of Drok, pushing off Drok and breathing fire at Drake. Drake stuck his shield up, blocking the fire.

"Ice, Drok!" just then, Drok shot an iceball freezing Alex on the dragon, rendering him unable to move. Drake and Drok quickly chased after Borak while he carried the heavy weighted ice cube. Drake smashed the ice into millions of small pieces, unfreezing Alex.

Alex's whole face was pale, and he was shivering. "Fire!" Drake shouted as Drok breathed fire a Borak's wings. Spinning, Borak easily dodged the fire and wacked Drok in the face with his horny tail.

"The battle will never end like this," Drok said. "We've got to get Alex off Borak."

"Yes, the next time they breathe fire at me, I will jump and hold on to your right front leg. Then you throw me over onto Borak," Drake said. "Got it?"

"Got it," Drok replied.

Then, Drake heard Alex whisper something to Borak: "We've got to end this fight someway," Alex murmured to Borak.

"Yes, I will breathe a fire ball to distract them. Then you'll climb to my left front leg, and I'll throw you over to kill Drake," Borak said.

"OK," Alex replied.

Alex quickly drew out his second dagger and threw it at Drake, but Drake dodged it. Then Borak took one big deep breath, filling the air up to his chest, and released the fire. Drake quickly jumped onto Drok's right leg, and Alex leaped onto Borak's left leg. The two dragons threw their companions at the same time crashing in the air.

Alex and Drake fought in the air, swinging their weapons at each other. Alex took a big blow on Drake's shield, breaking it in half. *Now, he will have no protection against my storm hammer now.*

Before Alex could react, Drake quickly slashed his sword at Alex's right arm, causing a bloody cut. "Now you can only use your left hand, which you…hmm…what's the word? Stink at!" Drake smiled. Choking Alex gently, not wanting to kill him, they fell, almost hitting the ground.

"HELP, Drok!" Drake yelled with all his might. Drok quickly came and have them land on his back. By the time they landed, Drake was still holding onto Alex's neck. Pushing his arrogant older brother to the floor, Alex cried when he landed on his right arm just where his cut was. "So are you going to surrender to me or not? I can kill you right now if you refuse," Drake said.

"Fine, you win! I admit it. I can't believe I'm saying this. You're better than me, and mom should treat us equally, okay? Are you happy now?" Alex moaned.

"Not quite…there is one more thing," Drake stated. "The Draks and Drakos will have peace forever and will help one another when needed, agreed?" Drake asked.

"NO! NEVER!" Alex shouted as Borak growled agreeing to his opinion.

"Yes, but the problem is, I won and you lost, so you would have to listen to me now, or I can always kill you, right now, which I don't think you would want me to do. You have a family that cares for you; you have your friends and especially your girlfriend. I'm positive she wouldn't want to lose you," Drake teased.

"Fine!" Alex groaned.

Borak, Drok, Alex, and Drake traveled back to the unknown world, explaining to the Drakos and Draks about their challenging battle and how they had made a pact they would never fight again and would help each other when the time is needed.

"Hip Hip hooray! Hip Hip hooray!" the Draks and Drakos yelled, saluting Drake, their new king.

"I promise you all that Alex and I will visit you every month. Borak and Drok, will you stay with us?" Drake asked.

"Yes of course, but where will we stay?" Drok and Borak said at the same time.

"Jinx!" Borak exclaimed.

"I don't play jinx..."Drok muttered.

"We'll figure it out when we get back," Drake stated.

The four of them flew back like the four musketeers; their heads held high, the dragon's tails wiggled. They landed softly in the backyard about to surprise their mother that they were both alive.

"Hi, Mom!" Alex said as he hugged her.

"Wait, where did you guys go?" Alex's mom questioned.

"We had a battle, and I won. I considered whether or not I should kill Alex, but we made peace instead," Drake smiled.

"Oh my gosh! I was crying the whole time after you guys went to the forest to fight. I was afraid I would lose one of you," Drake's mom cried.

"Thanks Mom, for treating us equally," Alex said.

For the rest of their lives, there wasn't anything special anymore. They kept their dragons a secret and visited the unknown world every month to make sure there were peace and no fighting going on. News about spotting dragon footprints was being talked about around the city amusing everyone. No one bullied Drake anymore because every time someone did, Drake brought him to Drok and Borak and showed them how they would suffer if they did bully him. The mysterious island of dragons wasn't an unknown world anymore; it was now a world of peace.